VILLAINS & VIRTUES
BOOK 3

ECLIPSE
OF THE
CROWN

A.K. CAGGIANO

ISBN: 9798377057161

Eclipse of the Crown is a work of fiction. Names, characters, places, and incidents either are the product of the author's imagination or are used fictitiously. Any resemblance to actual persons, living or dead, events, or locales is entirely coincidental, and would, frankly, be pretty damn wild, don't you think?

Cover Art and Final Image by Anna Mariya Georgieva
Map by E. C. O'Connor

First printing 2023 by A. K. Caggiano

For more, please visit:
http://www.akcaggiano.com

ALSO BY A. K. CAGGIANO

STANDALONE NOVELS:
The Korinniad - An ancient Greek romcom
She's All Thaumaturgy - A sword and sorcery romcom
The Association - A supernatural murder mystery

VACANCY
A CONTEMPORARY (SUB)URBAN FANTASY TRILOGY:
Book One: The Weary Traveler
Book Two: The Wayward Deed
Book Three: The Willful Inheritor

VILLAINS & VIRTUES
A FANTASY ROMCOM TRILOGY:
Book One: Throne in the Dark
Book Two: Summoned to the Wilds
Book Three: Eclipse of the Crown

FOR MORE, PLEASE VISIT:
WWW.AKCAGGIANO.COM

To my husband,
who can always see the good,
and has since the very beginning.

Contents

AUTHOR'S NOTE:

This book contains sensitive content including, but not limited to, sexual assault and child death. Please see a complete list of sensitive content on the author's website:
www.akcaggiano.com/trigger-warnings

This book also contains explicit sexual content.

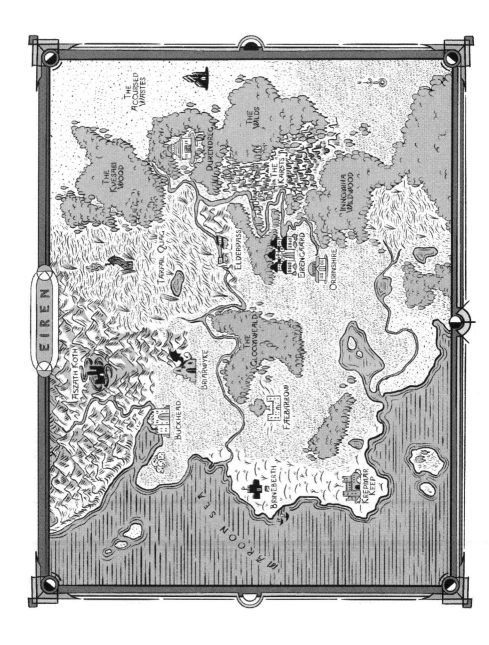

CHAPTER 1
THE FIRST CHAPTER AND WHAT IT ENTAILS

The Grand Order of Dread was established in a time before counting by an assemblage of beings that remain a mystery for their names alone would cause incurable madness and entire realms to collapse—at least, that's what the current iteration of the Grand Order has to say when asked about their history of poor record keeping. One certainly couldn't write things down once upon a time on account of the madness and the collapsing and the other inconvenient possibilities, so inadequate archives were just an unavoidable misfortune. The fault belonged with no one, least of all with any of the Grand Order's elusive and anonymous, six-member council, but someone was surely held accountable, tortured appropriately, and disposed of anyway.

The Grand Order of Dread, or GOoD, had since come to appreciate the art of documentation as failing to do so in the past lent itself to unmitigated disasters like Yvlcon two hundred and fifty-three when proper communication was not drafted and the meeting location turned out to be a direbadger mating ground or Yvlcon six hundred and eleven when a summons was sent to a direct descendant of a dominion instead of the intended demonic offspring due to an ill-placed apostrophe who subsequently slaughtered half of the attendees.

Eventually, the Grand Order evolved with the cycling of its council, and record keeping became not just an unfortunately necessary good, but unconditional. If one were an Yvlcon attendee, one would absolutely be accounted for in sextuplicate, and one who had failed to send the proper forms in via raven, shark, or viper post for approval to bring along a non-GOoD-sanctioned being to Yvlcon—especially a seemingly non-evil one—would soon learn things would become messy.

Damien Maleficus Bloodthorne knew this.

Baroness Ammalie Avington, however, did not.

Amma was by no means innocent. In fact, she had *just* killed a man, and had she been given longer than a few shaky breaths to think about it, she would have been delighted by not only knowing Marquis Cedric Caldor was dead, but that it was theoretically by her hand. This knowledge would have been quite interesting to the Grand Order, and as that dead man was trained in the holy ways of Osurehm, an inheritor of a march of Eiren, and a descendant of a dominion, it may have made her sudden and unapproved arrival at Yvlcon a tad bit easier, but Amma wasn't truly meant to be killing or maiming or overthrowing or really even spiting, and everything about her, from her soft but tangled blonde curls, to her frightened but bloodshot blue eyes, to her prey-animal thumping but sincere heart, screamed *good*. Not GOoD, just good. And to GOoD, that was bad. And not the preferable kind of bad that meant evil, just more of a sort of unacceptable atrocity.

Amma found herself being walked down a long, dimly-lit, windswept corridor, the vague sound of torturous howls echoing up into the forever-high darkness above. She had become used to forever-high darknesses and sourceless winds, but the screaming was new.

Damien's hand on the back of her neck was new too. His grip was tight, though not necessarily unpleasant, and if she had to admit, she would not say she *hated* it, rather she would have simply preferred it happening somewhere a bit more private.

While Damien's touch, even like this, was a comfort, she knew something was quite wrong. There had been a moment when his violet eyes went wide with distress as he tried to impress upon her the importance of doing exactly as he said, the implication that the consequence of not doing so would lead to something terribly unpleasant, like her death. Exaggeration was sort of his thing, especially when it came to Amma's life and the threatening of it, but he, nor anyone else, had killed her yet.

Yet.

Still, Amma sensed a shift the moment they translocated into the small chamber where Damien had gone from passed out to panicked wreck. He had since corrected his demeanor to carry himself with the cool confidence she was used to. In fact, he was downright chilly, back straight, eyes boring into the darkness ahead, mouth drawn into a tight line.

And those fingers. They burrowed into her flesh so tightly she couldn't have torn herself away if she tried. Amma dared to peek up at him, but his gaze did not flick back down to meet hers, his grip only digging in as if in warning. *Do nothing, do not even speak, without my permission*—that was what he said, and though she'd thought it a joke at first, the seriousness was hemming in as they traveled down the dark hall on the heels of an imp that was not Kaz. Those strangled, far-off screams continued to prod at the back of her head, and she clasped her hands to keep from fidgeting.

The hall's end opened up, and Amma was hit with a bracing breeze that made all of her already aching muscles go tight. This new chamber could hardly be called that at all, massive and going on into eternity to either side, blustery like they stood at the top of a cliff, but without egress to the outdoors. Thick columns of dark stone rose upward, illuminated at their bases by blue flames that danced in the gusting wind. The carvings laid into the pillars were unsettling though hard to decipher in the moving light, an agonized face, a ribcage rent from its chest, a kicked puppy.

The columns ran ahead of them, carving out a makeshift walkway in the otherwise empty expanse of a cavern. The imp led them onward, tiny in comparison, but Amma felt just as small as they passed several statues at least double the height of what they were crafted after. Though, she supposed, they could be to scale, as each statue was robed, and there were no visible features to tell her exactly what or who the creature beneath was meant to be. The bases had name-like carvings into them, and she recognized the Chthonic letters, but could only discern something like *council member* and a symbol she thought was a number, but then Amma's ability to translate the language of the dark gods was still fledgling.

It was a long walk across the cavern, but they eventually came to a wall that crawled up into the darkness above, and a small desk sitting just before it. The imp scurried off into the shadows, leaving them. Rather ordinary in relation to the imposing stonework and ominous darkness all around, the desk was wooden—cherry, if Amma wasn't mistaken in the low light—and behind it sat a woman.

"Running a little late," she said, lifting her eyes, all six of them, from a thick ledger.

3

Amma started, pressing back, but Damien's hand held her still.

Set into three rows up her forehead, each red eye flicked over Damien, and she grinned. Then they darted to Amma, and that grin plummeted off. "Registration?"

A pyramid-shaped crystal slid across the desk, and Damien pressed his thumb to its sharp point. As his blood seeped over the sides and was drawn in, the crystal's color deepened to violet, and the woman watched as words wrote themselves over the parchment in her book.

Her lips twisted into a deeper smile. "Lord Bloodthorne, welcome. We were afraid you wouldn't make it. You missed the opening ceremonies."

She turned then and glanced up at the wall behind her. Drawers were set into it, each marked with a symbol, and one pulsed in that same deep violet color as the crystal. It was much too high for her to reach, but as she stepped away from the desk, Amma saw that she did not need a ladder to access it.

A long, spindly, black leg reached up and poked itself into the wall followed by another and another until all eight were carrying the woman's mostly human torso atop a mostly-spider body vertically up the wall. Amma gasped, and she expected Damien to again squeeze her, but this time his fingers slid upward into the hair at the base of her skull, massaging in a small circle that sent pleasant tingles down her spine. She took a fuller breath, the tension in her shoulders lessening. As the woman descended, his hand slipped back down to hold her in place again.

The woman had retrieved a thin bit of metal that she held out. Damien offered up the hand he sliced on the crystal, thumb already healed, and she pressed the blade-like piece down over his wrist. The metal wrapped itself around him, and an arcane jolt encircled his arm, sealing the silver ring. Damien flexed his fingers, lip turned up at the unadorned band like it was there solely to offend him.

"There is only the one," the woman said. One pair of disapproving eyes was enough, but with all three narrowing on her, Amma wanted to shrink into the shadows and hide.

"She's unregistered. A very recent captive."

The woman's mouth fell open and revealed a set of fangs, much less of a surprise to Amma at this point, but then she gasped which did surprise her—that was a reasonable reaction to hearing someone was being held hostage. "You mean you didn't file form D2-WL3?" That reaction seemed slightly less reasonable.

Damien's stoic look barely faltered. "Why would I? She's here only to serve carnal needs."

Amma's stomach tightened, throat constricting, his touch suddenly prickly on the increasingly sweaty nape of her neck.

"And that requires at least three sub-forms." The woman flipped frantically through her ledger, but the sound of talons scurrying over stone made her look up. The maroon-skinned imp returned, waving a slate over his horned head, and he propelled himself up onto the desk. She tugged the tablet away from him, grumbled, then blew out a sharp breath.

"Well, if that's what they insist upon." She flung the slate over her shoulder, but it disintegrated before shattering against the wall, and she slammed the ledger on the desk shut, barely missing one of the imp's talons. "Protocol still demands confinement,"—she let her gazes run over Amma, distaste clear in each pair of her red eyes—"and a cleansing, thank darkness." A forced smile returned when she regarded Damien again. "And, of course, you will have the opportunity to refresh yourself before being granted an audience with the council about all of this."

"Fine. Provide me with a key, and I will see to it that she and I—"

"Ah, no." Tone terse, she gestured into the darkness at their side. "You, Lord Bloodthorne, are free to go to your chamber, but the captive must be taken into holding. If the council approves, then, and only then, will she be released."

Heavy footsteps approached, and a presence hemmed in at Amma's side where once there was only vast nothingness. She turned with Damien's hand still on her neck, and was immediately met with scales and fur. A long glance upward revealed two creatures, one covered in thick, brown bristles with an animalistic snout and horns, the other tinged green and sporting tusks that jutted up from a deep underbite. Both wore weighty axes strapped to their backs, blades stained. Amma pressed herself backward into Damien, and despite his warning, she grabbed onto his tunic. Whatever they expected of her, surely *both* of them were unnecessary.

There was a third form, one so small Amma had missed her with the appearance of the other two. Popping out from between the brutish ogre and minotaur, a woman with a shock of red hair flashed her a bright smile, amber eyes even brighter. "One for confinement?" She wrapped small hands around Amma's arm and tugged her forward.

Damien's grip was gone, and with it went what little command Amma had over her heart. It beat madly in her throat, even as the woman's delicate touch turned her about and hugged her to her side.

Hand out as if still gripping Amma's neck, Damien's jaw had gone so tight she thought his teeth might shatter. His fingers curled into a fist, knuckles cracking, and violet eyes trailed upward to meet those of the massive creatures standing just behind her. A callousness crawled over Damien's features. "If either of you touch her," he said, voice so cold even Amma shivered, "I will slice off whatever you did it with and shove it down the other one's throat. Understood?"

Both beings took a long step backward.

Damien turned to the woman at the desk, displeasure set deeply in his eyes. "Let's get this over with. Where is the council?"

"I assure you, a meeting is just a few short moments away. Let me show you to your room first, so you can make yourself…presentable." She started away from the desk, her many legs silent over the stone as she went.

Amma's stomach flipped—gods, he was about to leave her—and she opened her mouth.

Damien's gaze snapped to her, silencing whatever she might have pleaded of him, his warning reiterated without words. He followed after the woman into the darkness, and all Amma could do was watch him go.

CHAPTER 2
JUST AS A SNAKE SHEDS ITS SKIN, SO MUST A HUMAN SHED HER CLOTHES

Amma was tugged from her petrified state through the meager space between an at least seven-foot-tall minotaur and a just-as-hulking ogre. The monstrous men threw themselves out of the way to avoid even an accidental brush with her. Damien's warning had worked, but it didn't quell the frenzy with which Amma's heart was attempting to escape her chest.

"First time, huh? I can tell, it's in your eyes. And the rest of your face too." The woman trotted off, Amma caught in her clutches, gentle though they were.

Amma jogged to keep up but glanced over her shoulder. The massive guards followed behind, keeping their distance but cutting off any last glimpse she might have caught of Damien as he disappeared in the opposing direction.

"Listen, don't worry, you can totally leverage this if you play your cards right, trust me." She'd lowered her voice, but her lilt was sing-songy and not at all how Amma expected the person taking her into *confinement* would sound.

Amma was swept sideways and down a much more narrow corridor. The guards' steps continued to clang behind them but kept their distance. Amma had no idea what to even call the massive, maze-like place she'd ended up, every hall dark and windowless, but the slip of a woman dragging her through it meandered about with total confidence. Soon the way back was completely lost on Amma, not that turning and fleeing was an option with axe-wielding giants on her tail.

Pulled to a stop before a door, her guide turned sharply, holding a hand out to the two men. "Ladies only," she said with a grin and a wink, then pushed into the chamber and hauled Amma inside.

Shutting out the ogre and minotaur in the hall left the two of them alone, but the sound of gently running water filled up the empty space. The walls inside the new chamber danced with an ebbing reflection like glistening spiderwebs in a light breeze. It reminded Amma of the karsts' turquoise entrance, but here it was much brighter than the rest of the halls, and warmer too.

Three levels high, the central features of the chamber were tiered pools, each pouring into the next. The water's source spilled out from a long, narrow slit set high into the back wall, surrounded by snaking, metallic tentacles and inlaid with gems for eyes to represent a beast Amma hoped she would never come to meet. The whole place smelled of jasmine, and the heady, damp air made Amma's achy muscles relax.

"I'm Fryn!"

The woman at her side extended a hand, amber eyes unblinking and full of eager intent. She had her hair all bundled on the top of her head, but as she tipped it, a thick coil fell free. And then the coil looked right at Amma.

Throwing herself back, Amma's boot slipped on the tile, but Fryn caught her. "And that's Clio." Giggling, Fryn shook the hand she'd caught, pointing to the diamond-headed serpent wiggling its snout beside her ear.

Amma stammered out her own name, eyes tracked on the snake, the exact ginger color of Fryn's locks, but it wasn't a camouflage technique—the reptile was actually attached to her head. It was much smaller than the one that had tried to swallow Amma in the Innomina Wildwood, but for a moment struck the same fear. Then the snake's little tongue poked out, and its lipless mouth pulled back into something like a smile. Another snout rose from the mass of slithering bodies on Fryn's head, each with a distinct, banded pattern along its back the color of maple wood, bellies a lighter pine.

"Let's see, that one's Doris, and she's Thaleia, and this one's Neso, and those three are Eudore, Eunice, and Euagore."

"Oh, hi." Amma waved to them, and their heads bobbed back.

Fryn spun, and a whole host of snakes rose from the coils at the back of her head. "Then there's Arethusa, Calypso, Ploto and Proto, Halie, and Xantho." Little tongue zipped in and out of mouths turned up, and Fryn spun back around. She ran a finger under Clio's jaw. "We're all very pleased to meet you."

"Right, well I'm pleased to—um, what are you doing?"

Fryn's hands were on Amma's vest, pulling its tie free. "Well, you're kinda gross, no offense, and clothes don't go in the bathing pools, just bodies." Amma's vest was tossed over Fryn's shoulder, and then her tunic was pulled upward, blinding her. "I mean, yes, we're doing the '*have her bathed and brought to me*' shtick, which is a little cliche, but I think you're going to feel better cleaned up, and you'll definitely *do* a lot better if you smell nice." Fryn appeared again as the tunic was shucked off into the far corner of the room.

Amma's instinct was to push her away, not wanting to be touched, let alone stripped, after what had happened in Brineberth. But the sound of falling water meant that she had the opportunity to wash Cedric's hands off of her, and she suddenly desired nothing more than ducking below the surface and staying there until her lungs threatened to burst.

Fryn dropped to her knees and started working on Amma's boots. "Don't worry, though, I can fix you right up. You should have seen me my first time here."

Amma did look at her then, her strikingly pretty face despite being haloed by serpents, and her toned limbs and stomach, all of which were on display in what very little she wore. She was clad in what should have been undergarments but were adorned as if meant to be put on display in deep reds and violets with ornate chains and jewels that tinkled pleasantly when she moved. The woman's poise and confidence likely blinded Amma to how much of Fryn's skin was uncovered until then.

"Can you tell me where exactly here is?"

"Oh, I don't really know, the summons never says. It's just a temporary dimension or whatever, only lasts as long as Yvlcon, so it doesn't have a name." Fryn held one of Amma's boots up and poked at the scuffs, clicking her tongue. "Unless you mean *here*, here? At Yvlcon? You must have really been a last-minute decision. Happens sometimes." Too quick to be stopped, she reached up and pulled down Amma's breeches with a wink. "You must have some talent."

Amma tripped backward out of her pants, and they were tossed onto the pile in the room's corner. Left in just her chemise, Amma padded barefoot across the tiles, following Fryn to the first pool at the bottom of the tiered steps. A layer of steam blanketed the water, bubbles popping in its center like a stew, and Amma suddenly felt as though she'd enjoy being boiled.

"So, you, my friend, are at the Yearly Villainous Ledgeration and Convergence of Nefariosity, which is basically like a party. I mean, as much as these guys can ever have a party. Big, bad, evil guys from all over come together here, and they discuss new inventions and discoveries, make plans with one another, and basically just catch up. It's actually kind of boring during the day, serving drinks and waiting around while they talk, but at night it can get *very* fun." Fryn moved fast again, grabbing the hem of Amma's chemise and pulling it over her head. "Okay, hop in."

Naked, Amma was more than happy to cover herself by sinking into the pool. Muscles loosening in the heat, she groaned, eyes closing, nostrils filling with the jasmine-scented steam. "What kind of fun?"

"The kind you get paid to do." Amma's eyes popped back open to see the careful look Fryn was giving the lace on the neckline of Amma's underthings. "Wow, this is nice. What'd you have to do for it? Postern-gate stuff?"

Amma didn't know how to answer that. She didn't have to *do* anything for it, and she had no idea what the rear entrance to a fortification had to do with anything either. But Damien had said outright that Amma's presence was *carnal*, and Fryn's clothing, or lack thereof, suddenly made much more sense. She dipped a little lower into the water. "Um, I don't mean to be rude, but are you a…a prostitute?"

"Am I?" Fryn tapped fingers to her chin as she thought, then tossed Amma's chemise over her shoulder with a shrug. "Well, I do have *a lot* of sex, and I get paid very well for it, don't I?" She slipped a hand under the head of one of her snakes and tickled its chin. Its tongue darted out with a laugh-like hiss, and Fryn snickered back.

"But you, um…you choose who you…uh…" Amma rubbed her arms beneath the water.

"Oh, yeah! Things are way different than they were before." Fryn knelt then at the edge of the pool and tossed a small linen to Amma. "And I get paid for lots of other stuff too. I mean, you would *not* believe how much these guys like to yak. Sometimes that's all they want! It's like, world-domination this, and total-destruction that, and then, get this, sometimes they even *cry*. Which, by the way, you are *not* going to see coming the first time it happens, but you gotta be ready, because if you laugh? That's it, sister." She ran a finger over her throat and stuck out her tongue. "*But*, if you can be convincing enough like, *Oh, no, master, that sounds so hard, you must be totally overwhelmed having to manage so many nefarious plans and so many stupid minions*, they'll give you almost anything. It's great!"

Amma scrubbed at the dirtiest parts of her, perhaps a bit too hard as a distraction. "It's great?"

"Yup! I actually got a castle in Clarisseau off a guy who fell helmet over boots for me a couple years ago. I think he stole it from some nobles, I didn't ask for the details, ya know, it's better that way, but it's real nice, got a great view from the battlements and everything. The villain who gave it to me did end up getting himself killed when he tried to march on the Vouvusti temple in the territory next door though. I told him, I said, *Lucius, you can't just walk into a holy place to the goddess of a whole season and expect to turn it*, but did he listen? Of course not! I should have known, it's impossible to tell a necromancer anything—the whole bringing-stuff-back-from-the-dead thing *really* goes to their heads. He died choking on a bunch of dried leaves that the priestesses shoved down his throat and then set fire to. Can't cast yourself back to life when your lungs are burnt out, can you, Lucius?"

"Oh, um, I'm sorry?" Amma scrubbed at her face, peeking over the linen.

"Eh, it's fine. It's not like I was in *love* or anything." She squealed out laughter at that. "Most of 'em get themselves killed, so just don't get too attached. I think you got the worst grime off you—time for the next pool." Fryn stood, gesturing to the stairs set into the waterfall, and climbed up to the next tier on the tiled floor.

As the woman busied herself with a table covered in bottles, Amma ascended to the next pool. This one was just as warm, but smelled of citrus and made her skin tingle. Choking on burning leaves sounded like a terrible way to go, but the woman had been so flippant about it, like there were plenty to fill this Lucius's spot. Amma frowned—she wasn't here to find a replacement for Damien, but then she wasn't here to do any of the things it sounded like Fryn did—at least, she didn't think so.

"Also, games!" Fryn spun back around and jogged over, jars tucked into her arms. "We play a lot of cards, dice, Innkeepers and Imbeciles, you name it. I'm pretty good at Manticore and Mouse, but you have to make sure you don't beat the villains which can get rough. I mean, sometimes it's harder to figure out how to *not* win. It is important though, because most of these guys are really sore losers. But here's a secret for you: when you get to know one of them well enough, and you're all alone with them, that's when you play your best game and you totally obliterate them. Come here."

Amma approached the pool's edge, and Fryn gave the top of her head a push so that she completely went under. Amma sputtered when she was pulled back up, hair in her eyes, and Fryn laughed.

"It's weird, but sometimes they actually *like* losing," Fryn said, pouring out a thick liquid from one of the bottles and lathering it between her hands before working it into Amma's scalp. "I mean, what else would you do if you actually *did* dominate the whole of existence, right? Just sit around like some *king*? That sounds so boring! Nah, they gotta lose sometimes. It gives 'em something to work for."

Amma let Fryn's fingers work at the knots in her hair as she considered her words. Realm domination—that had been Damien's goal, but he never said what he would do if he got it.

"At least you only have one dark lord to try and figure out. Unless he brought you here to trade you off?" Amma's heart shot into her throat, but then Fryn shook her head as she rinsed her hands off in the water. "No, if he risked bringing you here unregistered, he probably wants to keep you. Plus, I've never seen Lord Bloodthorne take interest in any of us individually before."

"You know Damien?" Amma asked just as she was unceremoniously dunked under again.

Fryn was snort-laughing when she pulled Amma back out of the water. "You call him *Damien*? I don't know him like you do, apparently! Let's see, this is my sixth time to Yvlcon, and things have changed a lot since I was first captured—they don't even capture people anymore—but I think I've only been in one orgy with him. It's hard to remember since he's more sort of the strong, silent type, ya know? Well, I guess you *do* know."

Amma's mouth fell open, soapy water coating her tongue, a vague memory of him saying something about keeping track of a pile of bodies echoing in the back of her mind, but the words were wobbly and drowning in ale.

"He never hangs around much, always seems really unsatisfied, to be honest, but then there was that long stretch he was with Mistress Delacroix. You might have your work cut out for you. Okay, last pool for the final rinse." She gathered her bottles and returned them to the table.

Amma swam toward the highest pool, a frown creasing her face. "Who's Mistress Delacroix?"

"Oh, if you can avoid finding out, you should." Fryn's snakes hissed in agreement.

As Fryn replaced the bottles and gathered up more linens, Amma climbed into the last pool. Her stomach tightened at the cooler water, the scent much lighter, but the redness cleared from her skin, and no more dirt leeched off her arms when she moved them about. She leaned her head back, running fingers through wet hair and splashing her face, but her mind wandered, a jumble of too much information and not enough at once.

Fryn's call woke her of the muddled thoughts. She held out a fluffy linen, urging her to get out of the pool, and once she was wrapped up to dry, Fryn guided her to a chair and started running a comb through her hair. "I know just what to do with you."

As she picked up a hot, glowing stone, Amma leaned away. "Uh, are you sure?"

All the little serpents gravitated toward the stone, their eyes shining in its warm glow. "Oh, yeah. I didn't always have these,"—Fryn gestured to the snake nest—"it's a curse."

Amma's eyes went wide, but she fell still, and Fryn brought the stone to her hair, drying up the excess water from it while she simultaneously brushed it out.

"I know that look, but don't be sorry; I love my girls. I fell into the Everdarque like a decade ago, had no idea where I was, and I met this fae. He was real handsy, but what was I supposed to do? I was lost and alone and sixteen, so I just sort of did whatever he said. But then this other fae showed up real jealous-like, and boom, snake-hair." As Fryn came around to Amma's front, all the little serpents nuzzled against her neck and chin. "At first, it was awful when they sent me back to our plane—I couldn't even go home without my own parents being terrified of me, but then I met these lamia and they were so sweet, taught me how to take care of the girls and took care of me too. The only thing bad about it now is I gotta sleep on my stomach, but it's a small price to pay to be supported by thirteen ladies who will poison anybody who touches me without permission."

Amma eyed one of the snakes, its jaw dropping open to reveal pointy fangs, but then it closed up again and there was that cute, little smile. "That actually sounds nice."

"Sure is!" Fryn traded the stone for a jar of something red, dipping a finger into it to pat over Amma's lips and rub into her cheeks. "Makes me trustworthy to the villains too since, by everybody else's standards, we're all monsters, so, that means more gold for me. There! Let's get you dressed."

Amma followed Fryn back down to the lower level of the bath chamber where the woman dug through a wardrobe. Amma's actual clothes were still piled up in the corner. Fryn offered up a few pieces of fabric and made grabby hands for Amma's drying linen. She hesitantly made the trade, but clearly got less out of the deal, holding up the scraps of mostly transparent, crimson silk. "Um, what's this?"

"Clothes, duh." Fryn snickered and showed her how to wrap the material around her chest to cover up the most indecent bits, then used thin chains that rested on her hips to fasten two panels, one hanging between her legs and another, narrowly, over her backside. It could only justifiably be called an outfit if one squinted, but Fryn was thrilled with her work. She skipped back to the wardrobe, and Amma expected footwear, but instead returned with a thick, metal circlet. "So, I'm not happy about this part, but you have to go to jail now."

Amma's insides tightened right up, and the circlet went from mundane to harrowing.

"I mean, it's not *really* jail, I guess, it's just a cell where you have to wait until the Grand Order decides if you can stay or...whatever." She grimaced and moved again in her too quick way so that Amma didn't even think to stop her.

The circlet was pressed up against Amma's neck, there was a click and a jolt of arcana, and the collar was locked in place. Amma's hand flew to her throat, but there was no removing the thing, thick, sturdy, and pulsing ever so slightly with magic.

"Sorry. We don't really do slaves anymore since the slavers we used to get them from all got eaten by vampires, but sometimes the villains bring their own personal ones, and that's you. I'm sure you'll be fine though," Fryn insisted. "The Grand Order hasn't killed anybody who showed up unregistered in, like...four years? They haven't had anybody unregistered in, like, four years either, but that's not the point! Come on, I'll make sure you get the nicest cell."

Fryn's arm warmly looped into Amma's again, but the heat had drained right out of Amma's veins. One of Fryn's snakes gave Amma a piteous look, and she was swept back out into the dark corridors of the place that wasn't really anywhere, wearing clothes that weren't really anything, and wondering if she was still anybody at all.

CHAPTER 3
KILL, CACKLE, CONDEMN

Y OU ARE LATE.

Damien ground his jaw. It was all he could do to keep from barking back. *He* was late, but *they* had kept *him* waiting. Him. Damien Maleficus Bloodthorne, blood mage, son of Zagadoth the Tempestuous, Ninth Lord of the Infernal Darkness and Blah, Blah, Blah, half demon and wholly pissed. But then, that was what the Grand Order of Dread was wont to do in their own, private dimension when one deigned to break their insufferably arbitrary rules.

"I was...busy." Despite his fury, shouting would do Damien no good, so he kept his teeth clenched. There was a saying about how low voices lent themselves to closer heads which made them good for cleaving off, but Damien couldn't quite remember it, brain buzzing instead with irritation and time keeping. Four hours and thirty-nine minutes. It had been four fucking hours and thirty-nine abhorrent minutes since he'd walked away from Amma, and that was too long.

TOO BUSY FOR THE GRAND ORDER OF DREAD? asked the voice that was one and many at once, the voice of GOoD itself.

He would have liked to holler back that, yes, he was indeed far too busy for their pompous council and this ridiculous gathering. He had other concerns—breaking his father out of a crystal prison, exacting revenge on his rival, surviving a swirling vortex of chaotic destruction—and he only stood before the Grand Order now, bathed and dressed in attire they would approve of, because it was at the root of his greatest concern: the woman that was being kept from him.

But Damien instead just flared his nostrils, clenched his fists, and glared at the ground. The blood mage was familiar enough with the Grand Order's history of poor record keeping and the troubles that had once plagued Yvlcon because of it, so he knew bringing Amma along with him sans paperwork was indeed quite the fuck up. GOoD wasted more parchment on writing and revising regulations than committing actual atrocities—the council once lent him a chimera, the damn thing ate its own rental forms, and it took an extra moon and a half of feeding, bathing, and cleaning up its shit before he could return the dumb beast—so fixing *this* was going to require his complete composure.

Trying and succeeding only marginally to relax his brow, he lifted his gaze once more to the chamber he'd been summoned to for this dressing down. There were ornate illusions of some war gone past cast onto the grimy walls, a landscape painting of a hydra wreaking havoc in an armory hung at a slight but infuriating angle, and a pithy wood carving in Chthonic that read *Kill, Cackle, Condemn.* When his eye began to twitch, he focused on the council themselves instead.

Swathed in shadows, the beings that made up the preeminent order of evil sat atop a dais. Villains adored their daises, as did those considered heroic, he supposed—everybody wanted to be as high up as possible while still sitting down—but this dais was an unnecessarily tall, giant slab of stone raised just to the height of Damien's chin. Though he had to tip his head up to see them, their hooded robes still obscured the council members' faces, both fabric and arcana casting endless hollows in place of features.

Above, a miasmic cloud undulated with a faint pall of blue light. A constant presence of arcana, alive and throbbing with something like breath, it connected the members of the council to one another, allowing them to share a mind and a voice. That, at least, made Damien squirm instead of sneer.

He cleared his throat, flexing fingers and stretching shoulders. An excuse—he needed to come up with an excuse for being late. "I received the summons with little warning for this Yvlcon, and so—"

LITTLE WARNING? Only one leaned forward, but the voices still spoke in unison, shared amongst the whole and echoing off the walls. *IS THE IMPENDING ECLIPSE NOT NOTIFICATION ENOUGH?*

Damien's mouth opened, eyes darting down as he thought. The moons had been inching nearer one another, and, darkness, did the Grand Order ever love their astronomical anomalies.

Eclipses were popular in the villain community both for arcane and theatrical reasons. What better time than in the pitch black of the middle of the day to strike, really? The ignorant believed it was a god's wrath, and the educated were too intrigued by the event to notice evil preparing to strike. The fact arcana was heightened was beneficial too, if one knew how to capitalize upon it.

Yvlcon did not have annual dates, but instead preceded such anomalies, acting as a negotiation stage where a necromancer or alchemist could request assistance from a dragon tamer or a dark priest in return for a future favor. It was reciprocity in motion, and even as he stood before the council in defiance, Damien hoped he could twist this castigation into what GOoD liked best: a bargain.

His eyes shifted over the six seats before him, trying to glean anything he could off the robed, amorphous figures. The true identity of any council member was never revealed. Guesses could be made, especially when villains went missing, presumed dead otherwise, but there was never confirmation. GOoD members were sometimes rumored to be ancient, all-powerful beings who had been on earth since time's dawning but were also said to be whoever was available on any given day. Damien was unsure the members even knew who the others were, but there was one fact everyone knew: they were a council of six, and on this day, one seat was empty. "Seems I'm not the only one with other obligations."

There was an uneasy shuffling then, and he let the observation hang in the chamber along with that weird, arcane cloud. Damien stood a little straighter, arms crossing over his chest. If they were less powerful down by one, that could be a boon.

But the council would never acknowledge a mistake on their own part, despite reveling in holding everyone else to the coals for the most minor transgressions. Before the council's discomfort could grow into embarrassed rage, Damien took a deep breath and thought of Amma. "Extracurricular malfeasances aside, what can I do for you?"

The members shifted again, but this time with the slightest intrigue. *YOU WOULD OFFER THE GRAND ORDER YOUR SERVICES?*

"We all know that's the point of this—there has been a sort of miscommunication, and there is a price to be paid. In return for my...my concubine back, name your demand, and it will be—"

"I know, I know, I'm late, but I don't want to hear it: the transdimensional corridor is packed this time of—"

Damien turned to the opening chamber door behind him, and there stood a figure, cloaked in a significantly oversized robe like the five upon the dais, face obscured.

"How thoughtful of you to join us," Damien grumbled.

The figure remained there, letting the massive door fall closed with a long, low creak and a thunk that finally shook off his petrification. He hacked up bile into his throat and dropped his voice to a raspy, wet tone in a poor mockery of what the Grand Order sounded like. "What is this?"

LORD BLOODTHORNE HAS FAILED TO FILE FORMS D2-WL3, AR606, AND ALL SUBSEQUENT DOCUMENTATION.

The figure gave Damien a wide berth, yanking at his hood despite the spell over his face. He disappeared behind the dais, but his voice rose up, "Well, just kill her and get it over—"

—WITH. WE HAVE OTHER THINGS TO DO. The aggregate Grand Order voice took over as the figure reappeared and entered the miasma, huffing down into the empty seat.

Damien opened his mouth to object, but the Grand Order's voice broke back in.

LORD BLOODTHORNE HAS OFFERED US A DEAL IN TRADE. WHAT KIND OF DEAL? WE HAVEN'T GOTTEN THAT FAR YET. I CAN'T IMAGINE IT IS WORTHY—HE HAS TOTALLY DISREGARDED THE SANCTITY OF YVLCON. WELL, IF WE WOULD NOT HAVE BEEN INTERRUPTED, WE WOULD KNOW WHAT THE DEAL ENTAILS. IF WE HAD NOT BEEN INTERRUPTED, WE MIGHT HAVE BLINDLY TAKEN IT WITHOUT PROPER CONSIDERATION.

Damien rolled his eyes. If he had any idea who the late member was, he would put them on a personal list for immediate destruction. There had always been six council members, and their combined power was rumored to be great—it was said that only by fortune the Grand Order of Dread didn't take over the entirety of existence, but then that would require some sort of agreement they never seemed able to come to.

Instead of realm domination, the Grand Order doled out favors when requested and called them in when needed, creating a sort of balance that ultimately did very little in the grand scheme of villainy, which was likely how it ought to be. But they did have the power to make one, little woman disappear.

WE SHALL SEE, THEN, WHAT LORD BLOODTHORNE HAS TO OFFER.

Damien was tapping his foot when the Grand Order finally stopped arguing with itself. "It's my turn now? Right. Well, my father is—"

NOT YOUR FATHER. YOU.

Damien's jaw tightened right back up. He would need to see

someone about his teeth after all of this if he could handle even more evil than what he'd gotten himself into.

But as he stood there, annoyed and clenched and eager to be done, Damien came to an uncomfortable realization: what *did* he have to offer? To burn down a village? Assassinate a lord? Raze a temple to the ground? Amma wouldn't like any of those things, even done in trade for her. She was undoubtedly going to be upset about the whole stabbing-Kaz-to-death thing as it was, but to add yet another atrocity to the list? How many times could he say, *But I did it for you,* before she would request he do nothing for her at all? Ruining the entire realm to free his father was already pushing it.

Though there was one thing he had that theoretically hurt no one: information.

"You must be aware of the mysterious occurrence in the realm of Eiren. The one I translocated from."

The Grand Order was aware of most mysterious occurrences, if not directly responsible for them, and even if not, the stink of the incident was still probably all over him, bath notwithstanding. Council members shifted, some leaning closer. Interest. Good.

"There was a similar phenomenon in The Wilds that I had the displeasure of meeting. It knows me now, and I believe I have a name."

WE KNOW OF WHAT YOU SPEAK. The voices were lower, but Damien did not make the mistake of leaning in. *AND WE KNOW WHAT IT IS CALLED. YOU SAY IT KNOWS YOU?*

Damien nodded, slow but not hesitant.

SHOW US.

It was not a request, and though a bargain had yet to be struck, the Grand Order was going to take what it wanted.

The miasmic cloud expanded, filling the whole of the chamber and blurring Damien's vision. Blood pumped through him recklessly, noxscura mingling and heaving. He pressed fingers to his temples, fighting the arcana on instinct, but there would be no winning, only obscuring what he deemed most private, so he let the eyes in, and they saw...everything.

The pit was there before Damien again, tendrils lurching out and crushing men who tried to flee, the endless nothing at its core, and then the face, the one from The Wilds, the one that came out of his own reflection in the stump. Its voice asked again, *One of Us?* And the world was desolate and empty, razed cities, salted fields, crumbling cliffside, fear, chaos, destruction. Death.

Each image flashed atop one another, painting a grisly, unavoidable future if E'nloc were released, if It got what It wanted, to be free, to walk the earth, to inhabit a vessel. To inhabit *him*.

Damien's guts twisted. He'd not meant to share *that*, but then more of what he didn't intend to share spilled forward like intestines from a rent belly. Xander's tower, Kaz's heart, Amma's smile, Delphine cackling, Zagadoth calling him *Kiddo*, his mother wishing him a goodnight, shackles, scars, lips, a thankful draekin, a dagger piercing a finger, ice, feathers, blood, a kiss.

Damien pushed back, and the images wavered, a vision of Anomalous's lab shifting into some other alchemical setup he'd never seen, a scattering of graves across the courtyard at Bloodthorne Keep that weren't really there, liathau trees being felled in the orchard at Faebarrow and Amma's hand digging into his wrist, refusing to let go as she screamed her throat raw on his name.

The visions vanished, and Damien staggered back, a burst of silver behind his eyes as noxscura choked back the arcane cloud. He was shaking, but could not stop it, didn't want to stop it, and GOoD was…letting him?

With a sharp inhale, Damien straightened and called it all back. The noxscura obeyed, the miasma receded, and the chamber fell into a quiet, odd hum. Throats were cleared, robes shuffled, and Damien averted his gaze to focus on one of the chamber's paintings, a man with a rope about his ankle, dangling over a chasm, Chthonic words scrawled at its bottom to read, *Hang in there, baddy.*

WE NEED NOT LOOK FURTHER. ALL IN FAVOR? AYE. ALL OPPOSED? NAY. THE AYES HAVE IT.

It happened so quickly, Damien couldn't tell who or how many had opposed, nor did he truly know what they were agreeing to.

CONGRATULATIONS, LORD BLOODTHORNE, YOU HAVE BEEN CHOSEN. YOU WILL BE SUMMONED AND GIVEN INSTRUCTIONS WHEN THE FORGING IS COMPLETE.

Damien didn't like the sound of most of those words, not that any of them were specific enough to mean much, but at the moment he was really only concerned with one thing. "And?"

AND?

He held out his hands, waiting.

OH, YES, YOUR GIRLFRIEND. SHE WILL BE RELEASED ON THE CONTINGENCY YOU WILL COMPLETE THE TASK TO BE SET BEFORE YOU.

Face heating up, Damien stuttered too much to properly ask what that task would be.

YOU ARE DISMISSED. GO NOW, AND DO ENJOY THE REST OF YVLCON.

Enjoy was a loaded word.

Hours later, Damien found himself sitting in a plush chair amongst his peers, still waiting and doing absolutely no enjoying. If it was much longer, he was going to take to slitting throats, and he was going to start with conjuration mage Sceledrus Brack if the man didn't shut up about the latest terror he'd unleashed on his pointless corner of the realm. He was blathering on about making scorpions rain from the sky, but Damien couldn't concentrate with Amma still missing.

Nine hours and forty-two, no, forty-*three* minutes. His eyes flicked down to his drumming fingers, dagger still sheathed on his bracer, then to the silver band around his wrist. Well, slitting throats was out, he supposed, unless he wanted to forfeit his own life too, but he *could* write a strongly worded letter to the Grand Order about how long Amma's release was taking, and while submitting any kind of correspondence to GOoD would also require filling out a stack of frustrating and repetitive forms, he would do it if it meant each council member would have to suffer through reviewing them as well.

Damien began to compose the complaint in his mind to drown out Sceledrus's description of how delightful flesh appeared when stung and injected with venom. He sank a bit lower in his seat, the gaze he'd set on the hall's entry blurring, then smacked at his own cheek. How long had it been since he slept? To think, he had only woken beside Amma the day prior, attended a fae gathering in the Everdarque, lost her to his own foolish temper, spent the night flying to where she'd been taken, found her, and then when she was safely wrapped in his arms, she had finally—thrust a goblet into his face.

The second paragraph of Damien's mind-drafted letter which highlighted every heinous act he could have committed in the time it took to unlock one woman's cell door was interrupted by a servant girl handing him a cup of wine. Alcohol dulled Yvlcon's attendees' natural proclivities for violence, so there was a constant push to keep them all just a little boozed up. Damien sighed and took a swig before setting the goblet down with enough force to slosh half of it out and went right back to brooding. If anything happened to Amma, if just one golden hair on her head were displaced, he would be crushing skulls and dropping bodies into piranha ponds and—

"Um, Damien?"

He sat up, eyes snapping to the girl who wasn't a servant at all but Amma. The simultaneous burst of elation in his chest and the wave of relief at her voice left Damien frozen, though how she was dressed, or rather not, certainly didn't help his ability to function normally.

Barefoot, bare-legged, bare-stomached, all that covered her was a

21

narrow fall of crimson fabric hanging from a black chain perched low on her hips. Hips that he had seen in tight breeches but never looking so round and so soft and, well, so naked. She inhaled shallowly, her navel twitching with a nervous breath and chest swelling, a second swath of red silk barely containing her breasts.

Though the other Yvlcon servants dressed in variations of the same, he rarely took more than a cursory glance at just how little they wore. As much as his appreciation for it, amongst other things, suddenly grew, the way Amma stood there with pinched knees, clasped hands, and gnawed-on, painted lips made him want to rip every stitch off of her but somehow also bury her under a pile of linens before anyone else could touch her.

Which was about to happen.

Sceledrus had been eyeing the back of Amma even more salaciously than Damien did her front, and the miscreant made his move. Damien lunged simultaneously, yanking her out of Sceledrus's wandering reach for her ass. Amma squealed, knocked off balance and falling onto Damien's shoulder. He growled from beside her hip, the word feral on his tongue, "*Mine.*"

The mage gave him a protesting look. "You can't just lay claim to a servant like that. At least play me a round of dice for her."

It was far too easy for Damien to shift himself up against Amma's hip and lift her right off the ground. "I'll claim her however I want."

Amma's breathy gasp was in his ear, flailing until her hands gripped the back of his tunic as she slid into place over his shoulder, a perfect fit. He wrapped an arm around her knees, hand pressed to the back of her thigh. Skin soft and warm beneath his fingers, he gave it a squeeze, meaning to reassure her he hadn't actually devolved into the brutish villain he was playing at.

If only someone would assure *him* it was all an act.

Past the other attendees, most of whom didn't bat an eye at a dark lord throwing a servant girl over his shoulder to carry off to his bedchamber, and out into the hall where a few others lingered, he kept up the march to the stairs and straight to the quarters he'd been given. Fumbling only for a second one-handed with the key, he brought her inside and kicked the door shut behind them.

Damien stood there in the privacy of the room, breath coming hard, hands still clutching onto her thighs, noting how little the strip of fabric that hung over her backside covered, and then his eyes drifted over to the bed. While it was both a logical and opportune place for her, he knew he shouldn't, and like he had gone suddenly stupid and weak, dropped her right in front of him.

Amma squealed, wobbling but landing on her feet, hands catching onto his neck in the fall.

He pressed his back to the closed door to put a little more space between her nearly naked body and his own, but she didn't let go. Amma breathed as if she'd been the one to carry him upstairs, breasts straining against the too-small swath of crimson fabric. Damien ran a hand over his face, skin itchy, and he would have liked to adjust the tightness in his breeches if she'd just give him one or seven more inches of space between them, but she insisted on being right up against him, so he instead tried to conjure the least attractive image he possibly could in his mind.

"How many orgies have you been in?"

Well, that wasn't going to do it. "I've, uh…lost count?"

Amma's brow narrowed, and while that had clearly been the wrong answer, at least the look she gave him would help his trouser situation.

Damien ducked out of her grip and paced deeper into the dimly-lit bedchamber. "What I mean is, it has been years since the last, and anyway, those things are the incorrect solution to a problem that—wait, what's this got to do with anything?"

"I don't know, it's not really important." Amma had turned, worrying her thumbnail between her teeth, eyes darting all over the room. "It's just that we're in a temporary dimension, and apparently everyone here is a villain, and Fryn says there aren't slaves, but then she put this collar on me, and I didn't want to think about that in the jail cell, but then all I could think about instead was that giant pit of black goo that tried to eat you and how you almost died, but you didn't, which is great, but I was in that dungeon for a really long time, and I started to think you weren't going to come and get me because maybe you were in an orgy or something?" She took a huge breath, glassy eyes finding his. "You're not going to give me away to one of the other villains here, right?"

"Basest beasts, no." Damien swept back to her and took her by the wrists, pulling her close. "Why would you think that?"

"It's something Fryn said."

"Who in the Abyss is Fryn?"

Again, her features turned cold. "You slept with her in one of those orgies."

Damien's mouth went dry, and it was his turn to be wide-eyed as he released her. "Ah, well, no, you don't always,"—he brought his hands together awkwardly—"with every, single being at one of those things, and it's often dark, so, you know. But look, I did warn you about this, about the reputation I have to uphold here."

"Carrying off slaves to your bed?" She lifted a brow.

"No," he answered, quick and sharp. "Just general...villainous...*things*. And anyway, I intended only to remove you from that hall full of men like Sceledrus as swiftly as possible and bring you up here where we could finally...talk."

Face shifting back into unease, Amma nodded then paced away from the door as if lost in thought. Damien watched her, eyes drifting down her barely covered body, the room's dim candlelight dancing over her skin. Even mottled in the darkness, she was fucking perfect, and he longed to touch her again.

"You're really not going to trade me away? No matter what?"

He scoffed. "Amma, I would sooner be cleaved in two than allow anyone to take you from me."

Her fingers slid up to her neck and the collar she had gestured to in her nervous diatribe. Though it was similar to what had been sealed around his wrist, a warning to remain civil and a dulling of arcana, she'd been marked by the council as property. His property.

"Damien," she said, voice small, eyes wide. "I did something bad."

He swallowed. "You can't say those words, not dressed like that."

She pressed herself to the wall as if she could somehow disappear into it. "I think I...well, no, I *know*." Amma took a steeling breath. "I killed Cedric."

"You did? You drove that giant stake through his heart?" Damien squinted, recalling the scene of the marquis impaled against the wall over a thick pool of blood. The corner of his mouth ticked up, and he ran a hand over the back of his neck, skin there hot. "Oh, Ammalie."

"Well, the liathau technically did the impaling, but I asked it to. I mean, I wanted it to, at least, because I was afraid, and he was being awful, and then it just happened." She fidgeted against the wall, weight shifting from foot to foot. "And now he's dead because I...I *killed* him."

Damien wanted to take her by the hips, throw her onto the bed, and give her exactly what committing such a nefarious act deserved, but her hesitation put a dagger in those thoughts. He took a step closer to her, careful with his words. "And you are upset about this?"

"Can I tell you the truth?"

"Of course."

Amma's shoulders shifted back as she fell still and looked up into his eyes. "I'm glad he's dead, and I'm glad I'm the one who did it."

Her gaze held him, eroding the last modicum of restraint that kept his hands clenched at his sides and not lifting her up against the wall and fucking her right there.

"Is that okay?" She had lost the slant of confidence that had just radiated from her like arcana, timid sweetness taking over as she shrank in on herself.

Damien chuckled. "I may not be a dependable source of morality, but I, for one, am extraordinarily jealous."

Curiosity sparkled in her eyes.

"I would have liked to kill him, to slice off his head or hack him into a hundred useless pieces." He took a careful step toward her. "I wish I could have done it for you—slit his throat and cut out his heart to lay at your feet—however you might have ordered it be done."

"Oh," Amma said, breath catching, stepping away from the wall. "Well, maybe now I do regret doing it. Just a little."

"Is there anyone else?" Damien grinned, inching toward her still. "A life you would request I snuff out? I would gladly deliver you their head, simply give me a name, and—"

Amma took him by the tunic and jerked him down into a frantic kiss. Her lips and tongue worked at his like she was starved, and relief flooded Damien's chest at having her mouth on his again. It hadn't been an accident, inspired only because he had gone to her rescue, when she had previously kissed him, thank the dark gods.

She pressed herself against him, and he took her by the waist, skin bare and soft and hot. She had on so little it would take only the flick of his wrist to have her naked, and the way she clawed at his neck and tried to climb up him said she was keen on the very same idea. But then again, she had just asked him if he intended to trade her away, as if she were afraid she might have been brought to Yvlcon simply as some good to be sold when he was done with her.

"Amma," he breathed into her mouth as she kept kissing him, "Ammalie, stop." His words sounded like a plea though his hands roved over her bare flesh.

"You stop," she taunted, gripping the back of his head and nipping at his lip.

Groaning as he pulled back, he hooked a finger into the collar to hold her in place. "I can't."

Blue eyes heavy with lust, she searched his face for the answer. "Why not?"

"The talisman," he admitted, catching his own reflection in the metal clasped about her neck. "We both know it means I can have you however I please. It was easier to ignore before, but now look at you, wearing the evidence around your throat that you belong to me."

Amma's fingers grasped at him, drawing herself as close as he would allow, lips brushing his. "What if that's exactly what I want?"

CHAPTER 4
BEHAVING DECEITFULLY UNDER INESCAPABLE CIRCUMSTANCES

Damien's hands were underneath her, and Amma was lifted from the ground. She wrapped her legs around his waist and devoured his mouth again. Hot on her thighs, his fingers dug in, crushing her to him, but when her back came up against the wall, she winced and cried out.

"What happened?" He pulled back. "Did I hurt you?"

Amma had her elbows on his shoulders, leaning into him, breathing hard. "Nothing, I just—" She sucked in a sharp breath as his hold on her shifted, a spasm shooting up her spine.

Carefully, Damien guided her to the ground, fingers light as they slid along her back, and he walked her toward the closest wall sconce. "Bloody Abyss," he mumbled, touching her side. "How did I miss all this?"

Amma couldn't see what it was his palms glanced over, but she could feel a tightness in her skin. His hands did not return to ardently grab at her, instead hovering carefully at her waist as he urged her across the room.

"Get on the bed." He began to pull off his boots. "On your stomach."

She watched him a moment then climbed up onto the decadent linens. Easing herself onto her belly, she glanced back as he removed his belt. "This feels like the opposite of what you just said we can't do."

Damien made a thoughtful noise in the back of his throat, but as he continued to undress, the fervor he'd had moments before was gone. He stripped off his tunic, breeches still on but leaving himself nearly as naked as she was, and when he knelt on the bed at her side, her face flashed with heat. He was studying her body laid out before him, hair falling into his eyes as he tipped his head down, and then the warmth of his hand covered her low back. "Does this hurt?"

"No," she said, a soft sigh into the linens. It actually felt wonderful, the heat off his skin, the weight of his hand, the comfort of his presence so close, and then—yes, right there, that stung, and she jerked beneath his touch with a feeble cry.

"This bruising,"—he swallowed—"I can take care of this." Damien shifted beside her, and both of his hands gently pressed to the most sensitive spot on her low back. There was a tickle under his palms and then that familiar arcana of his. As it seeped into her skin, her limbs loosened, and she rested her cheek on the bed.

Damien's hands glided over places she didn't even know hurt until they were touched, but with sibilant, Chthonic whispers, the ache faded. Fingers exploring her skin, he treated a spot below her shoulder, her elbow, a place on her calf, and soon the discomfort was banished by pleasant tingles.

"This one is persistent and largest," he said when his hands returned to her low back. "One spell was not enough to heal it. What caused this?"

Amma drew her arms into her sides and curled fists under her chin at the sharp memory of escaping Cedric's grasp by plunging backward off the bed in Krepmar Keep. "I fell," she said simply, focusing hard on the fluffy linens to blot the image from her mind.

Damien grunted out a skeptical sound but didn't inquire further. His palms slid over her low back and beneath the chain that held up what little she wore, pulsing arcana into her hip and the fleshiest part of her. She sucked in a sharp breath, the much more intimate touch making her muscles tense.

He pulled away. "Apologies. The bruising is...lower."

"It's fine." When his hands didn't return, she peeked upward to see Damien gnawing his lip—hesitation still so strange on his face. "Please," she said quietly, "don't stop."

After a slow exhale, Damien's fingers found the worst bruise again, and she remained slack beneath them, even when they tickled. She knew he had meager spells to heal, despite that a blood mage had little use for them, but she supposed none of her injuries were grievous, which made mending them easier.

"Shift onto your back for me," he said.

Amma carefully rolled over, being sure to keep what little she wore in place, and when she was mostly satisfied that she was covered, she glanced up to see him inspecting her. It had been different on her stomach, pressing her face into the linens, but the way his brow knit as his gaze traveled over her body made her want to hide under the blankets.

Too exposed, she pulled her knees up and arms in. She may have been wanting to rip her clothes off moments earlier, but this felt immensely more intimate. At least with his own chest bared, she was slightly less flustered at being so close to naked.

Damien gently took her wrists and placed her hands at her sides instead of on her stomach. Then he touched her knees, but before he pressed them back down, asked, "Is this too much?"

She shook her head and let him ease her legs into the linens. He gave the length of her a long look, but there was melancholy in his eyes, not desire, as he lifted her arm to survey the marks and treat them. She had developed minor scrapes and bruises on their trek well before what happened at Krepmar Keep, of course. Stumbling clumsily or catching herself on a briar, she thought little of the nicks and purple splotches that would come and go, tender for a few days until they healed. Damien, however, never remained marred for longer than a few hours, and as he studied the marks he arcanely tended to, he muttered to himself between Chthonic spells.

He worked his way down, stopping at her thigh and a long scrape there. She let her eyelids flutter closed, heat building in her stomach and traveling lower as his fingers inched closer to the only concealed part of her. She pressed her lips together to keep from sighing out the suggestive noise building in her throat.

Then Damien's voice disrupted the quiet of the chamber, strangely raw. "Amma, I broke my vow to you."

Her mind was beginning to melt, the pain driven out by his touch now glancing over her other thigh and lightly massaging where the bruises had been. "I don't care if I never go back to Faebarrow as long as you keep doing that," she mumbled.

"I don't mean returning you to your home." Defeat was thick in his voice. "I swore to not use the talisman again, but I did."

Amma opened her eyes to see him looking utterly distraught.

"My broken promise led to your abduction." His hand came to her face, thumb sliding over her cheek. "And it left you wounded, even here."

Amma's tongue instinctively slid over the cut inside her mouth where her teeth had sliced in. "It was my own anger that made me run off, and it wasn't your fault that Cedric struck me. He'd done it before, and it's not the worst thing he..." Her voice trailed off as she watched Damien's eyes go cold.

"Tomorrow I will find a necromancer, I will bring that bastard back, and I will torture him so meticulously that he will beg his gods to return him to the Abyss."

She shook her head, laying her hand on his wrist. "No, Damien, please leave him dead."

The blood mage stared down at her like he would never rest until it was done, but she squeezed his arm, and his features finally softened. "It would not truly be his soul anyway." Damien whispered out another spell, thumb skimming over her cheek. The metallic tang inside her mouth disappeared. "I wish I could properly express my remorse, Ammalie, but I am sincerely sorry."

She wanted to tell him to not be, that was always her impulse, but she knew he would not accept that, and also that his words meant more if left as they were. "Thank you."

"I know that he was callous to you, and it is not difficult to infer how," said Damien, voice hoarse so he had to clear his throat, "but if you are inclined to discuss it, I will listen."

"Maybe someday, but for now I just want to forget."

Damien nodded and slowly appraised her body again. More comfortable under his eyes, she let the rest of the tension wring itself out of her limbs, and when he brought a hand to her chest, she didn't hold her breath. His finger slipped into the band, but only tugged it down the slightest bit to reveal an angry, red slice between her breasts.

"I did that to myself," she said, "to summon you with the feather."

He knit his brow and ran a finger over the cut. "I can mend this."

"Leave it." She caught his hand with a quickness. "That, I want to remember."

Damien frowned but obliged, asking after any more pain, but there was none, and deep circles had formed under his eyes. He hesitated, looking out into the room and then back. "Is it all right if I share the bed with you?"

Amma nodded and moved aside, giving him more room.

"Good." Damien yawned and slid down beside her. "It will be safer this way."

"You don't think it's safe?" She sat up, gaze darting to the door.

"No, I—" He paused, cocking a brow, and then held up the linens

29

as if in invitation.

She scrambled beneath them and right up against him, and he covered them both. "Did you fasten the lock?"

"I don't remember," he sighed, wrapping arms around her.

He didn't remember? He may have been a blood mage, but that was far too lax for Amma. "Damien, if you don't think it's safe—"

His light chuckling cut her off as he settled in, eyes closed. "Don't worry: there's nothing to be concerned about."

"But you just said—"

"I lied." He pressed his lips to the top of her head as his fingers threaded themselves into her hair. "That's what villains do—we lie to get what we want."

The next morning, Amma tried to think of a lie herself that would keep Damien in bed with her. No longer achy-muscled and without her bruises, she woke feeling better than she had in quite a while, and finding Damien's arms around her had certainly helped, but then he grumbled about the time and pulled himself from beneath the linens to begin dressing.

She had very little to do in that department. While beneath the blankets, she stuffed her breasts back into what constituted her top and then only needed to straighten the panels hanging from her hips. It didn't take long, but it was frustrating. No amount of shifting really mattered—the middle was the middle and it just wasn't wide enough for her liking.

She had a good distraction, though, in Damien's nonstop chatter. He was striding back and forth across the chamber, placing things down and immediately forgetting where he'd left them, pulling his tunic on backward, and just in general having a very tough time. Coupled with his roundabout explanation for how he was meant to act at Yvlcon, it was actually a fair bit entertaining to see him so flustered.

But her mind pulled back to the keep in Brineberth and when she'd been dragged into that room with a stranger who turned out to be Damien. When the spell fell away to reveal his face and she learned he had come for her, she could do nothing but kiss him. He had returned that kiss so tenderly and began to say *something*. There was no good way to ask him to finish that thought, but probably no bad way either— he'd likely forgotten after almost being devoured by a pit of evil— though it did leave things very confusing.

"Again, so you understand, and I am perfectly clear: I have a certain reputation to keep up here."

Amma tipped her head to the side, watching him pull on a boot more aggressively than he needed to and wincing. "Yes, Damien, I understand."

"You must not allow the things I say or do to vex you because you can't go around making that scrunched-up, indignant face nor can you defy me here, or we'll both be in trouble, all right?"

She crossed her arms and grinned. "All right, Damien."

"It will only be a few days of relatively light suffering," he said, strapping on his dagger and striding up to her. "But I must play along for now."

"I really do understand, and I—" Amma pursed her lips. "What do you mean *play along*?"

He squinted upward, fastening the last buckle on his bracer. "Oh, you know, act a bit cruel and thoughtless, nod along with the others when they speak of committing atrocities,"—his eyes roved down to her—"treat you like my property."

"So, what you're saying is, you'll be *pretending* to be a villain." She pushed up onto her toes and leaned against his shoulder. "But you're not *really*."

He looked down his long nose, brows furrowing. "No, that is not what I am saying. The rest of these villains are just uncouth, and I prefer nuance to my cruelty."

She twisted up her lips with a wry smile. "I don't really think—"

"That's right, you don't think, you only follow my commands, or I'll show you exactly what I mean." He leaned past her and opened the door, his hand coming to her hip and nudging her to go out ahead of him.

She stuck her tongue out and darted into the hall, but was caught in the same instance by his hand once again clamping onto the back of her neck. His fingers slipped under the collar and tightened, and she gasped. Damien's touch wasn't cruel though, despite what he said.

As she was guided back down the stairs and into the main chamber of Yvlcon, she held her breath, the trepidation of being brought there by Fryn the day before after hours locked up in a cell returning. When she had laid eyes on Damien, sitting in a chair all slouched down and scowling, she had blocked out the others in the grand space, and then he had whisked her right away. But now she had the opportunity to take in the others. Most were clad in black, tall and spindly or broody and menacing, sporting pointed teeth or glowing eyes and openly wearing sigils of dark gods. Amma sidled even closer to Damien.

"No one will touch you," he assured her, a rumble to his voice she recognized from the Chthonic he used to slice through things with his magic. She didn't know how he would make sure of that after he'd explained that no one at Yvlcon had more or less power than anyone else due to the suppressive circlets they wore on their wrists, but she trusted him. She had to.

But all that trepidation ended up amounting to nothing.

Amma's most important job was carrying Damien's wine goblet. He didn't really bother drinking from it, but it gave her hands something to do as she trailed behind him while he politely greeted snake-tailed lamia, blue-skinned beings with additional limbs, and someone who was almost definitely dead but come back if their smell was any indication. Once she relaxed, she found it difficult to contain her laughter.

As they procured a meal, a sickly thin woman was droning on to Damien about arcane weaponry from across the buffet. "You know, the others complain about cursed swords not getting picked up and just sitting around, rusting in some skeleton's lap for a hundred years, but that's barely a problem compared to what happened to mine."

"Do tell," said Damien in a thoroughly unconvincing tone as he stabbed a hunk of meat and then slid it off onto the plate Amma held at his side.

"I put in a decade of work into the Obsidian Widow Maker—it's got sentience and bloodlust and an edge so sharp you could shave Percy's mustache with it." She gestured with her fork to a man with about three hairs on his upper lip and none anywhere else. "But the idiot who found the damned thing went and made *friends* with it. That knight was supposed to die, Bloodthorne, a very painful and slow, soul-sucking death so that his sorrowful essence would be added to the steel and then the next nincompoop who came along and picked up the Widow Maker would have an even worse time of it, but no! The two of them are out gallivanting around to this day. It's like you can't keep these heroic imbeciles down!"

Amma squeaked out half a laugh before a sweet, red berry was promptly shoved into her mouth. Damien held the fruit there while he offered up a few sympathetic words to the woman and then quickly maneuvered them away.

Amma might have complained if the fruit hadn't tasted so good, and, really, the villains were much more skilled at whining than she could ever hope to be. A man called Norasthmus covered in full body armor was telling Damien about a minor slight he had incurred. "So, do you know what I did?" he asked in a tinny voice from behind his metal mask.

"You gave them the plague?" Damien guessed, corner of his mouth ticking up.

"I gave them the plague!"

As Norasthmus laughed, the hollow sounds echoing as he threw his head back, Damien turned to her and whispered, "It's always the plague," to which she chuckled, and he nudged her like that wasn't what he expected to elicit despite grinning himself.

Norasthmus dipped his head back down as the two plastered on somber expressions. "But, you know, it's the strangest thing: they don't even care. I mean, they did care for about a fortnight, but now they act as if it's too much of a bother to take any additional precautions. It wasn't even a difficult plague to fight off, it just took getting bitten by these fuzzy, little creatures called vaxins who have antivenom in their saliva, but there was a whole campaign against them for one reason or another. Some of them thought *I* made the vaxins, others thought the vaxins were from a rival kingdom, and a good chunk of the villagers don't even believe the vaxins exist! I mean, look, they do!" He held up a gauntlet-covered hand, there was a puff of smoke, and an almost perfectly round rodent with two massive black eyes and even rounder ears appeared.

Amma gasped, shoving Damien's goblet at him to take and instinctively reached out. The vaxin jumped right into her hands. "Oh, look at him, he's precious," Amma squealed, scratching between its ears and making its long foot thump against her palm. "And his venom's an antidote? Laurel would love him. Oh, Damien, can I—" She clamped her mouth shut when she saw the look he was already giving her.

"Your concubine fancies herself an animal tamer?"

Amma grinned awkwardly and nodded, and Damien gave her a withering look. "She does possess the required skills, amongst others."

"Have that one then—we've got thousands. Half of the villagers act as though it's a human right to lose a limb instead of getting a quick nibble from one of these things and exorcising the evil from the land. At this point, I'd welcome an exorcising really, it's all getting quite boring watching them fight one another rather than me." Norasthmus sighed then, a heavy, tinny sound.

And then the vaxin disappeared from Amma's hands in a poof of brown fur.

"They do that," said Norasthmus. "It'll come back when it feels like it."

Damien excused them, whispering in her ear that she was lucky The Plague Bringer was so generous. She noted the upward tick to his lips. Each time she accidentally—or not so accidentally—defied him, his apprehension and sour mood seemed to lessen.

"Maybe you're the lucky one," she whispered back, "having such a cute concubine who can get away with anything."

He scowled, but she could see he was gnawing on the inside of his cheek before he broke into a grin as he quickly ushered her into another hall.

The chamber they entered was filled with long tables, though no one was eating at them. Instead, they were covered with tattered banners depicting words in Key or Chthonic, crudely painted images of potions and weapons, and littered with objects presumably for sale by the merchants seated behind them.

"If you see anything you want, it's yours," he said into her ear, his hand shifting down to her low back as they walked through the hall. "The bill will be sent to Aszath Koth and someone there will take care of it."

Her eyes passed over ornate scrolls, books, and a rack of ethereally glowing jewelry that gave her a vague sense of nausea. "I don't need anything."

"I didn't say need, I said *want*. And as pleased as I am to have you wrapped in only a thin layer of silk, I imagine you would prefer something that covers a bit more of this." His hand slid down and pinched her backside.

Amma jumped, but Damien only smirked and used his hands to instead inspect a bottle filled with brilliantly green liquid that turned deep blue when he shook it.

"What's it going to cost me?" she asked, voice low, following him.

"Nothing. As I said, Aszath Koth will pay, so you may have anything you like." The next table was covered in cages filled with orange-skinned lizards, the stink about it so thick it could practically be seen. One burped, and a puff of sulfuric smoke wafted out. "Well, preferably things that aren't alive—that vaxin's enough."

Amma eyed a display of sharp things that could be tucked away. She took a careful step toward them, running a finger along the edge of the table. She'd crushed her crossbow, her dagger had been stolen, and the knives there were making her nostalgic for the safety of a weapon strapped to her thigh. Then she noted the prices, and though she never had a good sense of the worth of gold, the numbers made her recoil right into Damien.

The blood mage, however, kept her in place between him and the table. He reached over her shoulder and picked up a dagger, unsheathing it to reveal a blade carved with filigree so that it appeared to be lace turned to steel by way of arcana. He tested the sharp edge on a finger, and it drew quick blood. "Beautiful, delicate, sharp,"—he turned it over, and the blade caught the blue lights in the hall—"it's your perfect match."

She shook her head but was entranced by its curve and point. "By Sestoth, it's even silver, isn't it?"

"Well, that makes it an easy choice. Room seven." He handed it off to the merchant, then guided her on. "You'll need a holster, yes?"

"Oh, Damien, I can't—you can't."

"I can do whatever I want, Amma; I'm a dark lord, and this is Yvlcon."

She swallowed, clasping hands in front of her. "Fine, but I'm not doing any *postern-gate* stuff to reciprocate."

"Postern?" Damien chuckled. "If I ask, feel free to use the dagger on me."

She scowled. "You cut into yourself all the time."

"Oh, that's right, I do, don't I?" He chucked her under the chin. "Now, wipe off that look and at least pretend to be pleased, or I'll be forced to make you that way." His hand snaked down to her low back again, tickling as it went and breaking her of the pout.

He guided her toward another merchant selling leathers and clothing. They both sifted through the wares, replacing the garments and armor they'd ruined traveling across Eiren, and Amma even managed to find a tunic dyed a pale enough shade of red to be considered pink. It wasn't for wearing at Yvlcon though, Damien reminded her.

"That's fine, I'm getting used to this," she said, turning from him and stretching arms overhead as she cocked a hip, but then her eyes fell on an overflowing table across the hall and the broad-shouldered and stick-thin forms of Anomalous Craven and Mudryth behind it. She grabbed Damien's wrist and hauled him through the crowd.

"If it isn't my favorite demon spawn!" Anomalous threw his huge hands into the air, standing and knocking into the table. Mudryth's eyes went white, a shadow bursting into existence to keep the hodgepodge upon it from crashing to the ground.

"That's the third time today." She smacked him, and he tiptoed backward.

A third lumbering figure shifted out of the shadows carrying three plates of food. The man limped slightly, head permanently cocked to the side, but when he saw Damien and Amma, opened his mouth and let out a startling noise that fell somewhere between elation and fear.

"Oh, look, Vick remembers you." Anomalous clapped as the amalgam of a man rounded the table and went right for Amma, throwing arms around her middle and lifting her off the ground.

Unable to breathe, Amma went lax under the incredibly tight

embrace, staggering backward when she was finally released, but then the strange being clapped, and she saw the finger of liathau wood made from the trinket she'd found in the alchemist's tower. "You're"—she panted—"from the goo?"

"Sure is!" Mudryth patted his shoulder and eased him back into a chair that creaked under his weight. She plied him with food, and he happily began chomping down. "Lasted way longer than any of the others. I think he's a keeper." Then she gestured between Damien and Amma. "This certainly escalated."

"It is a long and arduous story." Damien cut off Anomalous's attempt to embrace him, taking his hand instead and giving it a shake. "Anything interesting?"

Anomalous excitedly pointed out a number of strange things, and Damien appeared to be listening, but when he lifted a small bottle and sniffed at it, he immediately corked it back up and dropped it on the table.

"What is *that*?"

"They call this Elixir Eternea, say it's arcane and sends you temporarily to the afterlife, but it's actually just a neat, little tincture that slows the heart to an imperceptible degree, impedes respiration so it becomes unnecessary, and presents the body, for all intents and purposes, as dead."

Damien turned his lip up. "Are you certain? I've never heard of such a thing, but it smells familiar. And nauseating."

Anomalous shrugged. "Muddie took a dose for me to test it out, and after a couple of hours, I almost chopped her up for parts."

"Woke up with a hatchet in my face," she squawked, and even Vick laughed at that, mouth full.

Damien ushered Amma off again when he checked the time, stating they would be late. He guided her out of the more populated halls to a smaller chamber where matching, plush seats had been positioned in rows facing a platform. The room was similar to a very small theater with thick draperies on the walls, though it was just as dark as any of the other spaces, no windows to be seen and only candlelight set into the walls.

Most of the seats were taken, and Damien maneuvered the two of them through the chamber, explaining quietly that she may find herself bored in the coming few hours, but then cut himself off and stopped short. She followed his gaze to a dark figure at the head of the room, and while most of the Yvlcon attendees were ominous and frightening in their own right, this one carried an aura about them, face totally obscured by a hooded robe, and Amma's stomach was immediately unsettled.

Damien straightened, and his gentle touch on her waist shifted to a grip on her arm. A coldness passed through him and to her, and he tugged her roughly to one of the few empty seats on the far side of the chamber. He fell into one with a huff and glared at her. "On your knees."

CHAPTER 5
IT IS THE TORTURED WHO TURN INTO TORTURERS

A mma's gaze flicked to the ground, then to the others seated around them. None of the villains or the few companions there seemed to be paying much attention, especially under the low lighting, but she was still hesitant to follow Damien's command. "You mean, like, right here? Now?"

But he had told her she would do exactly as he said, and, apparently, did not intend to repeat himself. He reached up, and his fingers laced into her hair. With a tug, Amma was brought to her knees, landing on the floor just between his thighs.

Damien's brutal gaze swept out over the room, lingering on the place where the frightening figure had been, but from Amma's spot on the floor, she could only see him. His grasp on her hair was too tight for her to even swivel her head, drawing her toward him as he continued to take stock of the room. She pressed forward onto her hands and knees, letting her gaze travel down his body—one that had been clad in sleek, black clothing—to land on the bulge only a few inches from her face. She had come dangerously close to knowing what he looked like completely disrobed, what was under his breeches the only mystery left. Amma bit her lip—was she supposed to...

A pillow was thrust into her face, and, bewildered for only a moment, Amma took it when Damien more urgently gestured with the thing. She quickly slipped it under her while no one else was looking, though it seemed no bother to anyone else that he'd forced her to the ground between his legs.

A voice rose from the front of the room, a woman explaining that she would be presenting on a "new enthralled state" that had been, of all things, "in use by divine mages in temples devoted to the Empyrean gods." Amma half-listened as Damien's fingers continued to hold her still, the dim light in the room fading even darker.

A second presenter joined in, and the two droned on about enchanted wine and zealous devotion and all-consuming grief, about the immense power and intriguing longevity of this holy technique to enthrall. It required a relic, something fragile that, if broken, would bring the spell state to an intense and bitter halt, but they had yet to figure out how to leave the thrall entirely with its own mind. The two states were counter, the presenters said—having control of oneself and being controlled—but Amma knew that was untrue: Damien had done it to her. The vampire dame Lycoris and the witches in the Innomina Wildwood agreed that Amma's mind had not been permanently altered by the talisman inside her, yet he could command her to do anything.

But there were moments when Amma wondered if Bloodthorne's Talisman of Enthrallment actually had done something permanent to her, something to allow a darkness to creep inside. She didn't necessarily feel different, but when his fingers had ensnared themselves in her locks and brought her to the ground, she wanted to go. She knew she shouldn't allow it, and she definitely shouldn't like it, not when she had detested the last person who treated her like an object and reveled in her pain. So why would her heart flutter when Damien's features went cold? And why did she get a thrill when he whispered threats into her ear?

His attentive gaze flicked away from the speakers on the platform and down to her. Amma squeezed her thighs together, glad he didn't know they'd grown slick while she had been staring up at him, contemplating her position on her knees and all of the things he might do to her if she pushed him just a little more. He leaned forward, face close to her own, and detangled his fingers from her hair. Tipping her head up by her chin, he murmured with knit brows, "Are you comfortable?"

Well, that depended. Amma's mouth twitched, but she nodded. Damien guided her head to lean on his thigh, and he stroked the spot he'd snagged on her head as he sat back again. Amma wrapped her arms around his leg, resting fully against him and closing her eyes. Maybe it was dark, this thing inside her, but that didn't mean it was bad.

Amma was roused from her nap when Damien reached down and tugged at her arm, which was almost as good as her hair, but not quite.

She pouted and groused back, "Five more minutes."

Damien chuckled but gave her a shake. "Has half-assing all of my commands and giggling when you're meant to be silent truly exhausted you so?"

Amma only yawned in his face when he finally managed to pull her to her feet. They left the darkened chamber for the main, slightly-less-dark hall where it was busiest, the voices of the assembled all harsh whispers as if they knew no other way to speak other than ominously. She blinked at the passing cloaks and scaled limbs and rubbed sleep from her eyes. "You know, I don't see what the big deal is," she said, not bothering to keep her voice low. "Everyone here has been pretty nice."

Damien grimaced, leading her to a less-populated corner of the room. "If you were on your own, you would believe otherwise. They've only been respectful because you belong to me, and I am one of them."

She started at that word, *belong*, but shook her head. "Oh, Damien, you're really not." She leaned in close and tapped the end of his long nose. "And nobody here is as sweet as you."

He caught her hand, looking about in a panic. "Don't do that."

Amma rolled her eyes and dropped her voice to mimic his huffy growl. "I can do whatever I want, Damien; this is Yvlcon, and you're only pretending."

His flustered survey of the hall slowly turned back to her, features going cold. "Oh, am I?"

There, *that* was the look, the one that made her pulse race and her muscles jump. The one that said she was in danger.

"We need one more, Lord Bloodthorne," a voice called from a dark corner of the hall. There, three men were seated around a table with an additional, empty chair.

Damien's hand came to the back of her neck again, jerking her toward him. "We'll see about that," he whispered in her ear then turned her sharply.

Amma's stomach flipped as she was marched toward the table. Of the three there, each man lounged like a king on his throne, menacing in their own ways though starkly different from one another—a scaled creature with thin limbs who looked like he belonged underwater, a dwarf with a red beard so bushy his features were almost completely obscured, and directly across from the empty chair sat a man Amma had to assume was a vampire by his golden eyes, fanged teeth, and the way he sniffed the air, commenting on the "new blood" Damien was bringing over. A thin man came to join them, draping himself over the vampire's shoulders and nibbling at his ear, marks on his neck suggesting he'd been nibbled on himself earlier.

Damien dropped into the free seat, and the vampire began shuffling a deck of cards, the others watching as if expecting an extra to come out of his sleeve at any moment. Damien, however, was not watching the cards but Amma. He crooked a finger, leaning against the armrest. "Sit," he said with a sharpness, eyes flicking down to his knee then back up.

It wasn't a complicated command, but before she could begin to puzzle it out, Damien wrapped an arm around her middle and pulled her down onto his lap. Amma froze, stiff and awkward perched on his knee, and then his hand snaked around her stomach, sliding over her lower ribs until his thumb slipped under her banded top and nestled itself between her breasts—the perfect lever to get her to do exactly as he wanted, talisman or not.

Even with eyes held open wide, Amma saw nothing, her other senses blotted out as touch took over. The hand pressing into her ribs cupped under her breast, warm and firm, and it slid her up his thigh until she was nestled against his back. Damien breathed a satisfied sigh into her ear. "You took too long," he said, lips tickling her jaw.

Amma's body melted against the heat of his, tingles crawling over the bare skin of her back. She didn't notice how her legs fell away from one another as his knee parted them from beneath until there were fingertips skimming across her thigh, and she gasped.

"I'd suggest following my commands with a bit more eagerness," he husked, the vibration of his words rumbling through her, their intention lighting a fire between her legs.

"Or what?" she heard herself saying, tone sultry as if spoken from some stranger's mouth who was not in such a delicate position.

Damien's hand fell fully against her skin, squeezing. "Oh, you'd like consequences? Because I would be delighted to give them to you."

Amma's mouth went dry, her body erupting into goosebumps under the place he touched. And then, painfully, torturously, hatefully, Damien removed his hand from her thigh to pick up the cards he'd been dealt.

It should have been a relief—she didn't think she was going to be able to breathe much longer with it there—but desire for its return clawed at her stomach. She focused on his other hand instead, tickling absently below her breast, and her nipples tightened as he perused the cards.

The game at the table began, voices speaking to one another, but the words were a muffled cacophony, background to the sensations dancing across her skin. Damien threw in a card, his hand leaving her for only a moment, returning lower on her stomach. She twitched under the new touch, and he chuckled, his response to something said at the table rumbling through her as fingers roved even lower on her belly.

Amma sucked in a sharp breath, catching the eyes of the thin man across the table. He grinned as if he knew, and she was glad the table hid how her legs were spread over Damien's thigh. But if that was covered, then perhaps she could do a little touching herself. She boldly slid her hand between his legs, fingers just barely grazing him.

"I don't think this is punishment enough," Damien's voice rumbled too low for anyone else to hear as he snatched her wandering hand. His cards were slipped into her curious fingers, and he scooped her up. Sweeping one of her legs over the arm of the chair, she was swiveled sideways on his lap, and he dropped a hand to her inner thigh to keep her there.

She gasped again, squeezing her arms and legs in as his fingers came dangerously close to the place she wanted them.

"Ah, ah." Damien clicked his tongue, other hand sliding up to the back of her neck. "Squirm all you like, but you better keep those up where I can see them."

Amma's heart raced as she extended her arm to hold the cards high enough, but the look on his face was completely disinterested. He languidly stared at the table, and when it was his turn to play, he grazed her ever so slightly as he moved to choose a card.

Amma writhed under his brief touch, hip shifting into the hardness in his lap. That elicited a reaction from him, a quiet groan from the back of his throat that didn't read on his face. His fingers came back to rove over her inner thigh, painfully close but never slipping beneath the swath of fabric between her legs. A smirk finally began to crawl up his face as she wiggled her hips to rub against his length, but his hand clamped down hard, and she fell still.

Never had anyone teased Amma like this, coming so close to touching her over and over and then veering away, but if this were how Damien carried out consequences, maybe she had no idea how cruel he truly was. Her breathing had gone ragged, her arms weak from keeping the cards at eye level, and her breasts and core ached in need of even just the brush of his fingers.

She gnawed her lip, watching him, but he refused to meet her gaze, focused instead on the game, only acknowledging that he was doing anything at all when she squirmed and he smirked. Amma let her arms fall only once, and there was a pinch to her thigh, the pain making her snap back to attention.

She leaned her face closer to his then and whined quietly. His eyes flicked from the game to hers, and she knew she had to look desperate, but she didn't care, she wanted—no, *needed* him to touch her. If she didn't get some actual relief soon, she was afraid of what she might do to get his full attention.

Damien pouted, a look so on the cusp of sympathetic that it gave her the tiniest sliver of hope. "Are you suffering?" he asked lowly, throwing a card onto the table mindlessly but not taking his eyes from her. Instead of replacing his hand on her thigh, he brought it to his chin in contemplation.

She nodded, mouth open, unable to form the proper words to express what she needed.

"And you believe that I'm merciful enough to end your suffering, don't you?" Damien stuck his finger in his mouth, tongue running over it and leaving it wet.

Amma's eyes widened, core clenching, and she nodded much more vigorously. She couldn't watch as his hand descended between her legs, gnawing on her lip, heartbeat pounding in her ears.

"Well, I'm not." He tore his gaze from hers and chose another card from her hand to play, leaving her unspoiled.

Amma whimpered, and, totally frustrated, brought her legs together to end things.

Damien dug fingers into her hip and mumbled against her ear, "Don't you dare."

Her breath caught, and she slid her thighs apart again. He only ticked a brow and then went back to perusing his hand, the game continuing along with her suffering.

Finally, there was a shout and a bevy of swears as both the dwarf and the scaled man stood, throwing down the rest of their cards and pacing away. While she was captive on his lap, Amma hadn't been paying attention to the game at all, but it came to an end and Damien took the rest of the cards and threw them onto the table, finally turning his full attention on her. Eager, Amma sunk toward him, hands on his chest, but he only grabbed her waist and held her still.

"I expect you're willing to behave now that you know what happens to bad girls when they don't."

Heat prickled all over her. "Why would I?"

He cocked his head. "Because there might be something better in it for you if you do."

She opened her mouth, not sure what was going to come out, but his eyes suddenly darted away and then widened, making her fall silent. Amma began to look over her shoulder, but his hand shot up to grip her jaw, holding her there.

"Don't." His voice had lost its playful tone, eyes pulling back to her. "Stay here, and do not move. This is not a game." He shifted her to the side and stood, plopping her down into the empty chair. "Idris, keep an eye on her." Damien swept away, and the man at the table's far side nodded in agreement, his own captive having found his way into the vampire's lap.

Frustration flared in her belly. If this was some sort of test that would make Damien fulfill the last threat he'd made, she would absolutely turn herself to stone for him, but the urgency with which he'd left told her otherwise.

Amma sank into the chair, the largeness of it swallowing her. Fear began to replace her frustration, watching the back of Damien as he mingled into the crowd. He had promised no one would touch her because she was his, but if he was gone, then what? His form came to a stop across the hall where another figure stood partially shrouded.

"My, my, kitten, what a *lovely* surprise."

Amma's breath was stolen by dread. She prayed to Sestoth it was only her imagination, but when she gazed upward, there was Xander Sephiran Shadowhart, leaning down just beside her ear.

"And here I thought you'd be in your husband's bed by now, not in Bloodthorne's lap."

Amma squashed herself into the corner of the oversized chair as far from him as possible. In contrast to most of the others, Xander's white coat gleamed under the dim lights, matching his hair, gathered up into a braided knot atop his head. How she'd not seen him over the course of the day, she had no idea, but that was likely by Xander's design.

"No touching," rumbled the vampire Idris from across the table, golden eyes flicking to Xander only once then refocusing on the man in his lap who was happily digging around beneath the table.

Xander laughed, a high and joyous sound. "Don't worry, even though I would adore partaking in some catty shenanigans, I will abide by the truce." He held up his wrist, flashing the cuff they all wore. Then he rested his chin in his hand and leaned even closer. "Must say, though, if you are for sale, I would be delighted to take you to my chamber tonight. How much?"

Amma scoffed, all the anticipation between her legs immediately drying up.

"Suit yourself. I'm getting most of you for free as is." He leered down at her, and she threw arms over her chest, feeling her skin go as red as the silks. "Really, I'm disappointed to see the two of you. I thought I'd finished you off, and I never expected Bloodthorne to be in such a good mood after all that. Though…" Xander pouted, gesturing across the hall.

Amma followed his gaze to where Damien was standing, back to them as the other figure had taken a step into the light. It was a woman, nearly as tall as Damien with long, black hair falling in a perfectly straight cascade on either side of her sharp face.

"Now, why didn't I think of *that* angle?" Xander sighed, a sound like pleased exhaustion. "Probably because I can't stand even the thought of that monster, but it does look like he's tolerating her pretty well, doesn't it?"

The woman had taken a hand to Damien's chin, much like he had just done to Amma, and he wasn't knocking it away.

Steeling herself to speak to Xander, Amma swallowed. She pulled her knees up, pressing back into the chair even deeper to keep both blood mages in sight. "Who is she?"

"You don't already know? Well, I suppose he wouldn't say." Xander draped his elbows over the chair back, lazing even closer to her. "That would be Delphine Delacroix, and for anyone but a blood mage, I'd call her the love of his life. She nearly killed him, but what is that fictitious feeling you humans call *love* if it doesn't nearly put an end to you? Delphine is unscrupulous and conniving and downright evil."

Amma's mouth twisted into a frown. "Like you."

"Exactly!" Xander popped up and sauntered around the chair to drape himself over the arm opposite her. "But she even gives me the heebie-jeebies. She was the worst partner for him, not abductable *at all*, unlike you. Not that I like anything that can pull so many of Damien's strings." His dark eyes bore into her, lips turning down.

Amma wrapped arms around her bare legs, both getting a chill and breaking out in a sweat. She wished she had that dagger if only to flash it at him.

"So, if you're here, then that means I should sick my little friends on you again, right?"

Amma sat up, chest pounding. "Cedric's dead."

"Oh, my condolences, Widow Caldor."

"We weren't married, thank Osurehm, but how did you even know about any of that? And the Sentries too?"

"That ragtag team of adventurers happened upon me by happy accident because they thought I had something to do with you. I cut them a deal, and helping them, helped me. Or, it was supposed to, but you managed to sink your claws right back into Bloodthorne's weak will again." His amusement had all fallen away, a shrewd cast left on his pointed face. "A shame you'll still have to die so we can retrieve that talisman."

Amma's heart dropped into her stomach.

A huge grin cracked over his face. "Surprised I know that too? It's amazing what Bloodthorne was willing to admit when he was desperate for my companionship." He sighed, leaning back, eyes drifting to where the other blood mage stood. "Though it looks like he might replace the both of us."

Amma snapped her attention back to Damien. The woman was just up against him now, whispering in his ear.

"You wouldn't be interested in banding together, would you?" Xander asked the question so casually, as if he hadn't just had her abducted and given over to a man who would let his entire battalion assault her for revenge. "Just until we get rid of Delphine, I mean. Then I'll go right back to planning out how I might kill you off."

Amma's insides roiled, and she glared at him. "Do you have any idea what you put me through? What kind of person Cedric was?"

"No, of course not."

Traitorous tears sprang to her eyes as she took a deep, ragged breath. "What you did to me—"

"Save it." Xander loomed over her, eyes and voice gone cold. "I really could *not* care less."

CHAPTER 6
IF TRUE STRENGTH RESIDES IN SUBMISSION, THEN WHY DOES IT MAKE ONE'S KNEES ACHE?

Delphine Delacroix was a breath away from accosting them, Damien knew, and so he beat her to it. He only realized a moment too late that he had done exactly what she wanted. But there would be no pretending he hadn't seen her, and no avoiding her either—she would use whatever means she could to get his attention eventually, and even without access to noxscura, she would find a way. She always did.

"Slumming it, I see." Delphine took a step back, shadows covering her face as she raised a goblet to her lips. Her eyes shone from the dark, vibrantly silver like the serrated edge of a blade, flicking back to where he'd left Amma—or abandoned her, more like.

He didn't look back, trusting Idris, and he didn't acknowledge the comment—it would be a mistake to let Delphine know he cared, and she'd already seen too much. "I thought you didn't come to these anymore."

"And I thought you didn't fuck slaves." She wrinkled her nose, eyes slicing through him over the rim of her drink. "What happened to all of your superiority about where you put your cock?"

"Realized it was already blighted by where it's been." He gave her a quick look up and down. She was still, of course, perfect, but something always had to be sacrificed for perfection, and with Delphine, it was all the parts that made one human—a thing Damien hadn't realized he valued until recently.

She pursed her mouth, setting down her goblet, and then that smile broke out over her face, the one that she didn't ever really mean. "It's so good to see you, darling." Her lips grazed his cheek, and frigidness bolted down his spine, but he couldn't move, old habits as hard to break as his will once upon a time, but everything that had happened to his loins with Amma atop him was snuffed out like sand dumped on a brazier.

"Can't say the same."

"But you came to me regardless."

She was right. He had just tossed Amma to the side as soon as he'd seen her—what the fuck was he bloody thinking? Damien took a measured step back.

"Wait." Delphine pulled in a breath, eyelids fluttering downward, hand extended but not quite pressing to his chest. She was holding back, demure for a moment, and it threw him. "I really am quite glad to see you, Damien."

That was…well, it was *weird*, and he didn't like it. He clasped hands behind his back and glanced about the shadows around her. "No Celeste?"

Her timid look faltered with a frown. "My sister has returned to Clarisseau, as if there is anything for either of us there. We had a bit of a disagreement recently."

Now, that wasn't a surprise. Delphine's requisite for total control often took its greatest toll on her younger sister, and even meek Celeste would eventually tire of so much browbeating.

"She'll be back when she inevitably fails at surviving on her own. But I'm not here to talk about her—I came to Yvlcon hoping to see you." Silver eyes finally raised back up to meet his own. "To apologize."

Damien's stomach knotted, and the feeling went all out of his limbs. Apologize? *Delphine*? She had to be setting up a joke, and if not, something much worse.

"I know things ended…poorly, but I truly regret that." Her fingers were touching his chin, hesitant and careful. The last time she'd touched him had been extremely unpleasant, but as she ran a thumb over his jaw, he was reminded of other things she could do with those hands. "I certainly don't regret the pillaging or the passion, but some of my actions—of both of our actions—were lamentable."

Damien searched for the truth in her face, the tautness of it always difficult to read. He shifted his jaw away from her hand. "Well, I suppose we both have to live with the damages then."

"We were so young and foolish then, but could you really blame us? You may have been upset, but so was I, and you did that, Damien. I know you can't understand, but you broke my heart when you left." When she blinked, there was something like earnestness in the silvery swirling of her irises. Damien had misconstrued that look before, but he had recently given it too. "Our relationship may have been a little fraught, but it was only because we wanted one another so deeply, and I've never stopped."

The room's sounds quieted around Damien, and a twinge in his chest deepened. It had been so long since he'd even laid eyes on her, he supposed anything could have happened. Delphine was a master at saying things but only following through on the most heinous of her promises, but then so was Damien, and he had meant his most recent apology.

Delphine closed the space he'd put between them. "I understand you now, Damien. It took time, but now I know what you really need, and I know exactly how to give it to you. Let me."

As her hand fell fully onto his chest, it felt as though her request burrowed in beneath it. Because that's what it was, a request, wasn't it? She'd never really done that before, asked for permission to do anything to him, she only ever took whatever she wanted. The pinching at his skin and the squirming beneath her palm, it couldn't be real, it couldn't be arcane manipulation, not at Yvlcon, though it was nearly as uncomfortable.

Damien glanced down and saw no magic there, just her claws poised to dig in. "You hurt me." The words felt odd, and he hated the weakness in his voice.

"But you can't be hurt," she said with the kind of timbre one uses on a child. "You always said so yourself."

She wasn't wrong, at least about the fact he had expounded as much as the truth.

"But, if you feel that way, then I suppose I'm sorry. Forgive me?"

"Forgive you?" Blood rushed past his ears as his hands tightened into fists. "You think a few words are enough to absolve what you did to me? Keeping me mindless and locked away for—" He snapped his teeth when he heard his voice waver and rise. Any kind of altercation was unacceptable at Yvlcon, and she didn't need to hear it anyway— she knew as well as he what she'd done, and she would only get off on being reminded of the gory details. In fact, there was already a smile playing at the corners of her lips.

"As I said, I know what you *need*," she stressed, pain twisting under her hand though she wasn't moving it. "There's no shame in admitting you were wrong and coming back to where you belong."

For all his confusion, Damien knew one thing: belonging to Delphine had been utter torment.

"No," he said flatly, stepping back and relieving the pressure against his chest, his heart beating madly. "I would much rather slum it."

Damien turned, unwilling and unable to give her another look. A brief moment of satisfaction passed through him—not since he had finally left had he managed to turn down one of Delphine's advances. An entire year had gone by as he wasted untold arcana constantly casting for her presence every hour of the day so he could flee if he ever felt it. But actually telling her *no*—that had almost been easy, no arcana even needed. It may have turned out differently if magic were not kept in check by the Grand Order and their helpful, silver cuffs, but as it stood, Delphine had no power over him.

But that euphoric feeling of freedom only lasted a moment.

"Fucking Shadowhart."

Damien strode back across the hall, no regard for those in his way. The sorry excuse for a blood mage was perched on the arm of Amma's seat, bearing down on her as she'd squashed herself into the corner, glaring back like a feral animal.

The two were so absorbed with one another that they didn't notice his appearance. "Will the onslaught of inconveniences this evening never end?"

Amma turned to him, and that's when he saw the redness in her eyes, the tears preparing to spill down her cheeks, and he knew it was because of *him*. Damien didn't give Xander a moment to say whatever pithy remark danced on the tip of his tongue, clamping hands onto his coat's lapels and yanking him to his feet. "You rat-fucking bastard, I'll rip off your limbs and shove them—"

"Challenging me to a duel?" Xander's hands were up, announcing the words loud enough for those closest to hear, his smile too wide.

The ominous whispers around them quieted. *Fuck.*

Damien released him with as much force as he could shrug off as accidental. The blood mage barely staggered, frowning back. "Is that a no?"

Of course it was—a duel would almost certainly ensure both of their deaths if it took place at Yvlcon, GOoD would see to that.

Damien gestured to Amma. "Come."

Her reddened face fell into a scowl, and she settled back. She was angry, and at him, of all people.

"*Now.*"

With a huff, Amma pushed herself up out of the chair and swept past him. He chanced a glance at Xander who was grinning from ear to ear, mouth open like he had just been presented with the severed head of his greatest enemy—Damien's head.

Amma had begun to make her way across the hall, but rather than to the exit, she was headed right for Delphine. Her legs were short, but somehow she'd covered quite the distance, so he had to hurry behind. He caught the back of her neck a bit more roughly than he meant, and she squeaked under his touch.

"Apologies," he mumbled, but she was still scowling, gaze trained on where Delphine stood.

The two women were making eye contact that Damien would have had trouble slicing through with his arcane blood blades. At least, for a moment, he'd stopped existing, pulling neither of their ire, but there was no way the tension under his hand would last, Amma's sudden ferocity poised to snap like a bowstring.

He tugged at her, and though she relented, kept her features locked into a murderous glower. Damien guided her through the hall and back to the stairs. They strode along in icy silence, Amma still making the exact face he'd told her not to, and as soon as the door was shut in their private chamber, she loosened herself of his grip and turned on him.

"Who was *that*?"

"Nobody," he said, averting his gaze and removing his coat, a job he focused on intently.

She clicked her tongue. "Nobody certainly has a command over you."

Damien grunted, chewing his lip—Amma had no idea what she was saying, but damn if it didn't fill him with indignation. "She would have approached us had I not gone to her first, and I didn't want to subject you to her presence."

"So, she's not nobody."

Removing his coat took too little time, and he suddenly had nothing to do with his hands, holding them out, empty. "Of course not."

"Xander says her name is Delphine, and she was your—"

"Don't listen to Xander." He paced up to Amma. "And if you see Delphine again, don't scowl at her like you were doing."

"I wasn't scowling—"

"Yes, you were. You were challenging her, to what, darkness knows, but she won't take kindly to that."

"I'll look at whoever I want, however I want," she said, that same scowl melting into a pout, crossed arms going limp, her voice losing its venom.

He snorted. "Then be prepared for her to retaliate in the most heinous way possible. She *will* hurt you, and she'll enjoy every second of it."

"And you'd let her?"

"No, I wouldn't *let* her," he spat, standing straighter, but then his hand came to the back of his neck, heat there he needed to rub out. "But it may not be up to me."

Amma's brow furrowed, hands falling to her sides.

Damien turned from her, pacing to the bed and sitting on its edge. Amma waited quietly, head tipped, expecting, no—deserving an explanation. "Delphine is a rare creature, and I do not mean that as a compliment. She was human once, and I suppose she still is." He looked up at Amma carefully. "You remember the cup that the fae king offered you. The one that I...took away?"

She nodded, and he was thankful she didn't correct him about the violence he'd used to do so.

"That was noxscura, but in its purest form. What is inside the veins of a blood mage or even a demon isn't that refined, but without impurity, calling noxscura dangerous is a gross understatement. It kills nearly every creature it comes in contact with in that form, too powerful, too destructive, but the few who can survive ingesting it become something we call nox-touched." He took a deep, reluctant breath. "They gain the ability to manipulate noxscura, often to a formidable degree."

Amma took a step toward him. "Delphine can control your blood?"

He squinted, thinking. "The noxscura in it, yes, if I'm particularly susceptible. When she is strongest, and I am weakest, she can essentially turn me into a thrall. I did not know, did not expect, her to extend that power over me beyond the games we played, but she insisted on complete control. I was to do her bidding, slay her enemies, and remain chained to her bed until my services were required."

With another careful step, Amma came a bit closer. "She kept you prisoner? But you're so...you."

"By my own stupidity, yes. At first, I could come and go, but I was too enraptured to notice as things changed, and then I was asking to leave, begging even, planning an escape, *failing*." He scoffed at the memory. "But I don't mean to...that is, I am only trying to explain that under the most dire circumstances, I cannot protect you from her because I likely cannot protect myself from her."

She still looked confused. "Xander called her the love of your life."

Damien hesitated, sucking at his teeth and thinking, but there was really no other way around it, and he had to tell her. "I may not understand love, but I'm fairly certain it does not inspire this." He gestured vaguely to the scar across his face.

Amma closed the distance between them, taking his head in her hands and tipping it up. "She did this to you?" She held him so firmly, touching him without reluctance or disgust.

"Well, no,"—he swallowed, the admittance difficult—"she compelled me to do it to myself as penance for trying to leave. In order for it to remain, I was forced to reopen the wound every morning and evening for a moon."

Her careful fingers glided over the raised skin like when she had climbed atop him in the karsts drunk on magic. She'd been so tender then despite her lust, and now her face had gone even softer, a thoughtful bend to her brow that looked as though she might cry. But then everything changed, and her features scrunched up as she blew hard through her nostrils like a boar.

"What is this face you're making?" He sat up, afraid to incur whatever wrath she had building within.

Amma's hands cupped his face again, and she growled, "I'll kill her."

Damien surprised himself with a laugh, relieved, but only for a moment: there was no change to how her blue eyes cut into him like divine steel. She *had* killed a man, and recently too, after all. "Amma, I appreciate the chivalry, but you would not come out unscathed, if you survived at all."

She huffed, stomping a small foot. "You said everyone's powers are dulled here."

"But violent actions aren't tolerated unless you declare a formal duel, which no one does because the council nearly always ensures both party's deaths. Otherwise, I would have cut Xander's tongue out for daring to speak to you."

Amma groaned, hands sadly falling away from his face. "You would have killed Cedric for me too, so I just…"

He watched her head dip, a frustrated sort of defeat. He stood from the bed, looking down on her. "Yet you didn't need me to. You ran him through all on your own. I saw the gruesome aftermath. I know what you're capable of." A flood of hot blood pumped through his veins, rinsing away the much worse memories.

"So, I could do that to Delphine too." When Amma grinned up at him, she arched a single, blonde brow and bit down onto that thick bottom lip. He would have liked to be biting it instead, especially as she clasped her hands behind her back, pretending to be both sweet and vile at once. "Can't I at least make her bleed a little?"

Breasts barely contained and swaying hips on display, Amma was all venomous honey, and he flexed his fingers, wanting a taste more than anything in all the planes at that moment. The collar, the talisman, both stood in his way, but Amma wasn't truly helpless, was she? Stabbing Delphine would certainly give her some power back, though it would condemn her too, but there was, perhaps, another way he could give her what she craved that might even satisfy them both.

"I don't know that you could survive an altercation with anyone," Damien said, wanting to touch her but waiting. "When I had you captive this evening, you nearly came undone under my hands as is."

She gasped, dropping her mouth open. "A baroness does not *come undone*."

"Never? Not once? Not even by your own hand?" He watched the redness bloom across her cheeks that told him it wasn't true. "You see, without practice, you're too vulnerable. And you forget that here, you're not a baroness, you are a concubine. One that earned herself a little torture."

She took a deep breath, chest heaving toward him, so close he could feel the warmth off of her. "That was only a little?"

"Yes, and you put up nearly no defenses at all."

Amma swallowed, wiping the last vestiges of ferocity from her face. "I thought I wasn't supposed to, Master Bloodthorne."

Fuck, of course she had to say it like that.

"I suppose you managed to behave for a short while, didn't you?" Damien was quick, grabbing her beneath her thighs and in one, deft move, spinning her. Amma gasped as she was dropped backward onto the bed, and Damien climbed atop, pinning her there. "Congratulations, you've earned Master Bloodthorne's mercy. That is, if you will allow me to give it to you."

She held very still, trapped beneath him with wide eyes, but then that mischievousness sparked in them once again. Amma's grip on the back of his head was inescapable as she pulled him down, pressing soft but greedy lips to his own. Damien could barely hold himself up, knees on either side of her hips as she clung onto him by his hair. Her tongue darted into his mouth, such a pushy thing, and she arched her hips against his.

Damien took her wrists. Fingers released him immediately, and her arms went lax in his hold, too easy to press down on either side of her head and keep still. Pulling himself away to catch his breath, he smirked down at the flush across her cheeks and the heaviness of her eyelids.

"I knew you were wicked," he breathed, dipping his head to bite at her ear, nipping down her neck while she squirmed under his grasp. Her next inhale was sharp as he reached the smooth hollow of her throat, feeling her skin hitch.

A small, pleased sound broke out of her as he trailed his lips over her collarbones and down the swell of her breasts. He wanted to unravel her, to free her of those restraints that kept her tied to quiet gasps and timidity, and replace them with his own bonds, ones she could be wild beneath. Caught in his hold, the pulse in her wrists surged.

"Stay still," he commanded, releasing her.

Amma's next ragged breath tripped itself on a stuttered affirmation. She would do her best to obey, he knew, and if she didn't, even better.

With her head tipped back, eyes falling closed, she was arching her chest, and the thin material that had been teasing him all day went taut. She was practically begging to be released from it, and with the tie somewhere beneath her, there was only one, quick way.

Unsheathing his dagger, he sliced up through the fabric, and her breasts sprung free. Amma's eyes flew open with one of her delightfully stunned cries, the kind that made his cock twitch in response, but then he realized he was looming over her with a weapon and chucked the thing across the room. It pierced the wall, hilt quivering as it landed, and her eyes flicked to it then back, but she didn't get a moment to consider her nakedness. Damien dropped his mouth onto an attentive nipple, drawing another cry from her throat, the depth of it exactly what he wanted.

He needed to savor her, so Damien took his time, his painfully relentless curiosity finally given an opportunity for satisfaction. Beneath him, Amma panted, still holding back, fists clenching as she fought to keep them in place as he'd told her to. But grazing fingers and tongue over soft skin that shivered with each pinch and lick, he grew desperate to taste her elsewhere.

Damien took her by the waist and shifted her upward, such an easy, little thing to throw around, just as she'd been in his lap earlier. He had wanted to toss her on the table then, to slide himself inside her to show her what her wriggling and whining had been doing to him, but he had chosen to be callous then despite that punishing her meant he too had to suffer. At least as he slid her over the linens and trailed his mouth along her belly, he was inching closer to satisfaction for them both.

As soon as his lips touched her navel, she inhaled much sharper than before. He stopped, glancing up between her breasts, slick with his mouth's exploration. Amma lifted her head, arms coming away from the bed as if to go for him. "What, um...are you doing?"

He pounced on her, pressing her back into the linens and holding her down. "You won't remember since you were quite intoxicated," he said, nipping at her bottom lip, "but I threatened to kiss every inch of your body once. Now I'd like to follow through."

"Oh." Amma's breath was warm as it fell over his face with the simple word, all she seemed capable of saying. She settled under him, and he released her, shifting downward to caress the curve of her waist with his mouth. Then she started to make noises that weren't words at all, a giggle when he tickled her side, a shocked gasp when he ran hands up her thighs to part them, and finally a pleading moan when he took the chain about her hips and began to inch it downward, lips following after. She wasn't being nearly loud enough. Not yet.

A rap sounded at the door, short and loud, and Amma sat straight up with a squeak.

"Lord Bloodthorne, you have been summoned by the Grand Order," a raspy voice called from the other side of the door.

Damien dropped his head into Amma's lap and groaned right up against the warm, wet, rapturous place he'd nearly gotten to, fabric regrettably still sheathing her away from him. "Fucking bloody fucking Abyss of all the bloody possible fucking times." He dragged himself upward begrudgingly to meet her face. "Apologies, my sweet."

He kissed her quickly before sliding backward off the bed, eyes trailing down her body, breasts pink and pleading for him to return, legs spread and too terribly inviting. He nearly fell to his knees right there, ready to devote himself to a goddess for the first time, the whole of evil be damned, but another sharp knock reminded him the only way he could keep Amma at all was to bend to GOoD's will.

"Don't leave the room," he commanded, grabbing his coat, eyes remaining on her, "and don't even think of getting dressed."

CHAPTER 7
A MORATORIUM ON DECISION MAKING

I f the Grand Order wanted to see Damien, it needed only order him to come, but if they were not yet ready for his presence, why in the Abyss had they summoned him at all?

He stood outside their meeting chamber, hands on hips, scowl on lips, entire body wound tight. The maroon imp had retrieved him an hour prior, and he'd reluctantly left a panting, wriggling, moaning Amma due to what he'd believed was urgency, but as the minutes ticked by, all he could do was count the number of times he could have summoned her to come instead. GOoD was going to have to deal with a very frustrated, very reluctant Lord Bloodthorne when they finally did call him inside.

Just as Damien was mentally juggling quality versus quantity and weighing the results against the resilience of his jaw, there was a rumble, and the door he'd been pacing outside finally shifted, a slab of stone grinding against more stone, horrible, ominous, and annoying. The imp jumped to attention, scrambling to stand on the threshold, and when it was opened, swiftly moved to the side and bade Damien entry with a deep bow.

There they were, the bastards who had kept him waiting, all six this time sitting high upon their ridiculous dais. Which had been the faceless, nameless one to run late, he couldn't discern, not that it mattered—surely they reveled in making him wait yet again—but at least Amma was not rotting in some dirty, cold cell. Hopefully she had nestled her nearly naked body beneath the warm linens and—"Shit, I should have told her not to touch herself."

WHAT WAS THAT, LORD BLOODTHORNE?

Damien grimaced. "You called, oh, terrible council?"

The hooded figures traded glances that he suspected even they could not see, the miasmic cloud above shifting in the low, blue lights of the stagnant chamber.

THE FORGING IS COMPLETE, said the council's one voice that was also many, and arcana sizzled in the air.

"Oh, goody," he groused, arms crossing.

The imp scurried past Damien and up onto the dais the hardest way, claws sinking into the stone as he climbed. When he reached the top, he hurried to its center betwixt all six chairs and held spindly arms up overhead.

The cloud that held the council's consciousness began to swirl, a shock of arcana bolting through it. The magic jumped from edge to edge, and Damien watched it languidly until it arced to the center and burst downward, striking the imp. Smoke curled off his horns as he staggered, and Damien almost thought to help the wretched thing, but under the watchful eyes of the Grand Order, he decided it would be best to let him suffer. The imp righted himself and made it to the dais's edge, hesitating and then jumping to the ground with a splat.

As if unworthy of being higher than what he carried, the imp managed to keep arms raised, scurrying to Damien and falling to his knees. In his clawed hands lay a bit of stone atop a coil of thin chain.

Damien glanced back up at the council, and he presumed their blotted out faces were staring back by the way a few leaned forward from their hulking seats. He clicked his tongue and snatched the chain. The rough-cut gem was shaped a bit like an upended triangle though the top corners were rounded, and it had a crimson sheen when it dangled in the light yet was too cloudy to be of value.

As the imp scurried away, Damien tipped his head to the council. "You know, I very much expected this forging to result in some pointy thing I was meant to stab some other angry thing with, not a bit of ugly jewelry."

YOU HOLD, LORD BLOODTHORNE, THE DREADCOUNCIL'S FRAGMENTABLE PENDANT OF ACCURSED BONDAGE AND NEFARIOUS CONQUEST.

His lip turned up at the spinning pendant. "Don't like the sound of that."

IT IS THE ONLY ONE OF ITS KIND, FORGED FOR THE SOLE PURPOSE OF ITS TARGETS' UNION AND SUBJUGATION. PUT IT ON, WON'T YOU?

"And I *really* don't like the sound of *that*." He dropped his arm, and the pendant bounced against his leg.

THERE IS NO NEED TO BE DISTRESSED BY OUR NAMING CONVENTIONS. SECTION THIRTY-ONE B OF THE DREAD CHARTER READS—

"All right, all right, I'll put it on so long as no one recites the damn charter." Damien blew out a long breath and slipped the chain over his head. The gem was heavy, thunking against his chest and falling still. It was gaudy and too thick to be worn under his armor, likely taking on an even brighter shade in the light of day. "You know, I think my pocket would be—"

Damien's skin was on fire. He slapped a hand to the back of his neck where the chain seared into his flesh, but he could not remove it, and a resounding crack rose from his chest. The pendant split down its center with an arcane sizzle, and he expected the pieces to fall away, but both remained, a second chain supporting the new half. As he went to grab for them, one piece pulsed, and then it was gone.

"What the fuck was that?" Damien yanked his tunic away to assess his skin beneath, warm and weird but free of burn marks.

OUR INSURANCE POLICY.

Damien didn't know what that meant, but it sounded like it would have to do with quite a lot of parchment and would not result in his favor which was no good, but also very GOoD. He wasn't stupid though, he was attached to the pendant now, their way of being sure he didn't lose the thing too early, accidentally or otherwise.

Damien snatched off what was left of the pendant, thankful when the thing actually came away from his neck. Where it had been split in half, it had a ragged edge, even uglier than before. "Well, it's a bit sharper now, I suppose."

THE DREADCOUNCIL'S FRAGMENTABLE PENDANT OF ACCURSED BONDAGE AND NEFARIOUS CONQUEST IS NOT FOR STABBING.

He stood there with it held out again, waiting. The council stared back facelessly. "What is it to be used for then?"

THE DREADCOUNCIL'S FRAGMENTABLE PENDANT OF ACCURSED BONDAGE AND NEFARIOUS CONQUEST IS TO BE DEPOSITED INTO THE EARTHEN VEIL BETWIXT REALMS.

"It's to be thrown in a hole?" Damien shrugged. "That does seem like where it belongs."

NOT ANY HOLE. YOU WILL TREK TO THE PLACE MARKED UPON THIS MAP AT THE TIME APPOINTED.

The imp once again darted across the chamber, up the dais, extended hands, and was struck by arcana. The second blow was worse, and Damien snuffed out the smoldering tip of the imp's ear when he scurried over, roll of parchment offered up.

Unfurling the map, Damien groaned. "Really? Here?"

IT IS THE PLACE WHERE THE DREADCOUNCIL'S FRAGMENTABLE PEND—

"—Pendant of Accursed Blah and Blah, yes, yes, you said, but this goes right through harpy *and* goblin territory. Darkness, I'd really rather not have to charter a giant hawk, I abhor flying beasts, but—"

NO WINGED MOUNTS.

Damien didn't really want to use one to begin with, but once he was told no, the idea of a bird for riding was much more appealing. "Why the Abyss not? If I'm atop something that flies, won't tossing the pendant in a hole be exponentially easier?"

THIS IS OUR QUEST, LORD BLOODTHORNE, AND YOU SHALL TRAVERSE THE GROUND IF WE SAY YOU SHALL.

He rolled the map back up and smacked it against his thigh in frustration. "Fine. Is that all? Just chuck it, presumably, into another of E'nloc's attempted resurrection pits? What's it meant to do?"

At this, the members of the council sat back, heads swiveling. If one could hear blinking, surely then the chamber would be full of it.

"Yes, obviously I know this has to do with that One True Darkness entity," he said with a sigh. "Everything I get caught up in seems to lately."

CONTAINMENT, the shared voice finally said.

"Well, that's an extraordinarily unhelpful non-explanation. And when do I need to do this?"

YOU MUST COMPLETE THIS TASK WHEN THE BLOOD OF THE CHOSEN IS DRAWN. BEFORE THE ECLIPSE OF LO BY ERO, AFTER THE CONSTELLATION CHIMERUS HAS CROSSED THE CELESTIAL POLE, PRIOR TO THE REVEAL OF ABARATH IN THE NIGHT SKY, FOLLOWING—

"Don't make me do the math. You've an exact date in mind, yes?"

THE TWENTY-THIRD.

"Eleven days," he mumbled, nodding. The entire journey, the trek and the time, pushed him even farther from Eirengaard. He hadn't forgotten about the capital and his waiting father, but he had hoped he could get the talisman out of Amma safely before the eclipse which was looming near according to when last he'd seen the moons.

TIME IS OF THE ESSENCE, the one voice said, calling his attention back up to the council.

"So, you would prefer I leave? Now?"

WELL, LORD BLOODTHORNE, WE DID NOT SAY—THAT IS— YOU SHOULD ENDEAVOR TO REMAIN FOR THE FINAL DAY OF YVLCON AND THE FOLLOWING NIGHT'S FESTIVITIES. GO NOW, BUT NOT BACK TO YOUR PLANE. ENJOY YOURSELF.

Damien grumbled but nodded, pocketing what remained of the pendant, relieved to not be reminded he should wear the thing. He probably already was anyway, he knew, after that arcane atrocity, but pushed that thought away. There was enough to be concerned with, and half of a pendant forged by the Grand Order of Dread that had potentially sunk into his chest barely made the list.

The burnt imp scrambled to get ahead of Damien, bowing at the door that opened of its own accord, and began to escort him back. Once he was free of the chamber and heard the stone slide back into place, sealing the council inside, he assured the too-put-upon imp that he could find his own way, and Damien was left alone in a rarely-traversed hall.

In the quiet, he slipped the pendant from his pocket and looked it over once again. Surely, the Grand Order wanted him to remain through Yvlcon's end because they would be sending someone after him when he left. He would be a fool to ignore their directive and an even greater fool to think they did not have other ways to watch him, but he still did not want to be followed.

He hesitated, Amma's soft skin drawing his wandering mind, but prudence disappointingly won out, and instead of heading back for his room, he turned down a narrow corridor half hidden behind a tapestry of divine priests being stretched on a rack. Light flooded his eyes, burning much brighter in the braziers overhead, and there was a stale, acrid smell to the air. The doors here were smaller, no grandiosity to the bland design of the stone flooring and walls, and when he listened, he could hear the shuffling of parchment and heaving of sighs behind them. Clearly, this was where GOoD kept its bureaucracy.

He ran a hand along the wall as he went down it, tracing lightly over the doors to feel for what could be behind them with as little magic as possible, the cuff helping to subdue what he put out into the world. It would have been much easier with Amma—all things were, really— but a much bigger risk too, and she would be too willing to help.

Then there was a sound, nearly inaudible, but the padding was familiar, followed by a quiet trill. Above Damien's head ran a shelf

61

along the entirety of the hall, and atop it stood a cat. Sleek and covered in swirling, grey stripes, she fell still when her golden eyes found him.

"Hello, beautiful." He held out his hand.

The creature darted over, butting her head against his knuckles. In her mouth, she carried an envelope, and as he held her captive by way of scritches, he could just read that she was making a delivery to the Department of Lesser Tortures.

"Would you mind showing me where transportation is, gorgeous?"

With a chirp, she skittered off overhead, and he followed to a door that, even with his senses dulled, he could tell radiated a familiar if off-putting magic on its other side. The cat continued on, and Damien remained, shocked when the handle gave way under his grip. It led to a simple storage closet lined with many shelves covered in scrolls of glowing parchment. So much intensely powerful arcana should have been locked behind many enchantments, but the source of the closet's open state stood just in its center.

"Oh, fuck me."

Xander's ridiculous grin only grew in response, and Damien nearly stormed off, but the opening of some other door along the hall forced him to slip inside.

"Shut up," he said before Xander could retort, snapping closed the door and listening for the sound of boots to pass. When Damien was satisfied, Xander was still looking delighted. "What are you doing in here?"

"What do you think?" Xander held up one of the glowing scrolls.

"Translocation. Of course." Used for Yvlcon summonses, the rolls of parchment housed in the closet were of the Grand Order's own design with the ability to send Yvlcon's attendees back from where they'd come and likely allowed the members of GOoD to travel uninterrupted throughout the realm. "Will they work once you're out of this dimension or only from here?"

Xander took a long look at the one he held, jutting out a lip then shrugging. "A little studying of these untargeted ones, and I should be able to figure it out."

Well, if Xander could figure it out, then so could he.

Damien turned from him, not that there was much room to do so in the cramped space, and began scanning the shelves. The stacks were helpfully labeled with their destinations, and there was even one for Eirengaard, but he skipped over that in search of something close to where the Grand Order wanted him to end up.

"So, you went and got her." Xander's voice was like a dagger being driven into the base of his spine, thick and painful and paralyzing. He would have liked to just kill him, but the risk was too great. If he wanted to keep Amma safe, Xander would have to be allowed to live another day.

"I did what I wanted to do," he said, crouching to read the labels on the lower shelves. "What I *had* to do because of you. Allying yourself with the Righteous Sentries—pathetic."

"Well, we certainly pulled one over on you."

Damien's grip on a shelf went so tight he thought the wood might splinter. "You hurt *her*," he said, teeth grit, "abducting her and sending her back to that monster."

"You're the one who abducted her, Bloodthorne."

Damien could have spun and hit him, but reined the anger back in, standing. "It's more complex than that."

"Yes, I'm sure you could fill two, maybe even three whole tomes with all the complexities of your internal conflict, but what's the plan now? You're going to let the kitten live and leave our parents trapped in their crystal prisons forever?"

Damien groused, "It's not really any of your concern."

"I believe my mother is a little bit my concern."

"Birzuma's plight isn't my burden."

"Well, it should be considering all she's done for you, but you *do* care about Zagadoth. And about that little baroness." Xander clicked his tongue as Damien shoved him out of the way to continue checking the shelves. "I mean, it's not that I don't admire what you're doing, ruining her and all, I just worry about what you think you're going to get out of all of this."

"You've never worried about..." Damien's growl fell off as his eyes found a scroll labeled with a place name he recognized, but only because he'd been told of it. Orrinshire.

"If you think you're going to keep her, you're delusional. But you're smarter than that, aren't you? Tell me you're smarter than that—I can't have been coming up even against you all these years to find out you're an idiot."

Damien covertly snatched the scroll for Orrinshire and pocketed it. He turned to face Xander only because he needed a look at the other shelves, but the blood mage wasn't keen to move. "Yes, I'm a moron, is that what you want to hear? I'll say just about anything if it will make you get out of my way."

Xander's eyelids fluttered. "Declaring yourself inferior to me because you suddenly have *feelings* is absolutely not the way to get me to move, and I think you know it."

"Fine, I'm actually better than you because I *perhaps* feel things *on occasion.* Whatever you need to hear. Now move." He took Xander by the shoulder and pushed him into the shelving.

"You're a fool," snorted Xander, righting himself and brushing away fallen parchment. "The only thing you could do with that girl is corrupt her."

"I'm not corrupting her," he protested, though his mind pinged on the word. Is that what he'd been doing to Amma? Between the stealing and the murder and the…touching?

"But you are. And sure, she might seem willing now, and she might fall for your broodiness and the way you try to possess her, but it won't last. Not when she finds out what you really are."

Damien swallowed, Xander's voice like blades sinking into his skin. He still wanted him to shut up, but he didn't quite have the words to lash out this time.

"Humans are stupid and weak," Xander went on, repeating a truth Damien had been taught since he could remember truths. "They fall for what they want to see, but when they're all through with the rush of dabbling in evil themselves and they're left with the ire, the conceit, the hatefulness—you know, our best qualities—they run. She'll abandon you just like humans always do to demons."

Damien's stomach twisted, the words heavy in his gut. There was no precedent he could respond with. Zagadoth and Birzuma were both trapped interminably until a demon spawn would release them, their human mates, or contractual associates, or even prisoners, gone.

"That is," Xander said with a lilt, slipping back in front of Damien, "unless you've decided the talisman's staying in her permanently so you can keep her like a little dove in a cage. Because you know she won't be so willing to stay when she finally sees the prison bars, when she feels the ropes around her wrists. She'll hate you for it, and she'll hate herself for being stupid enough to let you trick her."

"She's not stupid," Damien mumbled, the only thing he felt capable of arguing against.

"Perhaps not, but she is good, and that's practically the same thing." Xander chuckled at himself, and then his lips fell into a serious line. "And she's kind and trusting and self sacrificial, and you and I are the exact kind of cruel bastards who revel in taking advantage of that. In using her to touch an artifact we can't, to do translations and traverse a temple, to gratify our sadistic desires."

Damien was shaking his head, gaze focused on the shelf behind Xander to block him out. There, a parchment labeled with the Gloomweald sat, a translocation spell that would take its user just outside of Faebarrow. He snatched it up and pocketed it with the other.

Xander grabbed the back of Damien's head, forcing him to meet his eye. "The only merciful thing you could possibly do for that woman now is kill her yourself and save her from what you really are."

Gutting Xander right there would have been pure bliss, but it wouldn't shut out Damien's own thoughts, the ones that had plagued him since he had first laid eyes on Amma in the alley of Aszath Koth, felt her fingers on his skin, heard the way she said his name. She had become his weakness, and he would do almost anything to hold onto her. Was the tiny sliver of humanity within him enough to stop him from hurting her in the name of keeping her? Or was it just an inconvenient necessity as Xander had once called it, only a protection from being subjugated like his father and not enough to allow him true compassion, affection, or even love?

Damien pulled his head from Xander's grasp, eyes finally finding a label that read Ashrein Rise. He blindly grabbed the first scroll on the stack and turned, but Xander slithered himself between Damien and the door, his own hand falling to the knob.

"If you don't kill her, and you don't manage to trap her, she will leave. At least if she's dead, you won't have to trudge along through life knowing she's existing happily without you."

Imagining Amma existing elsewhere in the realm, separate from him, wasn't a new thought by any means, but the way Xander said it made Damien feel so empty he felt thinking on it too long might just kill him.

"They *always* leave, Bloodthorne. It's what your mother did." Xander tipped his head in something like sympathy. "And doesn't it just eat away at you that her only joy comes from the freedom of abandoning Zagadoth and the mistake she made with a demon?"

Damien's fist connected with Xander's jaw so hard there was a crack, the door flying open, and the blood mage splayed out into the too-bright hall. Blood pumped with a fervor through Damien's veins, begging to be released from his skin, to rein down arcane terror onto Xander and shut him up for good, but the cuff around his wrist pulsed and contained it.

There were other figures who had poured out into the hall at the sound of the cracking door, a lamia whose jaw had fallen unhinged, an arachne hanging from the ceiling, and of course a robed figure with an arcanely blotted out face. Damien's stomach twisted—now *this* was a much bigger fuck up.

"Aren't you going to do something?" Xander spat from his place on the ground. He was gripping his own jaw, and if it had broken, it was setting itself right already. "Bloodthorne's violated the charter!"

The charter also included a zero-tolerance policy, but Xander was so incensed he'd forgotten about his own safety.

The council member shifted slightly, the void in their hood focusing on Damien and then Xander and back. "An anomaly," they said in a voice run through with husk. "You are granted one, Lord Bloodthorne, and no more."

Damien nodded, sweeping past Xander's exasperated form on the floor, the lamia and arachne slithering and skittering out of his way. His heart pounded, nausea roiling in his guts as he strode through the halls and back to his chamber. *Foolish.* Xander was exactly right. He was a fool for acting on his desires—all of them—and only by the greed of GOoD was he allowed to live for his mistake.

But he had obtained an out. He could send Amma back close enough to Faebarrow with one of the translocation parchments he had stolen. Anomalous and Mudryth would go with her if he asked, assuring her safety, and then she would be free of him.

His furious march to his chamber came to a halt outside the door, a hand pressed to the wood, but unable to push inside. The corridor was filled with other chambers, and one of them contained Delphine. That was an option when Amma was gone. A bad one, of course, but if Xander was right, it might be the exact thing he deserved—some punishment for what he had almost done, for what he'd been doing. Delphine would, at the very least, remind Damien of what he was: little more than a thrall himself, hateful, angry, empty.

He finally entered the room, pondering how best to tell Amma she would be returning home. He had promised once to bring her back, but the words were protesting in his mind, refusing to form well enough to be said at all. It was going to be even more difficult when he found her stretched out naked on the bed, but he would have to be stalwart.

The chamber, though, was dark, and Amma was tucked into the linens, body drawn into a ball. He crossed the room, footsteps light, watching for any sign she might wake, but the only movement came from the tiny vaxin from Norasthmus a few inches away on the pillow, stretching in its sleep. Amma looked so peaceful, it would be a crime to wake her, even if he imagined doing so with his head between her legs.

What's one more journey? he thought, removing his boots and coat and climbing in beside her. Amma had already proven herself quite useful in surviving one of E'nloc's pits of nothingness: he would likely need her to complete this task the Grand Order of Dread had thrust upon him, and if Xander was right, then taking advantage of her skills was exactly what Damien was meant to do.

Amma stirred, turning. Her eyes did not open, her hands only snaking around him, and she nuzzled her head against his chest. Damien's heart thumped beneath her cheek so loudly he was sure it would wake her, but she only mumbled sleepy words against his skin that he refused to decipher, too similar to ones that had been playing in his own mind for the last moon. Instead he focused on that tone she used, so delicate and sweet, and let it lull him to sleep.

How he would live without her voice and touch once he had to let her go, he didn't know, but for at least a little while longer, he didn't have to find out.

CHAPTER 8
MORATORIUM LIFTED

A finger tracing down the nape of Amma's neck roused her. "You're back," she said, blinking bleariness from her eyes. "I wasn't asleep."

Damien made a small, disbelieving sound. "Oh, no? If only I'd known—I've been lying here for hours."

She pouted after him as he slipped out of the bed, leaving her cold. "Why didn't you wake me?"

"Couldn't bring myself to." He grinned and began to pull on his tunic.

"Now that's just cruel," she muttered, sitting up and taking the blankets with her to cover her bare chest. She had waited for him to return, urgency in every thrash of her heart, but when he didn't come immediately back, she had climbed under the fluffy linens to keep warm. She could only assume Damien would be disappointed if she took care of her pressing need on her own, so she shut her eyes and tried to think of anything else, and eventually fell asleep.

Damien placed the pile of clothes and cloaks they'd purchased from the merchants on the bed. Atop the stack sat her old pouch and the new dagger. "It's a shame, but you'll need to wear these now instead of those concubine trappings."

"I don't think that top is salvageable anyway," said Amma, finding her cleaned chemise in the pile and pulling it over her head.

Damien grinned as he jerked his dagger from where it pierced the wall the night before. Sliding it into the sheath on his bracer, he turned for her and expressions passed quickly over his features, hunger, thoughtfulness, longing, and finally defeat. "An actual tunic will be most useful anyway. It should be just before dawn back in the realm."

She held his gaze, letting the linens fall away and leaving her just in her lacy underthings, a thickness in the air between them. Would he pounce on her again? Should she just run at him instead? But then Damien turned away, and the tension in Amma's shoulders moved on to frustrate other places.

She scratched the vaxin behind his tiny ears, and he yawned, revealing massive incisors. Just before she'd fallen asleep, he popped back into existence on her pillow, and she was happy to see he had remained there all night. When she stood from the bed, she hesitated before slipping off the chain and crimson fabric from her hips even though her chemise was long enough to cover her. Damien was still turned away though, slowly strapping on armor, both a shame and a relief. "So, is there some early morning, unholy ritual we're going to?"

"Oh, no, we're *leaving* leaving." He held up a small scroll over his shoulder. "The rest of them can have their last day of Yvlcon without us. We're going...well, I suppose we're going on a quest."

Amma's eyes widened—now, that sounded exciting. She was quick to pull on her pink-ish tunic and untorn breeches in a dark leather. The new vest cinched in around her waist with black straps, protective and, well, uplifting was a word for what it did for both her breasts and her mood. Holstering the new knife on her thigh was the final piece, and though it wasn't her silver dagger from Faebarrow, this one was intended for protection. It felt good to have the slight pressure against her leg again, a constant reminder she had a means of defense. She flexed her fingers, feeling as though something was missing, but the rest of the pile was simply her old, torn and stained clothes from their previous trek across the realm.

"Do you have everything you don't intend to leave behind?" Damien had finished dressing on the room's other side.

Amma checked herself then gasped, running to the pillow and scooping up the vaxin. "Can't forget Vanders."

"Oh, good, you've named it." Damien smirked at the rodent as he strode over. "Listen, you need to stay alive, all right? This one will get very upset otherwise." He nudged Amma, and she giggled, but then he had his dagger out and was slicing into his hand.

He wrapped bloody fingers around the scroll, whispered in

Chthonic, and there was a flash of black arcana before them. Watery, silver strands formed in a doorway-like frame, the center a shadow. It was just like the portal that had been their escape from the bleakness of the courtyard of Krepmar Keep only this time the wind was not whipping, there was no pit of darkness flailing tendrils of arcana a few yards away, and Damien wasn't nearly dead.

Damien was, in fact, looking quite alive at Amma's side even as he bled, the circles gone from under his eyes and a grin on his lips that seemed to have settled there rather than just passing by. With black hair brushed away from his face, his eyes held a new lightness when they looked on her. It was frankly unfair of him to look so handsome after he had made so many threats and had yet to follow through, but the parchment sizzled in his hand, and he was guiding her away from the bed and into the portal.

A pull behind Amma's navel drew a gasp out of her, the world wobbly beneath her feet, and then the shadows about her cleared. They were surrounded no longer by the candlelit, windowless gloom of a bedchamber in some imaginary, dark plane but the dusty glow of a sky pink with coming dawn. Bands of mountaintops, each lighter than the one before as they were swallowed up by fog, trailed down from the rosy sky, and at their feet, a lush patch of greenery sprawled up between crevices in the rock.

Amma breathed in the piney air, no longer feeling the collar about her neck, and she sighed, eyelids floating down with her gaze, and then her stomach completely dropped out. She squealed, jumping back from the cliff's edge, Damien's boots scuffing at her side as he too staggered backward.

The tops of pines and maples swayed far off in both directions, a gust slamming into their backs, and they dug into the rocky earth. Vanders poofed right out of existence yet again, and Amma's heart shot into her throat at the sight of the mountain ridge they stood upon running to either side.

"Didn't realize Ashrein Rise meant up this high," Damien said breathlessly, eyes wide.

Buffeted at their front by another gust, they turned toward each other and held on until it passed, and then found a narrow break downward to slide off the ridge and land in a flatter spot where they could press their backs into the rock.

The mountain ridges spread out before them, many much higher, and below, a valley thick with rolling forest. The wind had been cut off where they stood, and Amma took a deep gulp of air. "Not that I want to complain, but what are we doing here?"

Testing the ground and finally taking his arms off the cliffside, Damien dug into his satchel and pulled out a folded parchment. "This is not exactly where we need to be, but it was the closest translocation spot I could find."

He unfolded the parchment, and Amma took half of it, huddling close to survey what was drawn out there. New and clean with crisp edges, the map depicted what looked like the northwesternmost corner of Eiren, Ashrein Ridge cutting up through it, separating the western peninsula that jutted out into the Maroon Sea from the rest of the realm. A single city was marked, and though Amma could not read Chthonic, she knew it would be Buckhead, the capital of the northernmost barony of Eiren. Farther south where the ridge ended would be Brineberth and Faebarrow, and near the map's top lay the border of the realm, Aszath Koth beyond. Places were marked in Chthonic, but there was a little, bright red dot just on the ridge that pulled her eye in. "Is that us?"

"*You are here.*" Damien's finger traced under the Chthonic script surrounding the dot. "But we want to be here." He pointed to the peninsula on the other side of the range. There was a black squiggle drawn there, and as far as squiggles went, it was probably the most ominous one Amma had ever seen.

"What does that say below our destination?"

Damien groaned. "*Temple of the Void.*"

"Oh, I've seen this before!" Amma released her half of the map and flipped her own pouch open, surprised to find Vanders nestled inside. The vaxin scampered up to her shoulder when he noted the lack of wind, and Amma pulled out her own parchment. "That reminds me of the other bad thing I did."

Damien cocked a brow. "Please go on in excruciating detail."

Unfolding the crumpled parchment, she presented it proudly to him. "I can't believe I forgot about this, but I stole it from Cedric's chamber at the keep. It's a star chart, but the writing on it is in Chthonic which he shouldn't have had. Nobody in the realm is supposed to use that language."

"Not even you," he said, tucking the other map under his arm. But Damien's mischievous look fell away as he took the chart, eyes darting from one point to another written in the language of the infernal.

"There was a second map there too, but it was too big for me to steal. It had Krepmar Keep marked on it and a place in the Kvesari Wood, one in The Wilds, and you can probably guess that the fourth point was labeled The Temple of the Void."

"What a convenient coincidence." Damien's lips turned down. "This depicts the eclipse, doesn't it? It's only showing one moon, but

71

it's marked as both Lo and Ero."

Amma tipped her head. "Huh, yeah, I guess so. The moons have been getting closer to one another in the sky."

"The Grand Order said the pendant needs to be chucked into the pit prior to the eclipse," he mumbled.

"Excuse me?"

Damien swallowed, handing the chart back. "I'm not terribly familiar with astronomy, I only picked up a bit from Soren Darkmore's journals, and that was mostly solar activity, a little constellation renaming, some theories about balls of gas. Hold onto this, we may find someone who can actually read it."

"Damien, what was that about the Grand Order?"

With a hefty sigh, he once again went into his pouch, and instead of more parchment, pulled out a raggedly cut gemstone attached to a chain. Looking displeased at the thing as it hung from his hand, he told her begrudgingly, "This is the root of our quest."

"It looks broken."

He cleared his throat. "Does it?"

Amma carefully reached out for the gem. It was cloudy, but when she tipped it toward the rising sun, she caught Damien's reflection on one of the cleaves. "It's very pointy too," she mused.

"The Dreadcouncil's Fragmentable Pendant of Accursed Bondage and Nefarious Conquest is not for stabbing."

She dropped the stone. "The *what?*"

"Nevermind, it's only meant to sound intimidating, and the name's likely been randomly produced from a pool of sinister words. They want me to dispose of it in a very specific way."

"Why do you have to take their trash out for them?"

"Because if I don't, they'll probably try and kill me, but not before they attempt to do something even worse to you."

"Oh, geez." Amma snatched the map out from under his arm, holding it open again. "Well, okay, what's the fastest route there?"

As if she had been speaking directly to the map, it answered in swirling ink, drawing a dotted path from where they stood, down the ridge to meet a road that meandered away from the mountains and Buckhead at its base, and out to the ominous black squiggles on the peninsula, technically just on the edge of Throkull territory, disputed land that both the realm and the tribes of giants claimed.

Amma clicked her tongue appreciatively, but when she looked back at Damien, he was still staring at the pendant. "That's cursed or something, isn't it?"

He blinked over at her. "This? No, no, it's not...well?"

When he tipped his head in thought, Amma clicked her tongue again, this time decidedly less enthusiastic. "You don't know?"

He slowly raised his shoulders and dropped them back down.

"So, an evil organization gave you an ugly necklace with a horrible name that they want you to get rid of inside what we can only assume is another big, scary pit of doom, but you don't know what's going to happen when you do?"

From her shoulder, Vanders made a small, disapproving squeak.

"They said something about *containing* it."

"Okay…" Amma waited for more, but all he seemed capable of doing was continuing to stare at the stupid thing, and if she were honest, it made her a tad bit jealous. "When we were in Krepmar Keep with that thing—with E'nloc—you said It wanted a vessel. That It wanted you."

"I did say that." His words came out stilted.

"You said you thought you could destroy It from the inside."

He made a small sound, something like agreement.

"But that seems a good way to get you destroyed too. And you have to know that's unacceptable."

Damien stood there, the pendant hanging from his hand, and his eyes finally fell away from it. "Amma, I have not shared with you the specifics of the prophecy, the one I'm meant to be following. It's a little dark."

"I'm sure it's actually *very* dark, isn't it?"

"It speaks of me releasing my father, but there is some confusing wordage about the corners of the realm and rot and other…things." Damien cleared his throat, a light wind coming up around them and carrying his words away but not his reluctance. "If you remember, that pit opened up just after I arrived in Brineberth, and I didn't tell you this, but the chore the witches sent me on in the Wildwood brought me to a much smaller version of the same entity. That's how It knew me—we'd met before."

The void's tendrils at Krepmar Keep had indeed acted like they wanted Damien. Of course, they also wanted everything else in the general vicinity, grabbing and crushing bodies for fodder, but Damien, specifically, seemed to be a prized target.

The blood mage rubbed his chin, squinting out at the mountain ranges. "If this thing, E'nloc, is rotting out corners of the realm in accordance to these maps, and I am to bring about a great evil when those corners are rotted…"

Amma felt her eyes go wide. "That pit thing isn't your *dad*, right?"

"No, no, my father is only a demon, not a swirling vortex of entropy. At least that's not how I remember him." His face screwed up. "He would have said something by now, surely."

"Then what does any of this have to do with your father?"

Damien shrugged with a defeated sigh. "I feel I'm missing something, information, clarification, *something*. And I need that piece before going to Eirengaard."

Amma lowered the map, worrying her lip between her teeth. He still wanted to go to Eirengaard, wanted to enthrall the king, release his father, wreak havoc on the realm. Why she thought things might be different now, she didn't know, but Damien was right: clarification would be nice.

"Oh, my gods, I know what we should do! What we *have* to do!" She squealed and shook the map, snapping him out of his long, thoughtful gaze out at the forest below. "Enchanted Map, could you please show me the Denonfy Oracle?"

"Amma, the map is not meant to—"

A new dot rose up on the parchment, deep blue and nestled into the mountain range, and Chthonic words scratched themselves out around the mark.

"I suppose you're so polite even the vilest objects will do your bidding." Damien leaned over her shoulder to peer at the spot. "They are not terribly far from here, but quite out of the way of our quest."

Visiting the oracle would mean hiking through the mountains northward and then cutting down through the valley and the city of Buckhead to reach The Temple of the Void on the peninsula instead of heading directly westward.

"But they could tell you exactly what that pendant thing does, and I bet you have other questions for them too. You can ask about the prophecy."

He shook his head. "I appreciate your enthusiasm, but one can ask only a single question of the oracle per visit."

"Well, that's fine—you ask about your destiny and the prophecy or whatever, and I'll ask about the pendant."

Damien's face drew into a frown, but not one of displeasure. "You would be willing to forgo your opportunity to ask the Denonfy Oracle about your own destiny?"

Her eyes fell to the gem still hanging from his hand. "If that thing's bad news, it sort of affects me, destiny included."

"Well, yes, but I've already been to the oracle to try and clarify the prophecy. I would be wasting not only my visit but yours as well."

"It wouldn't be a waste," she said. "You're older now than the last time you went, and I'm here to help. We can put the pieces

74

together…together."

"That is too selfless, Amma." Damien's furrowed brow softened, and he chuckled. "You'll be giving up your opportunity to discover who you're meant to marry, you know. Laurel will be disappointed."

Amma laughed then, high and sharp. "You don't think I've come up with a better question after all this time?"

"Have you?"

She shook out the map, focusing on the blue dot and their destination. "Well, it's not important because I'll be asking about The Dreadcouncil's Fashionable Pendant of Accosted Bridges and Nonferrous Combat."

"That is *not* what it's called."

"You said what it's called doesn't matter." She squinted and oriented them, pointing. "Come on, now, the oracle's that way."

CHAPTER 9
NECESSARY LIES AND THEIR CONSEQUENCES

Amma was too damn cheery about everything. The way she smiled, how she laughed—actually laughed—at the idea of throwing away her opportunity to ask the Denonfy Oracle what her own destiny held in favor of a question that *he* had, made Damien...not at all furious. In fact, it made him inconceivably happy, and that, in turn, was sort of infuriating. If only she could just stop being so wonderful for a moment, he could figure out exactly what to do with all of his feelings for her.

Amma's choices shouldn't have surprised Damien; she was self-sacrificial, exactly what Xander had said of her, and Damien indeed intended to use that to his benefit. But he knew deep in his gut that when they got their answers, she wouldn't be smiling and laughing anymore.

The problem with prophecies was that they were true, and there wasn't much one could do about them. Damien claimed to put little stock in divinatory arcana, but he understood how well the Denonfy Oracle was regarded by those on both sides of the moral divide, and that often accounted for quite a lot. When the oracle said something was going to happen, it *was going to happen*. And that was rather final.

Finding one's place organically in the world allowed for possibility, and as much as Damien didn't like the not knowing—the apprehension that had been creeping up his spine since he'd set off to free his father—there was something appealing about not entirely understanding the prophecy.

That appealing thing was hope, of course, but feelings were to Damien as object permanence was to an infant—confusing, slightly frightening, and likely to inspire tantrums. But Amma wanted him to understand the prophecy, and Damien wanted to give her exactly what she wanted—a desire that had long surpassed dangerous and toppled right over into completely reckless.

Reckless too was her burglary of that star chart he professed to glean very little off of. He hadn't entirely lied about being unfamiliar with astronomy, but he could read Chthonic just fine. Eclipses were always arcanely charged, but this one would involve more than just the two moons. A more powerful event than those past, as Lo and Ero crossed they would simultaneously obscure the sun, and the predictions scribbled in the margins of the chart suggested the veils between the planes would be at their thinnest. He claimed someone more knowledgeable should read it, but he hoped they never found that person, preferring to shield Amma from that grimness for as long as possible. At least he knew the eclipse itself was officially a fortnight away.

The hike along Ashrein Ridge was a more difficult trek than what they had become used to, the incline in places steep, footing often unstable, but at his side, Amma managed to forgo frustration to instead marvel at how moss grew atop the rock formations and the way the sunshine stippled the earth as they climbed it. Plucking an acorn from the nearest tree, she handed it off to the vaxin riding on her shoulder. "That's from an iron oak," she told Vanders. "The squirrels in the north seem to prefer them to the white oak acorns, so I assume they taste better. If you like it, we'll collect some more since they're pretty rare."

What might she do if the oracle told them the pendant would bring E'nloc into their world, and it was Damien's destiny to be the harbinger of that kind of chaos and destruction—that he was born for this and nothing else? Would she run from him? Insist it weren't true? Try to stop him? He knew E'nloc couldn't be allowed freedom, but he was beholden to do the Grand Order's bidding for no other reason but to keep her safe. They knew too much about her after being inside his mind, and they would come for her if he failed.

"Amma, I have a request to make." He offered her his hand from atop a steep embankment.

She looked up, blue eyes wide and expectant, and slipped her fingers over his palm without hesitation.

"I'm unsure exactly how, but Xander and those fools he convinced to help him have found us twice now, so I think it would be prudent to stay close together." He squinted at her as she got her footing amongst the rocks below. "If you do become angry with me again, do you think you could remain within my range of vision?"

Her face reddened. "Oh, right, that storming off thing I did was a little risky, huh?"

"You were right to be upset." Damien held her steady as she began to climb upward. "I shouldn't have used magic on you at all, but especially not in the Everdarque where it so often goes wrong. It just seemed at the moment the only way to keep the noxscura away from you."

Amma took a last, long step upward to crest the ledge beside him. "I understand why you did that, but you know I wouldn't have turned into her, right?"

"I know you are a different person than Delphine—a *very* different person—but the prospect of someone with the ability to completely enthrall me, to compel me with so much power, to—"

Her eyes narrowed.

"Well, if anyone understands, it's you." He cleared his throat. "The purpose of my request is safety. To protect you from further abduction or foul play. It would be prudent to remain close."

"I don't mind that." She squeezed his hand, pressing herself right up against him, sunlight glittering off her hair and dappling her breasts.

Damien swallowed, tasting the memory of her skin on his tongue. He could so easily pull her into a long and passionate kiss that would hopefully lead to other long and passionate things, but he heard that word in Xander's smarmy voice—*corruption*—and it burrowed itself into the base of his skull to fester.

"We should address what happened at Yvlcon." He pulled his hand from hers and continued onward.

She followed. "What happened?"

Well, not enough, he thought with a frown, but then huffed. "When you kissed me."

"You kissed me too," Amma said, and the vaxin chirped in agreement. "In a lot of places."

Damien groaned in the back of his throat at the reminder. "I suppose I should say, when we kissed one another." He lifted his eyes skyward as a crow called out from above. It broke away from the trees, leaving the leafless branches quivering in the breeze. How in the Abyss was he supposed to say this? "The oracle," he blurted out, a clever thought striking him like an acorn falling from an oak, "in order to see them, you have to be chaste."

"But neither of us—"

"Just for a little while, for the, uh…the pilgrimage, as it were," he lied, continuing forward at a brisker pace so she couldn't see the clear deceit on his face. "Otherwise, they will not hear your question."

"Is that the *being worthy* part?" She struggled to catch up.

"Ah, yes?" He had heard that too, that the Denonfy Oracle only showed themself to those who were worthy, but he hadn't ever questioned what that meant; the oracle was just there when he showed up, as he expected.

Would they still consider Damien worthy? He had thrown himself so far off course, he had acted so disparately to who he had always been, he had…well, he had dabbled in being *good*.

"So kissing, and other things, will have to cease." Damien shook his head, vexed with himself, especially when the softness of Amma's skin still somehow ghosted against his fingertips when his eyes inevitably fell to her backside, but it was truly worse than all that. Proposing that they shouldn't engage in any kind of intimate behavior was disheartening, but the more troubling unsaid thing was that they couldn't actually *be* together.

It was a silly thought anyway, Damien knew, the two of them, *together*. So silly that he couldn't even laugh, it was just that wonderfully painful. But they couldn't, and despite the many reasons why, one stuck out to him: that damned cup of noxscura. She hadn't known what it was, what it did, but she was willing to be reckless and stupid and throw herself into danger for him.

And he didn't deserve an ounce of her perilous generosity.

"But after the oracle…" said Amma quietly, her hands clasped before her, rosiness in her cheeks and a sheen of wetness on her freshly bitten lip. She looked so ridiculously innocent he wanted nothing more than to ruin her right there.

After the oracle, I will drive you to madness with my tongue so that you believe you were born only for wickedness.

Damien cleared his throat, pulling his eyes away from her. "We shall see."

Regrettably, his words, hastened by their detached delivery, hung much too heavily in the otherwise light, mountain air. The cold sentiment floated about them like the Grand Order's arcane miasma, carving into Amma's cheery attitude. What he would have given to be asked an absurd question or told a superfluous story as they trudged up the mountainside, but instead his once vociferous companion fell into a bleak silence. At least she held true to their agreement: she remained

79

in his sight even when angry, though the frown creasing her face did nothing to help either of their moods.

"You know," Damien said as if a thought had just come to him and he hadn't been mulling over what to say for the past two hours, "I did not reciprocate during our initial getting-to-know-one-another discussion. I should have asked you the things you favored as well."

Amma's pout shifted, giving him a small shrug that Vanders found no difficulty riding out. "I guess not."

He grunted—she was going to make this difficult. He probably deserved that. "So, would you, *please*, tell me your, what was it, hobbies?"

"Embroidery, I guess. My mother says that's an attractive skill. I like to read too, but she says that's less attractive."

Damien wanted to say that her mother had no idea what she was talking about, but kept that to himself. "Your work with the liathau must have also been enjoyable, yes?"

"Oh, of course." The corners of her mouth tipped up at that. "Harvesting seeds is a lot of fun because you get to climb the trees, and tending to the saplings is relaxing."

"Those are quite impressive skills," he said with perhaps too much eagerness, and she cast suspicious eyes on him. "And I think you asked me what my favorite moon is too?"

Amma chuckled lightly. "Oh, gods, I did ask some silly things, but I was pretty nervous about you killing me and everything. I think I like Ero best, but it's a toss-up."

"Food?" he asked, more quickly as the questions came back to him.

"Anything sweet, but especially the little cakes for Midsummer Feast iced in sugar."

"And color? Wait, let me guess—surely it's pink."

"Actually, not anymore. Now it's—" Amma had finally begun to grin again, a look that told him everything would be all right, but then it swam right off her face, desolation left in its wake.

He waited for her to go on, the answer so obviously right on the tip of her tongue, but instead there was a wall of sorrow that built itself into her features so quickly he could hear the bricks being laid.

"I don't know, I like a lot of colors."

Damien had done something wrong again, but he wasn't sure what. At least this time, she didn't seem quite so angry when her eyes fell to the trail, watching every careful step upward, she was just sad, and, darkness, that was *much* worse. Wanting to leave that be, he continued, "I believe you also asked me about my ambitions. What is it you want to do, Amma?"

At this, she thought for a long moment. "I should say, *serve my people*, but that feels wrong now. I do want them to be happy and looked after and treated well, and I don't trust the crown to do those things, even with Cedric dead, but I don't know if I'll really get the choice, and I can't imagine standing by while terrible things happen to them. My parents were behaving so strangely, and they really wanted Brineberth's gold, so I'm not sure if—oh. Oh, *no*."

When she came to an abrupt halt, so did Damien. "What's wrong?"

"Roman, Cedric's brother. Do you think I'm going to be betrothed to *him* now?" Her face twisted up into a mask of horror.

"You mean that very large, very sad man from the keep?" Damien felt arcana pinch at his skin, and he went reflexively for his dagger. "Just ask, and I will put an end to him, slowly or quickly, whatever you believe suits his crimes best."

"You can't do that," she groaned, beginning off again, shoulders slumped and Vanders holding on.

He followed, brow narrowed, fists clenched. Certainly, she didn't…didn't *prefer* this man. "I assure you, I *can* kill him and would do so gladly."

"Oh, no, Damien, it's not like that." She let out a fraught, little sigh and rubbed her temples. "It's that he's…well? He's not very bright."

"What's that got to do with anything?"

Amma snorted and threw her hands up. "He's a complete idiot, all right? And it sort of makes him sweet, but he's like a *child*! He doesn't need a wife, he needs a mother, and if I have to marry him? Give him children?" She shuddered. "By Osurehm, there should be laws against that kind of thing."

Damien's ire melted, and a chuckle worked its way into his throat. "Well, he did seem quite devoted. If he's as stupid as you say, you could easily manipulate him into doing whatever you want." When she made a scoffing sound, Damien just chuckled more. "If you are truly concerned, you can ask the oracle to put your mind at ease."

"No, I don't want to know." She sighed so heavily that Damien felt it in his own chest. "I'd just never go back to Faebarrow if that's what's waiting for me. I was already considering alternatives anyway."

"You were?" he asked as casually as he could.

Amma's eyes went wide in the same way they'd done when she had been keeping secrets from him, accidentally dropping little hints at her identity and trying to cover them up. She busied herself with petting the vaxin and making nondescript noises in the back of her throat. "I don't know. Maybe. I like being out in the wilderness. Lots of trees out here I could build a little house in. But I guess if I'm lucky, you'll just release your father, he'll put an end to the whole realm, and I won't have to worry about being a baroness or a hermit out in the woods or anything."

When her face turned back down, he left it alone, afraid to prod at that sentiment in case it hadn't been a joke. She did not perk up again on her own though, and by the time they stopped for the night, he was getting quite worried. His words had failed at bringing her any long-term joy, and all that seemed left were his tongue and fingers, but he had already been desperately fighting himself to keep from touching her.

As he looked about for the flattest place for them to camp, he wondered how close the two could lay without accidentally brushing up against one another, searching for some branch or bush that could work as a deterrent. Maybe he could find some rash-inducing plant and rub it on his hands.

"Kaz!" he said suddenly, whipping toward her.

Amma straightened, a hand pressed to her chest. "I can't believe I forgot! What happened to him?"

"I killed him."

"Damien!"

"Not like that!" He held his hands up in defense, but her shock had settled into a quiet fury. "I mean, I did stab him because I needed his heart as the component for a spell, but I'm sure it didn't really hurt. Much."

Her face was growing all sorts of horror over it, and he knew he was only making things worse.

"Look, it really wasn't in anger or anything, and I *did* ask him if I could kill him, and he *did* tell me yes, and I acknowledge that I've got a very frustrating power imbalance with just about everyone, but I am sorry for it. Anyway, I was just thinking: I know he was rubbish to you, but you always seemed to inexplicably like him, so if we brought him back would that...would that make you happy?"

Amma's watery eyes blinked, but no tears fell, and she nodded.

"All right, good, good," he said to himself, dragging his boot across a leaf-strewn but flat spot to reveal soft earth below. He knelt and used a stick to draw out a circle and the symbols for summoning from the infernal plane. "It's not very difficult to summon an imp, though I've not done it in some time. Would you mind assisting me?" He paused a moment, wondering how Kaz's name might be spelled in Chthonic, and then scribbled in his gut decision. When he looked up, Amma was standing on the other side of the circle, the evening darkening around her.

"You want me to help summon an imp from the infernal plane?"

"Yes. We need a sacrifice." His eyes flicked to the vaxin on Amma's shoulder.

She gasped, raising her hands to cover Vanders' perfectly round ears. "Don't even think about it."

The little creature poofed out of existence.

Damien chuckled, speaking louder into the air. "No, never, not Vanders. I was actually thinking you could use some of that arcana of yours."

Big eyes stared down at him, unsure.

"Here." He placed an acorn in the center of the circle he'd made, an iron oak one, he presumed, as Vanders didn't reappear to scurry off with it. "To summon an imp, we must trade a living thing over to the infernal plane. I'm sure that place is already full of rats and goats, so they could probably use a tree."

"The things used for summoning don't die?"

"Well, if you consider being on the infernal plane death, then yes, but if not…" He gestured to the acorn and sat back.

"So, you want me to make that into a tree?"

"It doesn't need to be a very big one since Kaz is pretty small."

Amma settled onto her knees across from him. Her fingers toyed with her lip, eyes darting over the Chthonic he had written.

"For Kaz?" he asked in a voice meant to tug at that soft heart of hers.

"Oh, poor Kaz, yes, okay, of course." Amma lay her small hands on top of the acorn, lips pursing.

He felt the arcana before it came, a prickling in the earth and a crackle in the air around him. Damien leaned backward, eyes wide as the acorn cracked, and a white stalk shot up so quickly between her fingers that she had to pull her hands back too.

"Well, well, well," he said, smirking, "looks like someone was a mage all along."

In the center of his summoning circle, the sapling bobbed from its sudden growth, the dirt disturbed, but the symbols intact. Damien called up fire, only a small spark that ran along the circle, and then drew a cut across his palm to drip blood onto Amma's tree, whispering the Chthonic summoning words.

The flames enveloped the sapling, flickering over Amma's skin in the growing darkness as she watched. But Damien only watched her, how she marveled at the spell she'd taken part in, breath coming shallow in anticipation. And then she grinned as the silvery strands of noxscura from the infernal plane opened up, and the imp's shadow appeared in the column of fire that had grown up around the tree to devour it.

The flames and silver spun around one another, lapping above their heads, and then imploded, dousing their patch of forest into complete darkness.

"Kaz, welcome back!" cried Amma, throwing herself forward and scooping up the imp against her chest. Even in the shadows, he could see how happy she'd become, and once again Damien's jealousy gnawed at him. Oh, to be a newly summoned imp, squeezed between her breasts.

But then she inhaled sharply, holding the imp away from her. "Uh, Damien?"

In the wake of the intense fire, Damien's eyes readjusted. The thing she held was imp-shaped, with needlessly long forearms and curling talons on its feet, big batwing ears flopping down on either side of its head, but everything about the imp was floppy as it hung by its armpits from Amma's hands, including its color, a milky sort of blue-green.

Amma turned it slightly, and Damien could see its face, a set of fangs that grew down from its flat line of a mouth, much longer and larger than Kaz's crooked underbite. Wingless, Damien reasoned that in its last life, this imp probably had not been kicked off a parapet by a selfish, bratty, teen-aged dark lord, but it did have a tail with a little triangular end and dark, roving eyes that settled on Damien. "Master?" And that voice—that was not Kaz's wet gurgle, but an unsettlingly heavy groan.

Damien cocked his head. "Guess that's me. And you are?"

The imp took in a breath for so long Damien thought it might burst, followed by an even longer, slower sigh. "I am Katz, imp of the Infernal Darkness and servant of all those who hold the Sanguine Throne."

Amma's brows were knit, head tipping as she looked him over with a frown. "Are you okay, little guy?"

It was a more than fair question. Based on his voice alone, the imp had barely anything to live for, least of all his own station in life. Damien had always imagined this was what existence might be like for an imp but had never met one who was quite so depressed.

"Yes, Mistress," said Katz, head roving back to her slowly, the rest of his body remaining completely limp in her grasp. "This is just my affectation."

"Well, at least this one's a bit more respectful to you." Damien grinned. Darkness, did he like the sound of *Mistress Bloodthorne* when he looked on her.

Amma set the imp gently on the ground, and he practically melted into a puddle of himself, shoulders limp, arms dragging. She looked almost as pained as the imp. "I messed it up, didn't I?"

Damien's eyes darted back down to his circle. "No, Amma, you did perfectly. I failed to record Kaz's name correctly."

"You meant to summon someimp else?" Katz asked, turning his face to look on one and then the other with such a uniquely miserable quality that even Damien could take no joy in it. "That makes sense. Nobody ever wants Katz around."

"Oh, no, no!" Amma shook her head, patting the imp on his knobby shoulder. "I mean, yes, technically, we were trying to summon a different imp, but having you here is good too. Isn't it, Damien?"

Damien screwed up his face—no, it bloody was not—then wiped the look off before Katz completed the excruciatingly slow turn of his head in search of confirmation. The smile he tried to put on actually hurt. "Right, yeah, it's…fine. Unless, that is, you *want* to go back to the infernal plane?" He slid his dagger from his bracer.

Amma's eyes flashed at him, and she sliced a finger across her own neck. Damien sat up at that, encouraged—she had never been so eager to have him kill something before—but then as she lifted her other hand and waved both through the air frantically, he understood and resheathed the knife.

Katz, however, noticed none of it, too focused on the long, low groan he was producing. "I desire only what my master wishes of me."

"Ah, well, sure, you may stay with us for now." Damien squeezed his hand and the healing cut across his palm. "I didn't exactly intend to have a whole retinue of imps following us through the mountains though."

Amma yawned then. "I don't think I can make another tree right now anyway. Kaz won't be upset if he's down there for a little longer, will he?"

"I'm sure he's fine." With another look at their new imp, Damien grimaced. "You can keep watch tonight, yes?"

Katz nodded, slow and long as if the weight of his own head were too much. "As you wish, Master." He did not sound the least bit happy about it.

CHAPTER 10
THE AMOROUS EFFECTS OF VERY ORDINARY WATER

Vanders' reappeared the next morning beneath Amma's chin, all of his tiny paws nestled against her neck for warmth. She was curled up in a ball to generate heat too, beneath her cloak. She would have preferred curling up in Damien's arms, but he had made no invitation, and she was unsure if she were more upset at the oracle and their supposed rules of chastity or the blood mage himself for sticking to them.

Sleep had come easily despite her irritation. After the initial rush from sprouting the acorn, the conjuring weighed heavily on her, and when she woke, the sluggishness still hadn't wrung completely out of her bones.

Then there was Katz. In some ways, he was an improvement on Kaz, never implying Amma was any kind of prostitute, though after meeting Fryn at Yvlcon she supposed that wasn't such an insult. He instead called her only Mistress, which might have been pleasant if not done in a voice that made it sound like he were carrying the whole plane on his shoulders. She knew she shouldn't be upset with him for simply sighing and existing, but it was grating.

And their constant upward trajectory wasn't helping either.

"Why does the oracle have to be at the top of a mountain?" Amma annoyed even herself with her whine, but she couldn't help it.

"I suppose if it weren't arduous, everyone would attempt the trek. We are fortunate to have missed the direwolf packs that troll the base of the mountain and to avoid the dwarven tribes scattered about. To speak of grumpiness." Damien hefted a sigh, and his breath swirled before him in the chilly air.

Amma chuckled weakly at that and then nearly lost her footing on a slick rock. Mounds of perpetual snow dotted the terrain, the turning of the season making for a brisk march. They had left the larger trees behind as they scaled a higher peak, the mountainside rockier and covered in thick shrubs that didn't provide as much cover from the wind.

Taking her next step more carefully, Amma tied back her hair to keep it from whipping into her face. No longer with a shield, Vanders scurried down her shoulder and dove into the front of her tunic, curling up in the pocket between her breasts, just poking out his little muzzle to watch the way ahead. That made her chuckle a bit more deeply, and when she caught Damien staring at the vaxin—because that was clearly what he was staring at—asked, "He looks happy there, doesn't he?"

The redness that crawled over Damien's face was at least a bit satisfying.

But another two cold days and even colder nights, made exponentially worse by sweating despite the chill as the climb grew more strenuous, Amma found very little else to be satisfied by. In fact, a twinge in her stomach that grew into telltale cramping made her tolerance nearly bottom out, the spell she employed from medicinal mages back home to avoid such things choosing the absolute worse time to wear off. According to the map, they were at least coming upon their destination, their red dot inching closer to the stagnant deep blue one, but even enchanted maps did not account for verticalness.

Pulling herself up onto a plateau, Amma flopped right down on her stomach, Vanders smartly scurrying up to her shoulder, saving himself from being smooshed between her breasts. Damien's boots were just before her, Katz's taloned feet beside, and she just groaned, not bothering to lift her head. He tapped a toe on the ground, impatient.

"Your arms and legs are *so* much longer than mine," Amma whined, face flat against the stone, a surprisingly pleasant heat there. "I can't keep up."

"Must you be carried the rest of the way?"

Avoid more hiking *and* have a good excuse to finally touch Damien again? "Yes!" she squealed, not even caring how eager it came out as her head popped back up.

But in the space between Damien's legs, she could see the plateau was laid out differently from where they had been. A thin sheen of snow covered the rocks, a wall of stone rising at its back, overgrown thickly with vines and sheltering them from the wind, and just in the center a layer of steam hovered over a pool.

Amma pushed up onto her knees, knocking Damien out of the way. Ignoring his confused squawking, she scurried to the edge of the water and dipped a hand in, the perpetual cold of the last three days melting away. "By the grace of the gods, it's a hot spring." She peered back at Damien and didn't care how desperate she looked. "It'll be sundown soon, these rocks will be dangerous in the dark, and we should definitely try and be clean for the oracle too—please say we can stop here."

Damien was already unbuckling the shoulder straps of his armor. "You really don't need to convince me."

Amma jumped to her feet, kicked off her boots, and pulled at the leather cord that laced up her vest, but as it fell open, she caught it and froze.

Chest armor off, one boot abandoned, Damien grabbed the bottom of his tunic, but had also fallen completely still. They stared at one another, half undressed, and even the frigid gust that blew over them didn't cause either to sway.

Amma swallowed. "Maybe you can turn around?"

Damien hopped in a small circle so that his back was to her, otherwise holding completely still.

"You too Katz," she said, but the imp was already averting his gaze, just doing it in his painfully slow way. Damien mumbled out an order for the imp to do a wide perimeter check of the area, and Katz traipsed off.

She watched Damien's back for a moment longer, making sure he stayed still until Vanders tapped her on the neck as if to say get on with it. In a rush, she pulled off her tunic, shimmied out of her breeches, and abandoned her chemise in a small pile up on a dry rock before stepping into the water. Trepidation at Damien seeing her naked melted away as she sank in. An entire layer of grime peeled away from her skin, the knots in her muscles unraveling, and her lungs filled with a heady, warm mist. Even the cramping in her belly subsided, and she dreaded the coming days a little less. Gods, was it good, and she sighed aloud.

"Um, Amma?"

"Oh!" She spun, ducking down to her shoulders and giving Vanders her hands to jump into. "Go ahead, I'm in." She'd made it to the middle of the pool where the steam was a bit thicker, body totally submerged.

Damien kicked off his other boot and pulled off his tunic, and even in the falling light of the coming evening, nothing was hidden by shadows. Peering up over Vanders' ears, she watched the muscles of Damien's back curve and contract with the small act of removing the dagger strapped to his forearm. He turned to the rock he used for the rest of his things, carefully setting his bracer atop the pile, then straightened, every crease in his stomach sharp. Hands firmly took his belt, and as he unhitched it, there was a jolt between Amma's legs she hadn't been expecting as the leather fell away. Damien's thumbs hooked into the waist of his pants, revealing an extra inch of hips carved out like stone, and then Amma inhaled so sharply she nearly choked.

"Ouch, Vanders!" The vaxin's incisors were sharp, but they didn't puncture her thumb. Amma's palms had dipped down, flooding Vanders' sanctuary as she'd forgotten she had a hold of him at all.

The blood mage straightened, armorless, bootless, and poised to be breeches-less. "Amma, is some reciprocation not in order?"

She spun with a splash, face heating and not from the spring. "You should have told me I was being a lech," she whispered to Vanders as she went to the side of the pool where there was a rocky ledge.

He squeaked back as she set him down on a flat space beside a divot filled with water. The vaxin dipped a paw into the shallow puddle there and then slid into it, flopping over onto his back and sprawling out.

Lightly splashing water behind Amma told her Damien was getting in—and that he was completely, deliciously, heartachingly naked—but she was too appalled at herself to turn back around. Instead, she watched Vanders float on his back for as long as she thought seemed believable and then an extra moment longer before finally shifting away from the ledge.

Damien had waded in to his navel at the far end of the spring, and Amma grimaced. He needed to pick one—don't show her how naked he was or actually get up close and really show her. Annoyed, she undid the knot in her hair and ducked under the water to scrub at her scalp. Breath held, she remained submerged, eyes closed and weightless, heat pressing in on her, and just as her lungs began to ache, she broke the surface.

Still looming partly out of the water, Damien had come closer but was much too far off to touch—not that she should be thinking of doing any touching. Amma rubbed at her arms though the dirt had all gone, checking that the layer of steam mostly concealed her. She didn't know if she were being silly, maybe he didn't even care about her breasts anymore after his mouth had been all over them, but the thought of his tongue tracing her nipples made them tighten, and she remained firmly beneath the surface.

"Does it remind you of home?"

Amma glanced about at the stones glazed with melted snow and the swirling mists. It was cozy and comforting in the little alcove they'd found along the otherwise dreary and draining mountain, but she knew Damien meant Faebarrow specifically. "We don't have springs like this, not that I know of."

He lifted a hand, water pouring off it. "I suppose I meant the bathing chambers. I remember sitting in a very large, very hot tub in Faebarrow." He snorted. "And feeling very sorry for myself."

At that, Amma chuckled. "Right, when you were Tia's prisoner. Don't you have bathtubs in Aszath Koth?"

"Of course, I just rarely thought to make them warm."

"A lifetime of cold baths sure explains a lot about you." When he smirked, she relaxed a bit and began dragging fingers through her hair to detangle it. "You live in that huge, temple-looking building in the center of the city, don't you? The one that's taller than everything else?"

He nodded. "That would be Bloodthorne Keep. It may look a little like a temple, but it's not so different from your own. It has an ostentatious entry hall and imposing throne room, bed chambers, torture chambers, bathing chambers——"

"Torture chambers?"

"Faebarrow's got a prison, I know that for certain, as does your friend Nicholas."

"Okay, but we don't torture people there."

"You're sure?" Damien's brows lifted, but before she could retort, her mind told her she truly didn't know, and she snapped her mouth back shut. Too pleased, he went on, "We do *have* hot water, though I will say, Bloodthorne Keep is not nearly as bright as Faebarrow. The city itself is shrouded, so we get very little sun which also means flowering things don't grow there. I suppose it could be brightened up with some paint? Can you paint black marble?" He dipped himself lower and rubbed at his shoulders, wincing. "It would likely not take. I doubt you would enjoy it much there."

Amma frowned though was intrigued that he cared at all what she would think of it. "I liked the karsts. I mean, it was cold, but it was beautiful, and there was a lot to do."

"But you did not want to stay."

The distance between them had shrunk, and surely the only way

Damien could not hear how Amma's heart raced was because it was being held below the water. "I didn't want to stay in the karsts by myself." She took a deep, steamy breath, throat tightening on the words. "Not without you."

"Well, yes, it would have been dangerous on your own," he said quickly, pulling arms through the water and watching how it moved intently. Damien was either much dumber than she'd always thought, or much more clever than she was willing to give him credit for just then.

Amma scrunched up her nose and said nothing. She could clarify that it wasn't fear that kept her tied to him, nor was it really the talisman, but did he even want to know?

"These mountains are connected to the infernal range," he finally said, voice lower as the water moved him a bit closer. "Aszath Koth isn't terribly far from here. I would be lying if I didn't say that I've considered just...going home."

Amma blinked. "You mean instead of following the Grand Order's wishes? Instead of marching on Eirengaard and—"

"Instead of all of it, yes." Damien dipped even lower so that his chin touched the water. "It's despicable, isn't it?"

"I don't think it's *despicable*, Damien," she said with a snort, "but it is surprising. Do you miss home?"

His lip curled. "Not much, no. I am just *concerned* about what's ahead."

She maneuvered slightly closer to him. "Do you mean you're afraid?"

"No." The answer was quick, but then irritation passed over his features. "Well. Yes."

Amma's eyes went wide, waiting for some joke or pithy remark to follow.

"Afraid," he said carefully like the word were new, "for the outcome and...you."

She lifted a hand out of the water to poke her collarbone.

He nodded slowly, words coming stilted and awkward. "I know that neglecting the Grand Order's task is inviting them to retaliate, but Aszath Koth is well-protected, and I could keep you—ah, keep *them* away, I mean. Probably. I also fear that in fulfilling their order, you will be injured or worse, and it will be my fault."

"I think something's wrong with the spring."

"What? Why?" Damien stood suddenly, shoulders and chest bared, water pooling off of him as his brow narrowed.

Amma giggled at the way his eyes darted over the steamy surface.

91

"The Damien Maleficus Bloodthorne I know was threatening to kill me not so long ago, so clearly it's enchanted."

"Oh, very humorous." He sank back down, relief plain on his face both from an avoided danger and the out she had given him. But his gaze finally lifted to hers, piercing as his tongue ran over his lips. "But come now, you know I wouldn't have ever wasted you like that."

Amma swallowed hard, glad for the heat so he couldn't see how her face would have reddened otherwise. "Well, I'm not really a thief, my barony has lost most of its wealth and standing, and I'm in the way of your destiny, so I don't really know what good I am to you alive."

"You don't?" Damien's eyes roved downward as if he could see every inch of her body, and then he dunked under completely.

She remained huddled there, losing sight of the shadow that was his hair. The setting sun cast the sky in deep pinks and purples, stars beginning to dot the darkest layer, and the moons had come out, dangerously close together.

The water parted just before Amma, Damien resurfacing drenched. She held her spot, body flushing from an internal heat. An inch of movement would bring them right up against one another, naked.

He ran a hand through his black hair, and wet, it stayed out of his face for once as water dripped off his nose and chin and lips. She tried very hard to not imagine kissing those lips again, but the feeling of them on her mouth, her jaw, her throat came anyway, a corporeal memory so strong she feared that alone might break the oracle's insistence on chastity.

"Would you want to go there? To Aszath Koth with me? I mean to see it properly, not to be eaten by a lamia or sacrificed by a cult or abducted by a blood mage."

"You'd show me the keep?"

He wiped at his face and nodded.

Amma made a thoughtful sound. "Could I see that rug the Righteous Sentries said you stole?"

"The Azure Hide of Ruvyn?" Damien cocked a brow. "Well, *that* is in my bed chamber."

"Oh," she said, feigning innocence, "well, in that case, I definitely hope you show it to me."

The muscles at the corner of Damien's jaw tightened, easy to see so close, and she wished she were right up against him, grinding back. A hand touched her waist below the water's surface. Instead of surprise, it was relief that flooded her, and she reached out, placing fingertips against his chest.

A gust of wind swept through the air, a flurry of darkness against the brilliant pink of the sky, and a screech like the dying cry of some animal rained down from above. Amma ducked, and Damien whirled around as a squall of feathers and inhuman shrieking landed on the pool's edge. The gust off its immense wingspan scattered their clothes, blotting out the light of the setting sun.

"I knew we were too bloody lucky," Damien groaned, his hand blindly thrown behind him and pressing against Amma's stomach to push her backward.

"What in the Abyss is that?" she squeaked out, peeking around him.

Shadowed against the light, the creature was perched with taloned feet sinking into the stone, knees jutting up and out, and long, sinewy arms that tapered into claws. Its shoulders were hunched, and from its back sprouted russet wings, the largest feathers dotted with a pattern that looked to be hundreds of eyes staring down on them.

"Harpy," said Damien in a put-upon tone, then he raised his voice. "Katz? A little help?"

There was no impish sighing from the scrub brushes, but the winged creature let out a screech that rattled the very stones of the mountain. It had a face that was almost human save for the beak, a massive, pointed thing with a tongue that jutted out covered in rows of sharp teeth.

Damien swore, then he looked down at himself and swore again. He raised a hand with a sigh, black smoke forming in his palm, and then sent a wall of haziness at the creature as it lifted off to attack. Amma shielded her eyes from the terrible gust its wings produced, a cry choking on the darkness that entangled the creature, and then a splash.

"Shit." Damien's other hand was still pressed to Amma's belly, and he pushed her farther back from where the harpy plummeted into the pool. His fingers slid downward in the slickness of the water, and for a moment Amma was too aroused to be frightened, but then the harpy burst back up from the water, and she realized this was no time to be thinking with her...*heart*.

Screeching and twice as angry, soaked wings beat at the surface, but the harpy was unable to take to the air again, instead advancing on its long legs. Amma's excitement shifted right back to fear as she flung her hands around Damien's arm and yanked him back from the irate bird-person. He simultaneously called up more smoky arcana, but two more harpies landed on either side of the spring's rocky ledge, filling the air with angry screeching. When the shadows were released, feathers scattered, but the frantically beating wings of all three tore through the haze.

Backed right into the rock wall and squeezing Damien tight, Amma pressed herself to the vines there, wishing for a place to hide. There was a crack, and the pressure of the stone fell away from her back. Amma tumbled with a splash, taking Damien with her. Flailing underwater for only a moment, there were limbs everywhere, but thankfully none of them feathered, and when she and Damien popped back up above the surface, the harpies were gone.

Amma wiped hair out of her face to assess the darkened cave they'd fallen into. The spring continued on for a yard or so before becoming shallow very quickly, a ledge climbing out of the water and leveling off against the back of the cavern. The hollow behind the rock wall was small but enclosed, a shaft of silvery light filtering in from a crack above, and it was quiet until a terrible scratching had them clambering backward.

Out of the water and up onto the rocky bank, they pushed their backs against the wall. Much too small for any of the harpies to fit through, the remaining divot could only be pecked and clawed at. Amma held her breath, waiting, but they were unable to break away the rock. She sighed, tipping her head back and closing her eyes, safe for the moment. "I hope Vanders is all right. And Katz too."

The small cavern went quiet as if Damien already knew the worst had happened.

Amma bit her lip and opened her eyes. "Damien!"

His gaze snapped up from her chest.

"We're under duress for goodness's sake." She threw an arm over her breasts but was secretly at least a little pleased.

"No, we're not—the harpies are out there, and we are in here. Alone."

There was another intense scuffing at the stone.

"For now," he groaned and held up a pointed rock between the two. "Stab me."

Amma screwed up her face and struck out, knocking the stone from Damien's hand. There was a plop as it sank into the water. "No, I'm not really upset with you."

Damien rolled his eyes. "So I can do bloodcraft."

"Oh." She looked after where the makeshift weapon had gone. "But you always cut yourself."

"With a blade meant for slicing. I thought you might be able to help with a little added pressure. Do you think you can scratch me instead?"

Amma held her chewed and chipped nails close to his face so he could properly see their sad state in the dark. He frowned, but then both turned toward the entrance of the cavern. It had gone quiet.

"Should we—"

Damien raised a finger to his lips, and then muttered against it in Chthonic. After a moment, he shook his head, voice low. "They're still there."

Amma settled back awkwardly, thighs squeezed together and knees up. Damien's wet shoulder shifted against hers as he looked about in the dark for another rock. Amma pretended to assist, leaning over to check the far side of him but let her gaze linger down to his lap when his leg fell askew. There were a lot of shadows, but if he just shifted slightly to the left where the shaft of moonlight was streaming down—

"I know you think demons have tails, but *that* isn't one."

Amma thrust herself back against the wall, unable to hide the grin that plastered itself on her face.

"Nor is it a willing source of blood, whether we are under duress or not." He handed her a slightly blunter stone than the last. "Perhaps you can dig this into my thigh. There is a vein just along here that—"

"Oh, ew, we're not doing that." She tossed the stone into the spring right after the other, and Damien's mouth fell open.

Amma squinted into the darkness of the cave for an alternative, then glanced upward. More vines hung down, and she pulled some free from the cavern's ceiling. "I've an idea." Amma wrapped the vine around his forearm a few times, tugging lightly on both ends to be sure it didn't snap. "Are you ready? This is probably going to hurt."

He cocked his head and gave her a smile that was running thick with condescension.

"Okay." Amma pulsed arcana in the young briar vine and pulled it tight around his arm. The plant matured instantly, hardening and sprouting thorns that sunk into his skin all at once.

Damien sucked in a sharp breath between his teeth, eyes going wide with disbelief. "Amma, you—" He held up his arm, blood oozing up from multiple places.

"I'm so sorry," she whispered, slapping her hand over her mouth.

"You're brilliant," he breathed, a huge grin on his face, and then he pressed a quick kiss to her fingers where her mouth would have been had she not been covering it up. "Now stay here."

She watched him, too stunned to move as he pushed off the ledge and back into the water, wading to the small break in the wall and submerging completely.

Amma did wait, but only until she shook off the surprise of both the thorns and the kiss that she assumed would be acceptable to the oracle since it wasn't really a kiss at all. But when she heard a scuffle and a chorus of squawks, she splashed through the water and ducked under to escape the cave.

When Amma emerged, a harpy was falling out of the air, hitting the edge of the rock with a thunk, and then it tumbled down the far cliffside. Damien stood in the middle of the spring, half submerged, arm covered in rivulets of blood, the thorns still twisted about him as he cast.

For a moment she was relieved, and then there was swooping just overhead. Amma ducked away from it, twisting her hands up in the vines again. Greenery shot overhead, trapping the last harpy's talons. The bird-person screeched, struggled to free itself, and finally tore away just as Damien sent bloody blades to cut into it and send it over the mountain's edge.

Amma's pulse was flying, the heat of the water building to an almost intolerable degree, but the air was silent. She swayed, and there was a splash before it all went dark.

CHAPTER 11
TEN THOUSAND EYES, AND GODS
CHOOSE TO BE BLIND

A t least moonlight is incredibly flattering."
Amma groaned, rubbing at her face.
"As is being soaking wet."

She grumbled out something unintelligible with her head down, doting on Vanders who had reappeared that morning.

"And who knew you had a mole right on your—"

"By Osurehm and Sestoth and even the dark gods, *please* stop talking."

Damien knew he was acting all too blithe, but he couldn't help himself. "If it is any consolation, I am much less concerned about all of the horrible, impending possibilities now." He grinned, waiting for her to ask why, but she didn't, which was going to be a terrible waste of a very good joke, and he didn't get to deliver those often. "Don't you want to know why?"

"No, but I suppose you're going to tell me whether I ask or not."

"Because if it all does end up going wrong, I've properly seen you naked now, so I can die utterly satisfied."

That wasn't entirely true—Damien was far from being satisfied with the extremely short glimpse he'd gotten of Amma when he'd plucked her out of the water—but saying so did get a little, embarrassed chuckle out of her, and he was very proud of how red he could make her face go at reminding her about it.

Instead of lingering at her side, however, Damien picked up his pace on their final ascent along the ridge, leaving her just a few steps behind. He didn't mean to be cruel, though it would certainly be the first time, only to poke at her a bit, but it quickly did become cruel to himself. Yes, he had laid out the fabricated rule: chastity until they reached the oracle, but it was proving significantly harder than he expected. Her matched distress was a bit of a reprieve. Even knowing he was on a dark quest for the Grand Order of Dread and that he intended to free his demon father and destroy the realm, she still tried to take a peek at his cock, at the very least, and that was *something*.

After he confirmed the night prior that Amma had only fainted but was in no real peril, he'd wrapped her in their cloaks and tried to get some sleep himself, but it didn't come. Instead, his hand went into his satchel, rescued by Katz in the wake of the harpies, and he pulled out the occlusion crystal hidden there.

With Amma solidly out, he held the shard above his head, catching the moonlight in it. No yellow eye stared back, though he did feel watched by the stone and his father. He didn't slice himself on the shard's edge, but he did allow noxscura to seep up from his palm and feel for the magic it once had. Its power was sapped after being out of the infernal mountains for so long, but Ashrein Ridge bled right into them. He could have tried to refuel the shard, but had stuffed it back away instead, not ready to face Zagadoth.

"I passed out again." Amma's voice was small, pulling Damien from his thoughts.

"Well, the hot spring was…hot," he offered.

She only grunted.

"Perhaps you need a conduit for channeling your arcana. Most divine mages use weapons." Damien slowed, allowing her to catch up to him again. "These things do take practice."

"How can I practice if I go unconscious every time?" She was holding her hands up before her and glaring at them.

"Not every time," he reminded her. "And when you do faint, I'll be sure to drag you to safety as you've done for me."

Her lips twisted out of the frown they'd put on.

Damien was beginning to feel it, that lightness in his head that came from being up so high. It was a sort of clarity, the reason the oracle was purported to live in the mountain peaks, and while it didn't let Damien push any of his fraught thoughts away permanently, he did place them to the side for a moment.

Below, large swaths of treetops all moved together with the briskness of the wind, making them seem small and pliable. Clouds had moved in over the day, casting the world in greying hues, but Amma's face, when he did finally look back at it, was glowing with the same warmth it always held. The only difference now was the intrusive thought about what it would be like when she wasn't there, and how horrible that was going to be.

"What?" she asked, clearly still embarrassed though there was really no reason.

He shook his head. "We're nearly there."

When they crested the next ridge, they were met with a rabbit which wasn't unusual, but the small tray it held was a bit strange, even for Damien who had experienced this once before.

Resting back on its haunches, the rabbit extended the tray instead of bolting as creatures of its size and predisposition usually did. Amma and Damien traded looks then peered into the cups. Damien lifted one, took a sniff of something putrid, and immediately handed it off to Katz. The imp took it with a slowness, but for once his depression abated, looking as close to pleased as a creature of his makeup could muster, and he took a drink.

The other two were both filled with wine, one significantly sweeter than the other. That he handed to Amma and kept the third. There was a single blueberry left on the tray, and Damien handed it to Vanders, the fruit like an entire loaf of bread in its tiny paws.

"They know we're coming—pretty good oracle, I guess," Amma said and took a drink. "Oh, no, excuse me, great oracle."

"Greatest oracle." A young man darted out from around the bend ahead, eyes fixed on a scroll so long it trailed the ground behind him as he went. He paused only to push his spectacles up his long, pointed nose before they began to slide right back down. "Blessed with ninety-seven point three percent of the god Denonfy's foresight, by my calculation."

Damien didn't recognize him, but when last he had made the trek over a decade ago, the human assistant to the oracle was a withered, old man who made it clear he didn't like the look of Damien. The man thanked the rabbit, taking the tray from her, then tucked it behind his parchment as he looked up into the sky.

Above them, a hawk circled twice, then swooped down toward the neighboring valley. "It is you then, but of course it is—arrival on the wings of the hooked-beak twice encompassed will come The Cleansing Rodent, Death's Vessel, The Eclipse of Destruction, and The Wrong Cat. No, not *cat*,"—he squinted at the parchment—"that's Kaz? Well, whatever that means, it must be you lot. Come on, they're ready for you." Without a glance to make sure they followed, he turned and went back the way he'd come.

"One of us is Death's Vessel and the other is The Eclipse of Destruction?" asked Amma, lips reddened by the wine. "Which is which?"

Damien only shrugged, not really wanting to know, and they followed the bend in the way that led between two tall rocks. The plateau of the oracle's encampment had a sharp decline at its far end, nothing but sky beyond. Canvases were strung up along the rocky wall they popped out of, tented and darkened within, lanterns hanging at their entries and bits of carved wood beneath those, jingling pleasantly in the slight breeze. The middle of the plateau housed a large fire and a massive bowl strung over it that spiced the air with something savory.

An elven woman poked at the fire absently with what looked like a metal halberd, a scroll in her other hand. Her face, a russet color with sharp features and black hair, was familiar, but then elves didn't really age, even if they were assisting oracles. "The Eclipse of Destruction and Death's Vessel?" she asked without looking up from her pages.

"Yep." The skinny man was just rolling up the length of his scroll and finally looking on Damien and Amma properly. "But it wasn't a cat at all."

"I told you it'd be a raccoon," she said, but her grin fell off completely when she eyed Damien. "Uh oh."

Amma's grip tightened on her goblet, and Damien tried very hard to not look menacing.

"You've been here before." The elf stood, hurrying to the thin man and trading her parchment for his, letting it unravel to the ground again.

Damien nodded. "Eleven years ago. You remember?"

"We don't get that many visitors, only the worthy, all that," she said then frowned even deeper. "This was before your time, Geoff, but I could have sworn he wasn't called…well, no one's sobriquet ever changes."

"It's not like the oracle's gotten anything wrong." Geoff fidgeted, eyes darting over the scroll he'd been handed. The rabbit hopped by then, collecting Katz's empty mug.

Damien could only shrug, again wanting their eyes off of him.

Geoff finally huffed. "You better come with me."

They were brought to the largest canvas tent and immediately bombarded with the smell of something woodsy and fungal, a haziness to the air inside. Amma covertly wiped at her nose as she took the last sip from her cup, and the rabbit hopped up to take the goblet away. Bundles of herbs hung from the poles holding up the tent, and specks of light emanated off stones placed strategically about, but the heart of the space was filled with pillows stacked up and strewn about, all dyed in various, bright shades and intricately beaded at their edges, and sitting atop the highest stack was the oracle, almost exactly how Damien remembered them.

The Denonfy Oracle wasn't an elf, but they didn't seem to age, their blue skin smooth, two sets of arms slim and long, and face only creased with a perpetual, knowing grin. Tall and lanky, they were sprawled sideways and draped in a gauzy robe of many colors, belted loosely at the waist, white linens worn beneath. They took a long drag of a pipe then blew out a perfect ring that dispersed into the hanging haze.

Damien had forgotten the feeling in the intervening eleven years, but it came back with a vengeance then as he stood before what he knew was great power and knowledge. He threw back his wine and squared his shoulders, the cup slipped from his hand as the rabbit silently scampered by, but none of that stopped the feeling from coming. Fear. Not the same fear of being faced with harpies or arch-nemeses or even Damien himself, but the fear of what was to pass and not being able to do a thing about it. Staring at the Denonfy Oracle inspired something unique: the fear of total helplessness.

"You made it! Right on!"

And then the fear subsided. That was right—along with being all-knowing and imposing, the oracle was also strange. They pulled themselves up to sit, raising their four arms wide and taking a full breath of heady, smoky air.

"You knew we were coming," said Amma in an awe-struck whisper. At least she was impressed.

"Sure did. And during harpy mating season too, but you did okay." Their voice was smooth, words slow with a tinge of fascination as they looked them over. "Oh, yup, still got all your limbs even."

Amma's wide-eyed look went suspicious. "Were we supposed to not?"

The oracle shrugged. "It was only a slight possibility."

"Um, your divinatoriness?" said the elven woman as she ducked around one of the tent's poles. "This one's been here before, but…well, I'm not sure how to explain."

The oracle was nodding as the elf's voice went awkward. "Yeah, you're worried about his, uh, what is it you call 'em? His sobriquet?"

She nodded, thin brows pinched.

"For sure, for sure, for sure." They took a deep puff on their pipe, and Amma and Damien sneaked looks at one another. She was as confused but intrigued as he expected. "So, like, our greater purpose in life sorta…well, it *changes*. We don't get a lot of repeat customers, but if we did we'd see it more. Does that jive, Val'tiel?"

"I suppose, it just doesn't make for the cleanest records, your sight-blessed."

"Exactly."

The woman rolled her eyes. "Come on, Geoff, we need to prepare for the storm."

The skinny, young man followed her back out, and Damien and Amma were left alone with the oracle, plus one imp and vaxin.

"So, what can I do you two for, hmm?"

Before Damien heard her say it, he knew exactly what was about to come out of Amma's mouth, impossible to stop.

"Don't you already know?"

That helplessness crawled back up to the surface of Damien's skin, and he scratched at his neck.

But the oracle laughed, loud and genuine, then took another puff of their pipe. "Course I do. But if I don't ask, you, like, won't say it, and then past me can't have the vision of you asking, so present me can't know, so the only way I could have already known is if you ask at some point, and I have a vision of that request."

Amma thought a moment then seemed to accept with a confused sort of nod. "Convenient."

"Cool, cool, cool. So, sit. Let's hang." They gestured to the pillows before them and leaned back.

It was confusing for most who heard any true oracle speak, and not just because they often communicated in riddles. Oracles spent quite a lot of time in their visions of the future and often picked up on language that would not come about naturally for centuries. These anachronistic words worked themselves into an oracle's vernacular, and since most of what they said made little sense to others as it was, a few funny words here or there hardly mattered. The argument could be made that oracles themselves, in using future speech in past times, were the true sources of languages' evolution, but etymologists didn't want their careers to be obsolete, so would never confirm the paradox.

Damien awkwardly sat on the ground, crossing his legs and sitting up straight as Amma perched on her hip with knees folded. Katz sulked nearby, plopping down with a huff.

The oracle pointed at Damien with their pipe. "But, just so you know, if you ask about your destiny and your dad and all that again, I'll tell you the exact same thing as before: *when the day is night, and—*"

Damien cleared his throat. "The prophecy. Right. Yes."

"You won't tell Damien anything else about his fate?" The

indignation in Amma's voice rose out of the awe. "But you *do* know? You're just going to keep it from him?"

The oracle seemed neither bothered nor offended, they just took another long pull of their pipe and tipped their head back. The smoke in the tent thickened and then dissipated. "Prophecy is, like, *hard*," they finally said.

Amma grunted. "So is climbing a mountain."

Damien held back the laugh that wanted to burst out of him but gazed at her what he feared was probably a bit too fondly.

The oracle rested their chin on a fist and smirked at Amma, reminding Damien he was meant to be afraid. "Yeah, that's fair, I guess, but it's not exactly dealing-with-the-gods hard. Or maybe you two do know something about that."

A slight gust outside buffeted the canvas tent, the sound filling up the quiet. It was an odd thing to say, but so was most of what came out of the oracle's mouth, so it was passed over.

"So, here's the thing: if I were to tell you that in fifteen hours and thirty-seven minutes, you are going to stumble and cause a great calamity, what would you do?"

Amma's small mouth opened, eyes darting around, and then she cleared her throat. "Probably try to not stumble."

"Exactly," they said. "You'd do, like, everything you possibly could, count down the time, try real hard to keep yourself upright, all that. But prophecies are going to happen—that's their whole *thing*. And, like, I've tried it a lotta ways, trust me. I even had this phase where I focused on the good stuff, ya know? So instead, I might say to you, in fifteen hours and thirty-six minutes, you're gonna have a little accident with a rock, but you'll be crowned queen of a loyal and vast empire. And then you'd be like, *Amazing! Bring on that rock*! Right?"

"Well, not exactly like that," mumbled Amma.

"The thing is, though, when you know, that's all you focus on, and the gods hate that because it sort of gives away the ending and ruins their games." The oracle waved one of their hands, stopping Amma before she could ask. "You're just pieces on a board to them that they get to push around. It's a whole thing, but back to my example. If I tell you, instead of all that other stuff, that the wandering lady will displace the earth to upend tyranny and usurp the salvage throne, I create a mystery, everybody plays along, and by the time anybody ever figures it out, it's probably already happened."

Amma was staring back at the oracle, brow knit. "You're telling us that you purposefully shroud your visions in metaphor and extravagant language so your visitors *don't* understand them?"

The oracle was taking a very long drag and then coughed. "Totally."

"What's the point of prophecy then?"

The oracle shrugged. "I'unno."

"You don't know?" When she threw up her hands, Damien grit his teeth, but he didn't really want to stop her.

"Hey, I'm an oracle, not a philosopher. Maybe people just like thinking they have control. All I know is, the gods didn't like having omniscience, so they focused it into just one of them, Denonfy, and then that god got sick of it too, so one day I woke up with almost all of the god of fortune and destiny's sight. I thought I was supposed to tell people the future, but then Denonfy came to me and said I was being too clear, but it was too late, word had spread, so I had to come up here, and well,"—they took a puff of their pipe—"here we are."

Damien wasn't entirely sure he understood. If prophecy were prophecy and if everything the oracle saw was destined to occur, one couldn't reasonably change anything, big or little. But then he looked at Amma once again, the pout to her lips, her indignation at the oracle's refusal to help, the soft curve of her neck as she tipped her head and her hair fell away, and he did understand, at least a little bit, how possible change could be.

"So, you." The oracle pointed to Amma and snapped her out of the deep thought she was having. "You have a question for me?"

Amma nodded and gestured to Damien.

He pulled out the pendant but hesitated. "Perhaps, instead, I should ask about this since my question cannot be answered."

She shook her head. "You'll come up with something else."

"But, Amma, this is a once-in-a-lifetime—"

"Twice."

"Maybe, but I think—"

"My mind's made up," she said flexing her fingers.

"She wins," said the oracle and took another puff. Whether they were judging the conversation or divining the future, he wasn't sure, but Damien handed over the pendant.

Amma raised it up so the broken gem swung from its chain, shifting up onto her knees and looking very serious. "This is The Dreadcouncil's Fermentable Pendant of Approximated Bogholes and Noninfectious Corsets—"

"That's somehow wronger than the last time," Damien mumbled.

Amma pursed her lips. "The Dreadcouncil's Formidable Pendant?"

"One would think, but no."

"Forgettable?"

Damien chuckled. "Apparently."

The oracle put up a hand. "I know what it's called."

"Right, of course you do." Amma set her face stony again. "It was given to Damien by the Grand Order of Dread to be thrown into a pit that's actually an entity that we're pretty sure is called E'nloc. What will happen when it's thrown in?"

The oracle's long features fell slack, head tipping as they gazed at the pendant. "*Misery personified shall descend upon a winged beast to unknowingly rescue her own undoing, but when the pieces are reforged, the downfall of the hallowed son, the chosen, and the heartless mother is inevitable.*"

Amma waited to be sure they were done, then brought the pendant close to her face again, whispering. "I don't know what that means."

"Good." The oracle broke into laughter.

Damien felt the world go out from under him. The hallowed son, the one who would cause the realm to rot and bring about the harbinger of destruction—that was him.

Amma carefully turned back to Damien, but he feared he might destroy the pendant if he took it back. "Why don't you hold on to that for a little while?"

She nodded reluctantly, tucking it into her own pouch.

The Denonfy Oracle squinted upward through an opening at the top of the tent then picked up a small linen, shaking it out and pocketing it in their robe. "You'll need more time. Val'tiel and Geoff can keep The Eclipse of Destruction and The Wrong Kaz company, and you can come with me."

Based on how they gestured, Damien was meant to go along with the oracle. Their words had been loaded, but they stood and began to lumber off, so all Damien and Amma had time for was a quick trading of glances before he had to follow through the hazy wall of smoke.

There was a flap at the back of the tent opening up onto steps built into the stone wall that wound in a tight spiral and led to a final plateau. The mountain's peak was a small, flat space that fell off steeply to every side, the whole of existence laid out below, both inescapable and isolate. Above, the sky spread out in deepening greys as the light leeched away behind gathering clouds. A bird circled, its silhouette odd with a long tail, and feathers red in the sun's last rays.

"Take a load off." The oracle dropped down and splayed out, hands folded behind their head.

Damien carefully sat beside them, legs crossed again, back stiff.

"You gotta know, I *am* bummed for you," said the oracle with a sigh as they lay their pipe to the side, smoke fizzling out. "You came all the way up here, but, like, that prophecy? There probably isn't anything you can do about it."

"Yeah, you said."

"I just don't want you wasting your time, man."

Damien grunted, eyes flicking upward to watch the strange bird make a lazy loop in the darkening sky.

"And if you obsess over it too much, the gods are gonna get real cranky."

"I don't care what the gods think," said Damien, resting his chin on his fist. "No offense."

"Eh, none taken. I'm not one of 'em, just got saddled with one of their powers. Denonfy picked fortune and destiny out the pot and then figured out it's too heavy having all the answers."

"If you got all of Denonfy's powers, don't you have control over fortune and destiny?"

"He kept just enough to ensure I couldn't. But can I tell you a secret?" The oracle cocked a deeply indigo brow. "I don't actually know *everything*."

With a groan, Damien flopped down onto his back, splaying out on the stone.

The oracle sighed heavily like a weight had been lifted off of him. "Like, I know one of us is about to get shit on, but I'm not certain which."

"Wha—" Damien went to sit back up, but it was too late, a splat of white falling on him. "Bloody, fucking Abyss, you could have *said*." He looked about for anything to wipe the bird shit off his chest leathers, but the mountain peak was all smooth stone.

The oracle passed him the linen he'd brought from inside the tent. "Well, I did, but it didn't matter, my man, it was gonna happen."

"You just didn't know to which of us," Damien mocked, wiping himself off and glaring up at the creature still circling above them.

"Nope! But that's the kinda stuff I like—that's the stuff worth living for. There isn't a whole lotta point in doing much when you know exactly what'll come of it all."

Damien settled back again but the sneer fell away from his face, the oracle's words too sentimental to be angry over. "You should have told Amma that; she would have been more receptive."

The oracle just laughed. "She wouldn't accept that—once upon a time she might have said okay and just gone with the flow, but she's changing, and eventually no one, not even the gods, will be able to tell her no. It'll be right in time too." They closed their eyes. "Take all the time you need coming up with your question. Don't tell Val and Geoff, but it's nice to just sit up here in the quiet sometimes."

The sky darkened as the sun slipped away, stars winking into existence against the deepening purples as clouds gathered. Damien drummed fingers on his stomach, lying back, no idea what to ask. He was pondering the nature of things, but that wasn't an oracle's forte—what does it mean to be evil, to change, to experience an impossible feeling? Those things had been in that unfinished book that Anomalous had given him, but even Soren Darkmore hadn't found the answers. Or he had, but ripped them out because they were too awful for anyone else to ever read.

The moons hung in the sky so drastically close to one another, and he could feel the impending magic as noxscura prickled at his skin. Where was his mother? How did Xander find him? What did Marquis Caldor have to do with everything? He couldn't even ask the possible ways to purge the talisman from Amma, only how it would be done in the end, if at all, and he was afraid of that answer.

He'd never felt like such a coward.

Fear manifested in a blurry vision of E'nloc obscuring the future. He'd never thought of a future beyond the moment his father was released, but now he wanted something, even if it was just a filmy, uncertain feeling of safety and belonging. Because that future was where Amma was safe and they were together.

He snorted out a feeble laugh at that impossibility and thought instead about what Amma would ask if she'd not been burdened with Damien's problems. Now that—that would be much easier.

"You're really struggling," said the oracle, and for once they were not smiling as they pushed up onto an elbow to look on Damien. Without that frightening, all-knowing smirk, Damien's fear abated somewhat.

He nodded and sat up, head tipping down to look into his lap. He felt young and small and wished there were someone around to just do this for him. Then his head snapped back up. "You already know what I'm going to end up asking, don't you?"

It was the oracle's turn to nod. "Sure do. Bit of a waste, if you ask me, since it's so obvious, but it is, uh, delightfully frivolous."

Damien opened his mouth, but the right question refused to come out.

"If it makes it easier, I can just tell you the answer without you asking."

Relief flooded Damien's veins more completely than the noxscura. "Basest beasts, yes, please."

The oracle sat up to face Damien, legs crossed and fingers folded together. An imposing figure even on the ground, when they straightened their back with eyes closed, Damien could actually feel the arcana that flowed through them, ever-present, seeping out. Sitting straight for once, the oracle cleared their throat and shifted hands forward to point. "You."

The silence following the oracle's single-word prophecy was…well, it was bloody annoying. No more words came, and Damien could only lift a hand and poke himself in the chest. "Me? That's the answer? No creative epithet or flowery illusion? Just me?"

"Just you. Man, even though I knew you were going to look at me like that, I'm surprised—you really should be totally thrilled."

"Well, you didn't shroud it in any kind of mystery! After all your explanation and warning, you just—you *told* me! Gods, am I going to fuck it up now? Am I going to do it all wrong and ruin everything? Is fate going to reverse itself because I know?" Damien frantically pulled at the neck of his tunic to cool down despite the blustery winds.

The oracle placed a single hand on his shoulder, its weight instantly calming him. "Do you even know the question?"

Damien's breath hitched. "I…no?"

The oracle grinned, using Damien to push themself back up to stand. "Maybe this'll be my new thing. Answers, but no questions."

Watching the oracle walk away, disbelief quickly replaced itself with indignation as he scrambled to his feet. "But I thought you had to know the question to be able to answer it. If I never ask it, how can you possibly give me an answer?"

"Oh, you will ask, it just comes in the, hmm…" The oracle thought and then shrugged. "Well, if you'll excuse a little more mystery, it comes in the epilogue, I guess."

Damien had no idea what that meant, and he called after the oracle, but he was already headed back down the stairs.

CHAPTER 12
SOMETIMES GREATNESS IS NOT THRUST UPON ONE BUT PLACED GENTLY ATOP ONE'S HEAD

A mma ran a finger along the stupidly-named pendant's most jagged edge. It didn't really *feel* cursed, though she wasn't sure she would know if a thing was. When she moved it under the fading light, she caught a reflection that looked just like Damien, but he hadn't yet come out of the tent.

Stuffing it back into her pouch, Amma wandered across the oracle's encampment with Katz trailing behind. The elf had put away her scrolls and was stirring the large pot over the fire, a number of bowls stacked before her. When she saw Amma, she snapped her fingers at the skinny man and told him to take down Amma's prophecy.

Geoff scurried over, digging out a parchment from a deep pocket, checking, and then trading it off for another until he found a blank one. He felt around on his person, and Amma tapped her own ear. Geoff plucked the reed out from behind his where he'd stored it.

"Tell me *exactly* how it was said to you."

"*Misery personified shall descend upon a winged beast to unknowingly rescue her own undoing, but when the pieces are reforged, the downfall of the hallowed son, the chosen, and the heartless mother is inevitable.*" Amma blinked, surprised at how easily she repeated the prophecy she didn't even understand. She stuck out her tongue and tried to take a look at what she would assume to be arcana roving over it.

Geoff was already walking away from her, but she hurried after, catching how the writing on the scroll glowed. "Hey, uh, you wouldn't happen to know what that means, would you?"

He was rolling up the bit of parchment and disappeared into a tiny tent, calling back, "Not a clue."

Val'tiel was still invested in her stew, and Katz was slowly lowering himself onto a rock to rest from all the sighing he'd been doing, so Amma followed Geoff into the tent.

Beyond the canvas entrance, a cave carved out of the mountain led downward at a gentle slope. Lit by glowing stones, row after row of tightly wrapped scrolls were nestled into natural outcroppings in the rock walls, seven stuffed here, another three there, a single one rolled just thin enough to fit into a narrow hole right above her head. The air was dry and smelled so like the Grand Athenaeum that Amma fell still and could do nothing but take a deep breath.

Geoff was skittering away down the cave when Amma opened her eyes again, and an idea formed in her mind. She still didn't know the prophecy that Damien had once been told, the one he was toiling under and didn't seem to want her to hear. But if she accidentally read it...

"Geoff," she called, hurrying after. "Do you have *all* of the prophecies here?"

Startled as if he'd already forgotten she existed, he stopped short. "Only the pending ones," he finally said, a little shake to his voice. "We burn them after they've come true. What good's a prophecy after it's already happened, you know? Nobody believes you at that point." He was slipping Amma's prophecy into a crack alongside another rolled-up scroll.

"What does that other one say?"

"I shouldn't tell you..." Geoff tapped his reed to his lips then dropped his voice to a whisper. "Well, I can't tell you the exact wordage, but a knight of Valcord recently visited on a quest to discover how best to serve his god. The oracle told him to go cleanse a temple, basically, but the poor guy thought the whole thing was a lewd euphemism, and you know how holy knights can be, so he got real nervous and ran off."

Beyond where he stood, there were more crevasses but no more parchment. She took a few steps backward and pointed to a high-up cluster of scrolls. "And these?"

"Last year's big batch," he said, looking particularly proud. "Took some of those myself directly from the oracle. They're separated into ones requested by visitors and the oracle's dreams."

"So,"—she stepped backward and Geoff followed—"if I wanted to see something from, say, eleven-ish years ago, I would stop…"

Geoff watched her continue toward the cave's entrance, then held up a hand. "Right about there. I wasn't around then though."

"But surely you've read all of these." She nodded as if it had to be true.

"Not *all* of them."

"Well, let's see how many we can get through," she said plucking one out.

Geoff was standing before her in a blink, snatching the scroll away.

But Amma was just as quick, pulling another from the wall, unraveling it with nimble fingers and spinning around. The lines seemed to be written in Key, but they swam before her as if moving on the parchment, and she had to fall still to try and read them properly.

And then Geoff got that one from her too. "Prophecies are meant only to be read by official record keepers and those who are directly involved in their outcome."

Amma pouted but plucked a third one down, muttering to herself about the oddness in the script. "What language is this?"

"Key, obviously, but arcanely protected from prying eyes." Geoff was reaching over her shoulder for it, but she ducked away.

She tossed the one she had back to him and pulled out a whole armful of others from the section he'd suggested. "Can you read them to me then?"

"I can *not*." Geoff stuffed the three back into a random crack as Amma collected as many as possible. "I mean, I can, but I *won't*." In a frenzy, he went for the stack in her arms.

Vanders propelled himself from Amma's shoulder, giant back feet sending him smoothly through the air to land on Geoff's face. The man shrieked, he flailed, and he connected with the stack of scrolls. Parchment rained down onto the floor of the cave like soft, falling leaves, unraveling to reveal prophecies in wiggly, illegible writing.

Amma immediately began to apologize, but Geoff just threw himself to the ground, picking up the fallen scrolls one by one but with as much care as he could muster. As Amma helped, she felt her head go funny, the moving writing making her nauseated, but then a violet glow, the exact shade of Damien's eyes, glimmered from beneath the pile. Her favorite color called out to her, and Amma stuck her hand into the scrolls to pull out a parchment that had perfectly legible Key upon it.

When the day is night, and the corners of the realm have fallen into rot, the hallowed son shall release the Harbinger of Destruction upon earth once again. Only by the spilling of the descendants' blood may It rise, and by the spilling of the heart of the earth's blood to beseech the gods may It fall.

"Well, that's ominous."

Geoff snatched it right out of her hands so fast she actually let go, afraid it might tear. "You can try all you like, but the arcana will block you out: you're not a record keeper nor are you involved in this prophecy."

Amma opened her mouth to say that she could indeed read that one just fine, but her mind was working too hard at the words themselves. It had to be the right one—it just had to, it was *glowing* for goodness's sake, not to mention all the talk of blood and rot and destruction—but who in the realm was it actually about?

"Oh, Vanders!" Amma scooped the vaxin out of the pile where he'd landed.

"Get that rodent out of here before it chews through all this work."

Amma clicked her tongue and swept around, back the way she'd come. But halfway up the ramp, she ran back, stooping to help Geoff clean up the rest of the scrolls and apologizing profusely. Sometimes pushiness was necessary, she realized, but there was no reason not to be polite.

When Damien and the oracle finally emerged from the tent after the sun had set, Val'tiel invited everyone to eat. The light of the fire danced over the faces sitting around it, but Damien looked particularly frazzled. Amma wanted to ask him what he'd been told, but his eyes never found hers—never found anyone's. He simply ate and stared at the ground. It was too much, all of this destiny and destruction business, and when she read the fret on his features, she wished she could take back the suggestion they make such an ambitious pilgrimage at all.

It would be stormy that night, the oracle said, and unsafe for travel. There was an extra tent in the encampment that Damien and Amma could share, and when an oracle suggests one stay, one does. Inside, the tent was cramped, and lying beside one another brought them the closest they'd been since Yvlcon, but Damien was still thinking, flat on his back, hands folded on his stomach, staring up at the canvas in the dark.

Amma reached over and laid a hand atop one of his. "I know I'm not an oracle or anything, but it's going to be okay."

"How do you know?" It was the first time he'd spoken that evening, throat raw, but there was no bite to his voice.

Thunder rumbled out over the mountains, and she inched a little

112

closer to him. "When I'm with you, I just feel like things will be okay, I guess."

Damien said nothing, but his hand shifted under hers to entwine their fingers, and as the rain began to pelt the tent, they fell asleep.

The next morning, the sky was clear and the air was surprisingly warm if wet as they began their descent. The red dot on the enchanted map had moved with its clever arcana, and they could see themselves now headed toward their destination instead of around it. The Temple of the Void was to the west, the city of Buckhead set between the base of the mountains and the ominous squiggles, but they could avoid crowds and potential obstacles if they took a day to go around once they reached flat land.

Damien was still in a confused mood, saying very little until the sun was high in the sky. "You still have the pendant, yes?"

Amma touched her pouch, feeling it inside and nodding.

"Good. Keep it. No matter what I say, it needs to go into the pit. Don't return it to me, even if I ask, all right?"

Amma frowned, not liking that. "Why not?"

Running a hand through his hair as he stepped awkwardly over a rock, he hemmed and hawed before going on, "You know that I am evil—"

"Oh, my gods, Damien," Amma groused, her patience all eaten up by the ache in her belly, much worse upon waking and discovering the ease with which female blood mages probably functioned.

But he didn't even react, "—and it's not terribly often that evil *wins*, but they certainly try."

Amma pursed her lips, thinking of Fryn and her suggestion that evil didn't even like winning all that much.

"The oracle told us that the pendant is going to lead to my destruction, which I know is probably the right thing, in the grand scheme, but I've a feeling I won't throw it in the pit when the time comes because I'll think I can somehow supersede fate with my exceptional prowess or what have you, and then things will go sideways, and I won't even avoid the inevitable. I know it is a lot to ask, but I need you to keep me…honest? Good? I don't know, just don't let me let that *thing* break its way into our world."

"Damien, do you hear yourself?" She grabbed his arm and pulled him to a stop on a flat ledge. "You're asking me to make sure you don't do a bad thing, and in the same breath calling yourself bad. You don't want to allow E'nloc to be summoned, right?"

"Right," he said with a heaviness she could feel, staring out at the valley below them.

"Then *how* are you evil?"

Damien squinted, then slapped his hands over his face. "I don't know!"

"Yeah, me neither!" She shook him by the elbow, and when he peeked through his fingers, he might have been grinning. "And also, what do you mean the oracle told us the pendant would lead to your destruction?"

"The hallowed son," Damien mumbled and pointed to himself. "It's a whole thing."

"From the prophecy? The one who's supposed to release the Harbinger of Destruction? You think that's you?"

His eyes narrowed, all the sheepishness falling away from his face. "What did you do?"

"I went into the oracle's prophecy cave, found the one you refuse to tell me about, and I read it. You can be angry with me about that later." She swept a hand through the air, ignoring his sudden shift at an attempt at terror—nothing was as terrible as the twisting in her guts, and she just didn't have the patience for his foolishness. "Doesn't hallowed mean holy? I know I keep saying you're not evil, but your dad is a demon, not a dominion."

"What are demons and dominions if not the servants of the gods, dark or light?"

Amma tapped a finger to her lips. That was perhaps troubling and not something she had thought of. She looked to Vanders on her shoulder, and the vaxin was worrying his tail in his paws. Amma took to pacing along the ledge. "Okay, but the prophecy says the hallowed son will release the Harbinger of Destruction on earth. I thought your father was the numbered lord of temper tantrums or something?"

"Zagadoth the Tempestuous." He gave her a withering look. "Ninth Lord of the Infernal Darkness and Abyssal Tyrant of the Sanguine Throne."

"Sure, that." She paced a little faster, hands rolling over one another as she spoke. "And none of that is about destruction or harbingery. So, when he was here before, because the prophecy does say *again*, did your dad destroy a lot of stuff?"

Damien's eyes snapped to the cliff beside them. "I don't believe so. After The Brotherhood summoned him, he spent all his time in Aszath Koth protecting the city until he went to Eirengaard, but he does always complain that he hasn't done anything to be imprisoned."

Amma felt her mind work, turning swiftly and pacing across the small ledge again as she spoke with a quickness. "So, if your father isn't this harbinger fellow, and you aren't the hallowed son, then

114

throwing the pendant into the pit won't lead to *your* doom. It could all be about somebody else even though it was given to you—you just might have something tangential to do with it because I was able to read that prophecy too, but I'm not mentioned in it at all, so—"

Amma's feet went out from under her, and the ground came at her fast, Vanders poofing away as she fell. Damien was at her side in a heartbeat, pulling her back to her feet and away from the ledge as he dusted her off. He was touching her again, all over too, and she went a little stupid standing there, unable to even insist nothing hurt, he was being silly, she had only clumsily tripped and—

There was a rumble. It was small, minuscule really, barely able to be heard, but then it grew.

A not-insignificantly-sized rock began to roll. Amma's foot had dislodged a pebble wedged just beneath it in her stumble, and that had been all it needed. Too big to stop, not that either was quick enough to, the rock went right off the edge of the cliff, crumbling and rumbling its way down, and landing with a colossal thud somewhere below.

They remained still for a long moment, waiting, but nothing else came. Amma bit down on an already chewed-to-the-Abyss nail. "That was close," she mumbled around it.

Damien glanced over the ridge. "Actually, it was dead on."

Not liking whatever that could have possibly meant, she hurried to the edge of the cliff and fell to her knees. Some forty feet below lay the rock in a newly-made dent, around it a spattering of what one could optimistically just call liquid if one ignored the color.

"Oh, no," she whispered into her hand. "Did I…did I do that?"

"Um, well?" Damien tipped his head, still looking down at the accident. "Technically the rock did."

"Oh, gods." She scrambled over to where the edge of the mountain sloped a bit less intensely, lowering herself down.

"What are you doing?"

"Checking," she said, sliding backward to the next ledge, using thin branches that grew out of the rock face for balance.

Damien held his hands out as if asking the sky. "What? Why?"

"I don't know," she called back, heartbeat in her ears as she maneuvered to a path that led more safely downward.

"Amma, it's not worth it," he called, following after. "You'll only make yourself feel worse."

She grunted in annoyed agreement, but there was no stopping herself, not when her emotions were already so heightened. Gods, she'd forgotten how fraught bleeding without injury made her.

As she neared the site, there was a smell, rancid and pungent, though she was unsure how so quickly after the calamity she'd caused. Her stomach turned over as she set her feet solidly on the final ledge. The massive stone was cracked up its middle from the impact, and there was no denying the liquid splattered about was most certainly blood.

Damien slid to a stop behind her. "Amma, really," he said after taking a deep breath, "it was an accident."

Belly still aching, now with the added twist of guilt, she squeezed her hands into nervous fists. "Can you use magic to tell what it was?"

"And potentially make you feel worse?" He scoffed. "No."

She knelt beside a small pool of blood, thicker than she expected, but then there could have been bits of flesh or intestine within—it was hard to tell post-smashing. "Please?"

Damien heaved a sigh, coming to stand beside her. "Yes, fine, but I'm not promising I won't—" He cut himself off abruptly then clicked his tongue. "Well, I suppose I won't get a chance to lie about it."

Amma lifted her gaze to peer where he was gesturing. Katz had just reached the bottom of the ridge, and behind him, in the carved-out mouth of a darkened cave, shone a great number of eyes.

Carefully, Amma got to her feet and inched closer to Damien. "You think it was one of them?" she whispered, hands beginning to tremble as she clasped them before her.

"Oh, almost certainly," he said, tone slightly lower but with none of the fear she thought he should have had when looking on an uncountable number of creatures looming in the darkness. They were low to the ground and small, but there were *a lot* of them.

Amma cleared her throat and took a step forward. "Hi, there," she said, shakiness to her voice. "First, I want to say this was an accident, but I think it is my fault, and I'm very sor—"

"You do this?" asked a voice, scratchy and high-pitched.

Damien put a hand on Amma's arm. She nodded.

"That one died Jiblix," said a different voice.

Another piped up. "Jiblix is died?"

"Died?" asked another. "Jiblix?" And so the voices continued back into the cavern, echoing with curiosity more than anger.

One of the figures stepped forward, bringing itself into the sun. Green-skinned with massive ears that dwarfed its wide head, the creature was only about two feet tall and dressed in tattered leathers with skinny limbs and huge, bare feet. It blinked bulbous eyes in the brightness of the afternoon as it came to stand a few yards from Amma and Damien. She had seen a creature like it before in Aszath Koth, and she had been afraid then of being eaten, but this one looked so demure that even when it opened its mouth full of jagged, yellow teeth, she felt next to no fear.

"The king is died!" he announced, raising knobby hands above his head.

Three more skittered out from the darkness, just as small, running on feet so big she was sure they would trip. They were quick though, clambering around the fallen rock's other side and reappearing with strange objects in hand. Damien casually went for his dagger when the three swarmed them but waited to unsheathe it.

The creatures stopped short before Amma, one taking a low stance as another leapt onto its shoulders and the third scrambled up to perch at the top. The three swayed in a stack, and Amma spread out her hands, unsure if she would catch them or fend them off, but then a stick was thrust into her hand, and while she was distracted with the odd amalgam of rocks and feathers stuck to it, something was plopped onto her head.

"What called you?" squeaked out the one at the top of the stack just before it tumbled down.

Amma sucked in a sharp breath though it seemed unharmed by the fall.

"Go on," said Damien, nudging her, "tell them your name." He was grinning much too widely for how odd the situation appeared to be.

Hesitantly, she gave it over.

"All hail Amma," one of them called back to the rest in the cave, "King of the gobbies!"

CHAPTER 13
OF RECKONINGS AND OBSCENITY

O h, no."

Amma hadn't even really wanted to be a baroness when it came right down to it, but a king? That had never even crossed her mind. Faced with the prospect, kingship seemed significantly less enticing than baronhood, and eminence over goblins? Well, who even knew they had monarchies?

Not all goblin clans utilized the slaying of their king to determine their new sovereign, but enough followed the bizarre tradition that saying a thing like *not all goblins* was a rather ineffective argument. The practice of replacing a clan's ruler with that ruler's murderer led to very short reigns and very bloody histories with anomalous stretches of highly tyrannical governance by the strongest amongst goblinkind. There is much to be said for physical prowess, but finding a figure with matched mental aptitude was often difficult, a thing the goblins didn't really ponder on too long despite their suffering because they really appreciated height. And of all the kings of the goblin clan of Ashrein Ridge, never had one been so tall as Amma. It didn't even matter that she wasn't green.

Damien was still laughing, a reaction Amma thought she would have enjoyed if it weren't at her expense.

"It's not funny." She elbowed him.

"No, no, you're right," he said, wiping at his eyes. "It's bloody hilarious."

More goblins had crept out of the cave, and, goodness, there were a lot of them. They dressed in tattered clothes, many wearing makeshift armor composed of items one might have found abandoned in the back of a larder or along the roadside. Most stood only as tall as Amma's groin which made their congregation around her even more distressing. "Damien," she hissed, "they're *swarming.*"

"These are minikin goblins, not like those sinewy ones up north. They're completely harmless: a strong gust of wind could take them out."

Amma eyed one's sharp teeth as it grinned up at her. With a rusted chamber pot strapped to its head and a set of roofing shingles tied to its shoulders, that statement was dubious at best, but it grabbed her hand, long fingers wrapping around her own not entirely unlike a child save for all the callouses, and that sort of did make her heart melt. Of course, that could have also been her insides tugging at her emotions.

"Still, there are *so* many."

"Think of it like this," Damien said, eyes roving over the lot. "If a numerical attribute could be placed upon one's health, and in order to slay someone like me, I would need to be stabbed, say, one hundred and forty-two times, a minikin goblin wouldn't be able to endure even one attack. And it would probably be killed twice."

Amma was still holding onto the thing she supposed was meant to be a scepter. It was an admittedly nice branch of oak but had a roughly-cut, cloudy gem attached to its top with so much twine it was nearly obscured. Its thickness and heft reminded her of the staff she'd called up in the Innomina Wildwood.

"You come, you see vast empire. All yours now!" A goblin tugged her forward.

"Oh, please, no," she beseeched whichever goblin she thought might listen, "I only accidentally put an end to your Jiblix, and truly, I'm sorry, but I do *not* think that qualifies me for this job."

"You died him!" another called in a high voice, hopping so that he could be seen over the crowd of little, green faces. "All hail King Amma!"

The call was repeated by the assembled, voices rising with unrestrained joy.

"By all that's holy," she groaned, casting a pleading look over her shoulder as she was herded toward the cave. "A little help?"

Damien only shook his head, a ridiculous grin plastered on his face. "Oh, no, I am too invested in seeing where this goes, and it is quite a good distraction from the conversation we were just having."

Amma returned one of Damien's withering looks, slight regret at how amicable she'd encouraged him to become. She would have rather appreciated a surly version of the blood mage who insisted on storming off with her, preferably thrown over his shoulder again, and getting on with his most destructive plans.

But Damien didn't even complain when the goblins swarmed him too, giving his thighs a push to continue on. "Yes, yes, all right, I am but your king's humble servant." Gods, even his tone had turned jovial—what in all the planes had happened to him?

The darkness took Amma's sight as she was ushered into the cave. A chill came over her skin, and then she was hit with the slightly sweet smell of decay. Dampness in the air and surrounded by the newly energized creatures, she rubbed her eyes to better see the place she'd been brought.

The cavern opened up into an immensely hollow space like the mountain had been bored out completely. A ramp jutted off in either direction from where she stood at a low railing atop a balcony. Made for a much shorter being, Amma wavered at the drop, but then her breath caught. Hundreds—no, *thousands* of goblins bustled about in the basin below, tightly packed and chattering so their voices floated up and echoed off the walls in a low din like the rustling of many fallen leaves.

Amma's chest tightened—that sure was a large clan that was about to find out she had just murdered one of them.

"King Amma," said a voice from her side, and a new goblin was there, slightly taller than most of the others, limbs a bit longer, but skinnier too. "Will make announcement to clan on behalf."

The goblin tipped the scepter she held toward him and gave the yellow gem a thunk. A glow from betwixt the tightly woven twine pulsed, and when the goblin spoke next, his squeaky voice reverberated into the whole of the mountain. "Gobbies, King Jiblix is died!"

There was a collective gasp from below, a scattering of metallic things crashing to the floor, and thousands of shimmering eyes turned upward. Amma longed to shrink away from the balcony where she knew she was towering like a tyrant, but the many goblins gathered at her back made it impossible.

"All hail new king, dieder of old king! Bow to great and mighty Amma da Enormous, Wielder of da Boulder of Doom and King of da Gribtoss Clan!"

The goblins clamored to fall supplicant on their knees, more clanging and thuds until all of the eyes were finally turned down.

The scepter's dimly glowing crystal was tipped back toward

Amma's open mouth. "If wish, Majesty," he whispered, "address Gribtossians."

"Uh…" Amma's utterance reverberated over them, echoing through the cave much louder than the tiny goblin's. Every head turned back up, but they remained on their knees, waiting, silent, bated. Even the swallow she took echoed against the walls. "Hi?"

"Hi…" was repeated back to her on the lips of thousands of goblins, drawn out in a mirrored awe.

"Very great," said the goblin at her side, and he tapped the scepter to end the glow with a reverberating thunk. Then he fell into a deep bow at her feet. "Majesty Amma, me Gribtoss Visor to King. But, if wish, can call as old king called." At this, he peeked up sheepishly.

"What did your old king call you?"

"Shithead." He swallowed. "Sometime Big Dumb Shithead."

Amma covered her mouth to hold back a chuckle. "Please, no, what's your actual name?"

The goblin's lip trembled, still in a deep bow. "Mama call Skoob."

"Skoob? Oh, that's much better. Skoob will do."

He popped back up, positively beaming, then turned to the others. "Sentinel gobbies!" He clapped at the twenty or so surrounding them at the cavern's entrance, and the ones with the heaviest makeshift armor all stood at loudly-clanging attention. "Lots stuffs to do! New king need new banners, need new sleep space, need armor, weapons, cape, and all those need be big cause new king is *e-norm-us*."

At this Amma winced, but it was fair, relatively.

"Also need food, lots too, and need redo old tin-er-y to new king rule." As he doled out work, the remaining goblins dispersed one or two at a time.

No longer quite so surrounded, Amma edged over to Damien, the blood mage still much too terribly amused, and even Katz looked on the verge of cracking a smile. "I think the fun part is over now," she whispered. "There are so many of them down there. Enough to stand up to more than a strong gust of wind."

"You would abandon your subjects at a time like this?" Damien's eyes had gone wide with mock horror. "Quite irresponsible. And is this not just what the oracle said would happen? You can't possibly run away from this, your destiny."

Amma would have dragged him right out of the cave herself if what he said hadn't struck her so deeply. The oracle *had* said she would become the head of a vast empire, but that…that had only been an example at best, and a joke at worst.

"Now, Majesty," said Skoob, turning back to her, "take on tour of clan, show barracks, show dining hall, show far reach of cavern, and, uh,"—he lowered his voice and waggled the crinkly skin where his brows would have been—"show harem too."

"Oh, gods," Amma closed her eyes tight, pinching her nose.

At that, Damien broke once again into infuriating laughter. So, it had been a joke of the oracle's after all.

"Dis concubine?"

When Amma opened her eyes again, Skoob was pointing at Katz.

"By Sestoth, no! Oh, no offense, Katz." The imp did appear to be offended, but then that was how he always looked.

Skoob's eyes roved up to Damien then. He pointed at the blood mage, and his lip curled in a sort of repulsed way. "*Dis* concubine?"

Finally, the all-too-pleased smirk Damien had been sporting fell away and he crossed his arms tightly over his chest, giving Skoob *a look*. Too bad it was about five minutes too late.

Amma finally had a chance to giggle out a bit of relief. "No, no, that's—actually, yes, he is."

Damien was so stunned he was, for once, at a loss for words, mouth falling open and nothing coming out.

"No account for taste," Skoob muttered then gave Damien's leg a shove without moving him at all. "Go, join harem. Moghart take you."

Another goblin had appeared at the top of the ramp. Unlike most of the others, this one was female, dressed in softer fabrics, and had an even slighter build. She reached up for Damien's hand, but he snatched it away.

Amma clicked her tongue. "Now, Damien, what's wrong? *You* said they're harmless."

"Oh, Amma, be reasonable." Indignation had settled into his glare pinging from the new goblin who was hopping to try and grab his hand again to Skoob who was pointlessly attempting to push him away.

Amma bent, hands on her knees. "Moghart, you're going to be very kind to Damien, aren't you? You're not going to put him in prison or take away his powers with an enchanted collar or threaten to sell him, right?"

The female goblin shook her head very quickly, ears flopping.

"Good. But I do think he could use a bath. You know, maybe make him a little more presentable?"

Moghart nodded, finally managing to snatch Damien's hand and tugging hard enough to make him stumble behind her.

"I recognize the symbolism here," he said, eyes boring into her, "but you're better than this, Ammalie. You are benevolent and merciful, and *you* don't require retribution—"

"I would *never!*" She gasped, pressing a hand to her chest. "But you said you wanted to see where this goes. And it *is* what the oracle told us would happen, so I fully agree that we need to follow through."

Damien's features went icy as he allowed Moghart to pull him down the ramp. "You will be punished for this," he muttered in a voice reminiscent of the blood mage she had met in Aszath Koth.

Amma only grinned, wiggling her fingers in farewell. "I look forward to it."

Skoob jumped back into her vision and took her in the opposite direction down one of the ramps, little voice hurriedly explaining in broken Key how the Gribtoss clan owned the entire mountain. Well, most of the mountain. Half of the inside parts at least, but the best half. Except for that one part, the scariest part, because something called *Big Spicy* had stolen it, a problem for later.

With Katz dragging himself behind the two and Skoob's enthusiasm, Amma found herself less concerned even as they descended into the goblin den without Damien. Skoob brought her first to their barracks. Closest to the cave's entrance, they wound down a corridor bore out of the rock, hammocks strung three high along the wall surrounded by claw marks for climbing up. This led out to a more open space, though part of it had caved in, where a group cheered on a set of goblins who ran violently at one another.

Amma may have been appalled at the barbaric display if it weren't so reminiscent of the drunken brawl she'd seen in Krepmar Keep. This was just the same, only a little smaller. A broken dagger was wielded by one, an iron pan in the hands of the other, and, shieldless, the two crashed together. Their battle cries were abruptly cut off and replaced with groans as they bounced, the lumpy padding tied about their torsos getting in the way and sending them to the ground where they remained, stuck flailing on their backs like desperate turtles.

When Amma stepped forward, the cheering ring immediately broke for her, falling into supplication. Apparently, news of the shift in sovereignty traveled fast. The duelists tried valiantly to get up, but beyond being physically difficult, it appeared the one with the dagger had been bonked so generously on his head he didn't seem to know which way was up.

"Dis new gobbies." Skoob dragged one of them up to his giant, bare feet. "No understand good fight yet."

"Maybe helmets." Amma propped up the knocked-senseless one. "And blunted weapons for beginners?"

Skoob gasped. "Enormous king have enormous brain. Hear decree," he shouted at the others. "Do that!"

There was a lot of noise then as the rest bumped into one another, scrambling, she supposed, to enact her suggestion.

Amma finally got the injured goblin to stand.

"King?" he asked in a grating but horrified cry as he blinked one eye and then the other.

"I guess?"

The goblin plunged to his knees. "Must fall on weapon. Has dishonored King!" He was reaching out for the dagger, but his aim was off and couldn't seem to grab it.

"No!" She grabbed the broken dagger herself, noting that it was more of a sharpened butter knife. "You're not doing that—none of you are doing that!" She pointed at the rest of them with the broken bit of metal. "Understood?"

"King Amma make nother decree!" Skoob pulled himself to his full, nearly three-foot height. "No more died for bad fight! Only died if be made died!"

"Oh, thank the gods, but also don't *try* to make each other died— er, dead, okay?"

"Gobbies hear Majesty! Only died if be made died by Big Spicy!"

The goblins cheered in agreement, but Amma held up a finger. "That's the second time you've mentioned—"

"Quick, Majesty, lots need see!" Skoob's ears flopped as he scurried back into the main cavern, gesturing madly for her to follow.

Down the spiraling ramp to the massive, cluttered space below, Amma's presence brought everything to a halt which was slightly amusing if also mortifying. Even in Faebarrow, no one really treated her like this, and she much preferred pleasant greetings to fawning and bent heads.

The goblins had a sort of market scattered about, crates and stalls full of mismatched objects and foodstuffs. Part of it was interrupted by another cave-in, bits of destroyed cart sticking out from some older disaster. There was no gold, only other items for trade, the conversion rate impossible to understand. One goblin appeared to be handing over a dried-out wasp nest for a salamander in a twig and twine cage, and another had just given over a handful of berries for a set of stained tunic sleeves.

There were female goblins here, most toting around two or more little ones strapped to their backs or tethered on leashes, able to bolt off for a moment before sling-shotting back to their mother. They were much less likely to fall into a bow as Amma and Skoob passed, but they did wave. Skoob knocked one out of the way as they went.

When Amma told him that really wasn't necessary, Skoob nodded in agreement, but said, "He be fighter soon, must learn now."

"How old are goblins when they join the military?"

"Four," Skoob told her proudly.

"Uh huh…" She took a last look at the others before being led through an archway and away from the big, open market. Amma wanted to assume goblins matured at the age of four as well, but she wasn't sure there was an appropriate way to ask about the average life expectancy. None of the goblins appeared to be terribly old.

In the next space, there were many long tables covered in mounds of bent tools, ripped clothing, cracked pottery, and other, well…garbage. Goblins were lined up, carefully picking through the debris and assessing each piece to sort into slightly more useful piles, but fell still when Skoob announced the new Gribtoss King had arrived.

Amma quietly urged them back to work, and Skoob took a deep breath of the foul air. "Ah," he said, "commerce."

"Where does it all come from?"

"Mostly humies city," he said with a grin. "Also sometime woods, sometime trader cart, sometime dwarvies. Dwarvies give good commerce actually, just say, *take dis, gobbie, no need*, so gobbie do!"

Amma giggled at Skoob's gruff impression of a dwarf, wiggling fingers under his chin to mimic a beard and stomping. The goblins really were sort of cute if she squinted, and she didn't even notice the pang in her stomach telling her not to trust the sudden maternal feelings flooding in.

"Used to get good commerce from da big, scary part of da mountain too, but not no more."

"You mentioned that before. What exactly is—"

"Harem!" exploded Skoob, hurrying away. "I show you new wives. Is Jiblix's old wives, so can pick new new wives, but some is very nice, so maybe want keep."

Amma rubbed her temples and followed after. She grumbled in the back of her throat, voice low, "Okay, new decree: don't talk about *any* goblins like that anymore."

Skoob came to a quick stop, standing straight, turning to her with abject fear in his glistening eyes. "Skoob make King mad?" He fell to his knees before her at the doorway to the sorting room. "Skoob apologies. Skoob take beating now."

Amma cringed at the scepter in her hand and held it behind her back. "No, no! Please get up!"

Confused, Skoob rushed to follow her order, taloned toes clacking on the stone. "Enormous King Amma sure?"

"Yes, of course, Skoob, I don't…let's just go to the next thing, okay?"

A huge swell ran down Skoob's throat, and he led her back across the market and through a series of tunnels into which she had to duck, the walls there covered in a variety of mushrooms being harvested by goblins outfitted with rucksacks. Finally, they came out into an open hall-like space. A set of some of the biggest goblins stood at attention outside an actual door hanging precariously off hinges somehow nailed into the stone. The two fought one another to open it, and after a short brawl, eventually completed the act together.

The new chamber glittered with piles of metal objects, shined up to reflect the glow of many stubby candles, easy to mistake for gold at first glance. When Amma got a little closer, she could pick out kitchen tools, brass plates, and doorknobs amongst what she could only assume the goblins considered treasure.

"King Amma, Skoob present da Gribtoss throne."

A wooden chair carved from cherry, scuffed but with fanciful finials along its back, sat in the room's center. Additional scraps of wood, pine and oak, were tied on with leather cords to extend the back and arms. Shiny rocks and iridescent shells were stuck on with hardened sap, and the seat was balanced atop a stack of crates to form a dais.

Amma took a big breath that she immediately regretted and went up to it, taking a careful seat. It fit her perfectly, but she could imagine any one of the goblins in it, their feet sticking out and believing the throne made them seem big and menacing.

"Now, wives!" Skoob clapped twice, and from a side door, a line trailed in until half of the room was full of little, green-skinned, scantily-clad, lady goblins. Looking much more demure than even the market-goers with their heads bowed, they stood in rows before Amma and waited. "You pick which is good, and others…um, well? We figure what do others for King!"

Amma looked over the forty or so goblins and frowned. "Ya know what, Skoob? Why don't you take a little break, okay?"

This word seemed completely foreign to him. "But I visor to king," he said. "Need vise."

"Right, but I need a little break from kinging. Maybe you can go check on Damien for me? You know, my, um…*tall* concubine?"

"Oh!" Skoob winked at her. "Skoob get!" Then he scurried out of the room, and the door was closed.

Alone with the former partners of the recently deceased Jiblix, Amma was awash once again with guilt. Katz was standing in the midst of them, having silently followed all through the den, but for once didn't appear to be the most miserable creature in the room. She supposed it was probably her responsibility to say something first. "Um, hello, all."

A chorus of sweet but pinched goblin voices greeted her in return.

Amma's eye twitched—she recognized that tone meant to please even if one didn't really mean it. "So, were you all, like, married to Jiblix or…"

The goblins traded looks until one of them stepped forward. She had her hands clasped behind her back, eyes trailing the ground even as she came closer. "Some us wives," she said, voice honeyed and quiet. "Could be wife if had nuff babies."

Well, that won't work with me, Amma thought.

"I have most babies, so I head wife," she said, a little pride in her voice.

"What's your name?"

"Sometimes call Best Breeder, but also sometimes call Fu—"

"Nope, not that!" Amma threw her hands up. "I mean, what did your mother call you?"

The goblin froze then squeaked out, "Faazzi."

Amma pressed a hand to her chest and blew out a breath. "Faazzi. Wonderful. I love that if you love that, okay? And the rest of you, whatever your old king called you, it doesn't matter—you can go by whatever it is you'd like to be named now, all right?"

Faazzi and the others nodded sheepishly though they looked unsure.

Amma sighed, resting a hand on her fist. "Gods, Jiblix was just awful, wasn't he?"

Faazzi's pale eyes widened with terror. "King Jiblix?"

"Yeah. Everything I've heard and seen—he was terrible."

"Uh, well?" She looked for confirmation from the others, and got the tiniest nod, then turned back, puffing out her chest as her voice fell into a raspy growl. "Jiblix worst."

"Hate him," said another soon after.

"Glad died," agreed a number of goblins amongst the rows.

"Yeah, that's what I thought." Amma sat back, stretching. "So, ladies, here's the thing: I'm not really looking for a wife—or forty—though you all seem perfectly nice."

At this the goblins began fidgeting, some frantic whispers rising up.

"But," she cut back in, "I *am* looking for help at this whole king thing because, believe it or not, it's my first time, and I think you all might know this place and your people a little better than I do."

127

Faazzi wrung her hands. "King Amma ask for help?"

"Yeah, like, more advisers. Or, I guess, visors? Skoob's fine, but he seems overwhelmed. Maybe you could form a council or something?"

Many eyes lit up through the chamber, hushed voices growing excited. Though Amma had no intention of staying, this might leave the clan better than she found it.

A goblin had come up to Faazzi and had taken one of her massive ears in hand, whispering into it, big eyes darting to Amma. When she stepped back, Faazzi took a breath, brows knit. "We show King project now."

"Oh, okay." Amma stood, following her back into the low opening the women had come through. More snaking tunnels dotted with mushrooms and canvas-covered passageways took them to a neat arch chipped away at the tunnel's end.

"Jiblix say stupid," Faazzi sighed, "but we not allowed do anything except have baby. No fight, no cook, no sort, no even raise baby, just have. So, gobbie wives and concubines do projects with unwanted scraps to fill up time."

Ushered through the canvas covering the last archway, Amma stepped into a massive chamber, nearly as big as the market at the den's entry. Though it was also crammed with sorted garbage, there were little plateaus rising naturally here and there and atop these rocky ledges stood what they meant by projects.

Amma could not guess their uses, the contraptions cobbled together with all manner of disused, human junk, but they were nothing short of impressive. She wandered to the closest, admiring what was a machine of sorts made of long, metal tubes, broken shutters and crates, and two sets of axled wheels, cracked at one time and put back together using a hardened pine pitch, a cauldron of which Amma could smell simmering somewhere in the cavern.

"What is this for?"

"Not sure," said Faazzi, gesturing to another goblin who had scurried up to them and was holding open a book, the pages upside down. "We just make."

There was a diagram laid out in the book, though the words were in a different language, not Key or Chthonic, but one from across the sea. Amma gently flipped the book over in the goblin's hands and could see the resemblance plainly then. The components were much different, and the one they stood before was a little ugly in comparison, but it was otherwise spot on.

She took another long look around the chamber with a new

appreciation, each plateau no longer holding a cobbling together of junk, but a purposeful attempt at creation, even if they had no idea what to do with them.

"Ladies, this is amazing."

Faazzi's bulbous eyes went watery, claws clasped before her face. "Really think so? Can do mores?"

"Go wild," said Amma with a shrug.

There were happy noises from the goblins as they scattered about to work, and Amma watched until there was a tug at her shin. She looked down to see a rather small goblin who was panting quite hard. "Missus King? Presence requestered at throne, please."

Back through the tunnels with a small group of the female goblins and Katz still trailing behind, they all spilled into the main chamber where the shined-up trinkets and the fancy chair, er, *throne* sat. At the door stood Skoob again, looking very proud of himself, Moghart at his side, and just ducking through the opening, completely naked save for his bracer still dutifully strapped around his forearm and a swath of thin, black fabric wrapped precariously around his hips, was Damien, face pulled into a delicious scowl.

Amma inhaled a sharp breath and beamed back at him. "Everybody out!"

CHAPTER 14
IN SERVICE AND OUTDONE

Humiliating was a word for it. Damien knew he had nothing to be ashamed of when stripped, but he'd rather actually be naked than *this*. With what was essentially a washing linen hanging from his hips and nothing else, things were just too loose.

He also smelled too nice. The goblins had surprised him with the cleanliness of their bathing facility. He was shocked by its freezing temperature too, but after he'd been pushed into a pool of clean, mountain water, he became preoccupied with the tiny, blue flowers they sprinkled in to give it, and subsequently him, a sweet aroma. As Damien tried to scoop them out, Moghart and a retinue of other goblins started scrubbing him, and that was absolutely where he drew the line.

By the time he'd fended them off, insisting he was more than capable of rubbing dirt from his skin on his own, some enterprising goblin had absconded with his clothing and armor, the things too fast and small to properly keep track of.

His bracer had been dropped though, and he grabbed the sheathed dagger, convincing Moghart that their new king had a peculiar fondness for him wearing it. That only worked once though, and they refused to bring the rest of his clothing back when he insisted Amma preferred him dressed to naked. He supposed it wasn't a terribly convincing argument anyhow, especially with the reaction he'd just gotten from Her Majesty.

There was unparalleled delight on Amma's adorable face, and a struggle between pleasing her and debasing himself flared in his chest. A past version of Damien would have just wiped out the clan of minikin goblins ages earlier, but his amicability had earned him this, and his internal seething was so quiet and so deep, that he wondered if it were really a *seething* he felt at all.

He wanted to be angry, and maybe he should have been, but standing there in naught but a scrap of linen he'd had to sling dangerously low on his hips to cover the entirety of his length, without even *boots* for all the dark gods' sakes, he could really only smirk because Amma had ordered—actually *ordered*—everyone to leave.

The goblins scrambled, and Damien stood straighter at the insistence in her voice, but he knew she didn't mean for him to go. Chamber doors opened and closed, Katz trailing out last, and the two were left alone.

The vaxin popped into existence on Amma's shoulder. "Not now, Vanders," she said, and it poofed away again.

Amma was staring at him from across the room, still carrying around that ridiculous scepter and wearing that silly, little crown, but her eyes—well, her eyes actually frightened him for a moment. They'd never looked quite so hungry before, even when she'd climbed atop him in the karsts, made lusty and aggressive by a confidence potion. He didn't mind at all.

Taking a deep breath, Damien's bare chest expanded, and he tried to think very little of it as he opened his mouth.

"Wait!" Amma held up her hands, and he froze. She dropped the scepter, scurried across the messy chamber, and climbed up onto the raised, bizarrely-adorned chair in its center. Crossing her legs and draping herself backward, she tried to nonchalantly lean on her elbow but missed the armrest, flailed for half a second, and then composed herself again. "You may proceed."

Damien ran his tongue over his teeth, rolled his eyes, and tapped a bare foot. "This experience has been illuminating, but I think I've learned my lesson."

Her smirk said she did *not* believe him. "Oh, have you?"

He groaned. Perhaps she was torturing him because of the situation she'd been put in at Yvlcon, or because he'd been so withholding since they'd left, but didn't she know all of this was just as agonizing for him? "I'd like my armor back in any case."

Amma made a small, flippant sound. "There are things, I imagine, we would all like but can't have."

She had no fucking idea.

When she curled a finger, beckoning him closer, he didn't think, he simply went, an easy demand to give in to. She was meant to be raised high on the goblin's makeshift dais and throne, but with Damien's height, their gazes were simply matched as he came to stand just before her.

"Tell me why you think you deserve your clothes," she said, sitting back, arms crossed under her breasts, and he wasn't sure if she knew how well she pushed them together.

Damien's jaw tightened, but not quite in the way he'd become used to, not with ire incomprehensible, not even with trivial annoyance, but with a covert grin. He shouldn't have liked being at someone else's mercy, and while he perhaps was not truly her subject, it may have been the only chance he'd get to be at Amma's behest while the talisman was still inside her.

Damien Maleficus Bloodthorne was rarely brought to his knees willingly, and he could not remember a time he was sincerely happy about doing so, but as he lowered himself before Amma, a sort of euphoria spread out in his chest. He held Amma's gaze as he went, the haughty amusement chased off her delicate features. She uncrossed her arms and legs to lean forward and look down on him, shocked. No, of course, she wouldn't expect this, but then, if he'd ever worked up the courage to tell her the absolute torment her presence had been waging inside him, it would never have been a surprise to find him on his knees for her.

"Brilliant, gentle, beautiful Lady Avington," he said, voice low, "would that I be allowed only what you deem me worthy."

Amma's lips twitched with perhaps nervous laughter, satiation, regret, he didn't know, but her hand came up to pull the goblin's bent crown off and drop it over the edge of the throne. "Okay, you can have whatever you want."

"You would grant me anything?" His gaze roved down her body and back up.

She nodded, fingers tightening on the armrests as she leaned closer. "Anything, just name it."

Damien placed his palms on her knees, easing them apart. He had told her she would be punished, but there would be time for that later. "I could make a request," he said, sliding hands up along her thighs and gripping the waist of her breeches, "or I could show you."

Amma trembled under his touch as he began to tug, revealing the soft curve of her hip's flesh and making him bite his lip. Then her eyes widened, and she sucked in an inhale so sharp, he stopped. As he released her, the trembling continued only beneath his knees. Of course it wasn't her; it was the bloody cavern.

Damien dropped his elbows onto Amma's thighs and raked fingers through his hair. "It is as if some sadistic god refuses to allow this until an unknown objective is met," he grumbled. "What in all the planes must I do to—"

"Damien?" Amma tapped his shoulder with urgency, and the waver of her voice made him sit up. "Something bad is happening."

Indeed, something bad was happening.

The chamber shook, bits of rock and dust crumbling away from the craggy ceiling, the sounds of chaos echoing beyond the door. There was yelping and pounding, and then the entry swung open, goblins covered in makeshift armor tripping over one another until Amma's *visor*, fitted with a crusty rack tied to his chest, reached the front.

"Majesty!" he panted, "Is time! Is early, but *is* time."

Damien stood as Amma slid off her throne. "For what?"

"Big Spicy awake!"

"What's this now?" Damien asked.

Amma straightened her clothing, cheeks rosy. "I don't actually know, but they keep mentioning it."

"Must fight! Big danger!" called one of the goblins, towering behind the others but still a scrawny thing relative to any creature Damien would consider a threat.

From between the larger goblin's legs, a comparatively tiny one's head popped out and squeaked, "Make died!"

"Majesty!" Skoob had caught his breath and scrambled across the chamber to Amma where he fell to his knees, a poor replacement for Damien. "Apologies not tell, but Big Spicy only wake every..." He held up a hand, counting on his knobby fingers, then turned over his shoulder and called back, "What day is?"

"Four!"

"Thirteen!"

"Six and three halves!"

Skoob whined at the chorus of goblin voices, eyes watery as he cowered before the leader they had made. "Is not spose be now. But must fight!"

The cavern rumbled again, and the goblins cried out in response, rattling their broken weapons and dented shields.

"All right, but what *is* this Big Spicy?" Amma asked, leaning down as if speaking to a small child.

"Formidable." Skoob's voice was low and quavering as his knees knocked together. "Makes many gobbies died. Big Spicy is worst."

Amma put a hand on his little shoulder and squeezed. "It sounds very scary," she said in a soothing lilt. "Can you be brave enough to show us?"

Skoob still shook but nodded. There was another tremor then, but not from the cavern. This was just the sound of human garbage used as armor and shields clanging together as a small hoard of goblins quaked. Amma turned her face up to Damien and gave him *that* look.

He sighed, hands on his hips. "Yes, all right, let's go see this large, peppery thing."

The goblins hurried them through the cavernous tunnels of their den, Katz being jostled along and moving quicker than he would have liked. The way through was cramped for the humans, but the goblins hustled forward as if slowing down would cause them to overthink and turn back. Then again, overthinking was highly unlikely to be any goblin's first or even fifth issue.

"Oh, Damien, your armor." Amma touched his arm just above his bracer and brought him to a stop in the tunnel. A small contingency of goblins piled up behind him, running into his bare legs.

Having forgotten how near-naked he was, Damien shrugged but kept his voice low. "I'm sure it will be fine. This fear they have is likely founded for them, but for a blood mage?" He gestured to his bare chest and smirked. "You watched me slay harpies with less."

Amma gave him a wary look, but they continued on until the tunnel opened up to a wider space with a much higher ceiling. There was a stone wall a few yards ahead, the path diverting to either side around it. The largest goblin who had been leading them turned to address the others. "Dis Big Spicy lair."

The sentinels had come to stand in a row, a wave of awe-struck whispers rising up as they repeated, "Big Spicy."

"Battalion One, prepare charge. Battalion Two, prepare replace."

In a surprising show of stealth and organization, the goblins lined up in rows of five at the head of each path, just at the edge of the wall. Skoob remained beside them, wrapping little clawed hands around Amma's calf.

"Um, can I ask real quick," Amma whispered, "what do you mean by *replace*?"

"Most Battalion One be made died," said the biggest goblin with a grunt. At this, there was a gentle rattling amongst said battalion.

Before Amma could express whatever fearful sentiment she was about to, Damien announced loudly, "Oh, nonsense. Fall back, all of you. Just let me take care of it."

Amma's hand wrapped around his arm again, and she was shaking her head, but she should have known that touch only emboldened him.

"It will be fine," he assured her even as the entire cavern took to quaking again, the sound drowning out his own thoughts it was suddenly so loud.

"I will escort Master, Mistress," said Katz in his miserable way, and something hard hit Damien's chest, a pan thrust upward, an offering from one of the goblins.

Damien spun his new weapon by the handle. "You see? I am more than adequately equipped."

"Dat's a brave concubine," Skoob whispered, and the armored goblins agreed.

Amma managed to nod, calling back the goblins to gather around her like a horde of chicks to their mother hen. "Be careful," she said, voice so heavy it practically held him to the spot. A few short hours with the goblins had certainly gotten to her, but she needn't be afraid of whatever this clearly minor inconvenience was, not that he minded the opportunity to do just a bit of showing off.

"Big Spicy shall be defeated, Your Majesty." Damien bowed within the bounds of his insufficient attire. "And then perhaps you will see fit to reward me."

That made her blush, a much better state to leave her in than fear, and he turned for one of the pathways out and downward, readjusting the swath of fabric just in case.

Katz at his side, Damien sauntered around the stone wall silently thanks to being unburdened by his clothes or boots. It was significantly warmer there, odd for the wide, open space, but the thinning of the veil that ran through the mountains likely extended to this one. He clicked his tongue—Zagadoth's occlusion crystal shard could have potentially benefited from the energy here, but then again, it was perhaps a lucky thing he couldn't speak with his father.

He swung the pan he'd been given, testing its heft and gripping it tighter, annoyed with just the thought of the demon lord. He'd never really been this upset with him, though he wasn't even sure of the reason—it was that lack of a reason, that missing truth, that was at the crux of the problem.

Hey, Champ, I got a little job for you! Nope, nothing huge, I'm just gonna need you to spend every waking moment of your life collecting nigh-impossible-to-find ingredients and learning life-altering magics to free my stupid, trapped-in-a-stone ass. What did I do to get in here? Don't worry about that, Kiddo! And why can't your mom help? I'll explain that to you when you're older, Son, just do exactly as I say, and everything will be fiiiiine.

Well, Damien *was* older, but he'd never gotten that explanation, though he supposed twenty-seven was no different than seven to a thousands-of-years-old demon. Everything, however, was certainly not fine, nor had it ever really been, he'd just ignored the fact he knew next to nothing about his mother. Things had been easier that way, but never *fine*.

The smell of brimstone tickled at Damien's nostrils as he crept deeper into the cavern, replacing his tangential brood with intrigue. Shafts of light shone down into the cave through cracks above, broken and hazy in the darkness. The space went on well above his head, many stories, high enough for an entire flock of those harpies to have the upper wing. Perhaps that was what the goblins feared—a ginger-winged harpy who had decided to torment their little clan.

But harpies didn't smell like eternal death, and they didn't exactly rumble either. His eyes roved over the shadowed ground before him. It could be yet another angry pit, he supposed, and that would be right on theme. But he had none of the looming dread or nauseating fatigue of his previous encounters with that bottomless crater of destruction.

No, this fear the goblins had, this Big Spicy, was most likely an animal of sorts that came slithering through the tunnels for them if they did not strike upon hearing it wake. He knew of large worms, eyeless and mostly mouth, that tunneled and surfaced with little regard for what fell into their maw. Or, if the veil to the infernal plane were thinner here, an abyssal hound could have gnawed its way through, gotten stuck, and was now marking its territory all over the cavern. Acidic urine could account for the spiciness and the size too, relative to a minikin goblin. If the thing were small enough, Damien could just banish it, and if it were larger, he could injure it first and then cast a longer, ritualistic banishment, so he handed the pan off to Katz, opting to pull out his dagger instead.

But there was *nothing*.

He'd come to stand before a shaft of light in the huge space's middle, Katz beside him. The ground rose up in stony columns, but nothing seemed to hide behind them. Shadows were cast in crevasses and around corners, but nothing moved within.

The only point of interest was a small pile of junk, metal things, wooden things, and bits of cloth. He went to inspect it and found it was actually just the tip of a much larger accumulation that filled a sharply sloping basin. A graveyard of disused and ruined objects lay before him, and he crossed his arms, finally deciding it was worth the effort to cast for the blood of other creatures.

The cavern was huge, and there were many goblins infesting the rest of the mountain's innards to muddy his senses, but once he identified Amma and Katz with his spell, there was something else, something infernal tickling at the back of his head.

He squinted down at the scattering of broken tools, their state even worse than those in use by the goblins as armor as if they'd been chewed up and spit out, looking a bit, well...if he squinted, they actually looked a bit *burnt*.

"Master!" Katz's voice was quick for the first time. Damien turned just as the imp gave him a surprisingly strong shove, sending him to the ground. He slid backward down the pile of ruined miscellany, and there was a gust of wind overhead so strong that he could not stand back up. Katz, however, was not so lucky, perched on the ledge above as a thick tendril sailed through the darkness and collided with the comparably tiny imp.

Katz's body was launched into the air, and Damien was petrified, watching as a snout materialized from the shadows, leathery skin pulling back to reveal fangs as long as Damien's arm and a blackened gullet he could disappear down in one gulp. A scaled tail snapped through the air, flipping Katz into the height of the cavern. The moment passed too quickly for Damien to have even sliced into his skin had he not been frozen in fear, but he did catch the look on the imp's face as he descended toward the toothy maw that positioned itself below him.

The imp smiled, probably for the first time in his entire existence, and then was swallowed whole by an infernal dragon.

"Oh, fuck."

Damien bolted. *That* had been the infernal tickle to Damien's spell, *that* was what rumbled the entire mountain with its waking, *that* was Big Spicy. And the goblins were absolutely right to be afraid.

Never had Damien run so fast, though it was easier without the weight of leathers and buckles and boots. Armor or no, there was little that survived dragon fire, but it wasn't just the fear of a crispy death that had made him flee. There was a primal memory that came with reptilian, winged creatures—ridden, specifically, by scorned women—that was wedged so deeply into the base of his brain, he could only retreat instead of stand his ground and fight. He might have been ashamed of such a fear if it were of something ridiculous, but as far as things to be fearful of went, dragons were easily the most acceptable.

The great menace's growl vibrated up through his feet and into his gut, and he dared a peek over his shoulder as he fled. The dragon was just coughing up the pan Katz had been given and spat it into the hoard of chewed-up garbage. Then it turned the slivers of its pupils on the blood mage.

Damien's heart slammed into his ribs as he dodged between stalagmites to try and confuse the beast. He pulled the dagger across his chest in a messy, frantic wound and sheathed it, smearing the blood in his other hand and casting blindly behind him. He could only hope the wall of shadows would distract it as he took a sharp turn and darted away.

Little goblin heads were peeking out from around the corner of the wall atop the steep path upward. He waved blood-smeared arms through the air to signal for them to hide, heat rising in the cavern at his back. That was a bloody bad sign. With another glance back, its form had fully materialized from the shadows, hulking and massive and unmissable, head pulling back, gullet blazing with an internal glow.

His chest wound was healing, but his mind was fractured—what could he even do? Slicing into it would only piss it off, and banishing it would take an entire ritual. This was not a task he could do on his own without being burnt, swallowed, or worse, carried off.

With a final push, Damien dove forward to clamber up the ramp, a burst of flames behind him, and he threw himself around the stone wall.

The brightness was blinding, heat all-encompassing, and for a moment he thought he hadn't made it, but it cleared as soon as it came, and Damien found himself surrounded by goblins.

"Charge!" The voice was fearful and brash at once, and a small contingency of doomed creatures spilled out around him and down the ramp, right toward the monster.

"No, you morons!" Damien reached out, scooping up the goblin closest to him as he plastered himself against the cavern wall beside Amma. He threw his free arm out to pin her there so he could be sure she remained still, the thickness of infernal mountain stone between the two of them and the dragon their only safety. The littlest goblin struggled to be free of his grasp, but he had him wedged up into his elbow too tightly to join the others on their suicide mission. There were screams, a roar, and a piteous clatter as death was cast in the mountain's center.

"Damien, what—"

"Dragon," he said, all out of breath. "Big, and indeed, spicy."

"Second Battalion, ready," cried the largest goblin.

"No!" Damien shouted between shallow breaths. "You're just feeding the damn thing! Basest beasts, that's why it growls in the first place—it's calling you lot to dinner!"

But a goblin army general wasn't going to listen to a concubine. "Charge!" The second flood of goblins went scampering down both ends of the ramp into the cavern, and the tiny one in Damien's arm started beating him with the broken chair leg that was its weapon to gain its freedom. Pitiful screams, another blast of Abyssal fire, and then the snapping of what he could only assume were goblin bones before the cavern finally fell quiet.

Still adhered to the wall, Damien caught his breath, glancing over at Amma who was looking utterly horrified. The goblin he clutched fell still as the battalion leader nodded, and Skoob nodded back. Apparently it was done.

"Big Spicy defeated," said the larger goblin.

Damien let out a snort, half anger, half relief, wrapped a hand around Amma's arm, and began dragging her back the way they'd come through the tunnels. "Bloody, fucking imbeciles," he grumbled as he went.

"That was a *dragon*?" Amma asked. "Living inside the mountain?"

"An infernal one, half made of shadows, yes, and quite happily, I imagine, with its meals delivered on a faithful schedule thanks to these little, green idiots."

"Damien, please," Amma hissed into his ear as she pulled herself close to him. "A bunch of them just died, and—oh, gods, it's my fault, isn't it?"

She stopped short, and Damien's march with every intention of continuing right out and as far from the den as possible, was brought to a halt. "Your fault? Amma, don't be ridiculous. Their brains are about as big as acorns. They think they defeated the damn thing by *feeding* it." He glanced down at the little one still in his other arm. "No offense."

"Big Spicy defeated!" it cried, and raised its bit of wood aloft, knocking Damien in the nose.

"You see?" He dropped the goblin to the ground to rub his face, and it scurried off down the tunnel triumphantly.

"I could have stopped them, though," said Amma. "Oh, and Katz, did he—"

Damien nodded. "I wouldn't feel too bad about that; he's likely thrilled to be back in the infernal plane."

"Still. The poor, little—and you!" She slapped her hands onto his sweaty arms, lifting them up and looking him over, a tinge more embarrassing than if he'd been clothed. "You just ran in there without your armor, and look, you're bleeding!"

"I did this," he assured her.

Amma threw her arms around his neck and pulled him down to her height, squeezing him close. "You were actually scared," she whispered into his ear.

He cleared his throat, embracing her back. "No, no, just reacting reasonably."

"Please don't do something like that again." She pressed her lips to his cheek then pulled back to look on him with those earnest, blue eyes.

It was unfortunate he would have to lie to her as he'd grown to abhor the deed, but for the moment, seeing to her reassurance was what he wanted more. "I won't, Amma."

"Now what do we do?"

"We leave," he said, starting off again.

"Leave?" She hurried behind, that worried lilt to her voice, Skoob and the larger goblin on her heels. "But they need help."

"With a *dragon*. One *you* just asked me not to go near again. Which, by the way, they could just choose to stay away from as well."

She should have been glad he was so keen to follow her orders, but she only slapped her forehead and groaned, "Oh, I know I did, but it's definitely the reason their den is collapsing in places, and *just look at them.*"

As they entered the main cavern, the waiting goblins all fell supplicant except the youngest ones.

"I am," he mumbled. "They reproduce almost as quickly as they get eaten. They'll be fine."

She huffed and pulled him up a ramp and back to the throne chamber, Skoob and the battalion leader following. They would, apparently, neither be leaving nor going back to what they'd been doing, much to his disappointment.

Once they were shut inside, she brought Damien to the far side of the room to give them privacy. Amma pressed her hands to her chest. "Damien, listen, I know this whole thing has been very silly. Well, up until the last few moments, at least, but I…I just love them."

"You *love* the *goblins*?" He could scarcely believe that *this* was how he was destined to hear *that* word from Amma's lips. "Some of them eat humans, you know. The ones in Aszath Koth would have made a whole holiday out of you."

"Well, sure, but they're a lot bigger, and everyone has to eat. That's what you said about the draekins, and the goblins are just like them, aren't they? I know they have their problems, and they're a little messy, and maybe they're not the brightest…" She glanced over at where the remaining ones had gathered with a few concubines, all of them pathetic-looking, really. "But they're just trying to get by, and I wouldn't feel right leaving them like this. Can't we take them with us or something?"

"Take them with us? Do you hear yourself?" Damien ran his hands down his face, but he did consider, briefly, how useful it could be to have a thousand-strong meat shield, then quickly squashed the distasteful thought.

Just keeping Amma alive had been difficult enough, but a whole clan of goblins? That would be impossible, and though he wanted to give in to Amma's every whim, the depression she would fall into as the goblins picked themselves off every day by accidentally getting impaled on tree roots and falling off of cliffs and poisoning themselves with the wrong mushrooms would ensure she would never have another whim for him to give into.

"Amma," he began again, quietly and carefully as he took her hands into his own, "I appreciate your newfound admiration of this tribe, but I cannot imagine a future where allowing these...these *simple*, little creatures to accompany us would truly be charitable. They barely have a sense of self-preservation, not to mention how incredibly easy it was for you to kill off their *king*. Think about the kind of trouble we get into. I know you don't want to watch them keel over left and right, do you?"

His words were working, he could tell by the way she chewed on her lip and furrowed her brow, and it was likely because they were true. "But they're sort of keeling over left and right here too. Isn't there anything we can do?"

He could feel it as he looked on her, a quiet acceptance that she would have to abandon the goblins working its way into her heart even as she asked. It wasn't a whim, her desire to help the stupid, defenseless creatures, it was simply what was inside her, what made up the very best parts of her, the parts that drew him to her. And that was worth protecting. "Perhaps there is something we can do."

"Majesty?" Skoob was standing just beside them, fingers pressed together. "Moghart say Big Spicy wake again in thirteen hours."

"Oh, geez, that's a lot sooner than what you were saying before."

Moghart came forward, clearing her throat. "He on cycle, wake period smaller each time til begin again. Is always same though. Concubines keep best track."

Damien groaned, the inconsistency in the creatures' knowledge perhaps more frustrating than their general lack thereof. "Why do these ones know, but the ones who are supposed to fight it don't?"

Amma patted his arm. "Women are just better at keeping track of time." When he squinted at her, not understanding, she leaned a little closer. "You know that *thing* you were about to do back before the, uh, world started rocking?"

Damien grinned.

"Yeah, so, I know you're a blood mage and all, but I'd prefer you not make another attempt at that for another day or so, okay?"

"I don't see—oh." He swore under his breath. "Well, I suppose we'll have to pass the time some other way. Perhaps discussing how we might save your ridiculous subjects from being eaten into extinction."

Amma gasped. "Really? We're going to help them?"

"Well, of bloody course we are, Amma." Damien rubbed his face and groaned. "Now will someone please give me back my pants?"

CHAPTER 15
ONE MOLECULE OF MERCY

It was only a small dragon, at least that's what Damien told himself once he was clothed again. Still formidable, still almost impossible to banish, still capable of injury that even a blood mage would not come back from, but it could have been a lot bigger.

Except it was still quite big. So big that it needed to eat about two dozen goblins every few days. Or it just wanted to—some dragons were like that, vindictive for the fun of it. They were unlike wyverns in that way, more clever, their thoughts much more advanced and capable of communication when they felt like it.

This one was infernal, able to make itself one with the shadows and breathe Abyssal fire. Every plane had its dragons, and once, long ago, the great creatures came in all sorts of magical flavors, but the world had grown small around them in Eiren and the rest of Damien's home plane, and while one would expect a thing so big would lord over its domain, it turned out they were just easier to spot, and the Holy Knights of Osurehm had spent many years and many lives chasing them out. As such, they were infrequent nowadays.

Damien's great, great grandmother, Valgormoth the Blind Fury who walked the plane when it was icy, would never have run from a dragon. She would have subjugated it into her army of beasts. But she was a demon who had existed before The Expulsion, and things were

143

different then, at least that's what he told himself. He imagined what it was like to be frozen in one blast from a frost dragon's gullet— probably better than being burnt into nothingness, but both deaths would likely be quick.

"Oh, you're *kidding*."

Amma's breathy excitement brought Damien out of the morbid thought. The goblins had been toiling about their clunky, dangerous-looking machines, and one began to produce some kind of steam. For a moment he thought the creatures had simply set it on fire and the dragon's job would soon be done for it, but then huge swaths of canvas unfurled from its sides and began to beat just like wings, and the contraption that looked like it should have been in Anomalous's tower was lifting off of the plateau into the height of the cave.

"Basest beasts," Damien muttered. They were *flying*. The goblins were fucking flying.

It was the most ridiculous thing he'd ever seen, three goblins seated in a basket, one piloting while the other two worked some sort of lever to keep the thing aloft. Few things flew, things with wings, most of which he loathed, and things that could shift into things with wings, and that was about it. He supposed he would have to add goblins to the list.

Dragons flew too of course, and like creatures with that ability, they often used height to their advantage. If one was too far from the ground to be reached, one could certainly control the battlefield. Though the massive cavern the goblins' enemy was currently residing in was perfect for something like a dragon to fly through, hiding up on the rocky ledges and swooping down to breathe fire and gobble up, that hadn't been Damien's experience. No, the infernal terror had hidden itself instead, using its innate abilities to shift in and out of the shadows and simply give chase.

A group of goblins bustled over then to show off the spears they'd fashioned, the tips sharp, but incapable of breaking dragon scale. They were perhaps narrow enough to slide between the scales, but that would require aim. One of the goblins who had attempted to bathe Damien earlier claimed to be able to assist with that and showed them something like a massive crossbow, mountable to the ground and requiring two to load and shoot.

After touring the wild tools and machines that the goblins would be utilizing, they sat and attempted to strategize. The discussion was repeated until the goblins seemed to at least halfway understand, and for a few moments, Damien actually missed Xander's sharp mind, but then hated his memory again almost immediately. After, Damien and

Amma sat through a five-course, entirely mushroom-based meal, and then finally retired to a private chamber with a bed that had been expanded just enough by additional soft things stitched together to accommodate a human. Amma insisted he snuggle in beside her, and he had no qualms about that even when a forgotten needle poked him in the back—she was the king, after all.

Wrapped up together, Amma fell instantly asleep which only made sense—it was exhausting lording over things, especially ones so dumb—but Damien lay awake considering how he had organized what would essentially be the demise of so many of the goblins. Together, their actions might be just enough distraction to allow Damien to banish the dragon back to the infernal plane where it belonged. Someone had brought it here, for nefarious purposes surely, but then abandoned it, likely because it was impossible to control.

Poor thing, he thought, and then finally fell asleep too quickly to realize how ridiculous that thought was.

"It time." Skoob's seriousness, clad in a bandoleer filled with chipped eating utensils, would have been comical if not for the fact they stood outside a dragon's lair.

Some of the minikin goblins who had been enlisted to fight were lining the hall, many more spread throughout the cave in larger tunnels above that led to the dragon's cavern, waiting for their signal to begin the onslaught. Damien hoped they had been quiet enough to not alert the beast, though they were surprisingly stealthy even maneuvering huge contraptions through tight tunnels.

The largest goblin, Ewigog, was standing beside Skoob and had taken out the relatively massive hammer he carried, holding it outward, sledge first. Atop it, the few goblins who followed Ewigog's orders laid their own weapons, and even Skoob presented the fire poker he carried into the mix. They glanced up at Damien who only observed, and then Skoob gestured to the crossing of their weapons.

"You may be ugliest concubine, but also bravest."

Damien rolled his eyes but unsheathed his dagger, mimicking the others. Then a broken chair leg poked up from beneath the pile.

"Absolutely not." Damien plucked the tiniest goblin from the ground by the scruff of its neck and carried it to where Amma stood, Vanders sitting atop her shoulder again but looking like he might disappear at any moment. Damien thrust the goblin into her arms with instructions to hold it back at all costs, and then was abruptly grabbed and hauled toward her.

Amma pressed a kiss to his lips that made him forget dragons even existed. He melted into it, limbs going weak as fear was chased out of him by flaring passion.

When she pulled back, her eyes were steely. "Come back so I can do more of that."

"Yes, Your Majesty," he breathed, and then was unceremoniously bonked on the head by the tiny goblin's weapon.

A bit more confidence swirling in his guts, Damien strode out into the lair first. The dragon would be lurking, using the shadows as camouflage, but it would be there—it couldn't actually make itself immaterial. He was under no pretense that he prowled unseen, but the dragon only needed to see him, not the many, miniature attackers that would be its doom—or just its annoyance before it killed them all. Still, he moved silently, not even casting as his spells would be too loud for an infernal thing, carrying his dagger unsheathed, other hand wrapped around the blade and already biting in.

Blood dripped steadily across the stone floor as he went. His heart pounded, pumping more from the wound. The beast would smell it, it would wake if it weren't already, and it would come.

He brought himself to the largest beam of light pouring from an opening above and stood within it. Morning sun lit the small space, his blood pooling beside him, and he tipped his head up to peer into all the dark corners above, searching for any flicker of movement, any misplaced shadow that signaled the dragon was beginning its descent. He would have completely missed it if it weren't for the tinkling of a rogue bit of metal behind him.

He whipped around just to see the head of the thing lifting up over the hoard of trash it had collected. Scales black and shimmering like liquid as they formed out of the shadows, its body rose behind it. The talons sunk into the ledge, each so large they would leave a hole in Damien's middle big enough to stick his own head through.

No reason to be stealthy anymore, Damien shuffled backward as the beast pulled itself up. Fearsome horns spiraled and glinted in and out of unseen darkness, scales following suit, body there one moment and gone the next as the shadows about it flickered. But its eyes, poisonously green and shining, remained locked onto the blood mage.

Unfurling fingers, blood ran from his palm, and he brandished his dagger as if it might do anything to the beast. The dragon seemed to grin then, knowing it couldn't, and then Damien cast.

New shadows rose from the blood he had left splattered across the cave, each in the vague form of a man, and when Damien sprinted, so did they. If he were lucky, they would last long enough to confuse the beast, and if the goblins could remember, they would begin their attack as soon as the dragon struck out.

From behind him, there was a rumbling clatter, and then the cries of a hundred tiny voices made raucous by the echoing cave. Spears were flung, contraptions whirred to life, and all manner of chaos erupted around Damien as goblins flooded into the cavern.

The little beings struck out, darting toward their doom as Damien led the dragon, drawing its ire. The heat in the cave built, and there was a glint in the corner of his eye as he took a turn, fire burning in the thing's throat. Damien skidded to a stop, whipping blades across the cave as the dragon reared back, slicing into the soft flesh of its neck. They drew blood and smoke, but it was not enough to stop the thing, and flames erupted from its maw.

Damien dove behind a thick wall of stone, taking an errant goblin with him, fire licking at the place he had just been. Already sweat-drenched, the goblin slipped right out of his arms and sprinted away. There was a squawk and a crunch, and Damien could only assume it had been crushed by the massive set of claws that came down to rock the entire cavern just beside his hiding place.

Damien sprinted back out into the opening of the lair, just beneath the beast. It saw him go, but did not lift into the air as he expected to pick him off, only swung its tail and attempted to whip Damien into the wall. He ducked, casting a shadow as additional cover, and continued on. The way the ground shook told him the beast was chasing after on all fours.

Glancing upward, Damien spied it, the trap finally set, and he corrected course to run beneath. A massive net dropped, just barely missing him as he led the dragon right into the snare. There was no expectation that it would restrain the beast, but it would perhaps slow it for a moment, and the itchy vines woven into the ropes could provide annoyance if they touched unscaled skin. Damien was shocked then when he turned to see the dragon splay out flat on the ground beneath the web of shoddy knotted ropes and thorny tendrils.

But the goblins had somehow worked in tandem, catching the dragon's back legs on a longer, thicker rope pulled taut across the cave, tripping it forward in the same instance and assisting in taking it down. Spears already stuck out from between its scales, more than Damien would have expected hitting their mark, and a hefty blob of burning pitch sizzled as it dripped down the creature's back, pouring out from the flying machine above.

Damien stumbled to another stop, calling up shadows to hover about him as he appraised the beast. The chaotic onslaught of attacks continued around it, but it was not getting back up, a roar bellowing out into the cave, trailing off as another spear caught it in the throat. It was not enough to make it truly bleed, but its head fell to the ground, and a second net was cast over the dragon's snout.

This was his chance. Killing the thing would take much more, but it was subdued enough for banishment. He had prepared the circle on his forearm, pulling up his sleeve and beginning to carve along the lines he'd drawn out so he wouldn't have to think too hard in the moment. The broken skin emanated a crimson glow beyond just his seeping blood, the arcana prepared to reach out and take back what it had lost from the infernal plane.

Noxscura flooded Damien, banishment rarely performed but closely tied to his blood's origin, and he strode back toward the beast filled with a purpose. He would rip it from this world, he would snuff out its existence here, he would destroy all manner and memory of the thing, and he would give it over to the darkness.

Dozens of goblins had climbed upon it, pulling the nets taut to the ground. The tiny creatures were practically feral, throwing themselves atop it, never having gotten the upper hand. More climbed over its back, trying to stab it with whatever pointy thing they could find. Dragon scales were too hard to pierce, but a select few ground down between them and stabbed into the thing. The dragon could not breathe the fire that was building hotly in its gullet, it could not rip into Damien and spill his guts on the cavern floor as its irate eyes suggested was its intent, it could not even stick out its tongue to goad him on. The thing was helpless, and a horde of minikin goblins and one blood mage would be its undoing.

Noxscura swept through him, seeping out of the infernally touched cavern itself at his command to descend on the beast. The shadows turned into violet shards of arcana made corporeal, falling in chain-like forms over the beast's back. He carved the last line of Chthonic into his forearm, the spell burning inside and out, prepared to swallow up the beast when finally he dripped his blood onto it and said the words.

The dragon snorted out a breath, smoky and short, and then another, struggling. It tried to pull back, to escape Damien's hand as he extended it, to cower from the great and terrible power being brought down upon it. Damien smirked—not any power, *his* power—and it would be a shame to do so too quickly and not revel in banishing one of the most formidable beasts in existence.

He let his gaze rove over the snarl of its jaw, the sinister slits to its eyes, the muscles of its back, the breadth of its wings. Except one of those wings was damaged, not just torn in the present scuffle but missing an entire chunk. That was not new, the wound old and healed. And of those eyes, one was clouded and scarred, while its fangs were chipped, its jaw slightly askew.

The noxscura prodded at Damien, longing to attack, but he shifted it ever so slightly, choosing to reach out to the creature one last time before banishing it. Fear, so much fear, all-encompassing and calamitous.

"Wait," he called, and the goblins paused their onslaught though still held it secure. Damien was unsure if he had meant to command the green army or simply himself, but he had yet to touch the dragon and complete the spell.

"Who brought you here?" Damien asked it.

There was a voice in his mind, a rumbling flicker that said, *No one. Fate, perhaps. Mercy, more like. I simply arrived through a tear in the veil.*

"And your injuries?"

From that place you want to send me. Others of my kind did this. Kill me if you must, but do not send me back.

Damien groaned and dropped his hand. "Fuck."

The goblins murmured, and Ewigog appeared atop the dragon. "Make died!" he cried.

"Just hold on a bloody moment," Damien groused, rubbing a temple and smearing blood across it. "Look, are you saying other dragons did this to you, and you only accidentally ended up here?"

I was looking for escape, and the veil had thinned, so I left.

"And you can't fly out of here, can you?"

It grumbled out a noise, turning its head slightly in something like shame.

"So you took to eating the goblins?"

It moaned into Damien's mind, *I didn't want to eat them but they kept coming to hit me with sticks. Eventually, I got hungry.*

"Did you lot attack him first?"

Ewigog balled up fists and stomped making the dragon flinch. "Course attack! Is Big Spicy! Is danger! Make died!"

Damien dropped back his head and groaned into the shadows of the high-ceilinged cavern. "Darkness help me for what I am about to suggest, but this has become a massive misunderstanding, and I think there is a possibility we can all come to some kind of accord."

"Damien?" Amma was shuffling down the ramp at the back of the cave. "What's going on?"

"Ah, and here is our negotiator."

Dragons and goblins were not terribly different when it came right down to it, their love of garbage, especially the shiniest garbage, quite the unifying force. Communication was the biggest problem, as every time the dragon attempted to speak telepathically to them, confusion would overwhelm the goblins, and they assumed it was some god and not just the big, leathery beast standing before them.

After many explanations, a select few began to understand, and very awkward apologies were traded. How the goblins so easily came to accept the deaths of their comrades, Damien was unsure, but perhaps building a monarchy on death helped. The traded assistance the dragon promised them was also a boon.

But the rest of their problems would be their own as Amma made good on her promise to abdicate her throne the following morning. It was quite easy despite that no goblin had ever done it before, and Damien suspected they simply didn't understand the word in its entirety, so put up very little argument. Amma was a blubbering mess by the time they'd finally left, and there was only one thing he could think to fix things.

"I'm quite appreciative you did not want to bring any of them with us," Damien said once they were far enough away he was sure she wouldn't suggest turning back. "Not even the littlest one."

"Oh, Kadruk, don't remind me!" As Amma wiped at her eyes, Vanders squeezed her neck likely both in an attempt at consolation and a reminder he was there. "Thank Sestoth this will be over soon so I can stop being so sad about every little thing." She squeezed herself around the middle and grit her teeth.

"Well, perhaps we can help things along by summoning our own, little goblin?" Damien held out an acorn to her.

Amma stood straight again and plucked the seed from his hand. "Kaz!"

"I'll try to get it right this time." Damien cleared away a spot and etched in the summoning circle, not so different from banishment.

Amma eagerly sat on the other side, and together they enacted the spell. In the brightness of the day, it was not so blinding, but it was also simpler, and Amma didn't even waver when she arcanely blossomed a tree into life for sacrifice—a thing he thought not to point out to her just in case she convinced herself she wasn't as strong as he knew she was.

The imp burst onto their plane, and Amma grabbed him, crying out and hugging him. The thing in her arms wiggled wildly, and she dropped it. As soon as it landed it took off in a blur of red, scuffling up the mountain, disappearing, and then flying past them as it tumbled back down. Damien shot an arm out and caught it by the tail before it plummeted over the edge and to its death.

Hanging by its hind end, Damien held him up, and the imp swung, little clawed hands grabbing onto its little clawed feet. This one had wings, bigger than Kaz's, but most of the rest of it was small with pinched features and beady eyes and tiny serrated teeth. Even its horns were little nubs. It breathed as though its heart might explode at any moment, and its black eyes darted everywhere all at once.

"What in the Abyss," mumbled Damien, looking down at his circle. "Oh, shit. Quaz."

When he said the name he'd mistakenly written, the imp's head snapped to Damien and it fell still.

"That's what you're called?"

The imp nodded aggressively, whole body shaking with the move.

Damien offered the creature to Amma. "Apologies, My Liege, best I can apparently do."

CHAPTER 16
UNCOMMON NAMING
CONVENTIONS

To reach The Temple of the Void by the twenty-third, they would have to go right through the middle of Buckhead. While the almost-all-knowing oracle, the kingless tribe of goblins, and the bullied dragon had all secretly been welcome obstacles, they no longer had the time to trek around the barony at the base of the mountains. Damien did not look forward to being without distraction from his angsty thoughts of the pit, but after spending many nights sleeping on the rocky ground or barely improved, lumpy goblin bedding, an inn would be a nice change, especially if it were to be his last night alive.

Amma's presence was the only bright spark. She was thrilled to be entering a city, and her excitement was infectious. "Buckhead's known for mining. Oh, and this sweet syrup that comes from the trees." She pressed her hands to her chest and practically swooned. "That's what should be on the crest instead of those giant antlers."

Bannerettes hung from many of the shop doors displaying a silver and blue crest, the mark of the Solonedys, she explained, the northernmost ruling family that served the crown. There were no gates into Buckhead, the mountain range a good barrier between it and the rest of civilization. The populace too seemed a good protection—most of them were tall and broad-shouldered and built as if everyone from the town guard to the seamstresses did physical labor daily.

"The Throkulls," Amma explained quietly when she saw him eyeing a man who was at least two feet taller than Damien and carrying a donkey over his shoulder like it might have been a sack of flour. "The villagers got friendly with them a few hundred years ago, and they even intermarried with the Solonedys. The tribal lands in the mountains aren't really part of Eiren, though it's a point of contention with the crown."

Quaz nearly tripped Damien then, snaking between his feet. Amma scooped up the imp-turned-cat, the disguise she'd suggested for him before they entered town. It almost suited him, the ginger fur and accompanying dumb look, but he kept wagging his tail and letting his tongue hang out. Damien did prefer him this way though and rubbed under his chin.

"You're more familiar with this place than I expected."

"I'm supposed to be familiar with all the baronies and the earldoms and the marches." She sighed and rolled her eyes. "But Faebarrow is the closest barony to Buckhead, so when the Solonedys are called to Eirengaard to pay their annual respects, they stay at our keep during their travels. I also spent a summer here when I was fourteen. My parents exchanged me for Kaspar, the oldest, so we could each learn more about the realm. Laurel wasn't allowed to come—she'd sprinkled some sort of dust in my mother's face powder that turned her skin green—so I had to make friends."

"I'm sure you were quite good at that."

"Well, it wasn't that difficult. Everyone here looks scary, but they're really big softies." She grinned. "Like someone else I know."

Damien chose to ignore that despite the tickle it inspired in his chest, just like he'd tried to ignore her assessment of how he had handled things with the dragon. Yes, of course, his deeds were very praise-worthy and wonderful and all those other good things, but the more honeyed her words went, the hotter his face became, and climbing out of the mountains the previous day had been fatiguing enough.

According to their map, the city was laid out along a river that ran north to south, allowing them to pass through its narrow middle in just a few hours and then it would be less than a day's travel to their destination. If they continued at their pace, they would reach the temple in the middle of the night on the eve of the twenty-third which Damien wasn't keen on. He needed a more minor distraction.

"Amma, do you remember how you expertly gathered knowledge for us in Elderpass?"

"Asking after gossip?"

"Yes, that. Could you put your skills to use for us here and see if there are any rumors of what might be waiting for us out on the plains?" They were closing in on a wide bridge that crossed the river in the town's center, a number of busy market stalls and taverns on its far side.

Amma's grin turned feral as she slipped her hand around his elbow, and Damien found himself being dragged through the streets of Buckhead on her arm. First, they simply listened, meandering behind villagers as they purchased goods and greeted cohorts. Then, Amma boldly struck up conversations with merchants, shrouding her nosiest questions between interest in wares and overblown compliments made easier to believe when she delivered them so sweetly. As the afternoon wore on, she finally led them into a bustling tavern called The Scholar's Bane where Damien relegated himself to a back corner table, watching as she sat at the bar and flirted some information out of the men there. He reminded himself it was all in the name of gossip, but Quaz did sink his teeth into Damien's hand when he pet him a bit too hard.

"Things. Are. Wild." Amma dropped down beside him, pushing a drink across the small table that she explained was mead made from sweet tree sap. She fell immediately into a diatribe about the locals. Apparently, the apple harvest was especially good in the last season, one of the Palmers had married a Thornton, putting an end to a decades-long family feud, no one had heard from the Rimespelts in about a week which was odd since they were usually so social, and the litany of people having affairs was seemingly unending.

Damien listened, but he also stared, watching the curve of her mouth when she snickered, the darting of her tongue with a particularly tawdry bit of information, the expressiveness of her brows when she playacted being shocked as she delivered a twist in her tale. All of it amounted to very little, but that wasn't the point. They had been together all day, they had walked streets arm-in-arm, they had shared a meal, they had conspired without immediate, impending danger, they had laughed, and Amma was happy.

"And of course there's a rumor about skeletons down south, but no one's that worried about it." Amma chuckled and took a long drink, but when she pulled the stein away, she looked somber. "And I realize none of that really helps us at all."

"No, it does," he said quickly. "There was that bit about the apples, and that's probably something?"

Amma shook her head. "I didn't even find someone I thought could be trusted to ask about the temple, let alone that star chart."

"Amma, what you've done—" Damien swallowed, thickness in his throat. "You've no idea how helpful you've been."

She shrugged and drained the rest of her mead. "I'll get us another."

"Do you think that's a good idea?" He put a hand on her stein, keeping her from returning to the bar. "You don't hold your alcohol well."

"How would you know?" She smirked at him, leaning in, and he simply stared back at her, waiting. Her grin faltered. "How would you know, Damien?"

He considered her, the intensity in her gaze as nerves pricked at the edge of it, and decided it would do little harm in telling her the truth. "After we stole the Lux Codex, you got so drunk I nearly had to carry you to bed, though I'm not surprised you don't remember."

She swallowed, sitting back, clearing her throat. "No, I remember that. Sort of. I remember the headache after anyway."

He cocked a brow. "You remember how inquisitive you were?"

Amma wasn't looking at him, her interest suddenly in Vanders as he chewed through a crust of bread on the table. "Maybe."

"Go on, then, regale me."

Amma's mind was working, he could practically see it, and she tried to take another drink, but there was nothing left in her tankard. Just like back in that tavern. Adorable. She scrunched up her nose at him. "It couldn't have been that bad."

Damien hid his grin behind his own stein. "No, I suppose it wasn't. That time you only asked to kiss me."

Her eyes went wide, color flaring in her cheeks. "No, I didn't," she insisted as if he'd suggested something much more salacious. "Not back in Faebarrow. You *hated* me."

"I never hated you, Amma." Damien scoffed at the idea. "And really, your simple request—which I did not oblige, by the way—was nothing compared to the karsts. You remember that vivid dream you had in the vampire's den?"

The offense chased itself off her face, and her features went all mushy as she giggled. "Oh, yeah, I definitely—wait, how do *you* know about that?"

He tipped his head to either side, reveling in her surprise.

"Was it…was it *not* a dream?"

"Well, you did come to my chamber."

"Okay?"

"Wearing a very revealing dress."

"Uh huh?"

"You climbed yourself onto my lap." He grinned deeply at that memory in particular. She hadn't blinked for a long moment, fingers grasping her stein tightly, and he leaned in. "And you finally did kiss me."

Amma's mouth fell open. "But you acted as if *nothing* happened!"

"That was quite the challenge. Especially since you also asked me to do all sorts of other things to you too."

She covered her face and squealed into her hands. "Oh, my gods, stop it!"

"That's not what you were saying when you were shoving my hand between your thighs."

"Damien, please!"

"Ah, begging—that's more like it."

"Oh, this is so embarrassing!" Amma was so red she was nearly purple as she dropped her head onto the table.

He let her wallow there for a moment as Quaz knocked her empty stein onto the floor. "But," he said, wiggling a finger beneath her chin and lifting it, "there is nothing to be embarrassed by now."

"You just told me I failed to seduce you. Twice!"

Damien grinned back at her distress. He would have liked to tell her that, if she'd done those things sober, they would have gone quite differently, but that might not have been true, the talisman being what it was.

Then something changed, her gaze on him sharpening, and like she used arcana to do it, the alarm drained out of her face, and he felt it flooding into him.

"If that time in the karsts wasn't a dream," she said carefully, a blonde brow arching upward, "then that means all those things you said to me—"

"Maybe we do need more mead."

As Damien went to stand, Amma glommed onto the sides of his face with her hands and kept him still. "Oh, no you don't. You said *things* to me, Damien. You said—you said I made you *feel* stuff, and that,"—she gasped as if it had just come back to her—"you *care* about me."

"Of course I care for you," he said, heart beating madly, tongue swelling, sweat breaking out on his neck. "Surely I've said something to that effect recently...the talisman's still in you, after all."

She made a thoughtful sound and screwed up her face. "You said I made you feel like you were falling through the Abyss or something? That doesn't sound good, but I remember it being good. It's all a little fuzzy now since I didn't think it was real, but you definitely said we could talk about it."

Trapped in her grasp, he teetered on the edge of his seat. Damien had told her he felt as though he were falling interminably through the Abyss every moment he was not burying his cock in her, and also that her incessant kindness had broken him and made him *good.* Or something like that; who could really remember? It was not as if it were written down in some tome, and he could flip to chapter sixteen to repeat it. "I do not know how you expect me to recall my words when at the time all of my blood was in my…pulsing manhood."

Amma grinned at that, gripping his jaw and pulling him closer. "Actually, I think you called it your—" But then her head snapped quickly away. "Erick!"

"Well, I definitely didn't name it Erick," he groused, glancing through the smudged window at their side.

"I mean Lord Solonedy." Amma leaned over Damien so that she could see to the street beyond, practically crawling once again into his lap but with none of the lusty longing of the times before. "He's the baron's youngest son. He might actually know something that could help us, something better than local gossip."

Damien grit his teeth, looking on the group of men passing by, well-dressed and clearly noble but walking with little concern for possible threat around them, much like how he might stride through Aszath Koth.

Amma put a hand to his chest and snorted, her gaze overflowing with frustration. "That sadistic god's getting an earful when I finally meet them." Then she tugged him away from his seat, calling to Quaz and Vanders to follow.

The four were back out on the road as evening began to fall around them.

"Do I look all right?" Amma asked, maneuvering them to a fountain.

"Yes, always." He watched her splash her face. "Why are you so concerned?"

"Well, it's been quite a few moons, maybe closer to a year, and he may not recognize me."

He would have asked her what she hoped to get out of this, but she was moving too quickly, slipping around the villagers who were finishing up their purchases and closing their stalls. In the busyness of the street, Quaz scaled Damien's back and sat himself on his shoulder, Vanders nestled into the cat's fur, and Amma only put more space between them. She was so nimble, she actually slid between two of the men in the noble entourage, a thing even Damien would have advised against, placing herself right before them and falling into a perfect curtsy.

157

"Lady Ammalie!" a bright voice called from the group. Of course she was recognizable even in her dirtied travel clothing with all that golden hair and her brilliantly blue eyes sparkling as she greeted the man. He took the hand she offered and clasped it in both of his. "But you were—and you're—well, you're alive!"

"Yes, thanks to Damien." She gestured to the blood mage, and four heads turned back to him.

Damien tried to smile, but he was sure it came off as a grimace. The men were all hulking, at least his height or taller, their chests definitely wider, and they each sported nearly identical, roguish stubble on boxy jaws as if they were some band of bards.

And then the fucker holding Amma's hand actually smiled back. He was handsome—too handsome—and, worse, he was *nice*. Damien could tell immediately since he had been around so much earnest kindness lately, and it radiated off of the man like an arcane hum. So, Erick Solonedy was handsome, he was kind, and he was still holding Amma's hand.

And Damien had to be nice back.

Lord Solonedy quickly bustled them off the street and into an establishment with a back room that was emptied for them, his retinue of men standing guard outside the door. In the privacy of the warm chamber, Amma delicately explained that she was neither abducted nor dead, but she had escaped a marriage she was not interested in with a man who had nearly destroyed her home. Erick slapped his thigh, proclaiming that he knew it all along.

"That bastard Caldor," he said and then apologized to Amma for swearing. "I knew he was never to be trusted."

Damien stood a little straighter. "Did you?"

Erick nodded as if there were no dubious tone to Damien's question. "There was always something about him, something wrong. And the crown practically confirmed it with their edict."

"An edict from the crown? About the Caldors?"

"It was a strange thing to be sure, but the message denounced Cedric Caldor's recent actions, though none of them were specified, and it stated he was in league with dark forces that are still at large. My sister and I have been wary of everything that's come out of Archibald's court in the last few years though."

"Oh, I'd love to see Winnie!" Amma's eyes lit up.

"And Winnifred would hate to hear you call her that." The two laughed too familiarly, and Damien's jaw ticked. "But she left for Eirengaard half a moon ago with some of our most trusted cohorts. Kaspar's been acting strange, his visits to the capital more frequent, and she's searching for answers there."

Erick looked both of them over, discomforted, but not because of them. He paced in the empty room, and beside Damien, Amma stayed quiet, watching, and like she knew he would, he spoke again.

"Buckhead has always been, shall we say, separate from the rest of the realm. We provide for ourselves, we ask nothing, and we only give what we must to avoid aggression. Kaspar has challenged that thinking. He's even had nasty things to say about the Throkulls. Their blood is in his veins,"—a sharpness rose in his voice as he glared at the floor and paced—"yet he seeks to cut ties and expand the realm under the crown's direction, to claim the plains and the mountains under their banner."

"Is your brother in Eirengaard now too?" Amma asked.

Erick shook his head. "He's off hunting in the Throkull plains. Refuses to allow me to accompany him, though that is hardly a change. Still, I'd like to find some way to quell his intensified allegiance. He is the heir to the barony, and our mother and father are increasingly interested in abdicating under Kaspar's urging, but it's…well, perhaps not something we should discuss here. Where are you staying?"

"We don't have a room anywhere," she said a bit too eagerly.

"Yes, you do. It would be unwise for you to come to the keep; my parents would likely want to see to your return to Faebarrow." He eyed her sympathetically. "But I have a place that I find myself going to escape my parents' attention—it's a little much when Kaspar and Winnifred are both away, as if they suddenly remember I'm around and can be put to use in some marriage agreement with another barony."

The way Erick smiled at Amma then really made Damien's jaw tick, but he said nothing, and soon the man was leading them through the city.

CHAPTER 17
IN DEFENSE OF SELFISHNESS

Y ou are sure this is wise?" Damien did not like the tautness to his own voice, the way he kept it hushed, but least of all was the squeeze to his chest as he asked, fearful of what she might say as they sat in the private estate of Erick Solonedy in the heart of Buckhead. He had left them in the parlor as he fetched them some dinner, a thing Amma had commented on being admirable because of course it was.

"We've been friends since we were young, and you heard what he said—he doesn't trust the crown, and he never liked Cedric."

Ah, yes, another positive trait to attribute to the cordial, generous, strapping man. "Right, well, he should have done something about that then."

"He actually asked me not to marry him when he last visited Faebarrow."

Damien bristled, fingers pressed together before him, and noxscura swirled about their tips. Before he could retort that asking wasn't the same as putting a stop to it, Amma's hand clamped down on his, snuffing out the magic.

"I know this seems dangerous, and Erick isn't stupid, he can tell who you are, but he trusts me. I won't tell him anything about the temple or the maps if you don't want me to."

The man in question returned then, inviting them into the dining room, and the conversation turned to pleasant things. No one asked Damien about his heritage, Amma and Erick regaling him with tales of their annual visits, speaking of his sister Winnifred's brave stunts and broken bones, and of how Kaspar, when he was more amicable, enjoyed running with them through the plains.

It was good to hear Amma laugh, to know she was not dwelling on what lay ahead, but a solemn realization settled on Damien as the night wore on: this was where Amma would end up. Or rather, Faebarrow was where Erick would end up. He'd admitted his parents planned to marry him off to someone from another barony, calling himself a spare, a means for power as a pawn, and Damien knew that Amma's parents would want her wed to someone noble and wealthy.

It ate at him with the evening's span, even when she touched Damien's arm or nudged him with her elbow when she spoke of his deeds. She could beam at him and heap on all the praise in the plane, but it would account for nothing in the end, just as he had expected.

When the plates had been cleared and the three retired to another parlor, Amma gave Damien a look, and he nodded—if she trusted this man, then he would too. Amma told Erick she had something to ask him, but then sat in thoughtful silence for a long moment before lifting her head. "Buckhead Keep has an astronomy tower, doesn't it? Could we meet with one of the mages?"

Erick looked as though he wanted more information, but was too polite to ask, instead giving Amma exactly what she asked for because that was what she did to people. He would have someone—the best and most trusted someone—there in the morning. He stood then, proposing they retire for the evening. His estate was large, though not as sprawling as a keep, and took them upstairs where the manor split into two wings, pointing out his own one way but taking them down a separate corridor full of empty guest rooms.

Erick's friendliness was cloying as he smiled at Damien and gestured toward the chamber at the hall's far end. "There is no one to draw baths or bring linens, but if you can manage on your own, everything you could need will be inside."

"Many thanks," said Damien, a hand on the door, eager to be away from him.

Amma slipped under Damien's arm. "I am definitely jumping right in a bath."

"Um, Lady Ammalie? Your private chamber is just across the way."

She spun on her heel, an awkward grin on her face. "Oh, right! Of course, I wouldn't be sleeping in the same…I just…" She scurried across the hall, catching Damien's eye before disappearing behind her door. "Well, goodnight!"

There was no malice behind Erick's gaze when the two were left alone in the hall, but there was a question in his eyes, one that Damien was not willing to discuss. Instead, he offered his most gracious nod and shut himself up in the room. He stood against the door for a moment, listening as Erick's footsteps left, waited a moment longer, and went off to the bathing chamber where, indeed, he could manage for himself, thank you very much, Lord Solonedy.

Damien scrubbed harder than he meant when bathing, knowing Amma was doing the same, and he tried not to think of her, naked, wet, touching herself. It was impossible though, and eventually he sat back, mind wandering, and was only snapped out of it when Quaz, who'd maintained his cat form, jumped up onto the edge of the tub and slipped right into the water with him. "You know you actually have wings, for darkness's sake," he growled, lifting the soaked feline form as far away from his cock as possible. Even if it wasn't getting used, he didn't want claws anywhere near it.

But in the imp's cat mouth was a pulsing glow, and when Damien held out his hand, the shard of occlusion crystal was dropped into it.

"Well, you've not done that before," he said to the stone housing his father. Apparently, being deep in the mountains amongst the goblin dens had given it a little power back, but even when it was full strength, it hadn't ever blinked.

Depositing Quaz on a linen, he sat forward in the tub and tapped the shard to see if it would stop. There was a flutter of light and then his father's voice but no eye blinking back. Zagadoth was grumbling something and then cleared his throat. "Never done this before, but hopefully…hey, kiddo, I just wanted to check in."

The occlusion shard nearly slipped out of Damien's wet fingers and into the water as he stuttered back an awkward, nervous greeting to his father, but Zagadoth didn't acknowledge the response.

"Last we talked, you were in the Sanguine Tower in the Accursed Wastes, and I just didn't feel right about that, son."

"I'm not there anymore, I—"

"I haven't heard from you since, so I thought I'd try to leave you this message, just in case."

Damien flipped the stone over, then clicked his tongue. So, Zagadoth had found a way to essentially send him a raven.

"I've been thinking a lot, son, and, well…Damien, I just want you to know I'm proud of you, no matter what, and I really don't want you doing anything too risky for me."

At that Damien scoffed and nearly dropped the shard into the water, ready to abandon it.

"Basically, kiddo, if it's not looking good, I want you to head home, all right? I've been stuck in this thing for decades, but getting out isn't worth your life. Don't make bad deals or put yourself in the kinda trouble you can't get out of for me. I know I pushed you but I…well, I hope you hear this, son."

The pulsing glow to the shard softened and went out. Damien squeezed it, a quiet anger welling up in him though he didn't know why. How his father dared profess such sentimentality, such kindness, such…sincerity. Zagadoth always sounded sincere, and even then Damien felt his father meant every word.

He dragged himself out of the bath and stuffed the shard back in his pouch where it belonged. If he survived the pit the next day, that probably meant it was time to speak with him, and if the demon refused him answers, Damien knew that if he asked the right questions, he could glean the truth from Zagadoth's eye.

After drying himself and Quaz off, Damien found light, linen pants in the drawer of a wardrobe and collapsed onto the bed. Quaz hopped up beside him, spun in a circle, and flopped down hard, immediately asleep. In the quiet of the nearly empty manor, Damien stared up at the ceiling and tried emptying his mind. He watched the shadows above him, let them come to life with the slightest bit of noxscura, and tried to put himself to sleep with the subtle movements.

It didn't work.

Amma would marry Erick, he could already see it manifesting more clearly than the fucking shadows above. Lord Solonedy was charming and handsome and, Abyss, if he asked, Damien would even have had a difficult time saying no because the man was soft—soft like Amma. He was a human who was kind and thoughtful and practically made for her.

Murdering him was an option, though, the thought creeping in coldly then sparking an unscrupulous kindling in his brain. Killing Erick would be easy, the man probably wouldn't even put up much of a fight. He wouldn't be messy about it, just send in some shadows to smother his pretty face. But then what would he say to Amma?

Must have had an enemy.

Quaz did it.

I was afraid you might marry him once you've come to your senses about me.

"Oh, don't be so bloody pathetic," he groused to himself, dropping a hand on his chest where the other half of the Dreadcouncil's Fragmentable Pendant of Accursed Bondage and Nefarious Conquest had disappeared. The next day they would find the pit, *something* would happen, and he and Amma were spending what was potentially the last night they could ever be together, apart.

Utter foolishness.

"Vanders?" Damien called hesitantly. "Vanders, can you hear me?"

There was a fuzzy tickle on his chest as the vaxin appeared. Where the thing went when gone, and how it knew when to appear, he couldn't comprehend, but it was convenient.

"Is Amma asleep?"

The vaxin tipped his head to one side, snout working hard.

Damien had no idea if that meant yes or no. Less convenient. He narrowed his eyes, trying to discern something greater. "Is she still in her chamber?"

Vanders' head tipped the other way.

"Of course," Damien muttered to himself, nothing any clearer.

Beside him, Quaz stirred, reaching paws out in a long stretch toward the vaxin, every claw vicious and sharp, but the imp's feline snout only yawned. Vaxins were little more than mice when it came right down to it, but Quaz wasn't terribly good at being a cat and seemed to have no desire to eat him.

Vanders dove off of Damien's chest and nestled into Quaz's fluffy, white belly, apparently equally unconcerned about being eaten. Perhaps Vanders wasn't terribly good at being a mouse either.

"Keep one another company," Damien said to them and slipped out of the bed.

Damien's instinct told him to try the knob before knocking, but he was still surprised when the door to Amma's chamber gave way. Did that mean she was not inside? Had she left to find Erick in the night?

A pall of blue moonlight streamed in through the large windows that ran across one wall of the chamber, falling on the bed and the form lying there. She shifted slightly, and Damien stood in the doorway, noxscura slipping away from him and going to her, feeling her heart race too quickly to be anything but awake.

"You failed to lock your door," he finally said, voice low. "Dangerous."

She lifted her head. "Not if there's a blood mage in the room with me."

"On the contrary." He eased the door to behind him. "And what if it weren't me?"

There was a lilt to her voice in the dark. "Then I'd scream, and you would come running, and I'd have you here either way, just like I was hoping."

Damien shifted the lock into place. "Well, now no one can come in. And no one's getting out either."

She put her head back down. "Guess you have to sleep here then."

That was what he wanted, of course, to feel her pressed up against him, but the thought of it being the last time held him to the spot.

"Damien, come get in the bed, or we're going to finish that conversation we were having in the tavern."

He hurried over and slipped under the blankets while she snickered into her pillow. Damien drew her close in one swift move, fitting her back against his chest where she belonged, her skin searingly warm. He slid his other arm beneath her pillow so there would be nothing between them, and she made a content noise as she snuggled in, but he froze.

"Amma, where are your clothes?"

"They were dirty," she said with a sigh. "I'm too clean to put them back on."

He groaned into the nape of her neck as his fingers grazed her bare stomach. She twisted under his touch, rubbing against him and inspiring a tickle that crawled downward from his navel. He swallowed hard and ignored it.

Breathing in the sweetness coming off of her, he closed his eyes, determined to revel in how wonderful it was to simply have her close. That lower tickle grew into a throb, but the point was to hold her, not hump her, so he wriggled his hips backward a few inches even as he cupped his hand just under her breast, her heartbeat fluttering against her ribs as she took shallow breaths. She shifted in his arms, and then nimble fingers grazed his stomach.

"What do you think you're—"

Damien sucked in a sharp breath as fingers wrapped themselves around his length. Any hope of sleep was doomed as the subtle creep to attention he'd been doing happened all at once under her touch. Toying with him in much the same way he'd seen her fingers toy with her lips in deep thought, she sighed into the pillow, entirely too satisfied.

"That's very bad behavior," he grumbled into the back of her neck but thrust his hips into her grasp despite himself.

Amma giggled, sliding her hand along the rest of his fully hard length. "Call it bad if you'd like, but I can tell it feels good." Her fingers encircled him again with a painfully light touch at the base, teasing their way up and then down and up and—

Damien's sense came back to him at once, and he snatched her wrist. She let him go, his grip much tighter. If she were to start this, he would want her to finish it, and hadn't he been so sure all this time that she couldn't possibly do these things of her own accord?

He whispered Chthonic into her hair, the sibilant words snaking out of his mouth, arcana following and seeping into her. He kept it no secret, but unlike the reaction other creatures had to being invaded by his magic, Amma relished in it. She moaned and arched against him, her ass replacing her hand and cradling his cock between the two of them, nearly dousing the spell completely.

But Damien refocused, and she put up no resistance—she never did, not with him—and her blood told him everything. Desire, hunger, longing. But it wasn't enough.

With the arm wrapped beneath her, he lifted his free hand to her throat, fingers pressing in to hold her still. "Tell me what you want, Amma."

He had her pulse in two places, her neck and her wrist, and both quickened. "You," she said, voice vibrating against his palm as it husked out. "I want you to make love to me, Damien."

Love. Damien's heart knotted, his grip on her weakening. Amma may have acted insatiable, but that soft, little heart of hers wanted more than a carnal tumble. Swallowing hard, Damien pressed his lips against the back of her head. "I can't," he breathed.

"Yes, you can." She slipped her hand from his lax grip and captured him again, less gentle this time but with a firmness that said he must.

"You're enthralled," he groaned even as she ran her fingers over the anticipatory slickness at the head of his cock. "You can't tell me no." He snatched her hand away again.

"Because of the talisman?" The answer hung in the quiet between them, filled only with deep breathing and the shifting of their bodies beneath the linens. "But that's what keeps us together."

Damien still had a hand on her throat, and he slid it up to her jaw, turning her head so he could look down into her eyes. Her lips were wet and parted in the soft moonlight, her brows drawn with worry, and her gaze traveled over his face until it met his.

"If the talisman weren't inside me, we would be apart." She was whispering, but the arcana still lingering under her skin made her voice thunderous. "I haven't been able to separate myself from it because I don't want to be separate from you. Not ever."

Her words rumbled into Damien, and as if he'd been struck, his breath was stolen. The fissure that had drawn itself through his chest cracked fully, like hardened bark falling away, the raw and soft sapwood inside him exposed.

"I'm sorry," she said. "I know it's selfish and—"

Damien kissed her, the only way he could put an end to her pointless apology. She was startled beneath his mouth, her lips catching up as he pulled away. "If that is what keeps us together, then be selfish," he said, "but do not think I keep you around because of that talisman."

"But you always say—"

"I say a lot of idiotic things," he grumbled, grip on her wrist and jaw tightening. "What I mean is that I want to keep you, your body, your soul. I want every beat of your heart for my own, and I want to be consumed by you."

Amma had fallen still again, glassiness to her blue eyes.

"You've ruined me, Ammalie," he said with a chuckle. "Enthralled me completely without even using magic."

She hummed a sweet sound then, the vibration of her throat tickling his fingers. Delight broke on her face under the moonlight—not terror nor disgust at hearing how he wanted her, but satisfaction. "Not true," she said, trying to shake off his grip on her wrist as her smile turned playful, "if I had you enthralled, you would fuck me when I ask."

Damien was stunned but not enough to let her nimble fingers slip away again. "It seems our morals have completely flipped." Swiftly, he wrenched her arm up and pressed it against where her other hand lay on the bed. Releasing her neck, he caught both of her wrists together and trapped them in a more secure grip.

"It's your fault—you've made me wicked," she said, and he thought he might die by her words alone. Hands caught together in his grip, she instead wiggled her hips backward. With only the light fabric of his trousers between them, she fit his persistent length against her ass so perfectly he nearly didn't get the chance to give her what she wanted before coming undone himself.

Regardless of what they confessed to one another, though, the talisman was still inside her.

Damien jerked away, but she was ravenous. He clamped his free hand down on her hip and dug his fingers in, holding her still. Neither of them would be getting any bloody sleep at this rate—she *had* to be satisfied. Perhaps it was just his cock thinking, but it occurred to him then that she was correct: he was choosing to not take her despite her requests, or her demands, more like, and was that not the same? Removing her choice completely?

"Please, Lord Bloodthorne," Amma whined, fighting against his hold to wiggle up against him, "just let me be bad for you."

Perhaps there was something he could do, something that might even satisfy them both.

"If you insist on acting this way, I will be forced to respond in kind," he grunted through grit teeth.

He could hear the grin work its way across her lips in the darkness. "Do your worst."

CHAPTER 18
A NOT-SO-BRIEF WEAKENING OF CONSCIOUSNESS AND CONSCIENTIOUSNESS

For a single, glorious moment, Amma thought Damien had relented when his hand came away from her hip. She squealed happily, intending to roll toward him and rip off the hateful layer keeping his *pulsing manhood* from her. But instead, his grip on her wrists only tightened, and she remained pinned to the bed on her side as a sharp slap landed on her ass.

Amma gasped, shock running through her right alongside the brief sting of pain. She whined, or at least intended to, but it came out as a breathy catch in her throat.

Damien's chuckle crawled up the back of her. "Come now," he purred, "that wasn't nearly as hard as either of us would have really liked."

Amma thought she should protest, but his hand remained, rubbing over the place he'd swatted, sending tingles through her, though they didn't go very far, pulsing between her legs.

"Now, are you going to hold still and behave?" Damien's hand wandered lower to the soft flesh at the very top of her thigh. "Or am I going to have to make you behave?"

"I won't try anything again," she responded, perhaps too quickly. "Promise."

"You're lying," he said as if he knew, which, of course he did, because she absolutely was. His hand slid back up, grazing her stomach as it snaked around. She rolled her hips the moment his grip was gone, breaking the vow immediately. "Why would you lie to me when you're in such a precarious position?" Damien's hand found her breast, carefully cupping it and then giving her nipple a light pinch.

Amma gasped, but the pain barely came before pleasure flooded behind it. "I can't help it," she panted. "I want you."

"I would certainly like to be of assistance, Amma, but every time I attempt to gratify you, I am callously interrupted by some clandestine force." Damien slid his palm down along her belly again and laid it flat just below her navel, fingertips drumming so close to where she needed them. "And I cannot help but think it is because divinity knows that I would derive far too much pleasure from finally tasting you."

"Let me taste you then," she mewled, toes curling at the thought of wrapping lips around the length she had pressed herself to.

"If only I were deserving of that." His throaty laughter blanketed her in chills. "But perhaps the satisfaction of witnessing you come apart could be countered by the torture of feeling you writhe up against me with no relief." Damien shifted, this time closer, the length of him pressing firmly against her backside. She groaned as his hand skimmed her thigh to land on her knee. "Shall we experiment?"

Amma swallowed hard. The arcana was still pulsing between them, matching her shallow breaths and prodding at her insides as his hands did her skin. "Yes," she barely croaked out, words hard to find in her anticipation. "Now."

He lifted her leg and pushed his knee between hers from behind, spreading her thighs. His other hand gripped her wrists even tighter though she didn't dare attempt to escape. "I know you're quite distracted, but have you so quickly forgotten that you should be on your best behavior for me? Where are your manners?"

"Please?" she husked, licking her lips. "I need you, Master Bloodthorne. Please touch me."

"That's my good girl."

Damien's hand finally slid between Amma's thighs, and no longer could she hold still as she'd promised. She bucked against his fingers as they dipped down into her wetness, drawing a groan up out of his chest that vibrated into her back. Slick and methodical, he encircled her, and it would only take moments, she was already writhing and arching away from him.

But Damien would not let her go, pressing himself to her back and digging his grip into her wrists. She turned her face into the pillow, the

170

squeeze that kept her in place delicious and making her cry out.

He quickened his speed, and it was like being lifted suddenly into the sky, Amma's stomach flipping, her only anchor his grip, but it was everywhere, on her wrists, at her back, stroking her core. Being wound tighter and tighter, she could hardly breathe, knowing her squirming was anything but rhythmic back against him. She'd never been so wild, but there was safety there caught in his trap.

"So eager," he hummed, and his hand came away to caress the inside of her thigh.

Amma sucked in a breath and frantically wiggled her hips. "Don't stop, not now."

"No," he said, sharpness to his voice that made her fall still as he clamped onto her flesh. "You're not getting out of this quickly. You were promised punishment, and now you're going to endure exactly what I say you will."

Amma shivered as his touch played over her legs and her stomach and her breasts, every place but where she needed it, and she couldn't even squeeze her thighs together to relieve the growing ache. Ensnared, her longing as intense as ever, her skin was set alight under his fingers, but the place he neglected calmed.

And then he began again. Brought up so quickly, Amma cried out into the linens once more, and then Damien's touch came to another brutal halt. Her mind was cloudy with lust, but she finally understood that it was not satisfaction he intended to give her but suffering. Yet if this were how he had decided to punish her, she couldn't really think him cruel, even as he whispered into her ear that she wasn't allowed to come undone under the torment of his touch, not yet, not until, well…he would see if she could earn it, somehow, if she proved to him she was good enough.

And so Amma tried. She endured under stillness, breath held. She wriggled and gasped while softening into him. She arched against his length while feigning an attempt at escape. Time and time again she made pleas and promises, and he told her he was beginning to believe her with laughter that could have been sweet if it didn't throb at her back like she was lying on the earth as it quaked.

"Oh, gods," she breathed as the pressure under his fingers built for a countless time.

"Don't invite the gods here," he rumbled against her ear. "They would be very disappointed to know you were allowing a demon spawn to command you like this."

"I don't care," she moaned.

"Don't belong to your gods anymore, then?" There was a pleasure baser than any beast in his words as he pressed a finger deep into her core and drew it back out with a curl, lighting up a place inside her that she didn't know existed.

"No." She clenched her bound hands into fists, eyes closed, unsure she could brave him stopping again. "I belong to you."

Damien's hand slowed, but this time didn't abandon her, instead only drawing lazy circles. "Do you mean this? Truly?"

"Yes." She caught her breath, nodding, the words that had been pouring from her chest for so long but always catching in her throat finally freeing themselves. "I'm yours, Damien."

He exhaled against her neck, his length throbbing, fingers quickening. "*Mine*," he rasped, squeezing her wrists and pulling her even tighter against him. "My sweet Ammalie would do whatever I say, wouldn't she? Arcanely possessed or not?"

The truth broke out of her like a sprout reaching for the sun. "Yes. Anything."

"Come apart for me."

Amma cried out, body obeying, run through with relief and torment and exhaustion and bliss. Her legs trembled, chest barely containing a pounding heart as her body stiffened, but Damien kept her close, a roar from deep in his throat coursing up against her back.

Awash with heat and wetness and the release of a pressure that had been building inside her not just for the night but for moons, she collapsed, his name mumbled on her lips, dizzy, spent.

But this time his fingers didn't relent.

"I did as you said," she panted, the feeling harrowing as it rebuilt between her legs.

"I am well aware." Her wrists were released, and Amma was rolled onto her back. Damien pressed up to loom over her, dark hair spilled into his face, violet eyes boring into hers under the moonlight with a primal need. She'd not been able to look on him as he brought her to Empyrea, and only then did she realize the intensity and admiration she had missed. "But my good girl is going to come undone for me again."

Arcana wrapped itself around each of Amma's limbs, pressing her arms back on either side of her head, spreading her legs, exposing her to him completely. As her chest arched upward, Damien slid his free arm beneath her, his mouth fell to her breasts, and he compelled her on with fingers that knew exactly what her core needed.

A second wave drove up through Amma's body as she screamed with the pleasure of his touch until her cry was cut off by Damien's mouth as it crushed down onto hers. To speak of being consumed, she was devoured in that instant, her lips, her breath, her very being, and if she could speak, she would have told him to do what he wished with her now and forever.

The arcana on her wrists and ankles relented, and Amma pulled her limbs in, wrapping them around him as he crushed her to his chest and fell at her side. She shook, the world spun, and she could only hold onto him, moored, safe.

When her breathing came a bit more naturally, she clumsily slid a hand down his front to find him still engorged between them, the skin so soft, yet the length so hard.

"No, no," he said into her ear, all of the commanding bite wrung out of his voice, replaced with a tenderness mirrored in the way he took her gently by the wrist and removed her hand to squeeze it in his own. Fingers threaded into her hair and danced against her scalp as lips pressed to her forehead. "You've done so much already for me."

"But you…" Her tongue would not work properly which, she realized even in her dizzy state, could be a problem considering what she'd like to do.

"*You*," he said, clear and kind and full of adoration. "You are going to sleep now."

She nuzzled into his chest, and as if arcana had taken her again, her body could only obey.

Amma sat beside Damien the next morning in Erick Solonedy's parlor. She had her hands on her knees, sitting up stiffly, waiting for their host to return. "Do you think he heard us?"

"Surely, you mean, do I think he heard *you*?" Damien was lounging with his arms spread over the back of the sofa, an ankle thrown up over his knee, exuding more confidence than she had perhaps ever seen which was really saying something for a blood mage. "The Solonedy boy is far too polite to say, but I certainly hope he did."

She flashed her eyes at him, he grinned back, and the flutters in her stomach forced out a giggle. His hand squeezed her side, making her jump, and then footsteps were entering the parlor.

Damien and Amma both stood as Erick entered, an elderly woman at his side. He had advised them the evening before that there was a mage from the astronomer's tower at the keep that was trustworthy, someone who cared solely for magic with no interest in politics or the crown. The woman was tall even with her hunch and still muscled with the broad shoulders of a Throkull beneath withered skin. Dressed in furs, her gauzy eyes darted between Damien and Amma before turning back to Erick. "Where is it?"

"You see?" Erick grinned from half of his mouth. "Straight to business."

Amma handed over the star chart, bouncing on her toes, no idea how Damien stayed calm beside her, arms folded, head bent. She had been a wreck since reluctantly detangling herself from him that morning but bundled it inside. She didn't want him to know how she feared the date and the pit and the inevitability the oracle had handed down to them no matter how much she didn't believe Damien was this doomed hallowed son, but she checked her pouch every time he wasn't looking to be sure she still had the pendant.

"An eclipse," said the woman, finger tracing over the chart. "We have been expecting Ero to cross Lo, but this…"

Damien's shoulders went back, hands falling to his sides, and Amma could feel a new tension leeching off of him.

"This will be an eclipse of the sun, the day turned to night." The woman snorted. "Do you know when last our realm saw the sun blotted out by not just one but both moons?"

Breaths were drawn in and glances traded, but no one spoke.

"The Expulsion."

When the tale was told of all one hundred and forty-two gods last visiting the plane en masse, coming to their worst disagreement, and casting the dark gods into the Abyss, no one spoke of how the sky looked. But then, there was a lot of other stuff going on.

"Darkness will eclipse the plane," the woman breathed, head tipping side to side as she continued to study the chart. "The One True Darkness."

Amma stiffened, hand floundering until it found Damien's arm and squeezing to reassure herself.

"How do you know this?" Damien asked, voice sharp.

"The truth has been written in the stars." She handed the chart back, and Amma was hesitant to take it. "But there is nothing that speaks of the gods returning to save us once again, and nothing on that page to suggest they will either."

CHAPTER 19
A NOT-SO-RARE HUMAN AFTER ALL

As he approached the site of The Temple of the Void, Damien assumed one of two things would happen: he would live, or he would die. He was right, of course, as those are just about the only two things that can ever happen to any being, but he was rather more dramatic about the details.

Damien equated dying with a sort of unkind kindness, an ending that would be too soon but perhaps spare a whole lot of innocent, well-meaning folks including a particularly well-meaning one who was only slightly less innocent since he'd gotten his hands on her the night before. But the worst of it was that dying meant leaving her.

Subsequently, Damien equated living with the fulfillment of the prophecy that had plagued him most of his life. Evil was an inevitability, even after he professed to Amma she'd turned him good. Things would be easier if he were already evil, which he was, or, were, or would be again? The subjunctive verb conjugation was rarely used correctly in Key, and sometimes he got it confused with Chthonic, but the point remained the same: there was a state—*evil*—and Damien Maleficus Bloodthorne was destined to be evil or to be dead.

"Do you still have the pendant?"

At his side, Amma turned to him, wide-eyed but with a tightness to her features she'd been carrying around all morning. He really thought he'd wrung all of that out of her the night prior, and she had been as wild for him as he'd hoped then, but the twenty-third brought its own tension to them both. In the greying late afternoon of the plains beyond Buckhead, she was still a bright spot, intent on moving forward and insisting nothing could go wrong even if they were following the Grand Order of Dread's commands.

She nodded, smile stiff, eyes unblinking.

"May I see it for a moment?"

Amma went into her pouch and held up the pendant by its chain. It caught no light in its cloudy, crimson surfaces, but his own shadow reflected over it. "See?"

Damien held out his hand.

"You said not to."

He curled his fingers back. "Just testing your memory." Though he hated the thing, it felt better knowing it was in her hand, and as she slipped it into her pocket, he was calmed enough to focus on the way ahead again.

Quaz was rabidly running across the plain, springing around brambles and rocks, and tumbling over his paws more than half the time. The newest imp had taken to being a cat as well as a cat took to water, which wasn't very good, but still somehow capable of finding a way to survive.

Damien pulled out the map again, their moving dot finally overlapping the ominously marked destination. Aszath Koth was not so far from where they stood, though an inlet of the Maroon Sea and mountains lay between. "So close to home," he said. "How did I not know this place was here?"

But looking around, it seemed fairly obvious: there was nothing to know about at all.

The land was flat, the peninsula stretching out away from the city of Buckhead nestled into the base of the mountains. The shore would be somewhere farther off, but it could be neither seen nor heard where they stood, the landscape only made bleaker in the briskness of late fall. A bare tree dotted the horizon on occasion, but no sign of cultivated life sprung up amongst the tall, brown grasses.

"Are we sure it's *right* here?" Amma's voice was taken on the wind into the space where the temple and its pit were meant to be.

"Perhaps it must be revealed." Damien took careful steps, the ground below him solid unlike it had been in Krepmar Keep. He would have expected a crumbling, ancient structure that had once been the site of worship for some formidable being, but there was nothing, only the two of them standing out in an open field.

Damien's stomach twisted at the thought of reaching out with arcana, neither wanting to feel It nor wanting It to feel him back.

"Catacombs!" Amma jumped in front of him. "Roman's map, the four corners were marked on it, and beneath The Temple of the Void, it said *catacombs*."

"Buried dead? Underground?"

Amma was nodding, eyes wide, expectant, excited perhaps, but mostly terrified.

Damien took a deep breath. "Quaz, do you think you can find us an entrance?"

The imp snapped his head up to Damien, whiskers twitching, tongue poking out with delight as Vanders rode on his back, tiny paws clutching his fur. He fell low to the ground, nose snuffling right in the dirt like a hound, and he scurried off, leaving a trail parting the tall grasses in his wake.

Quaz serpentined, doubling back over his own path twice as fast as they could follow. That familiar foreboding hemmed in on Damien, carried in on a briny wind that brushed back his hair, the sensation of wings both fresh and adrift in his memory.

For the brief time that Damien had arcanely been a bird, he experienced a single, desperate compulsion: find Amma. Now that she walked along at his side, nudging rocks with her boots and looking so carefully for impending destruction, he imagined if he never had, chest hollowing out at the thought.

It would be like that eventually, he feared, and the guilt flooded him at not sending her home to Faebarrow when he'd had the chance. But selfishness had won out, just as it had the night before. He used her for companionship, just as he'd used her to transport the talisman, the pendant, his own morality, and what kind of evil creature kept someone they cared so deeply about in so much danger when safety was such an easy option? Someone who had buried herself inside him deserved more. Someone who had given him such goodness in return for less than nothing, someone who made him think, even if he knew it was impossible, that he could actually love.

By all that was grim and unholy, when had it happened? In the streets of Aszath Koth when her hands had tended to his self-inflicted wound? In the shadowed halls of the Grand Athenaeum when she'd proven herself a thief? When she had allied herself with him as they fled for The Wilds? Or in the Everdarque, vowing to protect him and never once wavering? Perhaps there was no moment, nothing that defined the lines between loathing and tolerance, friendship and love,

177

but there he stood, incapable of stepping backward once they'd been crossed. He told her he wanted to be consumed, but he already had been, his ensnarement as permanent as the noxscura that ran through his veins.

It may have not been in the way that humans were meant to, but he loved her.

So, what in the bloody, fucking Abyss was he supposed to *say*? That festering blight he'd met in The Wilds and Krepmar Keep was stabbing at the edges of his arcane sense—this could be his only chance to tell her, but *what*? She had broken him for the better, this she knew despite how pithy he had always been about the strange, new choices he made in longing for her approval and happiness, but he had not admitted to *loving* her because that…that was a lie he was deluding himself into, wasn't it?

There was a prickle at the back of his hand, and he didn't have to glance down to know it was noxscura seeping out, telling him that leaving the fantasy unsaid was best. If he died, she would be free of him, but if he lived and went on to do the unspeakable things he was meant for, it would be better if she were not beholden to a demon spawn who had lied to her. He would be no better than Cedric Caldor then— a monster she was bound to.

Because if he did say the words strangling him to be free, and she responded in kind, then what? She said she was his in a fit of passion, admitted to selfishly keeping him near, but not that she loved him. If he did hear those coveted words from her, that she loved him even though he was a blood mage, son of a demon, prophesied to bring destruction to the realm, wouldn't he do the absolute worst just to hold onto that sliver of goodness?

The noxscura seeping out of his palms told him, *Yes*.

He would cage her.

He would break her.

He would never allow her to leave unless he was imprisoned himself, because he was his father's son, in the end.

Damien pulled his gaze away from Amma to look back at the way they'd come. The rocky mountainside climbed up from the horizon beyond the now-unseen city. It was thick with trees, the kind that didn't lose their needles in the cold—Amma would know exactly what kind of pines they were—and he felt in them hidden eyes, watching and waiting for him to become his worst incarnation. He snarled at them and refused.

There was a yowl over the windswept plain, Quaz atop a small boulder, paws in the air, Vanders perched on his head. Damien and

Amma went quickly to the imp to see he had identified not much besides a rock. It was nice, he supposed, as far as rocks went, as wide across as two carts and only about as tall as his knee, but it would have been nicer if it were marked with, perhaps, a sigil suggesting it were a gateway to evil unknown.

"Underneath." Amma put a foot up on its edge and shoved with no avail. "We need to move it."

"Shadows could break through, but it will be loud when it cracks. We could also—"

"No," said Amma. "You can't use your magic or It will feel you too soon."

"You are probably correct, but—what are you doing?"

Amma had her eyes closed, hands pressed together.

"I do not think invoking that goddess—"

"Shh." Her brow furrowed for a moment. "I'm trying to hear the trees."

Damien glanced about. There was only one, and it was quite far off. "Should we move closer?"

"No. Quiet."

Wind blew, and Quaz crept to the rock's edge with a trill. A groaning came up from the ground, and Amma extended an arm. A length of greenery shot upward from the grasses, knocking into her hand so hard she was thrown backward.

Amma squealed, catching herself and taking the vine in two hands. Its green coloring shifted to a rich brown as it solidified, the top thickening into a bulb and shooting tiny, pink buds off of it, and Amma's face grew into utter delight. "I did it! Holy Sestoth, I actually made one again!"

Damien admired the staff, slightly taller than she was, a twisting branch of earthy darkness that looped over itself at the crown. It was covered in delicate, pink leaves so obviously those of a liathau, but the core in its bulbous top, visible through small knots in the wood, held something—something also obvious, but that Damien couldn't possibly believe.

He put a hand out to it, and as he waved, the silvery strings running at the staff's core followed. "H-how?"

"So, there's this place the witches taught me about. Well, it's only sorta a place, but it's called *hessach*, and I think that's where these things are from." Amma tossed the staff from one hand to the other. "I only made one once before in the Innomina Wildwood, but it wasn't as pretty as this one is."

"Amma, that's filled with noxscura."

"What, really?" She pulled the top of it close to her face, and he almost grabbed it away. It wouldn't spill out, she had *made* the damn thing, but, dark gods, that in and of itself was…well, it was sort of terrifying, but it also made him want to throw her down on that stone and claim her once and for all.

Damien shook that thought reluctantly from his head. "Because of the talisman?" he said mostly to himself.

Amma waggled her brows but shrugged. "Maybe. Let's put it to use."

With a force he was not expecting, Amma slammed the pointed end of the staff at an angle where the stone met the ground. She grunted, baring her teeth, and then grabbed its knobby top and leapt.

Damien laughed as she pulled herself off the ground, the staff bowing under her weight, a growl emanating from her throat ferociously. "Amma, a lever's a brilliant idea, but—"

There was a shifting beneath Damien's boots that made him jump away from the stone. From the deadened earth, the dried-out ivy snaking beneath the grasses bloomed into life, running through with its original deep purple color, and it curled about the base of the boulder. Slow and steady, the vines squeezed, and the boulder was lifted from Amma's fulcrum. She dropped back to the earth, and the rock continued to slide, Quaz and Vanders atop it and prancing along its edge with huge eyes, until it had been completely moved to a new spot.

He sighed, hands on his hips. "When am I going to accept I have no idea what you're capable of?"

Amma blew out a long breath, tongue lolling out. "Whoo, Damien, I don't know if I could have taken it if it'd been much bigger."

He cleared his throat, tucking the memory of her words away for the off chance he did survive all of this and found himself alone. "Yes, well, look at you, still conscious and everything."

But neither of them could bask in her success for long. Left behind in the space where the rock had been was a cavern cut out of the earth and steps leading downward. They listened for a moment but heard nothing over the whipping winds on the plain around them.

"If we are concerned about certain arcane forces feeling for familiar magic, you might want to put that away before we descend."

"Good point. I remember the witches doing this…" Amma lifted her staff overhead, awkwardly sliding it down her back as if sheathing it in a scabbard that wasn't there, and then it vanished. "Neat!"

Damien wondered if everything he thought he knew about arcana was wrong, but only for a moment. He gestured for the imp still digging nails into the rock's edge and marveling at the massive hole below.

"Quaz, can you give us some light?"

The imp blinked his catlike eyes, and then Damien was blinded by a daunting, green glow. When Quaz tipped his head into the hole, the way down was illuminated, and when he blinked again, the light blinked along with him. It wasn't exactly Kaz's tail, but it would do.

Damien scooped Quaz up, Vanders leaping away and onto Amma, and sat the imp on his shoulder. "Keep looking forward," he instructed as the creature nuzzled his chin, though his fur was soft and, admittedly, a bit of a comfort.

With each step downward, queasiness built in Damien's gut. There was no wall to hug, a drop on either side of the stairs falling away into nothing. Quaz's eyes illuminated the steps well enough, and when they reached the bottom, the cavern opened up before them.

Massive, even when only illuminated in spots by the green glow at Damien's shoulder, the ground was pocked with pools of water, and the stagnant air was cold and clammy. Somewhere far off there was a rhythmic beating, perhaps the sound of the sea.

Amma pressed into Damien's side, and there was a glint as she unsheathed her dagger.

"Feeling combative?"

"Aren't you?"

Damien smirked and pulled out his own. Metal in hand, both crept deeper into the cave, and Damien almost didn't notice as the walls changed until they were no longer surrounded by dark, wet stone. Thousands of bones were stacked along every surface, femurs in neat columns, lumbar joints in pyramids, skulls in rows with their jaws placed atop them like crowns. Catacombs were meant to be burial grounds, but this was more like a very morbid work of art.

"You don't think they'll come alive, do you?" Amma whispered in the dark, and then she gasped. "Oh, okay, bye, Vanders."

"Even if there is a necromancer down here, these bodies would have quite the time putting themselves back together. We could probably run out if necessary." The trepidation in Damien's belly had shifted into all-out dread. Whatever way these bones sought to cobble themselves together would have been preferable to the pit that he knew waited for them. "I should say, Amma, though I hate to, I am...concerned."

"Do you feel worse than before?" She touched his arm lightly in that way only she could, somehow quelling everything awful, if just for a moment.

He nodded. "This is not a word I use lightly, but I think I may be exceptionally weak here."

Amma gave him a squeeze. "Wait here. I'll go ahead, throw in the pendant—"

"No, no." He straightened. "You're not doing this alone. I just want to be honest."

"You'll be all right," she said, insistence to her voice. "I'll protect you."

The horribleness that had settled on him lifted then, just enough so that Damien could continue on.

Forward deeper still, the wide corridor lined with dismantled skeletons led to an archway built from more of the same, beautiful in its design, but grim in its existence. It was wide and tall, as if it were meant for moving through by monsters and not men. Beyond, there was a glow, and Damien tapped Quaz on the head, the imp's eyes going out.

Through the archway lay a ledge. To either side were many stairs curling downward along the cavern walls to meet at least forty feet below in a wide, open space that marked the end of the catacombs. There had been no other living beings on their descent, but here they finally found them, an assortment of robed figures circling the space below as it pulsed with a glowing aura. It wasn't E'nloc yet, Damien knew, but It was coming.

From where they stood, they could throw in the pendant and never have to approach it, a lucky thing considering how ill he felt, but they would have to wait, so Damien and Amma got down on their stomachs right at the ledge. Quaz hunkered beside them, tail swiping through the air. Below, three of the figures stepped away from the others and one pulled back his hood. Amma brought her hand over her mouth, but her eyes filled with the shock she'd silenced in her voice.

"Archibald," she finally said. "That's the King of Eiren."

The queasy nervousness balled itself up in Damien's stomach to rise like bile into his throat. Archibald, the ruler of the realm that opposed his very existence, the divine mage who had dared imprison his father, the enemy he had sworn to defeat, was standing just there, and, darkness, he looked so human, a full beard, age to his skin, just a man. He stood so small and so far below them, effortless to pick off.

Of course, Damien didn't want him dead, not yet—he was a descendant of a dominion with power passed down and honed over decades that allowed him to imprison demons, the only being capable of freeing his father. But to come across him outside of Eirengaard nearly drove the noxscura right out of Damien's skin.

"He must be here to destroy it," hissed Damien, torn at the idea. That was what Damien wanted as well, and it was strange to be allied with an enemy. He glanced at Amma—well, perhaps not that strange.

"Kaspar Solonedy," called Archibald, his voice rising up through the tall cavern, echoing back on itself as the man at his side dropped to a knee and pulled back his own hood, "your service to the realm and loyalty to the crown have never wavered. As a chosen one, we now ask for this last sacrifice to bring about the darkness so that we may all finally step into the light."

"That's Erik's brother," Amma whispered.

Kaspar exposed his forearm in offering toward the king. The third man came to stand between them, a blade in his hand, and ran it down Kaspar's skin, bright red pouring out as he hissed in pain.

Weakling, thought Damien, and then his thoughts went darker. "Those bastards are doing fucking bloodcraft," he growled. "Aren't they supposed to be holy men of Osurehm?"

Amma was gnawing on the tip of her dagger. "Oh, who knows anymore? Do we stop them?"

Kaspar's blood dripped to the ground, and the moment it did, the glow that filled the center of the cavern was shrouded in a violet light. If he hadn't already been on his stomach, Damien would have fallen, a pull from behind his navel so strong he nearly vomited.

"I don't think that's wise," he managed. "And we need the pit to be opened."

Amma shifted, pulling out the pendant and squeezing her fist about it. Damien was glad—he didn't want the temptation to grab it from her, though knowing what the darkness below them would become, he couldn't imagine intervening. He did *not* want E'nloc on this plane, that he knew for certain.

But he did want Amma. Even in this moment, feverish and ill and mind on the verge of being addled, he thought to whisper to her that, if he could love someone, it would be her. It was completely selfish, but the part of him that wanted her to know was growing in the wake of his weakness.

Damien hesitated a moment too long, and the decision to say nothing was made for him when the cavern rumbled. The aura of the pit swelled, that same, forever blackness opening up at the feet of the mages who had circled it. Even as high up as they were, it was imposing to look on nothing, and Damien's head spun. Fucking E'nloc had a hold on him even like this, even when he cast no magic and stayed away, but then he'd not had control over the noxscura that insisted on seeping out at thoughts of Amma.

There were voices below, agitation in them. Archibald spoke over the din, "Can you contain it?"

And then one answered him that they both were familiar with. "I've had practice, Your Majesty. It will be contained."

"Gilead?"

"The Grand Order?"

Damien and Amma looked sharply at one another.

Amma sucked in a shocked breath. "That's the mage who served Cedric."

"I could have sworn, that voice,"—Damien squinted out over the ledge—"it's so similar to the member of the Grand Order who…who was late." When they had arrived at Yvlcon, and he had been summoned before the Grand Order of Dread, a member was missing even after making him wait. Was it possible that had been Gilead, too tied up with E'nloc to be on time? "If that is him, he will know we're meant to be here, but if not—it doesn't matter. We have to do as the Grand Order requested."

Amma nodded, sat up, and chucked the pendant. Through the air it sailed, the ugly gem tumbling over itself, chain spinning, and arced downward, headed for the darkness. There was a sizzle in the air as arcana reached back up toward it, and Damien's chest grew tight, the cave pressing in and pulling at him. He too sat up, needing to see it disappear inside, needing to know it was done.

But a gust of wind at their backs made them both duck, a dark blur sweeping through the shadows above. Wings flapped, leathery and wide, and a scaled creature dove down toward the pit, a rider on its back. Damien gripped the ledge with white knuckles, earth crumbling beneath them. It couldn't be.

The pendant was snatched out of the air, and a wyvern pulled up sharply to hover above the pit, the darkness below it unchanged, their attempt to stop the chaos bubbling inside thwarted. The creature beat its wings and rose up before them, the woman on its back holding out the pendant by its chain.

"Oh, hello, lover," she said, and Delphine began to cast.

CHAPTER 20
MISERY PERSONIFIED

Voices chanted from below, and the rumbling of the darkest magics crawled up through the earth, but Amma could only focus on the violet arcana forming in Delphine Delacroix's hands. The woman muttered a spell, something absolutely horrendous no doubt, and Damien was transfixed.

Quaz scrambled over Amma's lap and sank his teeth into Damien's arm. The cat-shaped imp was given a shove, and he tumbled away from the ledge into the shadows, but Damien hadn't blinked. He could only stare at Delphine, body rigid, the veins in his neck and face flooding with a dark arcana against his pale skin.

Delphine sat atop her hovering creature, the claws at the ends of its flapping wings bat-like, and Amma had recently enough seen a dragon to know that this had to be a wyvern. The woman continued to mutter, a crackling all around her glinting with the same darkness as was in Damien's veins.

Amma grabbed his arm and shook, but he remained unmoving, trapped. She swore, standing and pointing her dagger out over the pit, eyeing Delphine. "Stop this," she called, arcana crackling in her own fingertips as it searched for flora in the depths of the cavern.

Delphine gave her only a cursory glance and scoffed.

Amma's outstretched arm was yanked back, the dagger clattering to the ground, and she was spun. Damien was there, forcing her backward and holding her forearm so tightly it made her cry out, but then her yelp was cut off as her foot slipped on the ledge.

She flailed her free hand and grabbed onto his tunic, stomach flipping as he leaned her back, but he only took that arm too, freeing it of him and bending her away. A quick glance over her shoulder revealed that the pit had formed, chaotic blackness and tentacles seeping out, but this time it was not grabbing and devouring whatever it could find. There was an order to this chaos, the entirety of the assembled below chanting, so intent they didn't acknowledge what was going on above.

"Damien," Amma cried, "what are you doing?"

He said nothing, but his veins pulsed with arcana, eyes transfixed on Delphine still hovering on her wyvern. Amma couldn't even get Damien to look at her as he prepared to toss her into the horrible nothingness below.

"Get *rid* of her!" Delphine spat.

"Gods, no, stop!" Amma thrashed, wanting to break out of his grasp but knowing freedom meant falling to her death. She'd felt like this before, teetering on the window ledge of Krepmar Keep in Cedric's cold grip, and terror ran through her anew. Every muscle tightened, sweat breaking out over her skin even as goosebumps erupted, panic tumbling in her stomach.

But Damien was not Cedric, and he was not doing this to her. It was Delphine.

Amma swallowed, finding her softest voice as she fell still. "Please, Damien, I know you're in there."

He blinked, violet gaze falling to hers. The darkness that had been crawling its way through his veins halted as he looked her over with a sort of wonder. Then she was pulled to him, grip still painfully tight, and Damien pressed a hard and desperate kiss to her lips.

Amma didn't know what to do, but it was natural to kiss him back now, to want him even in a moment that could have been her last. And then she was falling.

Amma shrieked, but she slammed into the ground and toppled over herself. Rolling away from the ledge and Damien, she came to a dizzying stop on her stomach, the wind knocked out of her lungs. She felt for her dagger, fingers clawing at the ground, but there was only rock and dirt and pain. Gasping for breath, arcana sparked in her chest, reaching out again for anything left alive in the corpse-filled cavern.

Through strands of hair that had fallen in her face and the stars bursting behind her eyes, Amma could just see Damien standing at the edge of the cliff. Her voice wouldn't come to scream for him to stop, lungs refusing to fill, but arcana pulsed through her stronger than it ever had. She had no strength to speak, to stand, to run for him, but her magic persisted and struck out for life.

And there it was. Amma couldn't see it, but she could feel the flora, and it was listening to her. A carpet of dark, fuzzy greenery crept up from between the cracks in the ledge. Damien's figure stood with his back to her, a black mist emanating all around him as Delphine continued to cast, and his head tipped downward as moss crawled up his boots and clung on.

But it wasn't enough.

The wyvern swooped downward out of sight, and Damien stepped off the ledge. A scream husked painfully up Amma's throat, but then it died as the wyvern pulled back up, Damien on its back just behind Delphine. Face lax, veins dark, he sat rigidly behind her, and the woman grinned as the beast swooped back the way they had come.

Amma pulled herself to her feet. She ran, away from the king and Kaspar and Gilead, away from the magic and the task to be done, away from E'nloc. She sped back through the arch and into the catacombs, darkness swallowing the wyvern. How could she catch them?

Amma slammed a hand onto a skull buried in the cavern wall. Arcana flooded away from her and called to the moss. It seeped out of every crack, blooming in the darkness with a luminescence that brought the cave to life with light. In its push to come to the surface, the moss dislodged bones and cracked through stalactites, breaking free and carving through the air. The wyvern rolled away from the cavern's dropping daggers, dodging as bones burst forth from the walls.

Delphine tore herself around, eyeing Amma's figure in the newly-lit space. The wyvern turned with a cry, wings pulling in as it dove. Amma's fingers were firmly planted on the skull at her side, willing the moss to dislodge anything it could and knock the woman out of the sky. She couldn't move, she couldn't give up the connection she had and allow Delphine to get away, even as the terrifying creature sped toward her.

A pall of darkness shot up in front of Amma, shadows solidifying between her and where the wyvern would be. There was another screech, and she heard the beast's wings beat as it was so close, but she felt nothing through the wall of shadows.

"What do you think you're doing?" Delphine's voice roared. "Sleep!" With a crackle of arcana in the air, the shadow began to disperse. Damien's figure had slumped forward onto Delphine's back, eyes closed. The wyvern's talons broke through the last of the darkness, coming down on Amma.

Hands grabbed her. Wrenched out of harm's way at a speed she was sure was impossible, the wyvern landed just where she had been, breaking through the wall of skulls, shattered bones dusting the air.

Delphine cackled, and the wyvern pulled back up, Damien still immobilized. Amma thrashed in the place she'd ended up, hidden in shadows yards away. The creature swooped yet again for the cavern's exit, and with no more obstacles, made quick work of flying between the remaining stalactites.

Tears sprung to Amma's eyes as the moss's light died around her, the wyvern's tail disappearing into the darkness, Damien gone with it. She was screaming after him, throat raw on pleas that he wake up, but she was trapped. How—*how* would she get to him now?

She flailed once more, and the arms released her. She fell to the ground hard and choked on a sob, the sounds of chanting filling up the cave in the wake of her screams. All at once, the weakness came. The arcana had sapped her, and she fought the exhaustion, trying to scuff up to her feet to run after where the wyvern had gone but only falling back to the ground on hands and knees. "No," she muttered, disgusted with the fragility in her voice. She was unable to stand, so she clawed at the rock, trying and failing to use her arcana—for what, she had no idea. "Please," she whispered, "please, come back."

"He's gone."

Even in Amma's weakness, she lifted her head, boots stepping into her clouded vision.

"And you won't catch him, not like that."

The voice was familiar, and Amma focused, glare traveling up thin legs, a trim torso, and landing on that smarmy, fucking smirk. "Xander?"

"At your disservice, baroness."

Amma's mind was filled with too many thoughts to think them all at once, so she didn't bother with a single one, rage flooding her instead of rationale. "You did this," she growled, ire giving her the strength to push up to her feet and take a wild swing at Xander's jaw.

A shadow no bigger than her fist appeared, separating the blood mage's disgustingly-punchable face from her all-too-eager fist. Her hand sunk into it, skin taken by a shock of cold before it went numb, but she continued to push, ice jolting down her arm until she could take no more and collapsed again onto her knees.

"Really," Xander scoffed. "After I *saved* you?"

The mess of thoughts slammed against one another in Amma's

head. "You held me back," she croaked, "I could have—"

"You most certainly could *not* have. *I* can't even stop Delphine, *obviously*. Your moldy, little trick was a surprise, to be sure, but what were you planning to do? Knock them *both* out of the air? Bloodthorne was being enthralled—do you think he would have had enough sense to protect himself from the detritus you were flinging so haphazardly into the air?" He snorted out a single laugh. "Now, wait here and get yourself together for darkness's sake."

Amma glanced up through strands of loose, sweat-drenched hair, and aberrant forms surrounded her. Shadow imps. Beyond, Xander was walking back into the depth of the catacombs. If she were lucky, E'nloc would swallow him whole like It would have done her if Damien—she pressed a hand to her chest, squeezing her eyes shut. Oh, gods, he'd almost thrown her in.

There was a tap to her knee, and through cloudy eyes, Quaz was climbing up onto her lap, carrying her dagger in his mouth.

Amma took the weapon, squeezing the hilt with whitened knuckles. At least now she had something to kill Xander with for what he'd done. But as she gathered Quaz's cat form into her lap with her other hand, she realized the shadow imps had allowed him through, and they didn't move to take the weapon from her.

Thoughts began to sort themselves in her mind, and she was reminded of her brief and infuriating conversation with the blood mage at Yvlcon, how he'd said then that he hated Delphine. She wouldn't put it past him to ally himself with someone he loathed for a mutual cause, but why not just kill Amma now? Why was he still here at all?

She sheathed the weapon on her thigh—the thought of saving it for Delphine bolstering her. Hugging Quaz to her chest, she tried to work out what to do next, but the shadow imps suddenly dispersed.

"Up! Get up!" Xander's voice was calling back from the dark, footsteps approaching rapidly.

Xander never once struck Amma as the kind to run, and yet there he went, dark eyes wide, white hair blowing back to reveal a glimpse of terror on his face.

"No one bloody told me there would be a whole host of divine fucking mages here, not to mention that *thing*. Well, come *on*." He skidded to a stop before her and dragged her up to her feet by the back of her tunic.

Knees wobbly, she could barely stand. "Don't touch me!" She flung an arm out, Quaz clasped in her other.

"Believe me, I'd like little more than to abandon you here, but you're coming with me." Xander's hold didn't waver as he reached into

189

the neck of his coat. The vial he wore on a cord fell out, a second clinking along beside it. Apparently, he had been prepared for quite the battle. But he pulled out a stone instead and threw it at their feet. The ground cracked, a portal expanding there. "I've been looking forward to doing this," he said, thrill running through his voice as he angled her toward the hole.

Amma was thrust forward, and once again, she was falling.

CHAPTER 21
THE MAKINGS OF A VIVID, RESTLESS, RESOLUTE CAPTIVE

Amma fell into a heap, and Quaz's furry form shimmied out from beneath her. She rolled onto her back and took in a deep gulp of air, free of brine but spiced with herbs. Blinking up at a ceiling covered in brass panels, candlelight flickered over the repeating designs making her too dizzy to react to the sounds of passing footsteps and muffled voices.

She sat up with a groan, a hand feeling for the dagger on her thigh but fingers too clumsy to pull it out. At least she was still conscious, but that use of arcana had nearly done her in. She rubbed her temple, a thin form dressed in white standing across from her. Amma blinked the cloudiness out of her eyes and fear shot through her belly.

"Stay back," she murmured, swiping a daggerless hand through the air. Quaz hissed, scrambling onto her shoulder and baring his fangs.

"Oh, hi, no, I'm here to help. You really don't look so good."

It wasn't Xander that stood before her, but a priestess. One that she loathed. "I don't need your help," she spat.

There was a quiet scoff from the far side of the room, and Amma found yet another of the Righteous Sentries huddled up on a counter, digging a knife into its otherwise pristine top. *Her* knife.

The priestess, Pippa she'd been called, worked her way closer and knelt, but Quaz swiped claws through the air. "Ah, call him off!"

"Why would I?" Amma leaned away from her, looking about for the other two but only finding the massive knight sitting at a table on the room's other side. "You, all of you, get away from me."

The knight groaned, leaning back in his chair as he took a bite of an apple. "Still doesn't know what's good for her."

Amma sucked in a breath, ready to scream, but Pippa's hand came down on her ankle, and Amma was run through with arcana. Her mind sharpened, and she could smell the sage and thyme cooking in the stew on the stove, could sense the potatoes on the counter were on the verge of going off, could see a mouse scurrying through the not-quite-shut larder door, could hear the groan of Barrett's chair—that was his name, the bastard, and the other one was Kori, she suddenly remembered, the sneaky one who she'd stolen a crossbow from.

Her pain evaporated, but Amma didn't move to get up. She instead wrapped an arm around Quaz to keep him from tearing the priestess apart. For now.

Pippa cocked her head. "Good?"

Amma gave her a single nod. "Why? And where am I?"

"You're in a country estate outside of Buckhead, and you're safe here, I swear it."

Though she was healed, Amma didn't feel very safe surrounded by the people who had handed her over to Cedric. But there was no Cedric to bring her to anymore, and the Righteous Sentries weren't converging. In fact, if they wanted to take her somewhere, leaving her weak and frazzled would have been much wiser. "What in the Abyss is going on?"

Pippa hesitated. "He says he needs you."

"Xander." Amma stood, only a little twinge left in her side. "You're still working for him?"

"'Course," Barrett said through a mouth full of fruit, chair falling flat as he leaned on the table. "Pay's way better, and I've never felt so strong."

"He's a blood mage, you know. Just like your so-called nemesis." Amma couldn't bare to say Damien's name.

"Your husband only paid us half." Kori clicked her tongue from her darkened corner. "Someone owes us."

There was a prickling in Amma's chest that made her want to lunge even surrounded by enemies, their flippancy enraging.

"They're not married," corrected Pippa, clasping her hands together. "And maybe she wasn't really as enthralled as I said she was…"

"She still stole and lost Pierce," murmured Kori.

The knight shrugged. "Well, no hard feelings, right?"

"Yes, hard feelings," Amma spat, turning on him and striding up to the table as Quaz wrapped himself around the back of her neck. When he rolled his eyes again, she struck out, knocking the apple from his hand. "Not least of all for calling me a stupid bitch."

Barrett looked after where the fruit splattered against the wall, mouth agog, then glared back at her. "Well, you were being a—"

"Don't you dare!" She slammed her hands on the table and bore down on him. "To speak of foolishness: all of you blindly followed the orders of a man who was forcing me into marriage and his bed."

"Oh, come off it." Barrett got to his feet, the chair clattering behind him as he towered over her. "He was a marquis. You were probably begging for it."

Even with the table between them, he could have flattened her with a single palm, but Amma didn't care. She brandished her dagger and had it under his chin in an instant. "I should slit your throat like the pig you are."

In a pall of sudden darkness, Kori appeared beside Amma, and metal pressed into her flesh. The bite of her dagger made Amma freeze, but she didn't pull away, and she didn't stop staring hatred into Barrett's stupid, fucking face.

"Now, now, children," Xander's voice called into the room, "do behave."

Amma refused to stand down. The metal came away from her neck, but she didn't flinch. Barrett's jaw worked, and then he finally stepped back, arms crossed with a pout like he wanted nothing more than to rip her limbs off.

"Darkness, who knew retaining non-imps would be so exhausting? Kitten, would you mind taking a little break from pointlessly threatening the help to come and have a more civilized conversation in the parlor?"

Amma stuffed her dagger into its holster, turning away from Barrett. She gave Kori a knowing look, eyes flicking to the dagger she carried, Amma's silver one from Faebarrow meant for tending to the liathau. Pippa was pressed against the counters looking horrified, and at the back of the room, Xander curled a finger then swept away.

Amma strode after him down a wide hall lit with arcane sconces and covered in gaudy wallpaper. Portraits stared down at her from ornate frames, but she recognized none of the subjects, they didn't resemble any of the Righteous Sentries, nor had any of Xander's white hair or tanned skin.

Crossing through a formal dining room with seating for twelve,

Amma maneuvered around the long table, over the brocade carpets, and past heavy draperies into a foyer with a winding staircase and massive entry doors. The place was opulent, but Amma had been to Xander's tower, and this was not it. "Where *are* we?"

Xander flicked his wrist, and a shadow imp curled itself around the handles to a set of double doors on the foyer's other end. "I believe the owners are called the Dewgrains or the Frostwheats or some such. We can ask them later for clarification if need be." He bade her entry with a slight bow at the doors.

Amma wished there were another option, but could only walk past him and into the lavish parlor. A fire was already burning there, crimson seating set around it, and she hesitated, her own clothes covered in dust from the catacombs. "The people who live here are letting you stay?"

"They've not got much of a choice, locked up in the basement."

Amma whipped around. "You're keeping them prisoner?"

With another gesture, the shadow imps closed the door behind Xander. "I know, I *know*, but the pious one convinced me not to kill them, so they're alive. For now."

Amma opened her mouth to tell him how awful he was, but the strength ran all out of her, concerned only with one thing. "Just tell me where you're keeping Damien."

"Me?" Xander poked his own chest with a pout. He'd changed out of the white jacket he'd been wearing in the catacombs, and was now clad in a silvery robe, one that fit him much better than when they'd first met, though she doubted this one belonged to him either. The set of blood-filled vials still hung from his neck, and she imagined that was the only thing he never took off. He wouldn't be powerless without them, but much less of a threat.

"Yes, you. And that Delphine woman. What are you two doing with him?" Quaz trilled angrily from her shoulder.

"No, no, kitten, you've got it all wrong. Well, mostly wrong. I do know where Bloodthorne is, but I'm not keeping him there."

"Oh, so it's a coincidence you and she showed up at the exact same time?"

"Not a coincidence, no—this was all very much arranged in a sort of clandestine, calculated…kerfuffle."

Amma snorted, pulling out her dagger again and stomping up to him, Quaz's little claws digging into her shoulder to hold on. "Quit speaking in circles, and just tell me why I'm here and Damien's not."

Xander actually held up his hands, taking a step back. Amma brandished the knife, arm steady, heartbeat in her ears. It was her third threat with it, but she would be happy to make it her first slice.

The blood mage's dark eyes flicked to the tip of her blade, tongue darting out to run over his bottom lip. "My, you've sure sharpened your claws, haven't you?"

Carefully, he brought the tip of his finger down onto the dagger's point, drawing his own blood. Amma realized a second too late, a shadow enveloping the weapon before she could pull back, and it was ripped away. She jumped after it as it was held aloft, but Xander only pulled the shadow up out of her reach.

"You're still a *delight* though!" He squealed with laughter, sending the weapon up onto a high shelf with the flick of his hand and striding deeper into the parlor. "But I suppose this whole thing does look sort of bad, and when have I been anything but? Where you're wrong is thinking that Delphine and I are in on anything together. If you believe either of us is capable of sharing, you are sorely mistaken."

Amma watched him roll his head on his shoulders as he stood behind a long couch, a frown creasing his face in disgust when he used the woman's name. Trusting Xander made little sense, but keeping Amma alive made even less. He had admitted to wanting the talisman that could only be fetched out with her death, yet she was standing there largely unscathed, better actually, thanks to his minions. Her only other option was to run across the plains back to Buckhead where she now knew Kaspar and possibly his parents were allied with the king and, in turn, Gilead. In the oddest reversal of fate, Xander was perhaps the only person close to an ally she had. "So, you're not working with Delphine?"

"I would rather have my cock blessed by that priestess out there." He gestured to the doors back into the rest of the house then snapped his fingers. In a poof of hazy blackness, a shadow imp appeared. "Dinner," he said to it before it vanished again.

"Then what, you were just following us?"

"No, I didn't need that bloody, little trick this time." He snorted and patted his chest. "It was all inspired by a hunch, really, and then confirmed from on high. Yvlcon was enlightening in a number of ways this year. First of all, your precious blood mage attacked me, and while the Grand Order has a zero-tolerance policy for violence between members at our gatherings, they let that slide, so I knew Bloodthorne was in deep with GOoD. But more impressively, watching Bloodthorne *walk away* from Delphine, while amusing, was a surprise I knew would return to stab him in the back. She was infuriated, and I wasn't the only one to take notice, so when I saw one of the members of the Grand Order pull her aside for a private chat, you bet your sweet, little ass I kept an eye on her after Yvlcon and did some sleuthing of my own."

Xander brought himself around the couch and sat, gesturing for Amma to join him with a deep smile. She crossed her arms and remained in her spot in the middle of the room.

"Suit yourself," he said, leaning back. "Anyway, Delphine was so obsessed with the chore she'd been given by GOoD, that she didn't notice yours truly following behind her on my own errand. She came out to this wretched, little place instead, so I schlepped my minions along too and set them up here while I tracked the witch, and let me tell you, hiding out on the side of that bloody mountain is boring after a few hours, nevermind multiple days, but I was committed, watching her watch out for the two of you. The only reprieve was those divine mages who went down a day or so earlier. I was supposed to follow along to do my own chore handed down from GOoD, but I couldn't because she just *kept sitting* until oops! There you were, hiking away from that city, finding the entrance, and disappearing inside."

Amma stepped closer to him, searching for the truth in his face. "Someone from the Grand Order sent Delphine after us? But the Grand Order sent Damien to the catacombs in the first place."

Xander cocked a white brow. "It isn't the first time a member's gone rogue. Probably isn't the hundredth. Never goes well for them, they always get taken out in the end, but it does explain why the organization gets so little done. Anyway, you know the rest, she enthralled him all over again, and then I saved your tail from becoming wyvern fodder, which you've yet to thank me for, I might add."

Amma grimaced. "Thanks."

"Don't lay it on so thick, kitten."

"I know you didn't save me out of the goodness of your heart, so what do you want?"

He winced at the ridiculous suggestion. "Well, finally you've got something completely right. I do sort of…I don't want to say *need*, but there exists a conundrum with which you may prove slightly useful in all of this."

Amma rubbed her temple, though she was reminded, however slightly, of Damien in that moment, and the corner of her mouth threatened to turn up until the knowledge that he wasn't there came crashing back down on her. "I just want Damien back, so tell me what you need me to do."

Behind her, the door opened, and a shadow imp carried in a tray with bowls and wine glasses.

"Just in time. Right now, kitten, I need you to join me for a meal while I regale you with a bit more exposition."

196

Amma moved to the oversized chair angled beside the couch Xander lounged across, planting herself down firmly and doing her best to show him she wasn't happy about it. Quaz hopped down to the chair's arm and sat as catlike as he could, but a little growl constantly emanated from him.

The shadow imp offered them bowls and goblets, and Amma took them—Xander would have killed her by now if that's what he wanted, and poison didn't seem like a method he would favor anyway. She watched the blood mage take a bite of the stew, a sip from his glass, and then settle back.

"Well?"

"Oh, right." He took another sip and tipped his head to the side. "The thing is, it's not easy to explain unless you really know what noxscura is, so, do you?"

"Sure—it's demon blood."

Xander groaned. "Well, yes, but also, no. Noxscura is *in* demon blood and so is in the blood of demon spawn, but unrefined. True noxscura and luxerna are the purest forms of arcana, the basis of all magic and life, destruction and creation." At this, both of his brows raised and he took another spoonful of soup to his lips, watching her intently.

She nodded as she held her bowl out to Quaz to let him chomp on a chunk of meat. Damien had called refined noxscura a destructive and deadly force, and he had told her that was what sat idly in the cup, offered to her by the fae king. Those same strands of silver were what ran through the air when the veil was thinned between the planes and imps were summoned. And they ran inside the head of her staff when last she conjured it.

"So," continued Xander after he saw, or didn't, what he wanted in her, "human and demon blood don't typically take to mixing: one is so dreadfully mundane and the other is liquid magic, so blood mages are rare, and even when we do exist, existence can be...challenging. Now, I *can* control my noxscura, mostly, but Bloodthorne has always sort of had a *problem* with it."

Amma didn't like how he said that, and she stuck out her bottom lip.

"Don't look at me like that, I know you've seen it. He's just so tentative about things, you know? Noxscura just wants to be used. In fact, it *needs* to be used. I tried to take a break once, and it refused to let me."

"A break?" She took in how he was draped over the couch, feet up, wine goblet in hand. "From what?"

"Being evil, of course." His nostrils flared. "And everything else too: studying, conquering, being the greatest danger in the known realm. It was right after my mother was imprisoned, and I was just, you know, *overwhelmed.* Anyway, I was a few moons into my corruption hiatus, and I was only a little restless, and the next thing I knew, I had *built an entire oasis out in the middle of the Wastes.*" Xander leaned forward, a hand on his chest, astonishment on his face.

Amma swallowed a spoonful of stew. "Okay?"

He threw himself backward, head lolling to the side. "There were birds and trees and this big, freshwater lake fed by a natural spring. Oh, and these desert foxes with massive ears and teeny, tiny paws who would come to drink and play with each other on the bank."

"That actually sounds pretty nice."

"It. Was. Awful!" He splayed a hand out, tongue falling from his mouth as he retched. "Deepest darkness, it made me *sick.* Anyway, that was the noxscura's doing, trying to get me off my ass and out into the realm to continue on my Abyssal crusade to carry out evil."

"It sounds to me like the noxscura wanted you to do good if—"

"Evil," he insisted, sitting up and grabbing his bowl again, pointing at her with the spoon. "Now listen, none of that's the point, I just want you to understand what noxscura is so you're most useful to me."

"Okay, so noxscura is a neutral, motivational force of magic. Got it."

Xander's eyes rolled even harder. "Well, it's also a bloody poison, so add that to the list. In its purest form, it kills just about everything it touches."

Amma nodded. "Not Delphine though."

"So, you know something about the vile nox-touched and how they're your peoples' fault?" He sneered at her, taking another bite, and at that Amma screwed up her face. "Oh, no, you don't. Shocking. A couple of decades back, the followers of one of your gods came into an entire cauldron of pure noxscura. No idea how, but if you're in power, you don't let something like that go to waste, so your most devout rounded up orphans, most from that little island Clarisseau, and dipped each one in just to see what would happen."

The way he said it was so flippant, but Amma's stomach twisted, and she passed her half-eaten bowl of stew off to Quaz.

"It killed almost all of them, of course, most right away, though some languished for a few weeks until, you know, bleck,"—he stuck his tongue out in mock death—"but eventually they had a few survivors, and as a result, nox-touched were born. And that's how the realm was blessed with Delphine Delacroix."

Amma frowned. "That's awful."

"I know!" Xander looked too wistful. "And it made her into such a bitch."

"I'm sure it would anyone." She didn't want to offer Delphine any sympathy, but it was in her nature, even as she grit her teeth.

"Not her sister." He sat forward, smirking. "Celeste also survived the big, horrific dunk as a child. The priests and mages trained her up to fight evil while beating her for every little mistake and making her watch all the other orphaned riffraff die agonizing, noxscura-filled deaths too, and she's...well, she's like you. She's *nice*." The word looked like it burned his tongue to say.

"Let me guess, you hate her."

"I find her absolutely unbearable." Xander blew out a breath. "But we were friendly once."

Amma fell back into her chair. "Oh, my gods, is there anyone you *don't* sleep with?"

"I'm not stupid enough to fuck someone who could have complete control over the arcane blood running through my veins, unlike *some* blood mages. I just sort of abducted Celeste once back when Delphine and Bloodthorne were a *thing* because I wanted to know what in the Abyss was going on. She told me everything, her little sob story of a life and how they ruined the cauldron of noxscura that turned them. Impressive stuff, honestly." Xander put his empty bowl down and picked his wine up again, looking into the cup and swirling it about. "But she was boring, and too much of a risk to have around, so once I got what I needed from her, I sent her home."

For the first time that evening, Xander wouldn't make eye contact with her, hesitating before taking another drink. "She beat you up, didn't she?"

Xander choked on his next swallow. "What? No!"

"Yes, she did. You wouldn't just send someone home. She kicked your ass and escaped." A tiny tingle of delight raised Amma's spirits.

"Well, she didn't make living with her easy, that's for certain. Celeste insisted on planting flowers and baking these tooth-achingly sweet foods, and she taught the shadow imps to *sing*. Do you have any idea how dreadful an entire choir of infernal cretins sounds? She didn't even have the decency to teach them anything in a minor key. It was so...uplifting." Xander shuddered. "And I *did* let her go, I just didn't exactly do it of my own volition."

Chuckling, Amma took a sip. "She manipulated you into doing it."

"Yes, all right, that's what I'm trying to tell you—it's how the damned nox-touched work!" Xander threw his arms up, totally overwhelmed, wine sloshing. "If they can wheedle themselves into you, which is just what she did, filling my head with ideas about…about goodness and all that nonsense, then they can make you do things you would never otherwise dare. It's utterly abominable." He fell back again in a huff, head tilted up at the ceiling. "Sometimes I do miss the little tea cakes though."

Cake sounded pretty good to Amma. "Would she help us?"

"Celeste? No, definitely not. Even if I knew where to find her, she's as susceptible to Delphine's charms as Damien is, albeit in a totally different way. Celeste's mind or her heart or whatever it is that makes you humans all soft is weak, and the right word from Delphine is all she'd need to turn back into a simpering minion. It's better for her to stay away."

"You're probably right; two nox-touched working in tandem would be worse than just one."

"Hmm? Oh, yes, of course." Xander's brow was knit as if lost in thought, but he shook it off. "Anyway, I assume Delphine waited to enthrall Bloodthorne after he was underground because of that thing those divine mages were summoning. Just being near it made me feel a little woozy myself." He touched his stomach at the memory. "I'm sure that only exacerbated his loose grip on his own noxscura—a problem he's clearly having because of *you*, I might add. Delphine's grip on his reins is probably tighter than it's ever been, so retrieving Bloodthorne will require beating him into submission first."

She didn't like the sound of that and frowned deeply.

"The pleasure in that will be all mine, but I can't deal with him *and* Delphine at once. If I'm too badly injured—not that I expect to be, but *if*—she might end up controlling my noxscura as well. I need her distracted, which is where you come in."

Amma blinked, remembering Damien's warning that Delphine would destroy her. "How exactly?"

"I don't know, pull her hair, scratch her, make fun of her outfit? Delphine's strength is in her puppetry, but you don't have the kind of noxscura the rest of us do living inside you. Even with that talisman, you're still entirely you somehow. If you get in close to her, there's not a lot she can do. I mean, she could stab you, I guess, but as long as she's distracted plunging in the knife, that's all I need to get Bloodthorne free."

She didn't intend to acknowledge that dig. "Are the Sentries coming too?"

"What's left of them." Amma waited then, and Xander clicked his tongue. "Look, I gave all of them the power to do more—that mage is the one who went and blew himself up with it. Those big, bell sleeves look fancy but they're quite flammable."

Amma wasn't sad to know the elven mage was dead, but she would have liked the additional assistance. "You know I have to ask—I thought you wanted Damien dead, so why do you want to do this at all?"

"I want Bloodthorne dead by *my* hand, and I mean actually dead, not just dead inside because his girlfriend is killing his will to live. But before any of that, I want him—and consequently you—to get my mother out of her prison in Eirengaard. You remember that? The supposed A-plot, as it were? The whole reason, presumably, the two of you ended up stuck together to begin with?"

Amma bit her lip. "Right, that whole thing." That, at least, answered the question she was too nervous to ask: what guaranteed her own safety in all this from Xander himself? Killing off Amma too early wouldn't help him free any demons Archibald had locked away, but if he made it look like someone else's doing, Damien might still be willing to help him. Well, she would just have to look out for herself then.

Xander grinned, and a yawn caught him. "But I do need sleep first if I'm going to get us all the way to that witch's lair and then be useful once we're there." He stood with a stretch then closed the short distance between them to loom over Amma. "Now, kitten, why don't you come and spend the night in my quarters, hmm?"

Amma smacked his hand away as it grazed her chin. "Ew, no!"

Xander's grin fell sharply off, and he scoffed, still trapping her there in the chair, a hand on each armrest. "But I thought we were getting on so well."

Quaz hissed, jumping onto the back of the chair.

"Not that well—never *that* well." Amma leaned back and lifted a foot, kicking him squarely in the chest.

Xander coughed, stumbling backward, but then he actually laughed. "Gods, if the two of you weren't just made for one another." He rubbed at the imprint her boot had left on his robe. "Do you *really* like Bloodthorne that much?"

Amma got to her feet, taking Quaz with her. "Yes, of course I do."

"Even though he's off with Delphine right now, probably doing unspeakable, earth-shattering things to her? This is the best revenge on Bloodthorne you could possibly ever get, you know, letting his rival fuck you silly."

"Gods, you're revolting," she spat. "I don't want to get *revenge* on Damien, I want to rescue him. I promised that I would protect him, and

201

I…" Amma squeezed Quaz tighter, heart hitching. "I didn't."

The quiet of the parlor pressed in on Amma, the distant ticking of the room's clock echoing into the emptiness. She had failed, but she would make it right.

"You are nice, but you're also very stupid, kitten." Xander's disappointment had no bearing, his voice like a fly buzzing around her head. "The fondness you have for him is sort of cute, but when he shows you who he really is—"

"He has." Amma set her jaw hard and glared at him. "All this talk of being evil and vengeance and who gets to kill who, it's ridiculous. You can do this for whatever reason you want, Xander, but I'm here because I love Damien." Tears pricked at her eyes, the truth slamming into her as the words burst out.

She'd known this truth, of course, for some time, so it was not the suddenness that drove fear into her heart with its admittance. Amma had resisted saying that she loved Damien for fear of the much more painful truth that blood mages could not return those feelings. She'd sliced through the thin veil of protection she'd hidden behind with the word, and then discovered something wonderful if shocking. Amma didn't want protection from whatever would come of loving Damien. It was simply true, and that was enough.

As Xander opened his mouth again to spit out something undoubtedly pithy and cold, she cut him off. "If you want to keep being caught in this miserable, heartless spiral, go ahead, but don't try to tell me I'm stupid or confused. Pretend not to understand all you want, but I've never been more sure of a thing in my life."

Xander's mouth hung open, eyes boring into her, but they were seeing the truth, and she didn't care. He looked, for a moment, like he might bite back, and then the blood mage just let out an exasperated sigh. "Fine! But it's your cage, kitten, and I hope the two of you are very happy in it."

CHAPTER 22
THERAPEUTIC PHLEBOTOMY

There was a gentle tapping at the side of Damien's face. Feather soft, the touch slowly roused him from a deep if not restorative sleep, but his eyes wouldn't fully open. He heard his name being called from far off, a hush of a voice eerily familiar, but he couldn't go to it. Not yet. Still sleepy. Just a few minutes more.

Then there was a sharp crack across his cheek, and Damien was thrust into the waking world. "Fuck."

"Darling, you're awake!" Delphine had a hot hand under his chin, pulling his bleary gaze to hers. "Oh, I'm so glad. It's been ages."

She was crouched before him, and she was *smiling*. That was always a bad sign as it meant she'd managed to get what it was she wanted. And usually what Delphine wanted was to cause Damien excruciating pain and misery.

Everything hurt. That wasn't rare for being in Delphine's presence, but none of it was the good kind of hurt. This was a deep, lethargic ache that made Damien want to go back to sleep for about a century. The tightness in his shoulders and pressure on his wrists told him she'd tied his arms behind his back, and of course she'd done it exactly right, he'd fucking taught her. As he shifted, a jolt of pain let him know she'd used ropes enchanted to suppress arcana. She always thought of everything.

203

But she had dropped her arcane manipulation of his noxscura, and his mind was clear enough to have negative thoughts about her. Every hateful curse flooded into his cloudy brain alongside a heaping dose of panic. He had to get away, had to stop her, had to kill her.

When Damien lunged, Delphine only pulled back an inch with a perturbed gasp. "Now, now," she said, shaking a finger at him, "I didn't give you back your mind to have you biting me. Not yet anyway."

The lurch had taken nearly all he had, and he was thankful to already be collapsed on the ground, back against a wall, legs splayed out. His head was too heavy to keep aloft, and even breathing was a challenge. All he could do was watch his bare chest rise and fall shallowly. When had his tunic come off? At least he still had his pants, but no armor from what he could see. His vision went in and out, black spots in his eyes.

Except they weren't just spots, and they weren't in his eyes.

"Get them off," he mumbled, rolling his head back.

"What, darling?" She was using that voice, the one that was too pleasant to be genuine.

"The leeches," he stressed, jaw going tight as he glared between strands of black, sweat-drenched hair. "Take. Them. Off." With each word, he knocked the back of his head against the wall for emphasis. He could barely feel it. Not good.

"You know I can't do that *and* have you in your own mind. It's one or the other, dear: anemia or enthrallment. But it does look like this one's full." Delphine slipped long fingers beneath the leech across his chest and pried its tiny jaws from his skin. He bit his lip as she ripped it away with a squelch, refusing to give her the satisfaction of a pained grunt. Blood splattered down his chest, the only solace that his magic wasn't also inside that nasty thing. The bite pulsed, and he could feel arcana ooze through his body toward it, intending to heal whenever it finally got there, but it was going to be a slow process.

Delphine held the parasite in the air between them, its faceless end wriggling in search of a vein to latch onto and suck the life out of. Her metallic irises watched the slimy thing with a sickening joy. "We'll be using this one," she said, and carefully placed it into a scarlet-colored box with delicate filigree carved into its top.

As she snapped the lid shut, she focused back on him, a cascade of black hair catching the light and shimmering on either side of a pointed face. "You're a much better guest than most. No asking where you are, why you're here, what's going to happen. It's a lovely change of pace." She ran a hand up his neck, and he jerked away with a growl. "Okay, big boy, take it down a notch."

Damien knew the answers to those questions already, more or less. He was in her home, because she wanted him there, and bad things were going to happen. The specifics didn't really matter because there wouldn't be any bargaining with her, there would only be escape, if he could figure out how. Again. *Fuck.*

And there were other questions he cared about far more, specifically, where was Amma? He'd managed to fend off Delphine's enchantment in the catacombs twice, not dropping her into the pit and shielding her from the wyvern's attack. He hoped he hadn't injured her when he threw her away from the ledge, but he expected her to be angry for that—an anger he would be glad to have. He'd welcome *anything* of Amma then just to know she was alive.

But if Amma were dead, Delphine would have already said something—she loved delivering her variety of good news. And if Amma were dead, Damien was certain he would feel it. The talisman would have been shucked out of her, for one, but more importantly, the world would feel empty. His desire to flee from Delphine would likely not even exist if Amma were not somewhere out there, alive. But there was no gaping hole in his chest, no pointlessness to living, so he knew she wasn't beyond reach.

"Now, what is this?" The pendant fell from Delphine's hand, hanging from its chain, ugly and jagged.

He'd forgotten about that. "Oh, the Grand Order's gonna be mad," Damien slurred. "Shoulda gone in the pit."

She cocked a black brow at the cloudy gem then her eyes flashed to him. "Don't lie to me." Sharp nails dug into his cheek as she squeezed his jaw. "I was commanded by The Order to retrieve this from you, and in return, I could do what I wanted with you for a long weekend, not that I intend to give you back. Now, what *is* it?"

Damien's mind worked though it was slow. She wasn't lying—that was her I-told-you-my-bit-and-now-I'm-annoyed-I'm-not-getting-the-answer-I-expect face. He snorted. They'd been pitted on opposite sides of the Dread. Shocking. "I dunno."

He expected another slap, but Delphine instead rubbed at the place she'd dug in on his cheek. "Well, doesn't matter. I got what I want, so they can have this." Whistling as she stood, a flutter of black wings dove down from one of the rafters high above. A wyvern, much smaller than the one she'd appeared on in the catacombs, hovered before her and took the pendant before flitting back off out of sight. Well, if Damien survived Delphine, GOoD would be next in line to sever his head.

Taking a calculated step away from him, she glanced back over her shoulder. Her dress clung to her curves and spilled behind her like oil, raven feathers woven into the train and a nest of thin straps running up her back so that her flesh was on display from neck to hip. It had been his favorite on her once upon a time, and she had always known to pull it out when things were...complicated between them. "You are wondering why you're here though, aren't you?"

He rolled the back of his head against the cool stone wall, senses clearing a bit more. "No, I'm really not."

"I was just so disappointed when we spoke at Yvlcon," she went on, gazing up into the high ceilings of the space. "You disregarded my offer as if it were some two-copper whore you bedded and not the solution to all of your problems."

"Whores are more virtuous than whatever your solutions might be."

She bared fangs like a wolf, then quickly recovered. "I understand your reluctance, but as I said, I know what you *need* now, what will finally show you that this is where you belong. Eventually, you'll understand what's best for you, but until then, I'd like your true reaction to the work I've done and the sacrifices I've made to help you."

The last time Delphine had tried to *help* him, he ended up with an unmendable scar across his face and a three-moon's-long recuperation in the darkest basement of Aszath Koth. "No thanks."

"You haven't even heard it yet," she snapped, then sucked in a breath and sauntered back to him with another terrifying smile. She wanted him to ask. She *needed* him to ask.

He *wasn't* going to ask.

"Did you redecorate?"

Delphine lowered herself before him with a quickness and gripped his face in both hands. "Darling," she said rottenly, "you are truly testing me."

She held him so hard he thought she might just snap his neck, but then her hand shifted to brush sweaty strands of hair from his eyes, trailing fingers over his scalp. Her touch was rarely so gentle, but then her fingers came back to trace along the scar she'd given him. Or rather, made him give himself. There was an awestruck marvel in her silver eyes as she studied her work, her desire for pain, at least for the moment, sated.

"I know what was missing before," she said, a dreamy lilt to her voice. "What will make you complete. In fact, I've already given it to you, and you don't even know it yet."

Damien was suddenly afraid to jerk away from her touch. "Fine.

What?"

With the kind of joy a madwoman might have when declaring the existence of only one, true god, Delphine grinned. "Fatherhood."

What little blood was left in Damien drained away, leaving him so frigid he couldn't even shiver, struck still there on the floor of her hall. "You,"—he swallowed, throat dry—"you've already given it to me?" Unable to look away from her metallic pupils for fear he might see some tiny creature with black hair and soulless eyes come toddling through one of the hall's archways, he could only hope he had misheard.

"Mmhmm." She tapped her fingertips along his jaw. "And I just know you're going to love them. Well, not *love*,"—at this, she laughed once, low and throaty—"but I've already explained to them that daddy's not capable of that."

"Them?" Damien's leaden mind attempted to do some mathematics, none of which made sense, not that it should have mattered since he was always so careful, faithfully casting infertility spells on himself *for this exact reason*. How she had kept *multiple* children a secret from him for so long, he had no idea—she could manipulate his blood, yes, but could she also manipulate his—dark gods, he hoped not. Regardless, he had avoided her for over a year after their final tryst; long enough to not know.

She was nodding, a whimsical look to her face that he supposed might have come with motherhood. *Fuck.*

"Why didn't you ever *say*?" Utterly disgusted, his mind ran with what he had to do. Maybe…maybe there was some way to abduct them away? Aszath Koth was well fortified enough to keep her out and keep them safe from her, if he could get them there. But how? He shook his head—whatever the plan, no child could ever be left in her care, of that he knew for certain. "How could I not know? Celeste didn't even send a message."

"Oh, Celeste doesn't know." The grin fell off her face at the mention of her sister. "We haven't spoken in moons."

"How could *she* not know?" Either Damien had lost all ability to count or he knew nothing about pregnancy, either possible in his anemic state.

"I made them after she left." Her voice had gone cold, eyes sharp, the normal flippancy she used to refer to her sister replaced with a callousness. "Honestly, they've been quite the good distraction in both of your steads, but they need a father, and you need a tether. Hence why you are here."

Damien squinted. "Need. So, I'm not…already?"

207

"Hmm?" Delphine pouted, and then she gasped. "Oh! You thought I meant an actual baby? One that we made? Like a little three-quarters-human, quarter-demon, half-nox-touched, half-nox-blooded abomination that came *out* of me? No, of course not!"

She laughed lighter, and relief flooded him so that he almost passed out again, eyes closing, head lolling back.

"Though now that you mention it."

Damien was yanked back into consciousness for a second, violent instance by Delphine's hand only this time it was between his legs. He retched, blinded by the pain.

"Guess you'll need your blood back for that to work." Delphine sighed dramatically. "Later then, when you're reasonable enough to come off the leeches. For now, I want you to meet the family."

Despite his exhaustion, Damien had no choice but to get to his feet if he wanted his cock to stay attached. He levied his back against the wall, and, thank the dark gods, she released him when he stood. There was a shove at his back, the last vestiges of his noxscura she kept under her will.

Still sluggish, he traipsed behind her, wrists bound at his back, muscles aching. There was a time when he would have looked forward to being in this position—not that he preferred submission, but there was no choice with Delphine, and what came after was worth it back then—but now there was only dread and panic in his gut, neither of which assisted in plotting an escape, and the anemia wasn't helping.

He had no blood to give up for arcana, not that it was his to use anyway. Magic was out, so running would unfortunately have to do again. The vastness of Delphine's home lent itself to many hiding spots but was difficult to traverse, especially with those miniature wyverns patrolling the halls and that bloody big one in the courtyard.

Damien took in the space as he went, a repurposed temple to one god or another. Delphine had liked the building's placement nestled into the woody outskirts of a village already on the verge of collapse. The deity had fallen out of fashion with Archibald's rule, so when she ran the priests off, they had little recourse to take the temple back. The surrounding town of Briarwyke was half-abandoned when he'd been to it last, but they provided for her, and in turn, she offered enough arcane assistance to keep the most necessary around.

The main floor was an open space with many beams overhead and high-up windows that would have allowed for quite a bit of sunlight if not for the ivy that had climbed all over the exterior of the temple. Damien squinted at the bright streams that managed to peek through. He could climb the columns that led up to them, the carvings along them good footholds, but even with the windows clear, he would need strength for that.

At the chamber's back, there was once an altar, a flat-topped block of amber citrine with wings carved into its base, but it had been augmented into a wide seat with a slab of marble at the back and velvety cushions. Damien swallowed, a flash of the things they'd done there in defiance of whatever god the place was meant to serve running through his mind, and for the moment he was grateful for the leeches.

But there was something else there, something new. A trench was dug out of the stone floor, running in a crescent shape before her altar-turned-throne. At least ten feet wide at its thickest spot, a bridge of the flooring remained in the center for direct access to her seat, and Delphine walked out onto it. Damien stopped short, not trusting his balance so near a ledge, but with a small gesture of Delphine's hand, he was manhandled by arcana right to the edge and forced to peer down.

The pit was only about ten or so feet deep, but that was more than enough to contain what it held. The perhaps twenty shadows inside were small, milling about slowly in the cramped space, bumping into one another and the walls, but then they seemed to sense the presences above. Falling still all at once, their heads tilted back, and a beam of patchy sunlight fell across their faces.

With squat features on round heads atop bodies that hadn't quite grown into their proportions, they looked almost like children, but there were hints of something else, something *wrong*, with each one: a significantly oversized ear, a jaw that jutted out too far, movement of an extra limb.

But most odd were the eyes. Like the color in Delphine's, they had that silver liquidity to them, only the children had no whites nor pupils, just overly large sockets filled with swirling masses of pure noxscura.

Damien's heart raced despite having little to pump, and he felt doubly woozy. "Where did they come from?"

"Out back," she said, gesturing haphazardly over her shoulder. If he remembered right, there had been a small graveyard at the temple's rear.

"Necromancy?"

"A little of this, a little of that." She lifted the scarlet box from before, tapping her nails on its sides absently. "*This* being orphan corpses, and *that* being imps. They're actually very well-behaved."

Dressed in tattered clothing with patches of wild hair and smudges on their faces, he could see now the odd ear and tail had come from imps, creatures also ruled by noxscura that he should never have taught

Delphine how to summon. They hadn't moved since looking up at the two of them, though it was difficult to tell exactly what they were looking at without pupils.

"I'm sure being completely under your will makes them very pliable."

"Actually, I messed them up a little, and they have freedom of mind, hence the playpen." Delphine opened the box, and Damien grunted—lucky, little bastards. She plucked the leech from inside and dangled it over the pit. "But they're very responsive to treats."

The reanimated children reacted then, eyes and mouths widening. Chapped lips pulled back to reveal impish fangs in two twisted rows as the lot crowded under where Delphine brandished the offering. Fat with blood and still wriggling, the leech was released, and there was a frenzy. The bodies dove into one another, the slimy parasite disappearing into the shadowed bottom of the pit as blood spurt upward. The mania ceased, and the silvery eyes turned up again, a few of the Abyssal children now donning smears of blood—Damien's blood—across their grave-dirt-smudged faces like a nest of malnourished vulture chicks.

Not much turned Damien's stomach, but bile rose in his throat. He took a step back, pushing against the arcana and shaking his head.

Delphine sauntered back to him and fit her arm around one of his, caught securely at his back still. As she leaned her head on his shoulder, the noxscura stiffened around him so that he couldn't move away. "Aren't they precious?"

Of course, she saw no irony in what she'd done. She had been just like them as a child, an experiment, treated worse than an animal. She'd killed those involved in her subjugation, a thing he'd admired her for, yet here she was, perpetuating more of the same and looking utterly enraptured by it. "What will you do with them?" he asked bleakly.

"Whatever I want. Sometimes they do tricks for me. Watch." She peeled another leech off his bicep, the snap of its jaws from his flesh making him wince, and then wiggled it over the pit. "Who loves mommy the most, hmm?"

There were hungry growls from below as they reached, clambering atop one another. Some tried to dig into the stone walls of the pit for leverage, but the best only a few could do was manage to stand atop a pile of the others until the ones on the bottom shucked them off. A slightly bigger one put the two advantages together, calloused and stubby fingers clawing highest.

"Oh, is it you? Yes, of course it is, my little monster." She dropped the leech right onto its face, and it fell, blinded, as another pounced.

210

The frenzy was shorter this time, and the blood left on the two could have been their own along with the leech's. "The rest of you," Delphine said so sharply it even made Damien snap to attention, "try harder next time."

With a coldness he knew intimately, Delphine swept away from the pit, arm still linked around his. He glanced back, and when they were far enough from the trench, it was like the creatures weren't even there. "Do you plan on letting them out?"

"Why would I do that?" She laughed lightly.

They were constantly at her feet trapped in that crescent-shaped pit, so it was a silly question, he supposed, but still. "They're your children," he said hesitantly. "They need...tending to."

"I just fed them, Damien, what more could they need? Are you suggesting I...I *touch* them?" She shivered. "No, they'll spoil. They're fine right where they are for now."

"They may decide otherwise on their own," he cautioned, not wanting to be around when they did.

"Oh, no, I don't think so. When they get close to the edge, I just remind the ones on the bottom that when the ones on the top make it out, they'll leave them behind, and then their whole plan implodes. It's quite a bit of fun to watch them get into fights with their tiny fists and pointy teeth. Their mangled parts mostly grow back in a week or so, but I would like it to be faster which is where their father comes in. Enough of your blood should help them heal quicker, and then, of course, they'll finally have some of you in them too, and I bet that makes them more manageable for me."

She'd brought him to a couch that was positioned in the middle of the temple, a few other chairs there too encircling a fire that crackled warmly. There was a snap, the pressure on his wrists released, and the noxscura pushed him forward. Hands free but body weak, he fell onto the sofa with a huff.

"It will probably take quite a bit more than that," she said, gesturing to the leeches still covering him. He went to pick one off, fingers feeble, but she slapped his hand away from it. "We'll have to do some trials to see how much is needed, but I bet you've learned all sorts of fun spells that can help our babies."

Damien groaned. Even with his arms free, he'd never felt so weak.

"Give it time, darling: they grow on you. Soon they'll be reliant on your blood to survive, and once you're regularly feeding them, the bond will come naturally."

Her figure standing before him was hazy in the shadowed sunlight, and his vision swam. Even when he created the talisman he hadn't felt as sapped as this. If she enthralled him again, he wasn't sure he would be able to break out of it at all.

"Won't it just be wonderful when we're a complete family?"

If he had the strength, he could have vomited at just the thought, but Damien had few options. He wasn't sure if he were smiling, but he was at least managing not to grimace. "Y-yes."

"Yes, what?"

"Yes, that would be…*wonderful*." He swallowed back the choleric taste in his mouth.

She took a step closer to him, her form still fuzzy. "And you can see how this helps you, my dear?"

Damien's head moved in a way that might have been a nod. "And how hard you've worked. You must be exhausted."

Delphine pressed a knee into the couch, leaning over him. "I really am," she said, voice low and throaty.

"Let me help you now." He feebly lifted a hand to her thigh.

She climbed up onto him, and he vaguely felt her weight on his lap. "Tell me how." Her face dipped close to his ear as she grabbed the back of his head and forced him to look on her.

"Combined, the two of us, our powers." Dry-throated, he grasped at the words, pulling out ones he knew she would like even if they made no sense. "Immortal. W-we could make them immortal. And have *so* many more. An entire army."

"Can we?" Delphine knocked her forehead to his, staring hard into his eyes. This close, he could see the noxscura moving in her irises, could practically feel it prod at him, keeping him awake yet sapping away his will.

"Together, we can do anything. Just like you always said."

She ground her hips against his. "That *is* what I always said."

Damien took a deep breath. "But these leeches. I need my blood to help you." He swallowed, sickened with himself but desperate. "With arcana and with…this."

A deep chuckle rose out of Delphine as she fell still. Even through his haze, he could see the adoration on her face, but then her smile sharpened. "Oh, Damien, your memory is quite good, but you must have forgotten,"—a shock of pain ran through his veins, flooding him with enthrallment—"I'm not that easy."

The ache intensified, and then it left, followed by the sounds and then his vision, and even his thoughts evaporated as Damien was plunged into darkness.

CHAPTER 23
THE ART OF WAR AND WIRE PULLING

Amma was glad to have avoided Briarwyke on her original journey to Aszath Koth. The sky, the earth, the trees were all grey as if the life had been burnt out of the place and not even in that pre-winter way where pines at least kept their color and red birds still flit. There was a different kind of stagnation there, an arcane one, and it clung like smoke in the air and ash on the ground.

Xander had translocated them to the village at the very foot of Ashrein Ridge that Delphine called home. Briarwyke was small, fallen into disrepair, and half-abandoned. The structures held themselves up with shoddy work, but there were villagers, toiling, trading, and going about their lives, not that anyone seemed very happy about it.

No one gave their group a second look as they strode through town, bizarre as they were. Xander led them, pristine in his white coat against the moody hues of the road. Amma had managed to deeply clean her rosy tunic and shine up the rest of her things while she failed to sleep the night before. Barrett gleamed and clanked in his plate, the annoying bastard, and Pippa's eyes nervously darted everywhere, a devotional symbol about her neck that she normally hid beneath her robes clasped in both hands. Kori was there one moment and then gone the next, perhaps the least conspicuous, but Amma always noticed when her black cloak reappeared, looking for her chance to reclaim her dagger.

"There is a non-zero chance Delphine felt the pulse of noxscura when we arrived." Xander frowned at the bend in the road ahead that led away from the village, brambles thick on either side.

Amma hurried to keep up with his long strides, Quaz curled up on her shoulder, out of his cat form and a spindly imp once again, another odd thing none of the villagers cared to gawk at. "Will she know it's you specifically?"

"There are few of us who would willingly come here." Xander ran his tongue over his teeth. "Then again, she may be so busy riding Bloodthorne that she doesn't notice."

When Xander waggled his brows, she only snorted. He had failed to convince her twice more to engage in increasingly debaucherous activities, citing the likelihood of Damien's disloyalty as grounds. Amma had not said, but while she promised Damien that she was his, his intentions hadn't been so clear. But even if he'd pledged the world to her, anything that happened under Delphine's control couldn't possibly be deemed betrayal, and Xander was disgusting for suggesting otherwise.

Thinking of that woman hurting Damien, though—it did things to Amma. She wrapped fingers around the hilt of her dagger, nails digging into her skin the way she'd like to dig the blade into Delphine Delacroix's heart. She would cut it out, show it to her, make her watch it slow to an agonizing stop before allowing her to finally die. Amma wasn't sure if cutting out someone's heart worked like that, but it did in her gruesome fantasies, and even knowing the sorrowful origin of the nox-touched didn't make her the least bit sorry for it.

The violent imaginings spurred Amma on, away from the village until they reached a wall of dried brambles that had woven themselves all over a fence. A sickly brown, thorns blanketed the tall bars, but the gate was laid open. The temples of most towns were typically accessible for pilgrims and worshipers, and that was clearly what this had been at one time, but the overgrowth was exceptionally uninviting, the way in narrow and prickly. Xander brought them to a stop just at its edge.

"As we discussed." The blood mage turned to Barrett, and the knight unsheathed his long sword. Amma backed herself away, but he had his light eyes set on the gate's opening.

Arcana crackled at the hilt of his sword, and he stormed inside with a monstrous war cry. So much for any kind of stealth. Bits of dried bramble broke off on his plate as he blindly swung and charged.

Xander closed his eyes and blew out a breath. "Idiot," he

murmured, and for once Amma completely agreed with him.

The blood mage eased himself between the tangles in the wider space the knight had made. Amma followed, Kori and Pippa on her heels. The front of the temple stood tall across from them, covered in more greying vines, and the walled yard went long in opposing directions. Barrett came to a stop in the middle of it, sword brandished, waiting. Wind whipped over the empty space, dead, gnarled trees giving up no sound, but the dried-out grasses hissed, and then a mass of black wings and leathery skin came swooping from around the corner of the temple.

Pippa and Amma pulled back behind the briars, Quaz's clawed hands wrapping around her neck. Kori disappeared completely, but Xander continued to just stand there, arms crossed, watching. The wyvern Delphine had ridden was fast and screeching. Barrett swung too soon, the moron, but then a burst of arcana pulsed off the sword's tip. The creature dodged the bulk of it, but its wing was nicked, and it rolled.

Barrett's victorious cry was nearly as loud as the pained scream of the beast as it lost height and skidded into the earth, kicking up brambles and carving long troughs in the dirt. The knight charged fearlessly, and Amma's eyes widened; for as much as she hated Barrett, she wouldn't have gone running at a wyvern like that. It was, of course, not in her to remember how she actually had stood her ground before the very same creature when she thought it would have saved Damien.

The wyvern slashed at Barrett, and the knight skillfully dodged, running his sword along the side of the beast, blood in its wake.

"Now, go," said Xander, and they fled across the open yard to the temple's front. It was a mad dash, Amma's blood pumping in her ears as they tripped up the steps and fell against the wide doors of the temple just in time to see the wyvern swooping back into the sky, blood raining down from it. It turned sharply and soared back down, talons first, and the knight was not so quick, clipped on his shoulder and sent to the dirt.

Pippa pushed herself out from below the overhang at the entry doors, but Xander dragged her back by the elbow. "You have a job," he barked, and Pippa relented though worry creased her brow.

"Over here." Kori had somehow fled ahead of them, and only a slip of her shadow gestured from around the corner before disappearing again.

Xander went first, and Amma followed, Pippa hesitating before taking up the rear as they clung to the wall while trying to avoid stray brambles to stay out of the wyvern's sight. Screeches and grunts echoed out in the yard, quieter when they passed around the corner and were hemmed in by the much closer fencing that ran along the wall. Kori was working with two bits of metal at the lock of a door, one likely used by priests when the temple functioned to tend the once-fruiting plants that grew over the gate there. With a pop and sizzle of arcana, the woman snorted a short laugh and swung open the door.

Amma went for the entrance, but Xander's spindly fingers dug into her shoulder. She pulled out of his grasp but waited as Kori went in first and Pippa was encouraged to follow. There was a plan, of course, one they had agreed to over an uncomfortable breakfast, but she was eager to find Damien.

The two women disappeared into the darkness of the temple as Xander and Amma stood on the threshold, eyes adjusting too slowly to see where they'd gone. Amma drummed fingers on her dagger's hilt, chewing her lip.

"If Delphine doesn't feel me coming through the noxscura in the air, she's going to feel your jitters vibrating through the earth. Relax."

"Can she do that?" Amma's head snapped to him.

"No." Xander rolled his eyes. "But you do need to calm down so you don't get yourself killed. Remember what we discussed: observe first, run through the options in your mind at least twice, and only then act if it's opportune. They're expendable; you're not."

Amma scoffed, crossing and uncrossing her arms, shifting from foot to foot. "As if you want me alive at the end of this."

She could actually hear the smile breaking out on Xander's lips. "We could only be so lucky. And remember to save your best plan for last that way you've got it when all else fails."

"I still don't understand that," she squinted into the darkness, eager to get on with it. "Why wouldn't I do the smartest thing right away?"

A yelp from inside appeared to be their cue, Xander striding in and giving her a wink. "Well, it's for drama's sake, kitten. Otherwise, what's the point of *anything*?"

Amma followed, hackles raised and even more annoyed with Xander than usual. They passed through a corridor filled with closed doors to its end, following the sound of screaming. The hall spilled into a round room that had once been used as a small library but was currently a battlefield.

Bats darted through the air, Pippa cowering in the room's center. She had her arms over her head as they scratched at her with every pass, blood already spattered all over the floor.

"Do something," Amma urged in a hiss, Quaz on her shoulder squealing in agreement as they stopped short before falling out into the fray.

"Then what are they for?" Xander gestured, and just as he did, there was a flicker in the shadowed corner of the room. Kori appeared, and a knife flew through the air, spearing a bat to the wall just beside the entry.

Amma gasped at the impaled creature, not actually a bat but a tiny wyvern, as it choked out its last breath and fell limp on the knife.

"You see?" said Xander as if it were obvious.

Kori had pulled open a flap on her cloak, two rows of minuscule daggers there, and began whipping them at the flying menaces, cutting them down through the air, some impaled against the books, others littering the floor with heads and wings shorn off. The creatures turned their attention on her, finally leaving Pippa alone, though the priestess had crumpled to the ground in a ball, covered in weeping scratches.

"Let's go." Xander strolled across the room, using a single spell to flick away one of the wyverns as the rest converged on Kori who was running low on daggers. "Up," he commanded to Pippa, the woman barely catching her breath.

There were only a few left, but there was a fluttering coming from somewhere down the hall, another flock on the way. Amma ran to the opposing wall and pulled out as many daggers as she could from the shelves, Quaz helping from her shoulder and wyvern parts dropping to the ground as they were freed. She slid the daggers across the room to Kori's feet then went to Pippa and pulled her up.

"I cannot stand this dawdling." Xander's hand was on her again, and he yanked her around a corner just as the second flock of wyverns passed by. Pippa was practically hyperventilating, falling into Amma and squashing her up against Xander in the cramped space. The blood mage grinned down at her, and she would have scoffed if Quaz didn't gnash his teeth instead, and then Amma ducked away.

Xander took a hold of Pippa's arms when she fell against him in a quivering mess. "Really, Pips, isn't your god more inspiring than this?"

The priestess took a breath, fingers going to the symbol around her neck and smearing blood on it. Behind her, there was an opening into a much larger chamber, brightness there. "Goddess," she corrected, looking up at Xander, eyes glistening, braided hair askew, robes torn.

"Sure, whatever." He nodded with something like sympathy, his knowing smirk almost convincing. "Remember, this is your chance to destroy a great evil."

Pippa's features went, well, not steely, but at least a little coppery, and Xander turned her to face the hall, giving her a shove out into the light.

Amma waited at Xander's side as the priestess eased deeper into the room beyond. "She's so scared."

"She'll be fine."

A shriek pierced through the air, and Amma lunged after, but Xander stopped her yet again. They watched as Pippa fell to the ground, convulsing, her bloodied arms covering her face, a crackling of blue light over her.

"Was that the plan?" Amma gestured wildly, remembering how the blood mage had told the priestess she would draw Delphine out with her divine magic, and that since she was her goddess's disciple, she would be untouchable.

"Yes. She's drawing Delphine's power, and the more distractions the witch has, the better for the both of us." Xander was uncorking one of the vials around his neck and pouring blood into his palm, slow and steady, watching it drip. "I laced the priestess's powers with enough noxscura to allow Delphine to manipulate her."

"You set her up?" Amma hissed.

Xander scoffed, recorking the vial. "I figured she'd be strong enough to attack, or weak enough to be enthralled and pull Delphine's power. Either way, she's helping. Now, shall we?"

Amma hesitated. Xander had abandoned each of the Sentries, twisting his original intentions—surely none of them expected to be where they were. What he actually had in store for Amma, she didn't know, but then she remembered Damien, and none of it mattered. They could all be gobbled up by flying squirrels, she didn't care, as long as she got him back.

Midday sun filtered into the main hall of the temple through high windows, a white glow over the sandy stones that made up the place, quartz running through and catching the light to shimmer like pink streams. So much brightness for what they'd found hidden within, but Delphine did no hiding. At the back of the room she sat up high on a wide throne, and beside her stood Damien.

Amma's heart hitched seeing him there, eyes boring straight ahead. Like the stone carvings on the pillars lining the worship space, he remained motionless when she entered the room—not even a quirk of a brow acknowledging she was there at all—yet her own heart broke at seeing him all over again. It had barely been a day, and the ache in her chest was tremendous, staggering, frightening, but as she looked for a recognition that didn't come, that ache was replaced with a wholly new fear that he might never be the person she knew again, the one she'd grown to love.

"Xander, what an unwelcome surprise," Delphine called, voice carrying joyfully over the collection of furniture surrounding a brazier in the hall's center. "Oh, and you brought that little harlot." Who did she think she was, Kaz?

Amma unsheathed her dagger, holding it so tightly the hilt bit into her hand, the urge to scream, to sprint across the temple and strike out like that idiot Barrett so strong she almost couldn't hold back. But Xander had told her that scheming was twice as important as striking, and he'd managed to stay alive this long despite being very murderable. She scanned the room's narrow length, its corners and crevasses, the stone pillars that climbed up to the ceiling along the walls, Delphine's throne, and the divot before it meant to protect her. It was a long way to go before she could sink her blade in, but it would be done.

"Delphie, doll, darling, dear,"—Xander's smile was so sharp, his canines bit at his bottom lip—"how *have* you been?"

"Great," she said flatly. "But you're not here for pleasantries, or you would have sent a viper first."

Behind them, Pippa groaned, and the priestess began to shuffle up to her feet. "Wretched evil..." she moaned out.

"Don't interrupt!" Delphine flicked a hand, blackness pulsing around it, and Pippa fell into another heap of convulsions covered in a painful-looking arcana.

"Well, I haven't come on a social call exactly." Xander clasped his hands behind his back and sauntered deeper into the hall, pausing at the couch. "Is this salamander leather?"

"Draekin actually." Her eyes were sharp, darting from Xander to Amma, but letting him come closer. "If you and Damien have gotten into another tiff, it'll have to wait. Come back later and get killed then, why don't you?"

"I don't intend to do that at all." Xander pulled his hands out from behind him, and a vast cloud of smoke billowed out from his blood-smeared palms, the temple plunged into obscurity.

Quaz's eyes blinked into light, and Amma darted toward one of the many columns lining the room, behind them a corridor that ran its length. Cover wouldn't be full, but it would be enough to be lost by Delphine for the moment. The emerald glow of Quaz's eyes reflected off the wall of clouds, guiding Amma to the first pillar of stone where she ducked behind it. Her heart pounded, a sound like thunder rumbling through the temple as there was a flash of blinding light, but the darkness remained, and Amma slipped herself around the column and shot over to the next and the next, sprinting closer to Delphine and to Damien.

The haziness began to fade then, and Amma gave Quaz's head a tap, flattening herself against a column. Unable to see, but hopefully hidden, she stared hard at the marble wall ahead of her and willed her breathing to quiet so she could listen.

"Darling," Delphine was saying, "take out the trash, will you?"

Amma heard the familiar sound of Damien's dagger leaving his bracer, and she gripped her own that much tighter. She worked up the courage and leaned around the pillar to see him striding away from Delphine as he casually cut into his palm, none of that overly-confident smirking he normally did when intending to run someone through. The crimson sword he rarely called up formed in his hand in place of the dagger, arcana swirling and solidifying around it, but there was no flicker of acknowledgment that he was striding toward Xander, his nemesis. No joy, no trepidation even, just the heartless carrying out of an order to attack. Delphine, however, looked absolutely delighted in her seat.

Xander tipped his head, rolled his shoulders, and collected another pool of blood. A weapon formed in his hand, but unlike mimicking metal, a long tendril snaked down to the ground, and he took a low stance.

Of course it was a whip. Amma rolled her eyes and pulled back behind the column. There were three more lining the wall in the direction of Delphine's chair, but running across the open space between them would reveal her, and Xander had told her to keep herself hidden until she was close enough to get right up on Delphine and attack, so she took a breath and waited.

There was a crack out in the temple and the sizzle of arcana against arcana. Amma gasped, peeking out again to see the blood mages falling into combat. Xander had struck out with the whip's length and Damien had apparently done little to avoid it, grunting and rolling a shoulder, but continuing forward. Xander looked quite pleased.

Damien struck out then, and the grin was wiped off of Xander's face just as quickly. He went to dodge, but a shadow appeared at his back and boxed him in. Pressing his willowy body into the haze, the sword slashed, cutting down his arm and spilling more blood than Xander was probably ever used to losing, planned or otherwise.

With a hiss, he ducked under Damien's arm and away from the shadow, putting space between the two. Scarlet spread out on his white coat and splattered as he went, but as it hit the temple floor, it crackled and blossomed into a new haze, more shadows filling the whole of the temple as he laughed.

Xander hadn't forgotten Amma, it seemed, giving her more cover, and she darted to the next pillar unseen. The shadows were doused quickly though, and Amma barely made it before sunlight broke through again.

"Stop that," Delphine called. "I want to watch."

The only thing she and the woman had in common besides their taste in men, Amma thought, glancing around the pillar to watch from a slightly different angle. Damien should have been angry, he should have been *anything*, but his eyes were dead.

He raised his crimson blade again, but Xander struck out with the whip. Focused only on his attack, Damien did nothing to block it, and the whip wrapped around his neck. He slashed at the tether, but magic sparked at the weapons' meeting and neither yielded. Xander yanked on the whip, wrapping excess around his forearm and knocking Damien off balance. Self-preservation finally won out, and the sword clattered away before vanishing as he brought hands to the cord around his throat, the blue veins filled with Delphine's control of him pulsing.

By Sestoth, Xander, don't kill him, Amma thought, watching Damien be pulled right up against the other blood mage. With a last yank, Xander flung his elbow forward and cracked Damien across the face, the sound making Amma inhale so sharply that Xander's eyes flicked right to her.

Xander's mouth moved, holding Damien right up against him, whispering in his ear. It could have been Chthonic or Key, Amma couldn't tell, but there was the slightest narrowing of Damien's eyes, and his hands came away from his neck.

The whip went lax at his throat, and Xander grinned. He opened his mouth to speak, but then Damien hauled his fist right into Xander's face, knocking him to the ground. Amma had no doubt, whatever he said, the punch was absolutely deserved. From his spot on the ground, Xander swept his blood-soaked arm over the stone floor. Crimson crawled away from him, and a dozen shadow imps popped up into life.

Like a finger running up Amma's spine, a feathery touch made her whirl around, but no one was behind her. A deep dread ran through her veins as her heart was chased up into her throat.

That had been Delphine's magic prodding at Amma's back, and though it hadn't been able to compel her, she'd been discovered. Amma was meant to be closer before attacking, she knew that. She glanced to her right, noting Pippa far back at the temple's entrance still being tortured under arcana. To her left there were two more columns to hide behind, impossible to reach without being seen, thorny brambles twisting down one of them from the windows above making it doubly dangerous.

No other choice, Amma stepped out from around the pillar to face Delphine.

"Oh, there you are." Delphine twisted lazily toward her, legs crossed, unconcerned.

But Delphine had no control over Amma, and so she sprinted, knife brandished.

The woman's eyes flashed, and she snapped. A glint of arcana bolted through the air, and Xander's shadow imps popped up just before Amma. Even without features, the amorphous blobs of haze looked confused, but only for a moment before their rounded edges turned pointy and menacing.

Amma slashed through the first creature, refusing to stop. The shadows only dispersed around her blade, but she could see through to Delphine still seated on her throne, amused. The shadows reconvened, blocking her, and claws dug into her arms. Amma grit her teeth and slashed again, this time cutting through the parts of the imp it had made corporeal to grab her. Something like blood spilled out of it, and it hissed, releasing her. But there were more, and her wielding hand was twisted against her back. She kicked through a pall of smoke, nothing there, and rammed her head backward, connecting with only more haze.

"Xander," she shouted, "make them solid or call them off!"

"They're not mine to control any—" Xander's shout was cut off with a grunt, and Amma knew he would be no use. The imps were Delphine's.

But Quaz wasn't. He propelled himself off Amma's shoulder, and his manic screeches filled the air as the pressure on Amma's arms was released. She stumbled away from the cloud of imps and growing carnage. That bloody, black sludge Amma had cut out of one of them was flying everywhere. Quaz was but a blur of red amongst the haze, somehow tearing through shadow imp after shadow imp as they converged until it was only his diminutive form left, breathing hard and covered in infernal goo.

Elated, Amma almost went to him, but a shock of arcana overcame the imp, and he rose up without the use of his wings.

"Quaz!" Amma reached out, but the imp was dragged through the air, mimicking the flick of Delphine's hand, and then the magic around him dispersed, and he fell into the divot at Delphine's feet. Amma could not see into the pit where he had landed, but Quaz had wings, and once he recovered, he would fly out, she was sure.

Nothing left between them, Amma ran again, and Delphine actually stood from her chair, the amusement struck from her face. More shadow imps blocked the path, and Amma skidded to a stop— these were the last of the ones Xander summoned, but there was nothing to help her if she got too close, her dagger mostly useless against their arcana. She needed to fight magic with magic.

Amma sheathed her weapon on her thigh and turned back, running for the pillars.

"Kitten, what are you doing? You're meant to stab her!" Xander choked out, but despite that he was clearly in pain, it told Amma he was still alive, both fortunate and not.

Amma reached the column covered in tangled briars and grabbed the lowest of the dried-out tendrils. Thorns pierced her fingers and palms, and arcana flooded out of her. Glass burst overhead as the vines came to life, trailing over the ceiling rafters and shooting downward, finding the imps and strangling them until they exploded into nothingness. Amma groaned as she felt her energy drain away, but it didn't matter as she looked back over her shoulder, watching the greenery snake out of every crevasse in the temple and shoot toward Delphine.

The woman's face blanched as the vines converged, and she jumped up onto her throne as if standing on the seat would be enough to get away from them. Amma grinned, sweat on her brow. If she was meant to stab her, she would just have to do it her way.

But then Delphine's face took on a stark coldness, and she screamed as she ripped both of her hands through the air. The struggle between the blood mages stopped, and Damien turned from Xander as if he weren't there at all, striding back across the temple. Amma felt the magic freeze in her veins, trapped under Damien's dead gaze, absolutely no recognition it was her he marched toward with ill intent. It had been so long since she'd been afraid of him, if she ever really had been, but now?

She whispered his name, stumbling away from the pillar. The blood mage said nothing, his strides long and fast, but then he stopped short, slipping backward.

Xander was there, the whip doubled over in his hands and brought over Damien's head. In a choke hold, Damien was dragged back against Xander. "Oh, no, you're not ignoring me for her *again*," he groused, white hair wild as he struggled to hold the blood mage back. Damien's lifeless eyes remained trained right on Amma as if Xander were not even there.

"Enough!" Delphine shouted, and Xander and Damien were thrown apart by a burst of arcana that pulsed so strongly it cracked the stone floor. The men splayed out away from one another, and Xander spat blood as he tried to stand, slipping in the gore already there. "Did you forget that your injuries give me control?" Delphine ripped a hand downward from her spot high on her throne, and Xander groaned, a bolt of arcana running over him and pressing him into the ground.

Amma was woozy, so much arcana drained from her, but she still had her knife, unsheathing it and sprinting once again. With everything she had, she charged the woman, so close, and then she was rent right off her feet.

Damien had her by the arm, yanked backward painfully. Amma raised her free arm with the dagger, then gasped, quickly resheathing it on her thigh. "No, it's *me*," she cried, but Damien didn't give her a second glance, dragging her toward where Quaz had fallen.

Amma's feet scuffed as she fought against him, but arcana that she had so recently delighted in wrapped once again around her limbs, forcing her to stand before him, that divot at her back. Amma was dangled backward, just like before, and then she looked over her shoulder.

CHAPTER 24
REVENGE-SEEKING BEHAVIOR AND ITS CONSEQUENCES

Forty eyes blinked up at Amma on faces smeared with dirt and, if she wasn't mistaken—and she'd seen enough of it to know— blood. Quaz's blood, most likely, since he'd fallen into the divot that she was now teetering on the edge of. Damien bared down on her, Delphine willing him on from atop her throne surrounded by thorns.

"Well, do it already!" Delphine's voice was tight as she settled herself back down in her seat and eased her skirts around her. Lips twisted into a pout, she clasped her hands in her lap and waited, but Damien's grip on Amma's arm loosened.

Amma ripped her head back toward Damien. He *had* to recognize her, even with that deadened look, those violet eyes that said nothing, the tiny cuts and bruises on his cheek that weren't healing like she knew they would if he were fully in control. She threw her free hand around the back of his head, unable to pull him closer, but she could touch him. It didn't need to be harsh, she didn't need to dig claws into his neck or tug at his hair, she just needed to make contact.

"Bloodthorne, don't drop her!" Xander's sputtering voice came from across the temple's hall. It was a surprise to all of them, even Damien's brows twitching at the blood mage advocating for her life. "Think of the talisman—it would be such a waste!"

Amma groaned in the back of her throat.

But Damien tugged her away from the pit and the hungry mouths inside. Amma staggered again, and there was a brush over her thigh followed by the cold bite of metal against her throat.

Amma's voice caught at the sting of her own blade pressed to her skin. Her body wanted to flee though it was held impossibly tight under his grip, and her own hand on him shuddered and pulled back.

Delphine tutted. "Oh, by all the ridiculous gods, who cares how you do it, just *do it*. I want to see her blood spill, darling, one way or another." There was a crackle of violet in Delphine's hand, and arcana sizzled through the air.

Damien's grip on her arm tightened, but the blade didn't move, and she could just see its delicate filigree with the flick of her gaze downward. At least if she were going to die, it would be to something so pretty, the tiniest consolation. Amma met his eyes again, dead as they were, and gave her head a shake.

"No, Bloodthorne, not like this," Xander droned, the sounds of him struggling to stand filling the chamber. "Remember, we don't like messy things. Bring her back to my place first, and we'll sort out the details there." With a hazy flash and the wave of Xander's hand, a shadow imp materialized and swooped over their heads toward Delphine.

There was a twitch of recognition in Damien's face, a narrowing of eyes and a curl to his lip, that cruel look he'd had so long ago when they first met reemerging.

"Don't listen to him," Delphine snapped, waving the ball of arcana she held and snuffing the imp right out of existence. "Xander has *never* had your best interests at heart. Just kill the harlot and be done with it already."

Another twitch on his face, fingers digging into Amma's arm as she held her breath, afraid if she moved, she might accidentally do the job for them all.

Xander had made it to his feet, and with a flourish, he called up two more imps. "Damien," he said, the name nothing short of a demand, "drop her, and come here."

At that, pressure was taken off Amma's neck, and she sucked in a breath.

Delphine gasped, jumping to her feet. "Damien, no, you slit her throat right now and come over *here*." More erratically, the woman cast on the imps, striking down one while the other maneuvered around Damien and Amma, getting much closer before it too disappeared under Delphine's magic.

The blood mage's brow creased, eyes darting to the ground. The laxness to his features was retreating, cruelty replaced with confusion.

"Damien," Amma whispered, and his gaze snapped back up to hers, the knife still hovering between them. She carefully reached a hand up to feel the stickiness of her own blood on her neck that had been brought up by the blade.

Xander whistled sharply as he stepped nearer, drawing Damien's actual gaze. He injected his voice with a lightness though he struggled to breathe. "Over here, boy, come on! Come to Shadowhart, you know you want to."

Delphine screeched, her arcana arcing over them to make Xander convulse under a strike. She strode from her throne, crossing the bridge over the pit, and cleared her throat, trying to mimic Xander's sweetness. "Now, dearest, if you come to Delphine, you might get a treat!" Her dress caught on a thorn and she grunted, ripping it away. "Just cut the bitch already."

Amma rubbed her bloodied fingers together. She bled so infrequently, yet Damien constantly drew his own to cast. There were no plants close enough for Amma to call on for help, no imp left to assist her, there was only Damien and blood and...and the talisman.

A memory bloomed into her mind, a tree with golden tendrils reaching inside her, wrapping around the foreign stone, intending to sever her connection to it and to him. Amma had chosen to keep it.

That's my blood in there now too. That was what Damien had said in Tarfail Quag when he'd not wanted the swamp to get a taste for her, haughty, arrogant, and absolutely right.

Arcana shot over their heads as the blood mage and nox-touched traded spells, still calling to Damien to command him, though their focus even as each crept closer, seemed to be on one another and who might triumph. Damien's face contorted, struggling, eyes closed, completely overwhelmed.

"*Sanguinisui,*" Amma whispered, taking her bloodied fingers and pressing them gently to a cut on his cheek, "wake up."

Damien's eyes shot open, the lifelessness gone. They filled with everything at once, fear, anger, shock, elation, lost one moment and then found, finally landing on a softness that made Amma's heart swell. Her name was on his lips, but full of adoration as the blue-black veins receded from his skin.

"I wouldn't," he said, the words breaking in his throat as he lowered the dagger. "Never."

"I know." Amma clung to him and pulled him close.

The air sizzled, a frigid jolt running between the two. Delphine strode right up to them, her hands alight with arcana. "I said, kill her," she snapped, and the veins along Damien's skin pulsed anew, his eyes flashing with an anger Amma had never seen before. The dagger gleamed, brilliant as it slashed through the air too quickly for Amma to avoid. He would never, he had just said, and yet.

Amma's hand went to her neck, then slid to her chest, but there was no blood and no hilt. Her gaze fell to Damien's outstretched arm, taut with the strike he had just made.

Delphine sucked in a breath, metallic eyes falling to her chest where Amma's dagger had finally found its target by Damien's hand. Blood didn't seep out of the wound, not at first, as if it were as stunned as she. Damien dragged Amma up against him as the woman's magic fizzled, arms falling lax at her sides. She stumbled a step backward and then another.

"How could you?" There was a shakiness to her voice, all of the certainty wrung out of it, eyes still transfixed on the delicate hilt. Wetness blossomed away from the wound. "But, darling," she managed weakly, "I only wanted to help."

"Perhaps you finally will," said Damien, gesturing to the ground.

A small hand poked up from the trough and wrapped around her ankle. She screeched as if she'd been burned, blood bubbling up out of her mouth. As she kicked at it, there was another hand that gripped her shin.

Silvery eyes crested the pit's edge, staring up adoringly as they climbed. The woman flailed, but there were more little hands working together to cling on, tiny fingers sticky with dirt and blood clutching at the ripped train of her dress, and Delphine plunged backward. Her shrieking howls filled the desecrated temple, layered over the horrific sounds of tearing flesh and gnashing teeth.

Damien and Amma pulled away from the pit, the noises more than enough to tell them what was happening within. When the screaming and chewing died away, they stood in the silence, arms around each other, and then he turned to her. "Deepest darkness, Amma, please forgive me."

"There's nothing to forgive," she said, pressing her lips to his.

"Finally!" A hand slapped down on Amma's back, Xander's voice right in her ear. The blood mage pushed himself between the two, an arm swung up and over Damien's shoulders as he tugged them away from one another and up against him. "Look at the three of us, eh? Back together again as the dark gods intended."

"Fuck off, Xander." Damien slammed an elbow into his chest, pulling Amma away from him.

"But I *just* saved you," Xander whined, rubbing the spot and looking significantly worse for wear. "And her too, technically."

"No, she did," Damien said, dropping his own dagger into his free hand and brandishing it at the other blood mage.

"He helped," Amma cut in quickly, seeing the tremble to Damien's hand. The cuts on his face were still unhealed, and she could feel a weakness in him as he clung to her. He was in no place to fight, even with Xander so spent himself, the risk too great. "He brought me and the Righteous Sentries here to rescue you from Delphine."

Damien's teeth were clenched, eyes boring into Xander, but he flipped his dagger around.

Xander brushed hands down his blood-spattered coat and took a deep breath. "And I was much kinder to your kitten than she deserved." He sauntered around them for the pit and leaned over the edge.

Damien looked like he wanted to kick him in, but remained at Amma's side, hugging her to him.

"What a spectacular way to go." Xander clicked his tongue. "Looks like they ate her, and then died off themselves. Understandable, she was essentially made up of poison, but what were those things?"

"Abominations," said Damien, swallowing. "She resurrected the dead with noxscura, mixed them with imps. When she died they must have lost whatever magic she'd given them."

"Dreadfully poetic." Xander spun back to them with a sickening grin. "Oh, and speaking of minions."

Pippa was staggering toward them from across the temple. Delphine's spell had worn off of her too, but the priestess looked exhausted.

With more vigor, Xander met her in the hall's center and dropped himself into a chair. "Fancy a little healing, Pips?"

The priestess tended to Xander first, working sluggishly but not sapped of her abilities. With a little tugging, Amma convinced Damien to join them, pulling him down onto the sofa. He landed in a heap then dug a hand down the back of his tunic, wincing and pulling out a long, black, wriggling thing. "Fucking leeches," he groused and flung it across the temple where it splatted into a bloody mess on the stone floor.

Amma shifted up onto her knees beside him and yanked at his neckline. "Oh, gods, are there any more?"

Damien chuckled as she shoved her arm down between his tunic and back. "Ah, maybe you can check me more thoroughly later."

"Oh, right." She sat back, feeling her cheeks heat up, but still ran hands over his face and through his hair. "I just want to make sure you're all right. I mean, I know you're not all right, but I…well, are you all right?"

"Now?" He took her hands. "Yes."

Xander scoffed from across the fire, sitting forward with a quickness and giving Pippa a fright. "Please, spare us, we're recuperating here, not attempting to induce vomiting."

Damien ignored him, pulling her closer, breath still shallow. "Amma, I need to…we should have a…a discussion." The warm squeeze of his hands on her was reassuring, but her heart still shuddered. Something was wrong, and he was having trouble finding the words.

Pippa's presence lingered nearby. "You're hurt," she said when they glanced at her. "I can help."

Warily, Damien allowed her to touch him, but he looked the exact opposite of happy about it. As the priestess leaned down, the symbol she wore around her neck fell out of her robes, and when Damien eyed it, that unhappiness was replaced with curiosity. He grabbed the bit of metal and pulled it close to his face, ignoring how he knocked Pippa off balance, and then flipped it over to look on it upside down. "What is this?" he snapped.

"It was my great-great grandmother's," she said, a shake to her voice. "We've always been healers, all of the women in my family, blessed by the goddess."

"This is one of your god's symbols?" He thrust it back at her.

Pippa took it and stepped away as she flipped it right side up again. "Like this it is. For Isldrah."

Damien wiped a hand over his face and sat back. "She couldn't have been a priestess," he whispered to himself, staring off at the far wall of the temple.

"Um, it's okay," Amma said to Pippa as confused tears sprung to the woman's eyes, "he's just going through some stuff."

Xander slapped hands onto his thighs as he stood. "If you're quite finished, shouldn't we be heading to Eirengaard now?"

Of course that was what he wanted—Xander hadn't yet given up on getting Damien's help despite that he clearly wasn't going to get it.

"You have a way to get there?"

Or maybe he was.

From her spot on the sofa, Amma could only watch Damien as he stood, staring down the other blood mage, waiting for an answer. Pippa's touch made her stiffen, a healing spell making her heart race even more than Damien's words. Freeing the demons trapped in Eirengaard meant a whole heap of problems, but amongst them was still her death if she didn't purge the talisman herself.

Xander felt around in his pockets. "I'm only carrying empty stones right now, but I'm sure one of us has been there before, yes? With a day or two, I can craft a new translocation stone, and in the meantime, we can just sleep in this place, and—"

"I'm not spending another moment here." Damien waved a hand and traipsed across the temple to its head. He ripped through the cushions on the seat and found his pouch, digging through it as he carried it back. When he pulled out two small slips of parchment, he gestured for Amma to come to him, and when she did, he held one in each hand. "I have been selfishly carrying this on me since Yvlcon. This will take you to the Gloomweald. The elves will remember you, they will keep you safe, and they will escort you home. I should have given it to you right away, but I just could not bear—" He swallowed back what he was saying and shook his head. "The pendant is gone, and I failed in the task I was given by the Grand Order. They will not let that stand, and I suspect they will have an eye on Eirengaard during the eclipse for whatever it is Archibald and the others are up to, but that must be stopped. You should not pay for my failure. Faebarrow is far enough from Eirengaard to avoid whatever may happen there, and it is too far for me to call on that talisman inside you in the event that I..." Damien was staring at her hard, but his mouth seemed incapable of saying the words. "Amma, I just want you to have a choice."

She gently took the parchment he was thrusting at her. Warm arcana thrummed through it, and for a moment she felt home in her hands, the comfort of her bed, the laughter of her friends, the faces of her parents. "You won't come with me," she said, not a question. She nodded at the other parchment he held. "And what about that one?"

"This will take us to danger."

"Us," she said and tore the bit of parchment that led to the Gloomweald in two, letting the pieces fall to the floor. "That's what I choose."

Damien's face fought a smile, eyes still trained on hers. That was fine—she would be happy enough for the both of them until he realized it was the right choice.

"Touching and disgusting." Xander dragged himself over to them and swiped the remaining parchment from Damien's hand. "This goes to Eirengaard then?"

"Nearby," groused Damien, his affectionate look turning sour. "But we're not laying waste to the city and overthrowing it or whatever first thing, all right?"

"Obviously," said Xander, eyeing Amma, "she's got to be offed first. I have a plan for that, by the way."

Damien cut his hand through the air. "We're not doing that at all. Listen, when we get to where that takes us, I have things to do. You can fuck off to Eirengaard while I take care of this,"—he gestured to Amma, and she wasn't exactly sure what to do with that—"and while you're in the capital, you can find out what in the Abyss Archibald and his *chosen* are up to. We've only got, what, three days until the eclipse? We need to know what that king has planned before we do anything else."

"You mean all that unpleasantness in the catacombs? I just want to free Birzuma—I don't give a damn about whatever silly antics the crown is up to."

"You ought to care since it's not only standing in the way, but will likely lead to all of our demises if that thing is released."

Xander yawned. "Well, I need a big nap first."

"One night to recuperate." Damien held up a finger. "Then you go ahead to Eirengaard, do some reconnaissance, and we'll reconvene in two days. Agreed?"

"How do I know you won't kick me into another portal and run off again?"

"You don't," Damien said flatly, "all you have is my word."

"That shouldn't really mean anything to me."

"Shouldn't it?"

Xander clicked his tongue. "You really care about that creepy void thing, don't you?" When Damien nodded, he heaved a sigh. "Fine. Come on, Pips, you'll love this—Bloodthorne thinks he's going to *save* the realm and not destroy it."

The four traipsed back through the temple the way they'd come, finding Kori still catching her breath up against a wall surrounded by at least a hundred miniature wyvern corpses. She was battered and bruised, too tired to even glare at the rest of them when they showed up, but Pippa took her hand, healed her as best she could, and the five returned to the courtyard.

It was silent on the grass as they carefully went around the corner of the building to find the corpse of a much larger wyvern. The black, leathery body had a long gash up its side, and lying beside it was Barrett, a similar gash up his own. Neither moved.

"Lost another one," Xander muttered. "Pity."

Kori groaned, stepping away from the rest of them. She unsheathed the dagger strapped to her thigh and threw it to the ground so it pierced the dirt at Amma's feet. "I'm not getting paid enough for this shit." She darted into a shadow, and then she was gone.

Amma just as quickly retrieved her original weapon, its heft and shape familiar and comforting in hand.

"Or rather two," said Xander. "What say you, Pips? Devastated the meaty one's dead too? Remember what we discussed, what you're carrying for me, what it's meant to do."

The priestess stared out at the fallen knight and only sighed. "I didn't really like him all that much, to be honest."

Pleased, Xander pulled out his vial and let a single drop of blood fall to the parchment he'd taken from Damien. It spread out over the small scroll, and then it was alight with magic. Xander dropped it to the ground, and it projected a shimmer of silvery light that made the world beyond it change, no longer displaying the courtyard wall and dying brambles, but trees and fields and a well-worn pathway cutting between hills.

Amma's hand was taken up by Damien's, and he squeezed it. "For the record," he said grimly, "I don't think I've ever liked anything less than doing this with you, Shadowhart."

Xander chuckled and backed through the portal, gesturing for them all to follow. "Oh, I'm sure you can think of *something* worse."

CHAPTER 25
THE SUBTLE MAGIC OF THE RIGHT WORDS

T his. This is significantly worse." Damien's arms were crossed tightly over his chest as he glared at the small room and the single bed therein. It would have been fine if it were just Amma—amazing even—but he had no interest in sleeping in the same cramped quarters with Xander and his priestess minion.

Of course, Damien never had any intention of bringing Xander there at all, there was just no getting away from the other blood mage. He'd not even been sure he would ever use the translocation scroll he'd stolen from the storage closet at Yvlcon.

But Orrinshire was, indeed, a *teeny, tiny, little village* as the vampire dame Lycoris had said, and it had only a single inn. As a popular resting point before one entered Eirengaard proper half a day's travel northward, there was just the one room available.

They had shared an awkward meal, during which Damien and Amma explained everything they knew about E'nloc to Xander and Pippa, one of whom listened intently while the other did exactly as expected and rolled his eyes every chance he got. Damien then insisted Amma sleep, intending to stay up and keep an eye on the other blood mage. She, of course, would have none of that, and they came to an agreement that he would wake her in a few hours so that they could take turns recuperating. This convinced Xander into doing the same with Pippa, and Damien was eventually left staring across a dark bed chamber into Xander's eyes once the rest of the tavern had fallen quiet.

They sat there for hours, glaring through the shadows at one another until Xander finally broke the silence. "You're not going to do it, are you?" He gestured in the dark to Amma's sleeping form but kept his voice low.

She was curled up on the ground next to Damien as he leaned against the wall, a hand on her head just to be sure she was there. He didn't answer because they both knew the truth already: he wasn't going to kill her, and, really, had that ever been the plan?

"Well, you were successful in tricking her at least," Xander said, covering up a yawn. "She's completely enamored of you, scar and all, the poor, stupid thing, and probably thinks you actually love her back."

Damien's fingers curled into her hair, and she moved slightly beneath his hand.

His features were obscured, but in the dark, Xander's voice changed, the biting antagonism falling away. "Do you...do you really believe it's possible?"

"I want to," Damien told him, and for once did not expect a pithy remark back.

Xander woke Pippa then, grumbling about being exhausted. Though Damien's eyelids were heavy, there was one more thing he needed to do. When he was sure Xander was actually asleep, he went into his pouch and pulled out the Lux Codex translations and notes he'd cobbled together, passing a sheet to Pippa.

"You're still in your goddess's good graces, yes?" he whispered.

She shrugged. "I think so."

"Can you imbue a weapon with this spell?"

The woman squinted in the dark, moving the parchment so that moonlight fell over the words. As she read them, her brows lifted just as he expected they would, and then her eyes found his. "Won't this kill—"

"Can you do it?"

When she nodded, he glanced down at Amma's sleeping form. She hadn't removed any of her clothing or belongings to sleep, but she was curled up on her side so that it was easy for him to slide her dagger from the holster on her thigh. She barely stirred—he supposed he learned a little something extra from her.

A few hours later when the spell was done and the dagger replaced, he woke Amma, and she allowed him to sleep until well into the next morning. Xander tarried for far too long when he woke, and it was midday before he was finally ready to leave. Damien and Amma walked the two to the edge of town, and Xander reiterated the entire time that he expected Damien to come find him in Eirengaard in two days.

"Because I *will* find you if you have a change of, well, *you know*." Xander laid a hand over his chest.

"Yes, I know, now fuck off."

Xander grinned at that, and he and the priestess continued along the road northward to Eirengaard.

It was quiet for perhaps the first time when the two walked away, the roadway not busy for the moment. Even in coming winter, there was color in Orrinshire, trees with red and maroon leaves, evergreen bushes dotting the edge of the wood, and golden banners for the realm's capital hanging from posts to mark the way. Too peaceful was the moment for what had happened and what was to come.

Finally alone, Damien turned to Amma. She'd been very quiet since waking him that morning. He could see she had a hundred questions pinging around her mind but kept them locked tight inside. Unfortunately, those questions would have to wait a few moments longer.

He led her away from the road to a hollow nestled into the trees, shielded in case anyone might pass by. "Amma," he said, resolute in the decision he had made, eyes flicking down to her dagger to be sure she still had it, "do you think you could take about twenty paces in that direction, turn around, and stick your fingers in your ears?"

She scrunched up her nose. "You do know I've heard you pee like a hundred times at this point, so there's really no reason to—"

"No, not that. Just, please, do this for me, all right?"

She gave him a long look then counted off the steps as he requested with her back to him, pressed hands to the sides of her head, and began to hum.

Damien stared at the back of her for a long moment, fingers flexing at his sides, noxscura prickling under his skin. Maybe he should have asked if this was a good idea. She would know, and if she didn't, she would make him feel good about whatever decision he was about to make. She tipped her head and sighed between hums. She wouldn't continue humoring him forever, and he knew he needed to just get on with it no matter how messy it would be.

When he brought it out of his pouch, the shard of occlusion crystal had the slightest vibration of arcana thanks to their accidental trip into the depths of the mountains and the weakened veil to the infernal plane. It stared back even without Zagadoth's eye visible, disapproving of how long it had gone unspoken to, but then he remembered the tautness to the demon's voice in the message left for him, the worry, the *care*, and he pressed his thumb to its sharpest edge and spilled his blood.

A yellow eye blinked to life. It darted from edge to edge, confused, then focused right on Damien. "Son! You're alive!"

Damien nodded, guilt squeezing at his chest, unable to speak.

"By all that's grim and unholy, champ, I'm just so fucking relieved. I thought—no, I didn't think that, I knew you were fine, I just…" Zagadoth sighed, and his eyelid went heavy. "It's good to see you, kiddo."

"Yeah," Damien mumbled, trying to cover the quiver in his voice. "You too."

"You're not in danger, are you? I see sky and trees and…and sunlight. Where are you?"

Swallowing hard, Damien ran a hand over his face. "Oh, it's, uh, just this village south of Eirengaard."

"South? Took a little detour, eh? Something wrong with the gates to the north?"

"Took a lot of detours actually." Damien's head swam with questions, his father's just adding to them.

"Sure, well, makes sense with divine mages swarming around like butterflies. Abyss, you made it out and back from The Accursed Wastes! Must have traipsed all over. You see basilisks out there? Or how 'bout a fire roc? You know I don't believe they're all dead. Your great aunt once—"

"Father, I'm in Orrinshire."

"Orrinshire?" The demon's tone practically singed his ears as it shifted. "What in the Abyss are you doing *there*?"

The anxiety seeped out of Damien, replaced with a mirrored anger. "I think you know why."

"Damien Maleficus Bloodthorne, you leave that place immediately!" Zagadoth's voice was booming, and Damien tried to muffle it under his hand.

"Or what?" he growled back, holding the stone close to his mouth to keep the entire conversation's tone down.

"Darkness help me, I will break out of this crystal and drag you back to Aszath Koth myself."

Damien quickly looked up to be sure Amma hadn't heard. Her head was rocking back and forth as she continued to hum. He grit his teeth. "That better be an absolutely hollow threat or I swear to the dark gods, I'll devote myself to Osurehm right now."

Zagadoth took a breath, but his eye fell still, the anger in it abating for the moment. "Of course it is, Damien," he said, voice a rumble, "but

237

you still *cannot* be in that Empyreahole of a place."

The demon's tone suggested the village was a cesspool of danger, like Damien might be run through or burnt alive, but he had walked its streets, slept in its inn, and was now standing by its roadside without even so much as a dirty look from the inhabitants. And if anyone garnered dirty looks in tiny villages, it was him.

But they both knew it had nothing to do with Orrinshire itself. "I need to ask you something, and for once I need the complete truth."

Zagadoth's eye widened, but it did not flick away. "Son, I don't know if—"

"Dad. Please."

There was a slight movement in the crystal, something like a nod.

Shallow and ragged in his chest, Damien's heart pounded so hard that he felt as though air couldn't pass it, like his body wanted to remain ignorant, too used to pondering and believing he would never, truly know. He took a breath, tensed his muscles, and prepared himself for the worst. "Zagadoth, is it really true that infernal creatures are incapable of love?"

His father's brow came down, and he choked on a strange, confused sound. "Wha-who…well, that's not exactly what I expected you to ask."

And that wasn't an answer.

"Love," Damien said a little louder. "Are demons, no—am *I* capable of it? You said we can't feel it, that the infernal plane makes it impossible, and we're too far removed from the gods and humanity, but I feel…" His voice caught, and he fell quiet, listening, waiting, hoping.

"Look, kiddo, is now *really* the time to—"

"Yes, *now*," Damien spat.

Zagadoth did not speak for a long moment, and Damien held the stone away and shook it to be sure he was still there at all. The yellow eye blinked back and grunted. "Son," he finally said, "I think if you're able to ask me that question, you already know the answer."

Damien squeezed the stone in both hands, a weird prickling in his chest—there was anger there, enough to possibly break the crystal into even tinier shards, but there was something else, something deeper and louder and so much greater. When he sighed, there was laughter to his voice even though frustration tickled at his words. "Why in the Abyss didn't you just tell me? Why have you always been so adamant that we couldn't? That *I* couldn't?"

"It is…a convenient lie," grumbled Zagadoth, his eye looking away. "Most living things already believe the myth, perpetuated by prejudice, even though I know for certain it's not true because I have felt…and even now do feel it, for you of course. I just wanted to protect you."

A pull in Damien's chest twisted sideways. "Protect me from what?"

"Look where love got me, Damien," the demon huffed. "Trapped in this crystal, separated from my son, all because of the weakness I felt for your mother."

"Because of mom?" Damien swallowed back the burn in his throat. It was the most Zagadoth had really ever said to him on the subject, and the questions poured out. "You mean she's the reason you're in there? And you really did love her? You didn't hurt her or imprison her, or—"

"Whoa, kiddo, breathe." Zagadoth clicked his tongue. "The reason I'm in here isn't entirely her fault, no, but she sure as Abyss hasn't come to get me out, has she?"

Damien opened his mouth, defense on his tongue for reasons he couldn't comprehend, but then he looked up to Amma again. She had taken to pacing in small circles, head down, ears still covered, humming a little louder. She'd not once given up on him, had thrust herself into every danger, and he knew if he were in some crystal, she would do everything in her power to release him.

"It isn't just that, Damien," Zagadoth went on, calmer. "The more shameful truth is that you just look so much like her. I see your mother every time I look at you, and I was afraid, after everything that happened, that I wouldn't treat you the way you deserved to be treated. I was so angry and heartbroken over her, and I felt it again and again every time I saw her smile in yours, and if I ever failed at showing it, if you ever felt like I didn't love you, then it would be better if you thought I just wasn't capable rather than thinking I chose not to."

Damien felt his brows knit. "So, you thought I should just live a life entirely devoid of love rather than risk me being disappointed in your parenting? That's kind of fucked up."

"Come on, son, I already said it was shameful!"

Damien huffed. Now wasn't the time, really. "Fine, but I never thought you didn't…"

"Yeah, well,"—Zagadoth snorted out a laugh—"turns out you're incredibly easy to love, kiddo."

Damien glanced upward, a stinging in his eyes he was sure was only the bracing breeze that swept through the little clearing. Amma still had hands over her ears, but she looked back at him, brows raised with concern. Damien straightened and motioned for her to turn around again, and she huffed, blowing blonde strands away from her face, but did as he asked. Her humming got a little louder and a little more off-key.

"All right, listen, I'm in Orrinshire, so obviously I'm expecting you to tell me everything about my mother, or I'll just go find out for myself."

The demon grumbled. "I feel like I'm being held hostage here. It's a little ruthless."

"I learned from the best."

"Where do I even start?" he sighed. "Well, about a thousand years ago, I—"

"Not there. Try when you met her. And focus on the facts."

"Fine, but it's going to be boring then." Zagadoth mumbled a bit to himself then began, "Aszath Koth was being attacked. Again. The Brotherhood had summoned me a few decades earlier to protect the place, and I'd been wiping out the divine infiltrators sent by whoever was in charge down in the realm. On the day we met, it was just a sort of regular, slay-the-holy massacre, many died before the rest fell back, but one was left behind. Your mother."

"So, she really was a priestess?"

Zagadoth's eye stared back.

"Are you nodding?"

"Yeah, sorry, kiddo, it's just so…well, you know. She was badly injured and completely at my mercy, but she'd been abandoned, and I just couldn't go through with killing her. There was something in the way she spoke and in her eyes—I could feel she didn't want to be there, and she just *hated* me so fucking much. So I, uh…"

Damien's throat tightened. "You what, dad?"

"Well, I sort of kept her."

"Oh, bloody, fucking—"

"Not like that! I had her nursed back to health, the lamia healed her, the draekin fed her, and I watched all of them and made sure they treated her properly. I didn't even keep her in the dungeon—she got a private chamber and anything she asked for. I mean, I still needed information out of her, so she was technically my prisoner, but she was taken care of! She was pissed about it though." Zagadoth's chuckle broke the intensity of how he had been trying to convince Damien, a thing he wanted very badly to believe. "She absolutely *hated* me, begged me to just kill her nonstop for those first few days which was actually kind of cute, but then it was like some curse wore off of her, and she completely mellowed out. Well, as mellow as Diana could ever manage to be."

Damien opened his mouth to stop him—Diana, that was his mother's name—but Zagadoth just continued on, voice falling into his regular jocularity.

"She was strong enough to leave soon after, but she wanted to know more about the city, so I brought her anywhere she asked, showed her how Aszath Koth functioned, the markets and the taverns, took her to the Sanctum a couple of times, and there was this one day we had a picnic in the ruins, and that was the first time we,"—he coughed and quickly changed the subject, thank the basest beasts—"I introduced her to The Brotherhood too. She wasn't too keen on them, but with the rest of it? She told me she'd fallen in love with the place, and consequently me, and didn't want to leave."

"So, she just never went back home? And you didn't use arcana to make her stay?"

"Oh, no, she returned to Eiren. Once. About six moons after she arrived, she decided to make the trek back. I was terrified, but she was determined to go to the crown in Eirengaard and explain that Aszath Koth should be left alone, that there was nothing to fear from us. I didn't think they would listen, but she thought she could convince them. That was the warrior in her, and to be fair, your mother was *very* good at convincing people of things. I couldn't leave the city unprotected, so for nearly a moon, I waited. Diana did come back, but as I expected, they didn't believe her, and her temple tried to imprison her—that same damned temple you're so close to now—but she was stronger, and she fled back to Aszath Koth. At least, that is what she told me. After that, she put her whole heart and her divine powers into protecting the city."

"The orb, with the dove."

"The one in the throne room, yes. Diana crafted that for Aszath Koth to keep those who would do harm out. The arcana in that thing, I can't even understand it, but she said it contained a piece of her heart. It was a wedding gift."

Damien sucked in a sharp breath at his father's admittance that they were married.

Amma turned around swiftly at the sound he made, eyes wide. "Are you all right?"

Damien shook his head, but then quickly corrected to nodding and tapped one of his ears.

She bit down hard on her lip, eyes darting to the stone in his hand, then slowly turned back around.

When Damien refocused on the shard, there was a haziness that worked its way over Zagadoth's eye and then cleared. Tears, he

241

thought, but for only a moment, feeling the arcana fizzle and then pulse under his fingers. "Damn it, this doesn't have much more time. Okay, jump ahead—you always told me my mother left, that the two of you just had a deal, and she changed her mind, but you're telling me now that she wanted to be there, so what happened?"

"Well, we had a…a slight disagreement."

"About?"

Zagadoth hesitated so long that Damien nearly shouted at him to get on with it, but then the demon sighed. "Birzuma."

"Do *not* tell me you were disloyal to my mother with Xander's." His stomach knotted right up.

"No! Nothing like that. Birzuma and I hated each other, and it wasn't the sexy kind of hate that Diana and I had going on at first—the kind that makes you so frustrated you just want to—"

"Trust me, you don't need to explain it, and I don't want to hear that."

"Right, well, your mother and I were trying to decide if we should have another baby. I said you needed a playmate, someone else like you, and she pointed out you had Xander to grow up with. At the time we'd allowed Birzuma back into Aszath Koth because she had her own little blood mage and wanted to keep him safe which was really an appeal to Diana's heart, so it won out. But I still said to your mother, *Xander's a little shit, Diana*, because even at six years old he absolutely was, and she said, *I know, Zag, but he just needs someone to love him.* She was like that, you know? Very human. Anyway, we ended up in a ridiculous argument that had nothing to do with what we were originally discussing, and it was right before bed which was an even bigger mistake—don't ever let the person you love go to bed angry because if you do, you'll end up wandering the desolate plains outside of Aszath Koth all night and then return the next morning to your entire family missing. Your mother was gone, and she'd taken you *and* Xander with her."

Damien stood there, mouth agog until the crystal shard hazed again and snapped him out of it. "You really think one argument like that made her want to leave?"

Zagadoth clicked his tongue. "No, I think it was an…an excuse? I'm not sure how to explain it, but when I stormed Eirengaard to get you back and beg her to return with me, she was a completely different person, as if the years we had spent together were all a ruse. We met on the battlefield, and I couldn't hurt her, Damien, no matter how she insisted I was evil and had to be banished. Archibald was there too, and by the time I ended up in this crystal, I realized she had been a plant all along. She was left behind on purpose to play some game with me, to beguile and trick me. I had fallen in love with her, I had learned that I *could* love, but she had only been toiling under the order of that goddess and the crown all along to bring about Aszath Koth's downfall. My downfall. And worse than all of that, she took you from me."

Damien remembered the feeling he'd had, a brief but strong one, when he thought Delphine had his child. Without even meeting the spawn, his instinct was to take it and run from a being he considered evil—perhaps the same instinct his mother had.

"But, Damien, I need you to know, I cannot help but love your mother to this day—at least I love the woman she pretended to be—and I am weak to her still because she gave me you. I don't regret it, not any of it. I mean, I *do* regret getting trapped in this crystal, but that was my fuck up. I would never have gotten you back if it weren't for Birzuma and The Brotherhood, but I'm forever thankful to the darkness that I did."

Damien ran a hand through his hair, blowing out a breath and staring hard at the ground. There was so much earnestness in his father's voice, yet it felt as though something had to be missing, like his father was only recalling the fluffiest bits of his memories, and they simply didn't amount to the outcome that was his mother leaving. "You kept this from me to protect me?"

The crystal shard blinked. "I couldn't have you going after her—doing just what you're doing now—not with me trapped in here and no way to get you if, darkness forbid, something were to happen to you."

"You just said you still love her. You think she would hurt me?" Zagadoth was quiet for another long moment, and the crystal's arcana pulsed and sizzled. "Father, please, tell me."

"No, I…I think she took you with her because she wanted to keep you. Diana wasn't devoid of love herself. The way she felt for you—that was the one thing I never questioned. But I was afraid if she kept you, she would turn you against me, and I couldn't have that."

There—there was that anger, the feeling he'd bitten back. "You couldn't let me make my own choice?"

"You were so young," he said, and then his voice went muffled.

"I'm an adult now," Damien retorted loudly, "and I have been for some time."

"…know, but…"

Damien pinched the bridge of his nose, listening to the excuse that he couldn't even understand as the arcana seeped out of the shard.

"…dangerous…Aszath…priestess…"

Zagadoth's eye blinked out, and Damien was left with only the sound of wind in the leaves and Amma's hum that had dwindled into a sort of warble as she'd sat herself down on the ground. Damien almost chucked the stupid shard into the trees, but he instead pocketed it and shut his eyes, clearing his thoughts with a single, long breath.

When he opened his eyes again, there was Amma. She was sitting in the dirt with her fingers stuffed in her ears and moaning out a painfully dissonant tune, but she was there. He went up behind her and tapped her on the head.

She tipped her face up at him. "Can I stop singing now?" she asked much too loudly.

"For all our sakes, yes," he chuckled and nodded.

She dropped her hands with a groan, falling back against his shins, the softness of her body pressing into him. It was such a simple thing, trusting that he would be there, that he wouldn't step away and allow her to fall, that she wanted to touch him at all knowing who he was, *what* he was, and it filled him with that warm, fuzzy feeling he now knew was love.

"Oh, thank the gods, my arms are killing me. How much did you have to drink?"

"You know I wasn't relieving myself." He reached down and hauled her to her feet, and she squealed playfully under the too-fast movement. "But I do find it compelling how willing you are to follow commands even when they are unpleasant." He spun her, keeping her close, and she caught herself on his chest.

"I just, um…did what you told me to." Her unblinking eyes sparkled up at him, her words striking him hard in the gut—he liked that, but it was also a problem.

"Amma, I've not properly thanked you for coming to my rescue." He cleared his throat, heat in his face at the admittance. "It turns out I may be just as abductable as you are, but if not for you, I would be…well, worse than dead, I believe. So, my deepest gratitude is owed to you. You must know that you have it, forever."

"Oh, sure," she said, biting back a grin and looking a little flustered. "Is that, um…is that what you wanted to discuss?"

Damien made a sound in the back of his throat, glancing toward the road through the trees. "I would like to eat. Would you like to eat? I think we should eat."

They sat through a meal together, but it was stilted and quiet, Damien asking Amma if she was comfortable many times. After, he encouraged her to bathe in the small chamber attached to their room, the one they now had to themselves, while he sat on the bed and thought about how he might say the things he intended to say. By the time she emerged, clean and smelling wonderful, his thoughts hadn't converged, so he too shut himself up in the separate chamber, bathed, double-checked himself for errant leeches, and continued to think until the water turned cold.

When he finally left the bathing chamber, half-dressed and wholly confused, he found Amma sitting on the bed as he had been, but a much more concerned look creased her face. She pressed her lips together so tightly, as if it were all she could do to keep the questions in, the sweet thing holding back despite looking like she might explode, all for him.

"I believe my mother is here, in Orrinshire, at the temple," burst out of him as if it were a living thing that had finally worked out how to free itself. Fuck, that wasn't at all what he'd meant to say, and yet.

Amma's face went blank for a full minute, and it seemed like she had stopped breathing. And then she jumped to her feet. "Damien, that's incredible!" She sprung herself at him and wrapped arms around his neck, then froze. "Unless—oh, are you worried? You shouldn't be—this is great! Unless it's not." She looked swiftly away, features screwed up, then shook her head. "No, it's amazing! Your mom! You found her!" He was pulled into a tight embrace that he went to return until she pulled back yet again. "Oh, no, unless you're *not* excited about it, then it's *not* amazing or great or incredible, and I am an *idiot* for saying any of those things. Oh, geez, Damien, please just tell me how you feel about it already."

"I, uh…I don't know."

She hung from around his neck, studying his face and chewing on her lip, all the anxiety he felt painted across her features so plainly. But then they fell off, and she narrowed her brow and patted his chest. "Well, that's fine. Let's figure it out."

Amma pulled him down to sit beside her on the bed, threaded her fingers into his, and smiled.

"How?"

"Talk."

CHAPTER 26
ALL RIGHT, FINE

As it turned out, Damien had *a lot* of feelings. Many, many hours worth that he repeated and rephrased and tried very hard to make sense of, and Amma listened to them all. He had spoken with his father, she guessed it had something to do with that stone out in the woods but didn't interrupt him to clarify how, and he told her what he knew. In many ways, the story lined up with what Lycoris had told him in the karsts.

But the potential betrayal was quite a lot, not to mention confusing. If Damien's mother had meant to let the crown capture Zagadoth, then why had she created that orb he'd mentioned that still protected Aszath Koth? Getting rid of the demon that protected the city was supposed to make Aszath Koth susceptible to attack, but Diana's spell kept the place as well guarded as ever. Damien didn't have an answer for that, only adding to his turmoil.

It would all require finding his mother and asking for clarification. And that was the scariest part.

Damien eventually fell backward onto the bed. Amma leaned on her elbow and watched his features as he continued to speak, how they would soften with worry and harden with anger, and his eyelids eventually grew heavy. The light through the single window in their chamber darkened with the setting of the sun, sounds beyond their door quieting, and in the shadows that crept in, his voice became quieter too.

"My father will be upset if I seek her out," he said with a sigh that sounded so finite. "He may never forgive me, in fact. And maybe I shouldn't—she hasn't tried to find me in all these years; maybe she truly wants nothing to do with me, and I would just be upsetting her if I showed up."

So concerned, Amma thought, with everyone else's upset, but what about his own?

When he turned to her and asked the inevitable, "Amma, what should I do?" with his eyes glassy, hair a mess from constant tugging, and a soul that groaned silently with exhaustion, she wished she had a better answer for him, but there was only the truth.

"You should do what *you* want to do, Damien." It was what he would have told her, and in this instance, she knew it was right. "Your father may or may not accept your choice, and your mother will have whatever reaction that she does, but what you decide is all that matters."

"What if I make the wrong decision?"

"I don't think there is a wrong decision." She watched his eyes fall away from hers, unconvinced.

"But there is a decision which ruins many things. One that will lead to pain and…being alone."

Amma scooted up against the pillow on the bed, and she grabbed him by the arm, tugging. He moved awkwardly under her attempt to manhandle him but fell on his stomach against her when she dragged him down to her chest.

"There's no way you can breathe like this," he chuckled, splayed out atop her.

Amma just settled in, wrapping her arms around his shoulders and nestling his head under her chin. "Of course I can, I'm very strong." He was much bigger and heavier, but it didn't matter, she made him fit and held him tightly.

He snorted, again not terribly convinced, but he wiggled arms around her waist, relaxing.

Amma ran fingers through Damien's hair with one hand and drew lazy circles on the bare skin of his back with the other. "No matter what you choose, and no matter what comes of that choice," she said quietly, "I will be beside you, and I will stay beside you for as long as you will have me. By Sestoth's roots, I swear it."

He did not respond, but she didn't expect him to—it was her oath to make, and he didn't need to accept it, it was sworn either way. Damien gave her middle a tight squeeze, and in the deepening silence of the little room in Orrinshire, they both fell asleep.

It would have been pitch black hours later when Amma woke if not for how close the two moons were together, their slant light coming in through the slightly open shutters in the middle of the night. She was roused by Damien's movements as he lifted his head from her chest.

Bleary-eyed, he blinked at her then pushed up onto his hands to hover over her. Amma took a full breath, chest expanding fully as she rubbed an eye. When she focused on him again, he was staring intently back, brows narrowed. "What's wrong?" she asked, heartbeat speeding up. "Bad dream?"

"I must tell you something." His voice was hoarse, hair falling in his face, jaw tight. He had an arm on either side of her, so she was beholden in that moment to stay and listen regardless, but her limbs were suddenly too stiff and heavy to move anyway.

Amma swallowed and pressed back into the pillow. "Um, okay?"

"Since our first meeting, you have infuriated me time and again with the things you say and do and insist upon. Be kind, be thoughtful, be considerate—your actions and persistence have vexed me to no end." The sharpness of his face was highlighted by the scant light through the window, and his words were nearly as cutting. "But worst of all was each and every time you demanded that you knew me better than I knew myself. That you knew I was something that it was impossible for an infernal creature to be. Yet you pushed me to an edge I was sure would be the death of us both."

Amma stared up into the intensity of his eyes, shining violet even in the dark. "Uh, Damien? I'm not exactly sure where you're going with this, but it sounds kinda bad…"

"Shit. Of course it does." He huffed and his head drooped between shoulders taut from holding himself up. "Let me try again. Amma, you are like a…a thorn."

"Damien—"

"Wait, this is better, I swear it." His eyes widened, and she pressed her lips together. "Like the briars you enchanted in the hot spring, you've pierced me, and yes, it was very painful and frankly quite annoying at first. I mean, really, *very* annoying. Do you remember at Anomalous's when you dared to *shout* at me? I seriously considered pitching you off that tower despite how exquisite your breasts were, but—"

"How is this better?"

"*But*,"—he fell to his elbows and clamped a hand over her mouth—"in piercing me, you have bled out that which was actually injuring me."

Amma took in a breath through her nose, his face much closer now, fingers pressed over her lips.

"You have burrowed yourself inside me, hollowed out those things I did not need, and taken up the space left behind with your…what do thorns inject into you? Poison?"

Her muffled objection under his hand only made him laugh.

"Well, I thought that metaphor was apt, but if it displeases you so, then I will say it plainly. Ammalie, I am…fond of you."

Amma waited, she squinted, and then she slid her mouth out from under his hand. "Is that all?"

"Uh, no, I've just never said this. Not to *anyone*." Damien's lip curled up as he looked down. "Oh, this feels very, very strange."

"If it's too hard——"

"No." He pushed up again onto his knees and placed hands on either side of her face. His breath fell over her lips, and Damien for once did not swallow back what he meant to say nor use his blustery words to exaggerate and distract. He simply spoke to her, and she listened. "I am in love with you, Amma, utterly and unconditionally, until my last breath and beyond."

Amma was surprised her heart still beat at all. Speaking was right out of the question, breathing already a struggle, and her thoughts were a complete wash, so she did exactly what her body told her to, and she kissed him. It was frenzied and desperate how she grabbed his head to pull him down or herself up, whichever got them closest, and she bit at his lips and tongue and nose and squealed right up against his mouth.

Damien chuckled, trying to pull back, but her grip was too strong. "Amma, do——"

She chased after his mouth, planting more kisses on his face as he tried to speak.

"——do you have——"

She slipped her tongue over his when his mouth was wide enough to wriggle it in.

"——any'ing 'erhaps 'oo——"

She grabbed the back of his head and squashed their faces together.

He mumbled out something incomprehensible, their lips pressed too tightly to tell.

"Of course I love you, you big idiot," she giggled when she pulled back. "I've loved you since you risked everything and came for me in Brineberth. Actually, no, before that, when you gave your blood to the vampires for their help. Or maybe when we saved that baby together in Durendreg? Oh, but when you raised the Army of the Undead in Faebarrow I thought I was going to make love to you right there on the balcony, so maybe that's when it started."

"Really? Back then?" He looked far too amused at the admittance.

Amma shrugged against the pillow, lacing her fingers together behind his neck. "I at least thought you were very cute at the time, but does it matter? I love you now more than I ever have, and deeper than I've ever felt."

He was smiling at her, not a smirk, not a chuckle, but a beam that struck her right in the heart, yet it suddenly fell away. "I am elated," he said, though the word carried only half of its meaning as his brows knit, "but I'm also afraid of what this means because, you know…I'm supposed to destroy the realm and everything."

Amma grunted. "Even if that stupid prophecy is about you, the eclipse isn't for, like, a *whole* day, and we can't do much about it right now. In fact, there's not much at all we can do in this little bed chamber in the middle of the night."

He made a thoughtful sound in the back of his throat. "Oh, can you really think of nothing?" His hands came around hers and slipped them from his neck to press down into the bed.

She arched her chest and squirmed beneath him. "Did you have something in mind?"

"Would you make love to me, Mistress Avington?"

"Well, when you ask like *that*, how could I possibly say no?"

Damien's mouth was on hers, and he was devouring her. She sank into the bed with him straddling her, holding her in place as he took the kiss she so desperately wanted to give him. Then his hands slid down to her waist, and he was pushing up her tunic as they both fumbled to free her of it. Her breeches were next, and then only her chemise was in the way, but he didn't let the thin fabric stop him from slipping her breast from behind the silk and bringing her nipple to attention under his tongue.

She wasn't sure how it happened, but a moment later Amma was naked, lying back and being tasted everywhere—well, almost everywhere. Damien worked his way down her body, each press of his lips to her skin a blossoming of tingles that called to the ache between her legs. He was going slowly—so damn slowly—that she whined out a word of beseeching, and of course that only made him stop.

Amma glanced down the length of herself to see him grinning up at her from between her legs, all pointed teeth and the most delicious malice she could imagine. She twitched and bit her lip and tried so hard to be patient, but it had been so long. "Damien?"

"Just waiting to see if the world comes crashing down around us first, but I do believe we may have finally pleased the gods." To speak of the world crashing down, Damien's tongue finally slid over her, and she nearly came apart right then. "Quiet, you'll wake the whole inn," he mumbled, vibrations of his words right up against her, and then took her firmly beneath one thigh and hooked her leg over his shoulder.

Amma hadn't even realized she had cried out, but much more aware, she gripped onto the linens as his tongue had its way with her core. Bucking against his mouth, his fingers dug into her hips to hold her at bay, and a warm chuckle resonated out of him as he slowed his licking, drawing her closer to an edge she would surely plunge off of at any moment.

"Oh, Amma, you're far too easy to please," he said, a hand sliding down the inside of her lifted thigh, ankle still hooked on his shoulder. "You're not allowed to fall apart on me so soon." His finger found its way inside her easily, the curl of it hitting a spot that made her whole body quiver, nearly impossible to hold back from falling into bliss, but followed his behest. She rocked against the gentle urging of his fingers as he flicked his tongue over her in painfully light strokes, and when she could take no more, she reached for his head and pressed herself fully against his mouth.

Damien was slick, both literally and figuratively, and escaped her grasp and her core. "Ah, ah, bad girl." He took her wrists, and she collapsed, only half spent and wholly frustrated. Leaning over her, his grin was utterly wicked. "That's not how you get what you want, and I think you know that by now."

In a daze, she lifted and kissed him, the taste of herself on his lips driving her into wildness. She escaped his grip and went for his belt. With a quick flick of her wrist, her hand was down his trousers, and she had him fully in her grip.

The commanding glare he wore was chased away as she stroked his length, tugging at his pants with her other hand. "I'm taking what's mine," she panted, and his surprisingly eager reaction made her snicker as he was soon completely naked himself.

Amma pushed at Damien's shoulder so that he would sit back, slipping out from under him and getting up onto her knees. With a deft hand, she ran the keen wetness from its tip down his length. He steadied himself, leaning back on the bed and taking a ragged breath. Biting into his lip, his eyes watched her hand, and she watched the rest of him, finally exposed to her there on his knees, the slanting moonlight falling over his muscled chest and hips and thighs as he tried to contain himself under her touch.

"Mine," she repeated, taking her free hand to his stomach and running fingers along the creases of his skin, feeling the hardness of

251

him under both palms. All of Damien's strength and command were subject to her in that moment, control relinquished. His breathing went harder, chest expanding, stomach twisting, reacting to every light touch she danced over his abdomen and traced down his thighs, completely at her mercy.

He groaned as she slid her other hand beneath his length and fully cupped the rest of him then finally leaned forward to treat him to what she'd enjoyed. Damien's hand fisted her hair as he swore at her tongue running over the head of his cock. She giggled, a pleasure beyond physical running through her, and hummed against him as she fully took him into her mouth. Her name fell off of his lips like a prayer, guiding her head along his length, and she delighted in watching the control he normally had melt away as he panted and grunted and growled into her. Gods, the *power* she had, it was bliss.

And then she was pulled off of him, tongue left hanging out as she gazed upward to see him struggling to contain himself. "I will be useless to you if you go on much longer," he gasped out. "Unless you've changed your mind."

Amma shook her head, licking her lips.

"Then come here so I can claim you as mine."

CHAPTER 27
ONE LITTLE DEATH AND ANOTHER VERY BIG ONE

Damien didn't need to have Amma's tongue or anything else on him to be pushed to the edge, the adoration in her eyes, that sparkle under the moonlight that said she wanted him, was enough. He released her hair, taking fingers to her chin and guiding her to sit up.

Moonlight splashed over her breasts, pink-tipped and swollen, and down along her trembling belly to the warm place he intended to fill. He only wanted to look on her a moment, to burn her into his mind like this, but the restlessness in her small, fidgety movements had to be tamed. He slid hands under her thighs, pulling her forward to straddle him, her knees pressing in on either side of his hips, but he kept her aloft, sliding fingers through the wetness coating the bottom of her thighs and gripping onto her ass.

She gasped as he teased her entrance with the head of his length, mouth devouring hers. Amma wriggled, trying to shimmy downward, but he refused to allow her. Instead, he drew himself back, sliding up over the spot she liked for him to play with so much, and drew out one of her enticing whines.

"Eager, little thing," he teased, pleasuring himself against how slick she was, making her head fall back as she cried out. He was just as eager, of course, but watching her writhe and listening to her moan in anticipation was almost as nice as he imagined being inside her would be.

Amma fell still then, eyes opening and finding his. "Please, Master Bloodthorne," she mewled, "I need you."

"Of course, my sweet." Damien brought his mouth to her neck, her pulse quickening under his lips, and purred up against her skin, "For you, anything."

He lifted her just enough to draw out a delighted squeal, and then his length found where it belonged. Arms trembling, he fought against himself to thrust wildly into her, instead savoring her slow descent until he was fully sheathed in the warmth between her legs.

Damien had been wrong. Watching her squirm and listening to her plead had been exceptionally nice, but it was leagues behind how *this* felt. Soft and warm, he was captured completely by the grip of her, held, possessed, consumed, and it was *good*.

Amma took deep breaths, breasts rubbing against his chest as her fingers tangled themselves in his hair, eyes heavy with a drunken ecstasy, but she held herself still against his lap. Damien had never thought too terribly much of fucking someone during the act—it was simply using or being used with the expectation to feel awful about it later—but this was like being held, being consumed as he had wished to be, and by the person he had longed for in the deepest Abyss of his heart.

"In the wildwood," Amma breathed, hips shifting slightly so that he moved inside her.

He could only grunt out an inquisitive noise.

"When I knew for certain,"—she swallowed and inhaled raggedly—"that I loved you." Amma pressed up, sliding him to his tip and then settled back down to the base, eyelids fluttering as she repeated the move with more force.

Damien lifted a hand to the back of her neck and gripped tightly, holding her still. "How?"

Her eyes opened again, and she pressed her forehead to his. "I couldn't bear to be without you." Licking her lips, her fingers traced over his jaw, his scar, and finally held his face. "When you returned, I knew I could never let you go again because I loved you."

Damien took her mouth with his, laying her onto her back, and drove deeply into her. She cried out, and soon their voices matched as they moved together, pulling bliss from one another. Amma's legs wrapped around his hips, and he braced himself on an elbow as he worked a hand between them to lay his fingers on the tender spot that would break her apart along with him.

"Together," he husked.

She nodded, bucking desperately under the play of his thumb. There was arcana in the room with them, not under either's control, primal and filling up the air, and the two came undone before collapsing into a sweaty, unbecoming heap. A jumble of limbs and wetness, they slid against one another, the magic dispersing, and then laughter bubbled up out of them when she poked him in the side too hard with an errant hand, and he slipped and squashed her.

After more thoughtful shifting, they fell into stillness, breaths caught but hands still exploring clumsily. Damien felt her fingers on his hip and back as he traced around her breasts and neck with his own. There were shadows shifting languidly in the knots of the wood that made up the walls, and within them, tiny leaves had sprouted up out of the boards. That was going to be difficult to explain to the innkeeper, surely.

They found their way against one another, drained but gratified, and Damien tucked Amma into his chest with a quiet murmur of sentimental words he would have never dreamed he could muster before, coming so naturally, so easily, so ardently from his lips as she pressed kisses to his collarbone. Quiet hemmed in around them, and then, finally, restful sleep took them both.

Damien woke the next morning in a dreamy, almost tipsy state. Somehow jolts of pleasure still rang through him, and he squirmed, confused at the phantom sensation of the previous night between his legs. But then he panicked—Amma wasn't in his arms. Had someone taken her? Was she in danger? Where in the bloody Abyss had she gone?

He tore back the linens to jump from the bed but instead found he was tethered to the mattress by another body. Amma glanced up at him with big, bright, blue eyes, her ass in the air as she knelt between his thighs, his cock in her mouth.

"'Ood 'ornin," she said, lips still around him.

"Best fucking morning," he groaned, eyes rolling back into his head.

An hour or so later, the two were finally dressed but continued to make eyes at one another over bread and sausages in the tavern downstairs. Damien's urge to toss Amma over his shoulder and haul her back to the chamber forever altered by arcana was strong, but the solemnity of Orrinshire finally dropped its weight on him when a robed figure entered the inn.

He watched the priestess make a delivery to the innkeeper, the holy woman too young to be his mother, but the realization struck him that,

255

of course, that was why he had come to Orrinshire. Amma's words, her promise, had brought him to his decision the night before—he would seek out Diana, take whatever answer she gave him, and then he would go to Eirengaard to deal with Xander and what fate held for him there.

Orrinshire did not make its temple the central focus of the village. Like Briarwyke, the shrine to the goddess was set off and cloistered at the edge of the wood. Isldrah lorded over health, her followers often caring for the infirmed, and along the pathway that led to the temple stood another building that appeared to be a ward. Damien was glad for the seclusion and for the walk with Amma. It did, of course, give him quite the opportunity to run in the other direction, but her arm looped around his kept him moving forward. When he saw that symbol carved into the stone above the temple's door, the same that floated on the orb that protected Aszath Koth, albeit upside down, he did not turn tail and flee.

"Are you...are you allowed to just walk in?" Damien asked as they came closer to the place's open entrance.

"Uh huh." Amma led him to the threshold in the long, stone wall that made up the temple's front. There were no windows, the blocks old, but newly painted and brilliantly white, and along the base of the wall sprouted lavender bushes, still hearty even in the cold. She patted his arm. "Don't worry, you can do this. You probably won't even catch on fire when you set foot on the hallowed ground."

Damien grunted at her gentle laughter, but it was the push he needed, and together they stepped through. He expected to be taken by nausea or a piercing pain in his brain like in Durendreg, but he only felt an intense trepidation as they entered a small but formal space filled with candles along every wall.

The room was wide, two exits along its back but no windows, the candles' glow flickering over the white stone. A statue, presumably of Isldrah, presided over the temple's foyer, climbing up to the ceiling just in the room's center. It was a massive and intricate thing, depicting a woman twice as tall as any human. She stood beneath a tree, the branches coiling out over the entirety of the room's ceiling and filled with doves.

But stepping closer to the goddess's carving showed him that they were not doves but all manner of birds sculpted out of the light-colored stone. Yes, there was a dove that sat daintily on Isldrah's hand, but also there sat a sparrow on her shoulder, an owl in the tree's hollow, fat chickens gathering at her feet, one of those round-bodied, flippered servants that King Wil of the fae had conjured hidden amongst them. He continued to search, eyes pinging from bird to bird, until he found a raven. Perched on a branch and peering down at him, there was no confusing its breed even carved from white stone—he had conjured Corben enough times to know—and it was still counted as one of Isldrah's flock.

"People come here to pray for ill loved ones," Amma whispered to him, pointing to a basin filled with slips of parchment. Beside it sat another basin with seeds and small fruits.

"And she answers?" He gestured to the statue with his chin.

"I imagine so, if you have the right medicine." Amma tugged his arm as a priest entered from deeper inside the temple. He nodded to them with a wide smile, then continued outside without questioning their presence.

Together they went through the opening he had used, and it led down a corridor that was much brighter, sunlight streaming in through open archways on either side of it, walled courtyards beyond. Despite the chill of coming winter, there was greenery here, and the open spaces were filled with birdbaths, ornamental trees, fruiting bushes, and priestesses tending to the plants.

Slowly, they began down the open hall, another room at the long corridor's far end. "Perhaps she is not here," said Damien, the words thick in his throat. "I don't know why I thought she absolutely would be. Maybe it would be best to come back later or to request someone else to deliver her a message—"

"Uh, Damien?" Amma's grip on his arm went tight, and she brought him to a stop. "I don't think we'll have to do that." Her finger was pointing subtly to a decorative archway that led to a courtyard central to the temple. A woman stood there, adding water to a lifted basin—a woman with hair as black as night coiled around the back of her head. When she felt their gazes on her and glanced up, her eyes were the same color Damien had always seen in the mirror.

The last of the priestess's water was poured, but she remained unmoving with her jug even as a sparrow came to land on the edge of the basin for a drink. Damien stared unblinking at Diana—because that's who this was, he knew it as surely as anything else on this and every other plane—and only when Amma gave him a little shove did he remember to breathe.

"Go on," she whispered into his ear. "I'll give you privacy. If you need me, just call."

Damien took a staggered step forward, boot falling off the stone walkway and onto the softness of the earth. Her mouth moved, and though no sound came out, he had seen his name on Amma's lips enough to know it was what Diana was whispering to herself. Another step, more soft earth, a wobble in his stomach, but if he stopped he might turn and flee, so he continued on until he was standing just before her.

The jug fell to the ground, and the woman threw arms around him. Damien didn't move—he wasn't exactly sure what he was meant to do when his mother hugged him because it had been so long—but then every muscle in his body relaxed. His mother was embracing him. His *mother*.

"You were dead," a voice said into his ear. A voice that he suddenly could hear in his memory singing him to sleep. "Because of my betrayal," she was saying, still holding him. "I didn't want to believe them, my heart had given you up, but, oh, my sweet boy." Sweet? Damien? Well, she'd not known him for the last twenty-three years.

His breath was shallow, afraid too much movement would make her disappear, but he glanced down to the top of her head. Black hair, as Lycoris had said, just like his own, but there was a thick streak of silver running from her temple and through the braids woven around her crown.

She pulled back, but her hands gripped his upper arms firmly. "When I was told you may be alive, I couldn't allow myself that hope." Her fingers were long and her hands corded, arms muscled, but then he had always remembered her being strong, lifting him so easily from the floor, carrying him everywhere, spinning him about and laughing. She was a warrior, he now knew, if his father had been honest about her original intent in Aszath Koth, and though she wore the simple robes of a priestess, they were fitted for easy movement, cowl down and hood pushed back, sleeves short and the skirt split, leggings and boots worn beneath. "But he told me, he said to be prepared for your coming, and it's true."

Damien raised his eyes to her face. Violet irises bore into him, glazed and reflecting his own fear. Now *that* was not how he ever remembered her. Though he never could truly recall her face, as it stared back the sharp angles and fine features seemed like they should have been held serenely. But they were hollow now and bent with a kind of fear.

"Who?" Damien's voice cracked on the single word, but his mind sharpened at hearing it, reminding him he was there and not in a dream even as another bird landed beside them in a bush flowering with berries. "Who said I was coming?"

"It doesn't matter," she shook her head, corner of her mouth ticking up. "You're here, and you're alive, and you're…you're so old."

Damien glanced down at his hands, trembling slightly. Well, that wasn't very becoming. He squeezed them into tight fists. "I'm only twenty-seven."

"Twenty..." Diana's eyes looked past him, staring into the middle distance, and then she bent and retrieved the jug from the ground. Seeing that it was empty, she gestured for Damien to follow, and crossed the courtyard to a fountain, massive and elegant and spouting water so crystalline that it reflected every color in its flow over tiered edges.

"Did you say I was dead?" Damien asked, tearing his gaze from the beauty of the rainbows in the water.

Diana held her jug beneath a stream, drawing a symbol over her chest with a free hand, one that must have been for her goddess. "So small, so innocent," she whispered. "The both of you." Diana took a drink from the jug, and then her eyes flashed back to him, glassy with tears but a grin on her face. "But you're not—you're here. Tell me, how did you escape being locked away in that awful place?"

He swallowed—she must have meant Aszath Koth.

"Is that when this happened to you?" Her hand went to his face but did not touch him, fingers moving slightly like they would have run down his scar.

Damien shook his head—that would be a discussion for another time, if ever—and he glanced around at the courtyard. It was like spring there, the colors and sun brighter, and he began to feel a pressure building in his temples. He cleared his throat. "So, uh, you're a priestess?"

She nodded, offering him the jug. "Yes. I serve Isldrah, and she has blessed me with great power. Though, while I am in mourning, my duties are being carried out by the others and the Osurehm priests who have come to help in this trying time."

Damien declined the water though his throat was dry. "You're in mourning?"

"For you," she said, and her body seemed to shrink as she gripped the jug tighter. "But my son is not dead. It was my penance for betraying the gods that you were, but through my service and devotion, you are alive again. Yet you've lost so much time."

"I've *not* been dead," Damien insisted slowly. "What exactly do you believe happened?"

Diana looked about, eyeing two other priestesses walking through the courtyard. Though they were in discussion with one another, she guided Damien to the fountain's other side. "Of course you would not remember, you were so young. I too would like to forget," she said, taking another drink, "but nothing can remove that awful vision from

259

my mind when I was brought to you that night. You'd gone missing, and she found the two of you. No marks, no blood—it was as if you'd simply fallen asleep, but you weren't breathing, and your heart, it didn't…" She thumped a hand on her chest. "All of the power Isldrah had ever given me was useless to bring you back. I'd never seen anything like it, and all I could think to do was bring you here and to pray that someone who had not fallen out of the goddess's favor could save you."

"Wait, are you talking about when you took me from Aszath Koth? You're saying I was dead?"

"Yes, you and another little boy just like you had been taken from your beds and—" Her voice hitched, and she closed her eyes. "That place had so many enemies, and I foolishly thought I could protect it, could protect you and your—" Again she stopped herself, shaking her head. "Something got through, and it left the two of you dead as a warning."

"You're speaking of both me and Xander?"

"You remember?" Her hand went to her chest, and she flicked her gaze nervously around the courtyard again.

"I just saw that bastard yesterday."

"Damien, language," she hissed, then sighed, glancing off into the middle distance again and taking another drink. "So, both of you have been brought back."

"Diana," Damien snapped, "please, be clear. Are you speaking of the same night that you and my father had an argument, and he left Bloodthorne Keep?"

She shuddered. "The night he was gone, yes. The other boy's mother came to me, frantic because she had found the two of you and knew I could—well, *thought* I could help. When I failed, she used that arcana of hers to travel quickly—"

"Translocation."

"Yes, that. She brought us here, and I begged for help. The priests and priestesses tried, but there was nothing they could do, and then…"

"Then?"

Diana took another long drink. "Then you walked into the temple," she said as if only just remembering.

"There are twenty-three years between then and now."

"Twenty hours, twenty years, what is time to the grief over a lost child?" she whispered.

"My father thinks you stole me and ran off. Didn't you want to return to Aszath Koth? To your husband?"

All of the sorrow drained off of Diana's face, fear splashing over it again. "Your father?"

"Yeah, Zagadoth, my dad."

Diana gasped. "You cannot speak the name of demons lest they be brought forth unto our plane."

"If it were that easy, I would have done it years ago."

"Damien, do not even joke about...but you are not joking, are you?" She appraised him, placing the jug on the edge of the fountain and wringing her hands. "That vile place has taken its hold on you just as he said it would."

"Aszath Koth isn't vile," he murmured though it was only partly true. There were parts of it, at least, that weren't, and according to Zagadoth, Diana herself had been enamored with it. "The orb in Bloodthorne Keep's throne room bears Isldrah's symbol. It still protects the city, and Zagadoth says it holds a piece of your heart."

She touched her chest, eyes no longer peering into his, brow creased with worry.

Damien swallowed hard, mouth dry as the questions piled up and fought to be asked in his beginning-to-pound head. He let them spill out before they put him in too much pain to ask. "Was Zagadoth lying? Did he keep you as his captive? Force you to—to create the orb? Did you not love Aszath Koth or...or him?"

"Love?" As Diana stared into the falling waters of the fountain, the prism reflected over her face, and he saw something in her features he had really only felt, a longing for something he hadn't believed he could have until very recently.

"Mother," he said with a renewed conviction, "Zagadoth loves you, even after everything. He would tell you himself." He pulled out the crystal shard from his pouch. "If I could show you, I would, but—"

"What is that?" she hissed, pushing his hand back toward him and scaring away the little birds that had settled on the fountain. "You cannot have that evil here."

"It's just a bit of rock."

"It's infernal—I can *feel* it."

He stuffed the shard back away, but her disgusted look did not dissolve. "Well, so am I. You must feel that too."

She smoothed her hands over her robes as if wiping something off of them, and then her body went stiff. "He said if you came that this would also happen."

Damien's mounting confusion and the throb in his temple bled into anger. "Who is this *he* you keep speaking of?"

Diana only reached into a pocket in her robes. A chain hung from her hand, and when she flipped it over, a jagged and cloudy gem cast

Damien's reflection back at him.

"Where in the Abyss did you get that?" He took a step back, hands going up in defense but empty.

Her eyes finally met his again, hollow. "Son, I am sorry."

"Why would you apologize?" Damien asked, a quiver in his voice. Her face had gone hard, the pendant in hand, and the pulse in the temple thrummed through him. Damien forgot in that moment that he had his own arcana, noxscura not even coming to his aid unbidden. He forgot everything, in fact, that he was good, that he was evil, that he was a man with magic and strength and power, and when he heard his own voice he forgot even that he could speak. "Why are you sorry, mom?"

"Transgressions still must be paid." Her hand tightened around the pendant, and there was a squeeze in Damien's chest as if his heart were being smothered. "Evil must be cleansed."

CHAPTER 28
CLERICAL ERRORS

Amma clasped her hands together, watching. She'd ducked behind the edge of the archway, toes fidgeting in her boots, saying silent prayers to whichever gods might be listening, dark ones included. *Be kind to him*, she thought, eyeing the woman, *or I will raze this temple to the ground.*

But the priestess who looked so like Damien was hugging him, and though he stood awkwardly beneath the embrace, his mother had accepted him. Amma pressed a hand over her mouth to hold in the cheer she wanted to squeal out. It was not perfect and *could* still go bad, she reminded herself, but she would put all of her hope into things working out.

She watched for another long moment and then began to feel odd, like perhaps even at this distance where she couldn't hear them, it was untoward to pry. Amma carefully walked the length of the corridor, glancing back to see them as they crossed the courtyard to a fountain in its center.

Amma hadn't noticed it before, but the structure was gorgeous, the water so clear, and at its top hovered an arcane depiction of a bird. The relic was made to look as though it was constantly in flight above the water's spout, giving off a gentle, blue glow. Beneath it, Damien and the priestess, Diana he had said his mother's name was, were deep in conversation.

Amma tore her gaze away and peeked out into the other courtyard. A pair of bluebirds flitted around one another, coming to land side by side on the branch of a dogwood, curiously still in bloom with white petals. Beneath it sat a woman in robes, needle and fabric in hand as she sewed peacefully in the sun, grinning down at her work. Amma had never been that happy when she was embroidering, but then she was similarly not interested in studying and serving the gods like these women presumably were.

A short stroll down the rest of the corridor brought her to another room of the temple, large with plenty of windows for light. A few tables were scattered in the space, and acolytes studied there together. Amma grinned, thinking of Perry and the Osurehm exams. They would be soon, and she wondered if he would be making his way to Eirengaard. A pang in her stomach told her she hoped he had somehow talked Laurel out of it, the potential danger in the capital making her uneasy, but they would stop it—whatever it was—she was sure.

No one gave Amma a second look, but the first that the acolytes did give her was quite enough. They each grinned and nodded, and she thought it was meant to be welcoming and kind, but it was a little weird. When they went back to their work, she took it as permission to wander through the bookcases there. Medical texts and herbal recipes lined the walls, and she ran fingers over spines, the smell of the thick, old tomes reminding her of the Grand Athenaeum and then of Damien's arms around her as they hid inside it, her stomach fluttering.

She'd told him she loved him, and she'd never meant anything more. The vows that were made in the temple she stood in were but pithy nothings in comparison to her own oath. Amma ran a finger down the spine of some text, tingles shooting up her arm and into her chest. He'd confessed to loving her as well, a thing she hadn't truly expected. What it meant, she didn't know, but for now, it was simply a quiet truth that they could share, and that was enough.

She took another deep breath of the pungent books, and there was something else, a scent that tickled at a memory, but not a good one. It came into her mind with panic, but she could only identify incense, a thing she had smelled many times, and perhaps a blacksmith? She found herself following it, fear being overridden by the more intense familiarity, to a narrow hall amongst the shelves. Where…where had she smelled that before?

"…delivered by the eclipse."

Amma came to a stop. Another voice spoke from down the hall, too muffled to hear, but then the first responded much too familiarly.

"No need. She will prepare him."

Gilead.

Amma turned and ran. How in the Abyss Gilead was there, she had no idea, but her boots would take her back to Damien, she would grab him and his mother, they would all flee as far from the temple, from Orrinshire, from the entire realm if need be, and then a squeezing in Amma's chest brought her to her knees.

The talisman. She slapped a hand over her heart, feeling the twinge of the stone inside her. Something had happened to Damien, she just knew it, and she stumbled as she tried to regain her footing.

A hand took her by the arm, and another was at her other side, questions of concern in her ears and white robes converging on her. Amma pulled away to be free of them, but there were so many. Panic took her, and she swung an elbow into a woman's face with a sickening crack. The sound brought the friendly frenzy at her sides to a halt, and even Amma stopped her wild flailing. These were priestesses of Isldrah, the goddess of health, and she had just collapsed in front of them—of course they only wanted to help.

"Gods, I'm sorry, but I must—"

The priestess turned back to her, blood dripping from her nose, but that was not what made Amma's own blood go cold. It was the priestess's face itself, the too-wide grin across it, the impassive, unobstructed elation still plastered on her face despite the assault.

The rest of the acolytes moved then, each offering her to sit, to breathe, to relax, every single one smiling too wide to be real. Multiple cups and jugs were being thrust at Amma, each filled with that water that was almost too beautiful to consume.

Don't drink the wine unless you'd like to end up a mindless devotee like them.

"Oh, fuck."

Amma thrashed into the chalices, and there was a clatter across the stone floors of drinkware and bodies toppling. She resumed her sprint through the study chambers and bowled through a set of priestesses blocking the archway to the corridor. The women shrieked even through their ridiculous grins, but Amma didn't care. She cut immediately into the courtyard, Damien's name bursting out of her throat as she dodged a birdbath and a fruiting berry bush, but then skidded to a stop when she saw him on his knees.

The blood mage was doubled over, a terrible, smoky blackness covering his form. Standing before him was the priestess, the woman who was meant to be his mother, and in her hands was that stupid, cursed pendant, the same black arcana surrounding it.

She propelled herself forward, every intention of tackling the woman, ripping the pendant from her grip, and freeing Damien of whatever this dark magic was, but then Amma was slammed into the courtyard's grass.

She screamed Damien's name into the dirt, lifting her head just enough to see that he was still stuck there on the ground. Only yards away, she reached out, clawing at the earth, and beneath, something solidified in her hand.

Amma swept the staff backward. A pulse of arcana shot away from her, knocking the acolytes off. She squeezed the branch of liathau to her chest as she rolled to her back, and she could hear the very grass growing all around as the earth trembled. Stone began to crack, and voices cried out as the branches of the nearest trees twisted and swung.

So, she would be razing the temple to the ground after all. They really should have been kind to him.

Gritting her teeth, Amma heaved herself upward. Diana had not moved from her place over a crippled Damien, but her arm was trembling as it held out the pendant, and tears streamed down her face. She was struggling to do this, whatever it was.

Amma sprinted, swinging her staff as she went and knocking an acolyte out of her path, the crack of the wood sending them into a tree that used branches to hold them back. She pounced, and even as Diana threw a free arm out to stop her, Amma tackled the woman to the ground. Magic swelled throughout the courtyard, and the temple walls shuddered.

Diana's hand pressed to Amma's throat, a blinding light emanating from it, but Amma could still see just enough that the pendant had been flung from the priestess's hand into the grass. She kicked and tried to scramble after it, but the priestess's grip tightened around her neck, both of them reaching for the stone. A vine slipped itself around the chain, dragging it closer to Amma, but then it was ripped right from the ground.

Gilead. Amma's arcana went wild, so strong then that she thought she might make the earth itself open up and swallow them all. Gilead faltered where he stood, but then he cast, and the sound Damien made struck Amma so deeply that she pulled back her own magic for fear of hurting him herself.

Damien had collapsed, face pressed to the earth. She called his name, but he did not move, even when a man wrenched him up from the ground, not a priest but someone noble—Kaspar Solonedy. She tried to cry out, but magic pulsed straight into her throat, paralyzing her, and then a frigid wave came crashing down onto her back. She sucked in a breath full of water, choking.

Amma spat, everything hazy. She had never felt so…good? Her limbs went wobbly, and she wondered what all the fuss was around her. People were yelling, but why? She rolled to her back, the earth beneath her muddy and wet, the sky above a pall of bright blue. A bird flitted through her vision. Nice. Things were…they were nice.

Then arms hauled her to her feet, and between strands of drenched hair, she saw him being dragged away by Kaspar and another nobleman. "Damien!" she called, voice hoarse. "Fight back!" But he was motionless.

Amma tore herself away from those that held her, staff still in hand as she slammed it into the ground, sending acolytes to their knees. She ran after him, but there was another priest and priestess and so much magic that the world shook. Diana caught her, and divine magic pulsed through Amma's staff.

The wood splintered right out of her grip, strands of silvery noxscura disintegrating into the air. "We will cleanse the evil from you," a voice called, and hands had her caught, forced to the ground, and there was water, so much water, being poured down her throat that she could only swallow and choke and silently scream until the blue sky faded into black.

Gone.

She raised a hand to her face and wiped at her eyes. She'd been crying, she could feel the rawness in her throat and the puffiness of her face as she swept up her forehead and…why was her hair wet?

"You're awake," said a voice, sweet and calming. "You must be thirsty."

Amma sat up, expecting her muscles to ache, but there was only a slight twinge. She wasn't even exhausted from the…wait, why would she be exhausted? Or even achy? Probably because she was sad.

So sad.

She accepted the copper cup from the woman who sat on the side of her bed and brought it to her lips. Cool and tasteless yet the most delicious thing she had ever had on her tongue, she swallowed.

The priestess's too-agreeable smile spread wide over her face. "It's good, isn't it?"

Amma nodded, tipping the cup further until it was empty then taking a gulp of air. Maybe she wasn't *that* sad.

"I have more." She reached for a jug on the closest table.

Amma let her fill the cup, but as she swallowed, her stomach flipped over. When had she last eaten? She blinked over at the only window in the little chamber, set high up near the ceiling, late afternoon sunlight streaming in. Last she remembered it was morning and she was coming...*coming*. She giggled. Wait, she was...coming to this place?

"Where—"

"Safe!" The woman refilled the small amount she had drained.

Amma placed the cup down, a bit sloshing over the edge and onto her thumb. She brought her hand to her mouth to lick it off then stopped—what was she wearing? Atop her normal clothing was another layer, white and embellished along the sleeves and hem with tiny, blue, embroidered birds. Priestess robes? That seemed like it might not be so good.

"I think I need to—"

"Something awful happened," the priestess said to her, suddenly taking her hands. "You're safe now, but you're very sick. You must rest. And you must drink."

The cup was in her hands again, and she nodded, taking another sip. It *was* delicious but made her tongue go numb. Things would be all right, though, numb tongue or not. Then she felt bile in her throat. "I don't think I can."

"If you don't, you'll remember the bad thing that happened," the woman said with the utmost concern. "And then you'll be crying again. Nobody cries here. It's not polite."

Amma pressed fingers to her face under an eye, puffiness there. "What bad thing?"

"Oh, see, no, I can't tell you because that will make it worse. It's better if you don't remember. Don't you feel better? Can you remember any bad things?"

Amma squinted. Bad things. There had been many. Or at least some...one? No, there wasn't really anything in her memory except a boy. A very handsome boy who she loved, which wasn't a bad thing at all. And yet.

"Drink." The woman pushed the cup up to Amma's mouth and water sloshed over her lips.

"I'm going to be sick," Amma sputtered, stomach rolling over again.

"Oh!" The priestess stood quickly. "I'll run to the kitchens and get you something to fill your belly, and then you can keep drinking."

When the priestess was gone, Amma gazed down at herself again, hands shaking. Her heart thumped in her ears, and a little buzzing in the back of her brain told her something was off.

Magic. There was magic inside her. And it wasn't...it wasn't hers. But that was okay. Everything was okay. But maybe she shouldn't have any more to drink. And maybe it wasn't okay that things were okay.

How…how far away were the kitchens?

She placed the cup on the side table, and when she glanced downward, a mouse had suddenly appeared in her lap as if out of nowhere. Amma went to sweep him right off of her with a squeal but froze. "V-vanders?"

Pain shot through her hand as the creature bit down on her thumb. Amma reacted without thinking, flinging her hand, but the vaxin held on, his little body flopping around. Blood pooled where his long teeth pinched in, a throbbing pain running down her arm, through her veins and into her chest. Blood. Pain. Arcana. Love.

"Damien!" Haze cleared from Amma's mind as she carefully eased Vanders into her hand, and he released her thumb. Her eyes darted to the cup filled with water, to the window set up too high to reach, to the robes she wore that were not her own. "Oh, those sneaky bitches."

There were sounds beyond the door, and her heart raced. "I am happy to see you, Vanders, but you need to hide again." The vaxin poofed into nonexistence, and she grabbed the jug. There was no basin to dispose of it, only a potted plant in the room's corner, and that would have to do. She hustled over and poured half of it out before the sound in the hall came too close, and she had to sprint back to the bed.

"We've got rye bread and raspberries and goat cheese," the priestess was saying as she backed into the room with a tray.

Amma sat up straight, plastering on a smile, the cup back in her hand and empty.

"Oh, you're looking much better." The woman set the tray on the bed and immediately filled Amma's cup.

Amma nodded absently, corners of her mouth curled up, eyes darting across the room at movement there. The potted fern was growing so quickly she could see it. "Oh, my gods."

The priestess's smile faltered, and she began to look over her shoulder. "What's wrong?"

Amma grabbed her arm, pulling her attention back. "I meant goddess. Isldrah, specifically. Isn't she great? And this water's just so good." She brought the freshly filled cup to her lips but kept them tightly pressed together. Arcana prodded at her mouth, and she nearly sputtered back.

"I'm so glad!" The priestess gave Amma's knee a pat and took the jug. "I'll bring you more in a little while. Eat up, and tomorrow morning we'll start on your studies. You need your rest tonight."

Amma continued to smile stupidly until the door was shut, and then the grin plummeted off her face. "No chance, sister."

CHAPTER 29
NO REST FOR THE WELL-BEHAVED

Amma couldn't carry the fern from the room's corner, the pot too sodden with the contents of multiple jugs of that frighteningly persuasive water, so she had to dig the plant out. The fern had tripled in size since she'd ferreted away what she'd pretended to drink in its soil, but it had hidden the liquid well, and luckily no one had questioned why her chamber pot was still empty, or why the little bush was sprawling so impressively all of a sudden. Throat dry, her jaw ached from all the ridiculous smiling she'd been doing when acolytes came to check on her throughout the evening, and now her arms would too, but she managed to pull the root-bound shrub away from the clay and carry it to the room's center where she had the most space.

She took an appraising look around the little chamber in the darkness and quiet of the night, the light-colored stone, the simple and clean trappings, the book of Empyrean songs sitting on the foot of the bed. Was she really going to do this? Would the temple even allow it?

"Okay, Isldrah," said Amma as she knelt before the plant, "I think we both know that whatever's going on here probably isn't what you intended." She picked up the book of songs and flipped through it, looking for something appropriate. "And I get that this isn't the way you'd probably like to fix things either, but I'm the best you've got, and, really, birds make their nests in trees all the time, so maybe Sestoth sent me to help."

She stopped on a page that spoke of curing madness by requesting the assistance of guardians devoted to Isldrah. Yup, that would work, it had to. She tore it out and set the rest of the book aside.

Dirt on her hands, muddied from the last dousing she'd given the plant, she took a deep breath and began to draw a circle on the light stone floor with the soil, mimicking how she'd seen Damien do it. The shapes came easily, the Chthonic writing itself under her fingers as if she were born knowing the language. But then she came to the name.

Amma traced what she remembered Damien's markings to look like in the mountains, but it seemed incorrect. Beneath it, she tried again, and again, something was wrong. Finally, she reverted to Key, and simply wrote out how she imagined the name would look in her own language. It was the best she could do, and if she could summon at all—a thing she wasn't terribly confident in—she would hopefully end up with some kind of help.

She sat back and took stock of her work, Vanders perched on her shoulder and finishing off a crust of rye bread. Under the candlelight and against the clean floors, the Chthonic scribbled in messy soil took on a creepy slant, but it was beautiful too.

Clearing her throat, she read aloud the Empyrean of the song she'd torn from Isldrah's book, beseeching the goddess for help but replacing *guardian* with *imp*. When she reached its end, she caught the page on fire with her candle and dropped the burning parchment atop the plant—Damien used fire, so she guessed she needed it too—and then offered her finger to Vanders.

"We're in this together," she said, and the vaxin nipped her again. Quickly, before the flame went out, she squeezed a drop of blood over the burning fern, and then a second and third, just to be sure. Finally, she buried her hands into the roots of the plant, whispered an apology to it, and pumped her arcana in.

Amma didn't expect the sudden burst of silver that came swirling up before her, but then she really should have as, for all she didn't know about arcana, she had gotten a pivotal thing correct—urgency. She needed help, and she needed it now.

Throwing herself back to avoid being blasted in the face by a portal to another plane, Amma held her breath, watching arcana and burning leaves swirl up to the chamber ceiling. Crawling backward a few more feet and gnawing on her lip as the portal grew, silvery strands licked all the way to the corners of the room overhead.

"Don't burn through," she muttered, eyes flicking to the door, but then the light doused itself, and she was left in the quiet of the dark with just her candle and a blobby shadow where the plant had been—or where it still was, she couldn't exactly tell as it very well could have just been the husk of the plant, burnt tendrils poking out oddly. And then one of the tendrils moved.

"Kaz?" Amma leaned forward carefully.

A ball of claws and fangs and red skin shot at her, wrapping around her neck so tightly she thought she was being attacked until she heard the familiar panting and snuffling of Quaz. A laugh broke out of her as the feral imp dragged its tongue up the side of her face. Help was help, she supposed, and scratched under his leathery chin.

But there was still movement in her circle, and another imp sat up out of the soil, slow and wretched. "Mistress," it said as if the absolute worst were about to happen, "I have been resummoned."

"Oh, my goodness," said Amma as Quaz clamored down her side and began to investigate the room by darting from corner to corner. "Or, badness, I guess."

"Get off, get off, I need to greet my master!" a gurgly, strangled whine called from below Katz, and the sallow imp was shifted away as a third rose from the ground, soil smeared all over his front and crooked jaw drawn into an intent grimace.

"Kaz!" Amma pushed up onto her knees and threw her arms out.

"Harlot!" Kaz bound toward Amma and wrapped long, spindly arms around her middle. Amma squeezed him back, tears in her eyes. His little wings flapped, and his tail wagged, and she couldn't bring herself to let him go even when he began to squirm away. "Okay, okay," he grumbled, slipping out from under her grasp. "Where is Master Bloodthorne?"

Amma wiped at her face. "Well, that's sort of why you're here."

Kaz stepped back to stand beside Katz, and Quaz came scurrying up to his other side. Six bulbous eyes shined back at her in the candlelight from the little row of infernal creatures, each varyingly invested in what she was about to say.

"So, Damien's been abducted."

Three vastly different noises erupted from the imps, but they all amounted to the same declaration of, *What in the Abyss are you talking about?*

"Quiet, please, you'll wake up the priestesses."

"Priestesses?" Kaz pressed claws to his rounded stomach. "I thought it was the summons that was making me feel so awful."

"No, that's probably the temple—don't make those faces, I'm pretty sure Isldrah herself let you in here, so at least pretend to be

272

grateful. Step one is breaking out of this place anyway, and then step two is finding Master Bloodthorne."

"You *lost* Master Bloodthorne, Mistress?" Katz's disappointment was immeasurable, and his summons was ruined. Quaz whined quietly, tail wrapped around him, and Kaz was tapping a clawed foot against the stone with his knobby arms crossed tight.

"Only a little, but it's not like it's the first time."

Kaz's massive eyes widened. "You said you would take care of him, and you lost Master twice?"

"I know!" she hissed back, his words weighing heavily in her chest. "I'm not happy about it either, but at least I have experience saving him now, okay? Also, I've been doing my best, but Damien has proven himself *quite* abductable lately. Like, maybe a little too abductable considering how close together these two abductions happened. In fact, if someone were telling me about this, I would probably think the pacing was a little off." She ran hands through her curls and cleared her throat. "But this is the problem the gods have dropped into our laps, and we need to deal with it. It's not like this next part's going to be very hard anyway. You three just need to sneak out, fly into the courtyard, and smash something for me. Kaz, I remember how especially good you are at throwing things on the ground from up high."

Kaz stuck out his tongue. "We were *just* summoned. No flying's happening tonight. And I don't know how you think imps are supposed to sneak around a temple."

"Oh, I already thought of that: disguise yourselves as birds—they *love* birds here, it's a whole thing."

"I don't think I can transform yet," droned Katz.

Quaz squeezed his eyes shut, clenched his fists, and started to shake. He emanated a low growl, but all that came of it was a puff of rank-smelling gas before he collapsed to the ground from the effort.

Kaz shoved at the other imp to put fresher air between them then gestured to his clearly infernal self. "Without Master granting us additional powers, this is all we are for at least a day."

"We don't have a day." Amma grit her teeth and glared up at the high window. "The eclipse is happening tomorrow, and I still need to get all the way to Eirengaard, and Damien's mother—"

"Master Bloodthorne's mother?" Kaz padded up to Amma, sticking his crooked jaw in her face. Amma remembered how he had spoken of human women in the past, stating they were deceitful and treacherous, and how that ill will extended to her. "She's here?"

"We need her, so you're going to be nice. I think she might be the only one with information on where Damien is, and I'm pretty sure this temple is enthralling her about a hundred times worse than I've ever been." Amma stood, pacing to the door. She needed to believe the woman was enthralled, really, otherwise the desire to pummel her for what she'd done to Damien until only holy water was left took over. "At least I know I can unlock this chamber. Are the three of you ready?"

When she turned, the row of imps actually straightened before her, even Kaz. They were truly ugly, wretched, feral creatures that behaved poorly and smelled worse, and she absolutely loved them. She took a deep breath, pressing a hand to her chest. "We're getting out of here, and we're rescuing Damien, and I don't know exactly how we're going to do it, and I don't even know if all of you will survive, but you've all died once, and you were very good at coming back, so..."—she scrunched up her nose, not quite sure where the speech was going— "Who wants to totally demolish this holy place?"

Six eyes shimmered, claws clacked, and the imps swore to follow Amma into battle.

After explaining just what she needed them to do, the door unlocked for Amma as easily as she knew it would, and she stuck her head out into the hall, Vanders tucked into the pocket of the priestess's robes she still wore just in case someone saw her. Each imp popped their heads out as well, but thankfully no one was coming. The narrow corridor was quiet, many doors along it where she assumed other acolytes slept, lay closed. It seemed the minor ruckus of her summoning didn't rouse anyone.

She pulled up her hood and silently sprinted down to the study room, finding it empty and dark, the moonlight dimmer as it spilled in through the wide windows at the back of the temple. She gestured to the imps, and they came scurrying behind, Kaz stopping short, Quaz running into him, and Katz slowly bringing up the rear. They weren't quite as steady on their taloned feet as she would have liked, but they could still serve some purpose, she was just waiting for that purpose to show itself. Another scurry brought her to the corridor that would take her to the courtyard, but there she stopped abruptly, knocked into by an imp against each calf.

There were two women in robes in the far courtyard on the right. The moonlight was odd, but of course the eclipse was coming, and it cast long, weird shadows from the bushes and basins. The trees had twisted under Amma's arcana, reaching upward and out at strange angles, and there were cracks running through the outer walls that made her grin. "I did that," she whispered, pointing out the destruction.

Kaz just rolled his bulbous eyes.

The priestesses were discussing something in whispers very close together that Amma strained to hear, but then one grabbed the other. Amma shrank back into the shadows, throwing a hand over her mouth, fearing they'd resorted to violence, but only after a moment did she realize she was simply watching the two from the shadows as they ferociously kissed one another.

"Oh," she whispered to herself then snorted, "okay, but why can't you go be frisky somewhere else?"

"Should we kill them?" asked Kaz, Katz waiting studiously behind him, and Quaz looked ready to bolt out into the moonlight, claws and fangs bared.

"No, we're not killing anybody, these people are enthralled, remember? Just come with me." They maneuvered quietly to the other archway and angled themselves so that the fountain was just in view, but a priestess was already sitting on the edge of it. "Why is everyone choosing tonight to wander around and be sneaky?" Amma groused and pulled the robes off over her head.

A short and stressful conversation with the three later, Amma pushed her shoulders back, held her chin up, and smiled. She belonged now, or at least, the priestess should have thought that she should think that she did, and so she was going to act like it, even if she wasn't wearing their vestments anymore. Distracting one priestess and convincing her to come away from the fountain should be easy enough, but then that priestess's head raised, and she saw it was Diana.

Amma's smile faltered, probably a plain enough thing to see in the moonlight, but Diana was not beaming ridiculously back at her either. In her lap, she held Amma's things, her pouch and her holstered dagger, and a cup sat beside her on the fountain's ledge.

When she stood, bringing the cup with her, Amma's muscles clenched, but the woman didn't move to unsheathe the weapon. Deep circles were under her eyes, so like Damien's that it made Amma's heart ache. She bit her lip, swallowing back a lump in her throat, and then peeled the corners of her mouth up.

"You came here with him," said Diana, her voice like a ghost wandering through some future version of the courtyard long after it had crumbled away to nothing. "You tried to help him."

Amma wasn't sure if it were an indictment or praise, or even if she was supposed to remember after so much mind-altering water, but the hollowness in Diana's face urged her to nod back because it was true— she had tried to help him, and she wasn't going to stop.

"He was my son," the priestess said taking a step closer.

She watched her fists tighten around Amma's things and the cup. "He still is."

Diana shook her head, eyes locked onto the ground. "I let them take him." She had moved a bit farther from the fountain, slowly going to where Amma stood. Another figure clad in priestess robes sauntered out into the courtyard.

"Where did they take him?" asked Amma, voice cracking. "And for what?"

"The will of the gods." There was exhaustion in Diana's face and words. Behind her, the robed figure came closer, and Amma's eyes went wide as it wavered like a drunkard but then corrected to stay aloft. At least its hood remained pulled forward.

What was she supposed to say now? "Isldrah's will?"

Diana shook her head again. "Osurehm. The crown." She brought the cup to her lips, and Amma wanted to bat it away from her, to watch it rain down on the earth and to free the woman of the hold the enthrallment had, but it was too soon.

The other figure made it to the fountain, swaying one way and then the other, body undulating strangely until it finally leaned against its edge. It lifted one very short and very strange leg and hopped up onto the bottom tier. It swayed again, so far back Amma was sure it would topple, but then two sets of spindly arms jutted out of the robe, and, spinning madly in the air, it straightened again. *Darkness, lightness, whatever*, she prayed silently, *help us*.

"You'll be happier here," Diana said then, a lilt to her voice as her chin lifted.

Amma forced herself to nod. "Yeah. Totally."

Diana extended her hand, and to Amma's disappointment, it was the cup she offered and not her dagger.

The figure on the fountain was wobbling as it stretched upward, and a tail poked out from the bottom of the robe, but it was getting closer.

Amma took the offered cup and plastered on an even wider smile. "So, a priestess, huh? That's interesting."

"I was raised in this temple when my parents died. Isldrah called me into her service shortly after." Diana's hands came around Amma's and eased the cup upward.

"Funny how that happens," Amma said, watching the water ascend and then flicking her gaze to the figure on the fountain. How they were lucky enough for no one else to notice the little, stacked idiots, she didn't know, but all three sets of arms were sticking out of the robes now, gripping and reaching and looking like they would topple at any minute.

The cup had reached her mouth, and Amma tipped it toward her lips though she held them tightly together. Diana was urging her on, grinning hollowly, tall enough to look down and possibly see she was only miming taking a drink. The priestess's eyes narrowed as the cold liquid splashed against Amma's face.

There was a screech, and Diana turned, eyeing the imps as they burst forth from the robe. From the top of the stack, Quaz wasted no time, pouncing off of Kaz's shoulders and knocking the other two to the ground. He grabbed the hovering bird as he flew and sailed over the fountain in an arc before plummeting, wings working but doing nothing to stop his fall.

Diana sucked in a sharp breath, lifting a hand that glowed with a brilliantly golden light, but it was too late. Quaz landed, and the relic shattered beneath him, shards and arcana in every color spilling out in the moonlight.

A pulse rolled over the courtyard's grass followed by a fluttering of wings, sleeping birds woken and scattering, crying out cacophonously. Nausea roiled in Amma's stomach, and Diana fell right to her knees. There was a seeping from the flora, color and life leeching away, and a chill settled down over everything like the first winter wind sweeping over a plain.

Amma dropped the cup and knelt beside Diana. The woman had a hold of her head, groaning, retching, tears streaming down her face, and for a moment Amma worried this had all been a terrible mistake. If Amma's assumptions were right, Damien's mother had been there for over twenty years, toiling under some false belief that had just been shattered in one go, and if the woman's mind weren't permanently altered already, suddenly shucking it into the present would certainly not help.

But then Diana's head popped up, and she gasped.

Amma sat very still in the quiet that followed, watching Diana's eyes widen as they stared blankly forward. Then slowly, her hands came to her face and pressed into her cheeks. "Oh, I fucked up."

Well, that was an understatement, but perhaps it held more weight coming from a priestess.

"My little boy," she said so quietly it was nearly inaudible, then swiftly got to her feet. When Diana stumbled, Amma caught her, and the woman looked at her like she'd appeared out of nowhere. "You," she said sharply, "you tried to help him."

"Yeah, um, we went over this, but—"

"And I could have killed him!" She bent and grabbed Amma's

things from the ground and thrust them at her. "Why did you let me do that?"

Amma's mouth fell open as the woman began to stomp away, then she blinked and caught up. "Excuse me, but I *tried*. All of your holy friends made it pretty difficult."

Diana huffed, gesturing to the pair of priestesses in the other courtyard who had fallen to the ground, one sobbing uncontrollably, the other looking like her mind might have melted as she stared up at the moons. "Oh, I know, I know, I just can't believe I've been so foolish and for so long!"

Amma struggled to belt her hip pouch as she followed Diana back into the temple. It wasn't exactly where she wanted to go, but the woman seemed to be on a mission. "Have you been here Damien's whole life?"

"I guess so, though it barely feels like it's been any time at all." There was a small effigy of Isldrah in the hall, and Diana threw her hands out at the thing as they passed. "I can't believe you let this happen!"

Amma made a weak, apologetic gesture to the statue then began working on her thigh holster as she hopped behind Diana into one of the smaller bed chambers.

"As soon as I see him, I am going to throttle him," Diana was growling as she stuffed things into a bag.

"Damien?" Amma straightened, hand on her dagger.

"No, Zagadoth!" She pulled the draw tight on her bag and slung it over her shoulder. "He just left me here as if I ever would have actually—Kaz?"

Amma glanced down to see all three imps huddled behind her in the doorway to the chamber. Kaz was just peeking out from behind Amma's legs, and his eyes went wide when the woman acknowledged him. "Remember what I said," Amma hissed, but the imp was already shooting toward the woman.

Amma tried to stop his attack, but Kaz was too fast, leaping into her outstretched arms. Squeezing him tight, Diana planted a kiss on the top of his head. "You terrible little beast, I am so glad to see you."

Kaz sniffled under her embrace, and when he was released, he was beaming up at the two of them like he'd been dunked into the fountain himself. Amma held her hands out as if in disbelief at what she was seeing. "I thought you hated human women?"

The imp just shrugged.

Diana stepped up onto the cot in the room and then reached atop the wardrobe at its side. "There you are," she sighed and pulled down something long and thin that she held in both hands with a reverence. Tugging on its end, she revealed a few inches of metal that shimmered in the slight light, and then quickly resheathed the blade.

"You have a sword?" Amma gawked.

"I'm a holy warrior of Isldrah—of course I have a sword. Don't you?"

"Uh, no." Amma scratched her head. "Sometimes I have a stick though. Except for when priestesses blow it up."

"Oh, right. Apologies. Who exactly are you anyway?" Diana hopped down from the bed and was striding again so quickly that Amma had to jog to keep up.

"She's Master Bloodthorne's trollop," said Kaz as he followed behind.

"Kaz, my son does not have a—" Diana halted her march back through the temple's study room and clicked her tongue. "Oh, gods, I haven't been around; he very well might."

Amma stomped past her and swung around. "My name is Amma, and *your son* abducted me after losing his enthrallment talisman under my skin. A talisman that was meant for King Archibald because he planned to destroy the whole realm with it by releasing *your husband*, a demon. He's stuck in a crystal, by the way, which is probably why he didn't come to get you. And whether I'm a prostitute or a baroness or a witch or whatever, it doesn't matter, because all I'm interested in being right now is the person who protects Damien and puts a stop to all this eclipse nonsense which needs its own, huge explanation, but I'm only talking if we're both moving because we need to get to Eirengaard, and it's half a day away. So, are you going to help me or not?"

Diana blinked back at her, and the corner of her mouth ticked up into a smirk. "Oh, I am going to help you, Amma, but I hope you are prepared for a little destruction, if need be."

"To get him back?" She scoffed. "I'm prepared to destroy the entire realm myself."

CHAPTER 30
THE DARK DAY OF THE SOUL

When Damien came to, he knew it was bad. And not the good kind of bad. Not even the bad kind, really. This was a wholly new measurement of bad, one he hadn't experienced before despite thinking all along he was the epitome of *the worst*. But Damien Maleficus Bloodthorne had been wrong.

He'd been wrong about a lot of things, a dose of truth that did him very little good when he was tied to a stake, but at least his maturing cognizance represented growth, and what more can one ask of a human man?

"Sorry," he mumbled, the word still rattling around in his head. He wasn't sure what for, but he knew he should have been, or he was, or would be later. It was as inevitable as the fulfillment of the prophecy.

"This isn't that Caldor asshole."

Damien lifted his head to see two blurry figures standing before him.

"He got himself killed," said a voice that was slightly familiar. Erick? No—Damien squinted—Kaspar Solonedy.

"I thought they were tricking that idiot brother of his into taking his place?" asked the other man.

"Guess not."

The air was stagnant and cold, smelling of wet earth and brimstone. Damien was someplace familiar, yet he'd never been exactly here. A tortuously slow turn of his head allowed him to gaze out over a muddy field and the tiered seating that surrounded it, an arena, but he'd never seen one so empty, and certainly never standing in its center.

Across the field, there were two other figures, and amongst the stands, an audience of only two more. The shadow of the otherwise empty seating crawled away from where Damien was trapped in the arena's middle as dawn broke beyond its high wall. He'd lost the entire night which meant—

Noxscura coursed through Damien, jolting him completely awake. For once, he let it come with abandon, desperate for escape. The bindings on his arms and chest and legs strained as arcana clouded his vision, his thoughts, stealing his breath and stilling his heart.

And then it was gone, sucked away even quicker than it came, dragging at Damien's limbs and his mind. If he weren't bound to a pole, he would have been pulled to his knees as the noxscura was drained down into the earth.

Kaspar and the other man recoiled, only then realizing Damien was conscious. The stranger went for his sword, but Kaspar stilled his hand. "Look."

At Damien's feet, the earth had gone black.

"Oh, fuck me," Damien grumbled.

The sun continued to climb, filling the sky with a bloody-colored haze. Kaspar and his companion backed away as the other two neared, Roman Caldor's hulking form amongst them, and soon four men were staring back at Damien with the kind of disgust Damien would have normally reserved for them instead.

Young, pretty, smug, the four wore crests from whatever places they lorded over across the realm, each dressed so cleanly that the mud of the field was especially offensive on the hems of white cloaks and shined boots. Sons of noble houses, they were clearly impressionable, entitled, egomaniacal, stupid. It was like leering into a pool and having four reflections sneer back.

"That's a blood mage, huh?" said the shortest amongst them, chest puffed out, louder than he needed to be and making Damien's ears ring. "Doesn't seem so dangerous." He came closer, hand raised, and there was a flash of golden light as he flicked Damien in the forehead. A spike of pain drove into his skull followed by the smell of burnt flesh.

Damien gnashed his teeth and struggled against the binds, noxscura flaring up once again. Hazy darkness surrounded all of them, the short man actually crying out and jumping back, and then the arcana was drawn down into the earth leaving Damien utterly drained.

"He was dangerous. Once."

Damien managed to rouse his head, tunneling vision honing in on the final two as they joined the others. Gilead, the mage who had played at serving Cedric, had his hood back, weathered skin warm in the red lights of a tumultuous sky. Beside him stood Archibald Lumier, divine mage, warden of his father, King of the Realm. Damien wasn't sure who he hated more.

Gilead stepped beyond the crescent the others stood in safely yards away. The only bold one now, the mage grabbed Damien beneath his jaw, and he couldn't move out from under the man's withered hand, smelling so like brimstone it burnt his throat. Gilead had stepped into the ring of blackness expanding at Damien's feet, but the shadows barely licked at him.

"Come on, now," said Gilead, a smirk on his dry, thin lips. "Feed It. It is your destiny."

Noxscura wrapped around the fingers that dug into his throat, but Damien willed it back, sweat pouring down his neck and muscles shaking. If that was what they wanted, then it was the last thing he was willing to give them, but he was struck by the fact he'd expected to be run through, his blood spilt, to be cleansed from the plane. But they weren't killing him—they were coaxing E'nloc into existence. Were they really that stupid?

"Do they know you're doing this for the Grand Order of Dread?" Damien spat back, throat raw. He looked for shock on the faces of the others, but nothing in their features changed.

"If I were to act in the Order's favor, it would have already been done in The Temple of the Void. They expected containment in a vessel, before It could come to full power, so that they could destroy It." He squeezed so tightly, Damien could not take another breath. "You should be thanking me, boy—that would have been your death."

The Order was going to *destroy* E'nloc? Damien scowled through his suffocation—that meant they were going to destroy *him* too. Gilead's hand finally released him.

"And this isn't meant to be my end?" he coughed, the growing pool of forever darkness lapping at his bound ankles. The magic was so intense, he no longer felt the nausea or the pain, only the ebbing of his own blood inside him, being drawn toward the dreaded inevitability below.

"Cooperation goes a long way," Gilead whispered, decaying breath on Damien's face, and then he backed toward the others. "Truly, what we do here today, the sacrifices we make for the holy light of Osurehm, is in service of the realm."

Murmurs rose up in agreement from the rest, though the words seemed hollow and repetitious. They were…they were *all* divine mages, weren't they? Perhaps further removed from their dominion forebears than Damien, but with veins that ran thick with luxerna in their blood.

And there Damien stood, alone and given up to *good.*

Dawn's crimson brightness that had been creeping over the stadium began to darken then. Over the edge of the arena's high wall, a black orb hung in the sky above the sun's ascent, slowly swallowing the light. As it rose, the sun would be blotted out when it passed behind the moons still hanging there, one before the other.

When the day is night…damn it.

The men stepped back, giving Damien space as if there were anything he could do in his bound state. Even if he could have bled himself, casting was out of the question; E'nloc would absorb it all. Defenseless, he watched the four noble sons and Archibald drawing various, pointed weapons to be brought to their forearms while Gilead looked on.

Only by the spilling of the descendants' blood may It rise…shit.

Blades cut into flesh. Bloodcraft done by divine mages. Hypocritical bastards. Bastards, all of them. Everyone, leaving him there to rot just like the corners of the world. Rot he had failed to stop— fuck, perhaps he had actually been feeding it, left to fester and grow, to follow him, find him, and consume him in the end just as he knew it would. However far he traveled, however much he changed, he couldn't escape the prophecy, couldn't escape who he knew he was meant to be. He'd not expected to become a sacrifice, of course, but then he had always been a tool of evil. Even his own mother knew it.

Blood splashed over the arena's mud as darkness ascended overhead, the sun rising into its own obscurity behind the double moons. The blood lost its color in the growing crimson shadows. No one moved to stab Damien though, the men, even Archibald, simply watching the void open at his feet.

Curiously, Damien did not sink into the darkness, and no tendril reached out to wrap around him. His racing heart did slow, though, breath calming. There was pressure on every limb, on his chest, on his head. Something was happening, but he had no idea what, the sound of wind whipping down through the arena's basin carried away into a hollow nothingness. An entire arena, and not a seat filled, only these six to watch as he could no longer hold back the noxscura, and they didn't even look pleased by the heinousness they were inflicting upon him.

"Can't you at least fucking enjoy this?" he gasped.

But no—they insisted on looking utterly terrified.

Only Gilead had the courtesy to grin as Damien succumbed to E'nloc, arcana flooding out of him so quickly that he only had a few seconds more before turning to a husk. The mage held up the pendant, the one his mother had used against him, the one Delphine had stolen, the one he had given to Amma for protection.

Amma. She'd done her best, really, if only he could say the same for himself.

The sun finally hid behind the moons completely, and darkness fell over Eiren. Damien wasn't a praying man, he wasn't even aware of what most of the gods were called, but he knew Thea, goddess of death, mostly because her name was easy to remember. As her fingers crawled up Damien's spine, the only thing he thought to lament was not telling Amma he loved her sooner. Because it had always been true, he had just been too stupid to realize and too afraid to say, and he mourned not having a moment longer with her.

Then there was nothing.

Well, no, there was an inky blackness. A bone-deep chill too. And the strange feeling of floating. If this was death, then perhaps it wasn't *that* terrible, but to experience this *forever*?

It wasn't death, of course, because Damien Maleficus Bloodthorne couldn't die that easily, and death was quite different than just floating in chilly darkness forever, but those details would be sorted later.

A tingle, something like noxscura, ran over the back of Damien's head—that was, if he had a head anymore. In the darkness, there was a flicker—half of an ugly, red stone that had a ridiculous name he probably should have paid a little more attention to. And then there was a voice.

"Finally," It said. "Ours."

The stone's other half floated up to meet the first before him in the nothingness.

"Oh, no, no, no," Damien groaned. "Just let me be dead."

"Destruction soon," It replied as the two halves of the rough-cut gem became one, no longer fragmented, "but first, existence."

Discord.

Domination.

Destruction.

These things flooded into Damien uninhibited and limitless. He'd gotten a taste of this kind of power in The Wilds when he had allowed his noxscura to erupt unbridled, but this—this was *so* much more. This was everything, the ability to strangle and crush and not just kill but make nonexistent. This wasn't breaking, wasn't death, but annihilation.

And it, or It, was inside Damien.

The ground was no longer soft, the stake at his back gone, and Damien could flex his fingers, roll his shoulders, straighten his back. He could do a lot more than that, actually: he could swallow the entire world if he liked, but he didn't need to, not with the looks he was getting in the dark.

We should kill them, It said into his mind.

Six men stood before him, but he only needed one. *At least give them a head start*, he said back to It. *It will be more fun that way.* "Run."

Roman Caldor was first to flee, his weapon dropped into the mud with a disappointing splat. He made it perhaps two yards off before a black tendril burst from the ground and ensnared him. There was a guttural scream, a crushing of bones, and then nothing was left of the final Caldor heir but blood.

Kaspar and the other two nobles scrambled, but Damien simply reached out. Or was it E'nloc who reached? Who took? Who killed? Two of them were gone just the same as Roman, and then only the little one was left. He was raised higher into the air, a second tendril working upward, curling as if to flick him in the head but instead impaling him through his face before he too was squashed.

The field was awash in darkness, but the blood of the four caught the slight ring of sunlight still visible in the arcane eclipse above the arena, shimmering beautifully in the shadows.

Damien grinned—darkness, that felt *good.*

Archibald hadn't fled, but he was gripping onto Gilead, his other arm unsheathing his sword. Magic was alight in the weapon, divine mages often choosing something sharp as a conduit for their strongest powers. Rather silly, such a little flicker in the dark, barely a candle held up against the expanse of the Abyss.

Damien shook his head. E'nloc flicked a thin tendril. The magic was snuffed out, and the sword was pulled from his grip, tossed across the field.

Archibald reared back, but he had nothing to be afraid of—Damien needed him. It was the mage he didn't need.

"Aren't you supposed to be able to control him?" Archibald cried.

Control Damien? With E'nloc inside him? *No one* would ever control him again.

Well…

Gilead snorted at the king's demand and simply squeezed his fist.

A pressure in Damien's chest mimicked the move, and his arm twitched. Oh, that was much, much less good.

Let us kill them.

Damien's head pounded with the demand. *Not Archibald. I need him.*

We need nothing. Complete the merger so We may destroy all.

So, the merger wasn't complete?

Gilead squeezed his hand again, such a nothing move for a nothing spell, and Damien fell to one knee.

"How?" he coughed.

"I've not been studying this entity for decades and drenching myself in protection after protection so that I would be at its mercy once summoned," spat Gilead.

That one knows, It spoke into Damien's mind, voice vicious, *but his manipulation works on the vessel alone. Relinquish control, and We can stop him.*

Archibald's relieved sigh cut through Damien as he was trapped there in the mud, ensnared all over again. "I was quite nervous there for a moment," said the king as if he were not surrounded by the splattered remains of four of his most loyal subjects. He wiped at a drop of blood on his cheek. "The crimes continue to accumulate for our villain, eh? At least there will be no question his death will be well deserved. Perhaps we'll even make a holiday out of it. Well, let's get this over with. Send him on his wild rampage, remember to avoid the places we discussed, and we'll reconvene in Eirengaard's square for the finale."

Gilead let out a long, low sigh. He turned swiftly to the king, his own arm raised, ill intent in it along with an arcana that would surely kill. With his other fist so tight, Damien could barely breathe let alone move, only glancing upward. "I didn't domesticate the greatest destructive force in existence to do the bidding of some pathetic monarch with a father complex."

Archibald took a step back, boot squelching in the mud. "You serve the crown." He spoke as if nothing else could be true.

"I've the combined knowledge of the Grand Order of Dread and the Benevolent Advising Descendants. I alone have combined the luxerna flowing in the veins of dominion offspring with a noxscura-filled vessel to bring E'nloc into our plane. I serve no one but myself."

Shocking, thought Damien.

Good for him, It replied.

"Now, let us see what this can do, shall we?" With a twist of Gilead's wrist, Damien felt the world fall out from under him. Arcana was no gentle thing unless willed to be, but when it was thrust through one so completely, it showed no mercy.

Damien screamed his throat raw as the veil was pulled taught over his body and then began to tear. Or he was tearing it, or he was being torn, he didn't know, but there were fissures, huge swaths of rent plane, and all manner of beasts flowed through on hooves and wings and claws. Damien could see them each, individually, and his will was placed into them, talisman unneeded. Each pledged allegiance to the one who had allowed them this, to him—well, to the him that was also E'nloc, but still—and they climbed into Eirengaard as the screams of the city's inhabitants filled the air. The creatures waited for Damien's command, but he had none to give, not without Gilead to tell him to give it.

The mage let out a triumphant sound as the arena came back into Damien's focus. He could see the silvery fissures that had broken in even there. Abyssal hounds bared fangs, hoards of imps readied themselves for battle, a serpent larger than a tavern coiled in wait, and a tiny, black cat rubbed itself against Damien's shin.

"What are you doing?" cried Archibald. "This isn't what we planned. Not *here*. Did you summon them in the estate district too? The keep? Are you mad?"

"Are you?" Gilead rounded on him. "You must be to believe that I would assist in your asinine plot to frame some blood mage for resurrecting the greatest evil to exist in ten-thousand years so that you can play savior to your realm and live up to the deeds of kings that came before you. You're the mad fool, and I've got no use for you."

No, not Archibald. Damien needed him, and worse, he did not want to be left with Gilead.

Give yourself over completely, and We can spare him.

Damien grit his teeth, trapped there on the ground, but wouldn't relent to It. *No.*

There was a flash of arcana, blood rained down onto the mud, a choking gasp seized the air, and Damien's limbs were free of their petrification.

Gilead lay in the mud, only identifiable because he'd been standing in the same spot moments earlier. His head was no more, a small cloud of arcana so similar to the Grand Order's miasma dispersing where it had been, Archibald still standing but utterly splattered in gore. Damien sucked in a breath, ragged, exhaustion running through him. "Huh," he coughed out quietly to himself, having really expected Gilead to be a bigger problem. "Suppose I'll take that one for free."

"What *have* you gotten yourself into, Bloodthorne?"

Apparently, it wouldn't be free.

Xander Shadowhart strode across the field, hands clasped behind his back, the priestess scurrying along behind him. Damien's hackles raised despite that he wanted to collapse into the bloodied, muddy ground and sleep for about a century.

This one is offensive, It said. *We should kill him.*

Now, *that* sounded splendid, but Damien hesitated—if E'nloc wanted to kill Xander, Damien probably shouldn't. Or he should at least think about it for a few more minutes while he caught his breath.

Now! We should kill him now!

"Fuck,"—he huffed—"off."

"Well, hello to you too." Xander rolled his eyes, but he was grinning. "Abyss, you are looking rough."

Damien glanced down at himself. He was still clad in black, but the skin of his hands was even sallower than normal. Grey, really. He pushed back up to his feet and shook out his arms. They tingled with newfound noxscura and something else, something lighter that burned from the inside.

"You, blood mage, demon, abomination—whatever you are, destroy this newcomer." Archibald spoke to Damien as if giving a command, gesturing to the approaching Xander.

Damien ignored him, rubbing at his forehead but feeling no injury there. "I could have used that assistance a moment earlier, Shadowhart."

Xander shrugged. "Well, I wanted to see what would happen, and, I must say, this is magnificent!" He spread his arms out, spinning. The infernal creatures filling up the arena seemed to breathe with one breath, like a single, living thing, waiting. Damien could make requests of them now that Gilead was dead, he could feel the freedom of the new powers inside as well as the willingness of the infernal beasts to follow their master, but he could feel something else too, something in his gut...chewing.

Archibald called up a spell, a weak one, but he didn't cast. He'd never planned to be alone, clearly, and was completely at a loss. "I said, destroy him." Somehow, the king's voice was still biting even when it was quiet.

Both blood mages glared at him, then looked back to one another.

"What did you do to Gilead?"

"Little something I picked up from the Grand Order." Xander wiped his hands off on his white coat, still pristine since last they'd seen one another. "One-time use, but they granted me a pretty powerful spell to assassinate their traitor. I was supposed to do it days ago though, and they're definitely going to be upset that I stalled. They'll be after you now too, so we should maybe consider some cover." He squinted skyward into the dark, Pippa cowering behind him.

Damien didn't need cover. If the Grand Order came, they would be destroyed.

Everything will be destroyed.

"Well, no, we're not doing that."

Xander pouted. "Oh, what, now you get to make all the decisions because you've got the end times inside you?"

"I wasn't speaking to you," said Damien.

Archibald raised his hands. "Infernals, I demand to know—"

"Shut up," Damien and Xander spat in unison, and the king fell silent.

"Look, the castle's just back there, they've got a little bridge running directly from the arena into it and everything. Come on, let's take Archie down to the vault and get to work on freeing our parents, and then we can have some real fun with all these cute, little beasties you've summoned." Xander crossed his arms, craning his neck. "Where's our kitten? Or have you already given her a nice, sharp stabbing and fetched out that talisman?"

Damien's heart thumped, and it reverberated through E'nloc and back.

Kitten, It said, even more hateful than the pet name had ever been on Xander's tongue. *Blood. Heart. Earth. Destroy.*

Damien couldn't stop his noxscura, made too powerful with It inside, from reaching out across the arena, the city, the realm, and he found Amma in seconds, her blood a persistent bright spot even when it coursed with worry and dread. Amma, so brilliant and lovely and sweet. Amma, still alive.

She was not in the city, thank the darkest gods, and it would stay that way.

Will it?

"She isn't here," he said to Xander.

"But the talisman! We need it to force his hand. You said—"

"I said that *I* would be here." Damien's gaze turned to Archibald. "There is another way."

CHAPTER 31
A STUDY IN DESPERATION

Xander was still talking. There were a lot of details coming from the blood mage, superfluous ones, mostly about how clever he was—and Pippa too, just a bit—to figure out where Archibald would be conducting his malfeasance, how it was obvious because the arena had been boarded up for construction that wasn't actually occurring, and how Damien should really be much more thankful than he was being, but that was all right because he'd make it up to him, in the end, by freeing his mother.

E'nloc, on the other hand, just chanted, *Kill him*, over and over into Damien's mind. Tempting, but not useful.

There were a few distractions though, and if not for them, Damien might have reduced the whole of Eirengaard Keep to rubble just for a moment of silence. Brave guards and mages dared to stand in their way, to rescue their king held hostage between the two demon spawn as they marched him to the vault. A retinue of basilisks and Abyssal hounds kept the do-gooders busy, an enterprising infernal rabbit with fanged incisors and glowing red eyes even chased off some of those attempting to become saviors, but a tentacle of E'nloc's here and there assisted in clearing the way.

It was messy though, and Damien hated mess, so he changed

course and called up shadows instead that pressed outward from around them, blanketing the keep. They drove away would-be heroes and those who just happened to get in the way, locking them up in stray larders and bathing chambers instead so that the castle felt like a tomb as they walked through it, empty and silent.

Eirengaard Keep's throne room was magnificent even under the darkness of the eclipse, as if the king of Eiren would sit and rule from anything less. A floor of hand-painted tiles, blue and silver, spread out before them covered in a length of burgundy carpeting run through with golden threads. Walls of blue-grey marble with veins of sapphire rose forty feet, a domed ceiling at its top inlaid with relief sculptures of dominions and guardians, none of which were there now to see what was slowly becoming of the city that dedicated itself to them. Massive windows along the back wall that should have filtered in sunlight through blue glass were illuminated only by pulsing arcana as infernals stalked the exterior courtyard. Crawling in behind to fill up the room were legions of them, beasts that slithered and flew and prowled with blackened hides and eyes the color of fire.

It all led to not one but two daises atop one another. Even the Grand Order could have taken notes. Twenty steps led to a platform that had no other purpose but to make the climber choose which of the additional curving staircases one would take to reach the throne at its top, gilded and glorious.

"Fancy." Xander nodded, giving the room an appraising look, Pippa timidly following behind him as if she were safe by his side. "Though it does scream overcompensation. Where's this vault I've heard so much about, Archie?"

The king's gaze fell onto his high seat. Behind them stood a row of creatures with the hulking bodies of bears but gator-like heads. The infernal beasts kept Archibald between the two blood mages, pawing at the ground with talons and snapping jaws at every errant move. The creases at the corners of the king's eyes deepened, his lips pulled into a tight line beneath his full beard, and then he continued forward across the long hall.

When they reached the stairs, Xander clicked his tongue. "No, old man, the *vault*. You know, where you keep your spoils of war otherwise known as *our parents*."

Damien held up a hand, watching Archibald ascend before them to stop on the platform. A banner hung from the upper dais that held the throne. A deep burgundy, the golden embroidery across it illustrated a sun with a set of swords beneath, the crest Damien had seen about the city honoring their god, Osurehm, he assumed. With a wave of the

291

king's hand, the banner swept aside revealing a set of doors. The blood mages climbed up behind him, the priestess following, and the gator-bears at the rear taking ground-rumbling steps.

Arcane flames burst into life around the newly-revealed room hidden beneath the throne. The space spread out and away from them, alight with a warm glow, the walls covered in dark, lacquered wood, the place almost homey if not for what it held. They were met with the head of a dragon, jaws open, eyes piercing, but it didn't move. The flickering flames danced off of its too-shiny hide, the scales doused in a clear resin. It was mounted to the wall at the far end of the room, but it was so enormous that it shocked one immediately upon entrance. After a slightly longer look, it became clear that the eyes were but painted glass domes, and one was pointed in a slightly different direction than the other.

More mounted heads adorned the walls, beasts mostly, but then there was a strangely-preserved one of a man, and without clarification, it looked only human. Damien imagined his own head mounted, and how it would be identical, really, no horns or anything else to tell the world he had been a blood mage once he'd been stuffed. Ghoulish, the trophies stared out with more of those glass beads for eyes, looking down on the rest of the chamber's plunder.

There were many pedestals housing glass cases, beneath each a trinket or jewel or weapon, some whole, others crushed, all significant. Damien could feel the arcana, even when it had all been spent, little memories of it in each piece. One case stood directly in the room's center, and despite the prestigious spot in the king's trophy room, only held a mound of ash. Damien was drawn to it. Or rather, E'nloc was. It nudged Damien, not enough to force him forward, but the blood mage was intrigued enough to approach.

All that was left, It said into Damien's mind, and It needn't go on—Damien knew he meant from The Expulsion.

Fog fell over the glass of the case as he breathed on it, and then he saw his own reflection. Xander had been right—he really was *not* looking good. His skin had gone grey, his veins blue, and his irises dark. The gnawing at his insides persisted, a hot, sharp grating against his organs that the noxscura was constantly responding to and quelling before the pain flared up again.

Don't worry about that.

"Well, I really expected a dungeon set about eight stories below ground, but this isn't too bad." Xander sauntered in, running fingers over everything like he already owned it, and then he let out a squeal of delight. "Mother!"

The blood mage skipped to one side of the room where there stood a crystal twice as tall as he. Deeply sapphire, within stood the shadow of a being even darker than the rest.

Damien scanned the chamber, similar crystals set against the walls, and then found a crimson one. Damien brought himself to it so that Zagadoth the Tempestuous, Ninth Lord of the Infernal Darkness and Abyssal Tyrant of the Sanguine Throne could loom over him. He held up the shard, the color matching, and pressed it to a divot just on the crystal's edge. It sealed itself in, and he expected some sort of reaction, but there was nothing. Perhaps that was better for now.

"Did you say the Grand Order is coming?" The room was a wide one, so when Damien glanced over his shoulder, he had to look past Archibald still standing in its middle, a small contingency of infernal gator-bears at his back, snuffling and dripping acidic saliva on the pristine carpets. Pippa had made her way into a corner to stand awkwardly, eyes unblinking, terrified.

"Oh, probably," Xander lilted, hands clasped under his chin as he turned. "They weren't too keen on this happening,"—he twirled a finger in Damien's general direction—"but I think they had the same idea as you, not wanting to let it out and wreck the whole world or whatever. You might be able to convince them to not kill you? Then again, they might want to keep this thing around: they're always changing their minds, and now they have a tie-breaking number of council members, so who knows?"

"It cannot be left alive." Archibald was apparently still brave, even surrounded by evil.

"How did you intend to kill It?" Damien cocked his head.

He doesn't know, It hissed.

"As if I would reveal your own downfall to you."

Damien rolled his eyes.

"What exactly was the plan, Archie." Xander sauntered over to the king and got right in his face. "You summon the same entity that supposedly brought about The Expulsion, stick it in my friend over there, and then what?"

Friend? It scoffed. *Kill him.*

Archibald's eyes shifted from one to the other, but his mouth didn't move.

Xander swore and gripped the king by the front of his coat. Arcana crackled through his hand, aiding in how he dragged the larger man across the room to a seat at the edge of the dragon's mouth. He slammed him down so hard, Damien thought the chair would shatter beneath him. "Spit it the fuck out, Archie," he growled, and shadows coalesced around the man's body, beginning to squeeze.

"It was only meant to be a show!" he sputtered. "The One True Darkness was to be controlled. That mage, Gilead, he swore to do it, to enthrall the entity so that it would only destroy the slums and a few market streets, and then it would be put down. The people, they would be...be happy, grateful, and their trust in the crown and its protection of them would be renewed."

Xander backed off, straightening, white brows raising. "You mean, you orchestrated all this and were willing to sacrifice your own people to reinvigorate their love of...you?"

The squeeze around him lessened, his eyes darting to the shadows across his chest and then up to the gator-bears that stalked toward him. "Not all of the realm's people, only some of the offensive places, the places that gave us trouble. I would never have allowed The One True Darkness to threaten the other nobles' estates or the keep or-or...or my *family*."

"Wow." Xander grinned, leaning up against one of the dragon's fangs. "Now, that truly is evil."

"Protecting my son isn't evil," he spat back.

"Oh, not that part, you asshole." Xander laughed as a shadow of arcana slapped the king across the face. "All the rest of it, though. I must say, I'm *impressed*."

The king sneered, clearly disagreeing, but turned to look at Damien, still on the far side of the room. "You cannot release It. The mage said It could only be controlled when It was inside a vessel."

That fool knows nothing. We must meld.

"Considering how demented that plan of yours was, releasing a couple of demons you've got trapped in here should be easy." Xander leaned there laxly, head hanging back. "So, go on, start drawing up the ritual. We've got some time, but who knows how long Bloodthorne's got until he, uh, releases the thing you're suddenly so worried about."

Archibald's knuckles were white as he gripped the arms of his seat. "I'm not releasing any demons."

"What?" Xander snapped back up to rigid attention. "You've suddenly developed morals?"

Eiren's king stared hollowly past the gator-bears, face creased into solemnity. "I will not be remembered for taking down the greatest evil in existence, the evil that required godly intervention when last it walked the scourged earth, but I still have my legacy of ensnaring the last demon lords. I will not sully that. Kill me if you must, but I will be remembered as a good king." Stalwart, his eyes seemed to be staring at the destiny he expected, the one he was willing to die for.

"Oh, this is bloody ridiculous." Xander pinched the bridge of his nose then he snarled. "That's it, I'm taking something." The shadows twisted, lifting Archibald's arm and weaving itself between his fingers, spreading them. Another shadow shattered a glass box, and Xander retrieved the blade that had been contained within, striking out without a second thought.

Blood spurt, and Archibald's littlest finger was severed cleanly, arcing through the air and landing on the carpet. Pippa's seemingly natural reaction was to heal, moving toward the cleaved flesh, but the nearest gator-bear was quicker and gobbled it up.

"Now," began Xander, brandishing the bloodied weapon, "you're going to—"

The King of Eiren let out a chamber-rattling scream. Trapped there in the chair, hand suspended, he could only stare and screech, the stub leftover still spurting blood with every frantic pump of the man's heart.

"Really, Archie," Xander groaned over the wailing, covering his ears, blade still in hand. "It's just *one*, little finger."

Kill them both, It said, and Damien almost agreed, head pounding with the man's guttural cries.

"Darkness!" Xander flicked a wrist, and the shadows contained the fresh wound, pulling the arm back down and away, and another tendril slapped over the king's mouth. "Clearly, you didn't like that, so I'll keep taking them until you comply."

The king's screams were muffled under the shadow, but Damien couldn't deal with another outburst. "He needs his hands to cast."

Incensed, Xander pressed his lips together and looked as though he wanted to yell, but knew he was right. "Fine, I'll take something else."

"No." Damien strode over to them, breathing heavily. "Even divine mages die from blood loss, and we need this one alive."

"This one." Xander's face went truly wicked, and he clamped a hand down on the king, pressing his forehead to Archibald's. "But he's told us he has a son somewhere in the keep. We'll have him found, brought here, and—"

"Xander, that's *enough*." Damien felt ill, and not just from the persistent gnawing at his innards.

The blood mage's fingers twisted into Archibald's coat then shoved him back. "Fine, then *you* make him. That's the whole point of that thing in you, isn't it? Limitless power?"

Pain ran through Damien and then was stifled once again. No, that was not Its point. What Xander didn't understand, and what Damien knew too intimately, was that E'nloc couldn't *make* anyone do anything. It wasn't enthrallment magic, it wasn't illusions or fire or anything else. It was destruction and destruction only. It tore at the planes, destroying them, It ensnared and consumed the descendants, destroying them, and It was eating away at Damien from the inside, destroying him.

Damien gestured with his head for Xander to step away. He took up the space before the king, Xander's shadows removing themselves from his mouth, and thankfully he had gone quiet. Pale and distressed, Archibald sobbed, and Damien placed a hand on his shoulder.

At his side, Xander reached out and grabbed Pippa, dragging her close to him in his excitement and forcing the terrified priestess to watch. "This is going to be so good," he whispered.

"Archibald," Damien grunted, meeting the man's eyes, "would you please consider releasing my father, Zagadoth the Tempestuous, from his occlusion crystal?"

The king sniffled, his brow pinched, and then shook his head.

Damien tipped his head slightly. "But...*please*?"

Archibald's horrified eyes went narrow. "No?"

Damien clicked his tongue, straightened, and crossed his arms. "Well, that didn't work."

"Are you fucking *kidding* me?" Xander threw his hands up so fast that Pippa collapsed to the ground in fear. The blood mage ignored her. "All the power in this and every other plane, and you ask? *Nicely?*"

"It was worth an attempt."

"Well, I bloody suppose so. Now do the real thing."

Damien chewed the inside of his mouth. There was no real thing. Not unless E'nloc took him over entirely, and then he would do the only real thing that could be done and destroy. Damien could drag in the king's most prized possessions, his closest companions, his family, and destroy them all one by one, but Archibald may never give in—he loved himself, and perhaps the realm, or at least his status in it, more than all of that. And all that destruction seemed awfully distasteful.

We should do it anyway.

"If it's what you want, it can't be bloody good," Damien mumbled.

"What was that, Bloodthorne?"

"Nothing." Damien took Archibald's wounded arm, freeing it of Xander's shadows. Not caring if he caused pain, he smeared the man's blood on his own hand and stomped over to Zagadoth's crystal, pressing a bloody print to the gem and pumping in noxscura behind it. The occlusion crystal pulsed and glowed, but nothing more happened. Damien swore under his breath and went back.

"Maybe we need more." Xander eagerly spun the dagger he'd commandeered around in his palm.

"No, he's not a blood mage. Priestess, do you have anything?"

Pippa sat up from the spot on the floor she'd yet to retrieve herself from. "Me? You think I have a spell to *free* a demon?" she squeaked out in a frustratingly familiar way and looked urgently at Xander. "You said I was here for—"

"She'll be no use in this," Xander snapped, and so the two fell into experimenting.

Time meant little in the windowless vault filled with arcane things that already made the air stagnant and strange. The blood mages toiled, paced, swore, cast, until Damien stated he needed a break.

"I'll come with—"

"No. You'll stay here. *Everyone* will stay here. I need a moment alone."

Futile.

Damien swept out of the vault, dropping the banner behind him and heading into the throne room proper. Infernal beasts still lined the halls, and he could feel them, each one individually, the gator-bears still in the vault below, the wyverns and serpents and Abyssal badgers in the courtyard, the chimeras and hounds and infernal otters trawling the streets. They all gnashed teeth and paced, keeping subjects trapped in their homes, waiting.

A gentle caress brushed against Damien's shin, and the little, black cat was there. He lifted it from under its front legs, holding it out. It blinked yellow eyes at him, and Damien was unsure if it was infernal or not—it was always exceptionally difficult to tell with cats—so he just shrugged and carried it upward to the throne.

Dropping himself into the only seat in the colossal room, he stared out on the opulent hall to think, and the Abyssal creatures slunk into the shadows, giving him the privacy he wanted. The cat circled in his lap and curled up, and Damien mindlessly pat the thing as he slouched in the throne of Eiren and pouted.

"Everything's gone to shit," he muttered.

So destroy it.

"Will you fucking stop it with that?"

The inevitable has no delay.

Damien readjusted in the throne. For all its pomp and accouterments, the damn thing wasn't even comfortable.

You have a choice, It said. *Merge.*

"Or I can die," Damien grumbled.

The cat in his lap chirped, and Damien made sure to be gentler as he scratched under its chin.

No.

"Oh, don't like that? I thought you loved destruction? Not so thrilled about your own though, eh?"

Everything will come to an end, even Us, but not until it is time.

Damien simmered on that for a long moment. It was true, he supposed, it was just the order that was important.

His skin was warm, burning from the inside, and then the noxscura flared again, healing the parts that E'nloc was eating away. It worked furiously, but it would eventually not be able to keep up. Gilead had said E'nloc was the result of luxerna and noxscura both, and so luxerna was almost certainly inside him now. If he could continue to contain E'nloc, it would eventually destroy its own vessel and be doomed to die within him. But death was frightening, and if Damien had learned anything, it was that he was weak, and a weak man would do quite a few things he wouldn't have believed he would otherwise, perhaps even merging with The One True Darkness in earnest.

Damien's hand went into his pouch and came out with a bit of white cloth. It had been buried in the bottom of his things for well over a moon, but always there, kept safe, just in case. In its center, the crest of Faebarrow—embroidered poorly, he noted and snickered—a dry smear of his blood across it. Amma would know what to do. In fact, he had set her up to do what he truly needed from her now, another disgustingly selfish act. But she was not there, safe beyond the borders of the city.

Staying away, however, was never an option, and one creature trolled Eirengaard's streets that he should have counted on, poised to prove Damien's virtue better than any darkness ever could.

CHAPTER 32
SO, HERE'S THE THING ABOUT BEING INDESTRUCTIBLE

It had been difficult to hear the details on horseback, but as Diana shared her returning memories, Amma pieced the past back together. Twenty-three years prior, Diana had taken Damien and Xander from Aszath Koth, but not for retribution or escape. Birzuma had found them lifeless, and the priestess's former temple seemed the only way to help. She remembered very little after, only that her son had not survived. Her intention had never been to leave Zagadoth, and when Amma told her the demon was trapped in a crystal in the capital, a new memory came back to her of assisting divine mages in trapping him.

That had made the woman swear so severely, Amma worried Isldrah might strike her down right there on the road.

An Osurehm priest had come to the temple and given her the pendant along with a prophecy that her son would return, but he would need to be cleansed of evil before she could have him back. Amma was getting sick of prophecies, not to mention sick of Gilead. That man had promised a number of people they could have Damien, which meant none of them could, his intent for the blood mage far more sinister.

As their stolen horses ran themselves ragged, the sun had risen at their backs, the sky a dusty red as the gentler lights of the double moons burnt away. Amma's stomach twisted at the bloodiness seeping out over the sky, dawn casting itself over the realm, yet on this day its coloring was a warning, and it inched toward where the moons still hung.

They dodged early-morning travelers headed at a more reasonable pace for the capital. *Turn back, you fools*, she thought, barreling toward the very place she wished they wouldn't go. When the rising sun began to dim, Amma refused to look over her shoulder, only driving forward harder as the day's darkness crept up her back.

Eirengaard was silent save for a quiet hum of arcana. Normally one would hear the distant sounds of a city well before reaching it, but there were not even bird calls in the air as they approached the gates. The sky had completely darkened, the aligned moons holding the sun captive in the eclipse, but a ring of red light still shone over the realm, giving everything a bloody glow. The horses were spent, and Amma dismounted at the unpatrolled city gates. There was no need for guards, a wall of shadows thickly shrouding the entrance instead. She knew those shadows.

At their feet, the three imps went right up to the arcane barrier, and Quaz bolted in. A second later, he returned, tail wagging.

"Noxscura," said Diana, raising a hand to it, and the shadowy wall bowed around her palm but didn't break. She unsheathed her sword, glimmering with radiant light. Holding it aloft, she was poised to swing, then froze.

A set of eyes flashed from the hazy darkness, and then another, and another. Nothing crossed the barrier, but they watched, waiting to strike at the divine magic.

"Don't attack them," said Amma, kneeling into the dirt of the road and laying her fingers flat. She felt the earth pulsing under her hand, tumultuous with so much noxscura so close, but that was, perhaps, good. It had been shattered, but she could bring her staff back, stronger than before, and it formed under her fingers, growing up from the ground as she stood. Silvery strands of noxscura pooled inside its head, gathering from the shadowy wall itself, and liathau leaves, red under the darkened sky, blossomed along its length.

The glinting eyes took stock of it and her, and then they faded away. Amma took a step toward the arcane gates, they bowed, and then began to clear. Hands steady around the staff, Amma led them through, and they passed into Eirengaard.

Silence still rang through the capital, the streets clear of villagers but not empty. All manner of beasts stalked openly from the smallest rat with eyes aglow to massive behemoths, three stories tall on legs as thick around as trees. Fire imps like Kaz and the others, but blobby shadow imps too, and others with wooden-like limbs and antlers instead of horns, a few that were scaled, and some with skin like stone. Nothing moved to attack them, but eyes watched as they crept along the main thoroughfare.

Fissures blinked in and out of existence, drawn messily across the sky or through the earth. Tears bubbling with silver noxscura at their edges, eyes peered through them, and then carefully a beast would emerge on spindly legs or leathery wings to join the rest.

Eirengaard was otherwise a clean, flat place, laid out thoughtfully so it was easy to traverse. The road into town continued down the city's middle, pathways jutting off of it to take one to markets and inns and specialty shops, but led directly to Eirengaard Keep which loomed over the entire city. In the distance they could see it, more fissures crackling over its spires and arcing about like lightning. That had to be their destination.

Columns dotted the main road at every intersection, banners that celebrated Osurehm hanging laxly, and under the reddened light, their burgundy had gone dark like pooling blood, the sun they depicted looking more like an eye, holding watch over all. Breezeless, the shadows that encircled the city held even the air captive.

Amma lowered her staff, confident they would be able to pass through the city unbothered so long as it was out. "I don't understand what happened here." Carts and market stands littered the thoroughfare, transactions abandoned on the road before them, coins and goods scattered.

Diana's sharp eyes darted from beast to beast, a hand on her hilt but the blade sheathed. "There are infernal things crawling everywhere," she said as if it were obvious which, to be fair, it was.

"Yes, but there's no destruction. None of the buildings have been touched, there's no blood in the streets or disembodied limbs hanging from the eaves. No fires have even been set. I mean, I expected carnage and mayhem, but look." She pointed to the window of a shop where the faces of two small children were pressed against the glass, eyes wide with wonder and unharmed. "They're trapped inside sure, but that's...it?"

Diana grunted in confused agreement, and they picked up their pace, finding that nothing challenged their steady march to the castle. The keep grew more foreboding as they approached the sprawling gardens at its front. A silver fissure streaked above it, and a sound like many trumpets being blown off key filled the air as a flock of infernal geese burst into Eirengaard. They swooped overhead in formation and landed themselves in the garden's pond, skimming across water that reflected the reddened sky, so like a pool of blood. Amma and Diana waited, but the birds only watched back ominously, floating on the unstilled waters, eyes like hollow sockets. It seemed infernal geese were not quite so different from ordinary ones.

The capital gardens that blanketed the keep's entrance were always pristine and beautiful no matter the season, open to all and constantly being tended to. On this day, however, there were no gardeners about, only more of those bark-skinned imps and the occasional slithering serpent. But even under the darkness of the odd, red lights, Amma could sense something different the moment they entered the high-hedged courtyard.

The garden once held ornamental trees in places of interest amongst the crossing pathways and flowering bushes, but those were gone now in favor of statues. She remembered, specifically, a plum willow she had always had affection for, but in its place now stood a massive pedestal holding a human figure. And it was...it was waving?

Amma came to a stop with a gasp, Diana taking a defensive stance at her side, but there was no apparent threat. Yet Amma could still feel a latent magic to the gardens she hadn't before, something friendly mingling with the infernal, but sad too.

Amma broke from the path and crossed the soft grass to the statue that moved of its own accord. Magic that animated objects was not uncommon, but this felt unique, so similar to the bend of a tree in the wind. She'd also never seen a statue with such a strange coloration or pattern across it, and squinted, reaching out to touch its base. As her fingers grazed its smooth surface, a tingle ran up her arm, and a pink petal bloomed out of the wood.

"Liathau?"

Auberon Lumier, read the plaque carved into the statue's base, more of the precious timber from her home. Amma's eyes trailed up the effigy of the previous king of Eiren and Archibald's father, depicted in full plate armor with a holy shield on one arm, the other extended in friendly greeting, forever immortalized in enchanted wood.

Bewildered, she sought out the other statues that dotted the gardens. More kings or knights or men of some repute were carved from liathau cores, moving with the arcana inherent to the trees. There was even one of a dog, its tail moving merrily in the breezeless air. "This is why they desecrated my orchard?" she breathed, voice hitching on the words. "For glory?"

"Amma?"

She spun despite thinking it could have only been her grief that cast the voice into her ear. Peeking out from behind a hedge was a set of pointed ears attached to a face still somehow pulled into mischief surrounded by so much chaos.

"Laurel!" Amma bound toward her, and the women collided, arms wrapped around each other, competing to see who could squeeze tightest. Laurel lifted her, and at her back there was Perry, staying close, irresolute and wide-eyed. Amma grabbed at his robes and tugged him into the embrace, tears springing to her eyes. "You came to Eirengaard?"

"I did say I would get Perry to the exams. But I think they might be canceled." Laurel's slick hair was pulled high on her head and trailing down her back, swishing as she looked at the acolyte beside her and hooked her arm into his. "We did have some help though. Stitches, come meet Amma."

A skeletal figure eased itself out from the hedge. It was hugely tall, likely due to its four-legged, lower half, and wore a bandoleer over its bony, human chest that was outfitted with daggers, needles, and thread. Stitches said nothing, but the skeleton centaur waved, and Amma politely waved back.

"He's from the Army of the Undead, isn't he?"

Laurel nodded with a grin. "And you should see his herringbone ladder."

Stitches pulled a small square of fabric from a pocket on his bandoleer covered in embroidery.

"Very nice." Amma tipped her head appreciatively, only noting then the set of knoggelvi trotting behind the massive skeletal centaur. "You found them too?" she squealed and ran to the creatures, their leathery skin no longer hidden under an illusion, and rubbed their long, toothy snouts, receiving nuzzles in return.

"Yeah, we did, and imagine our surprise when they weren't actually horses." Laurel laughed, but it quickly died away. "Oh, um, who's this then?"

Amma recognized the look Laurel was giving Diana and could practically see the half-elf's mind working out just how she might pretend to faint to be caught by her. "That's Damien's *mother*, Diana."

Laurel stiffened but still bit her lip. "So, where's Sir Scary-Surname then?"

Amma gestured vaguely all around.

"Shit." Laurel slapped her hands together. "Okay, what's the plan? All the beasties don't seem to care about us moving around the city, I think because of the creepy not-horses and Stitches, I have *all* my poisons on me, and Perry just memorized a new spell for punching holes in things."

303

"It's only supposed to make digging a garden easier," whispered Perry, though he straightened under Laurel's offer of help.

"These are your allies?" asked Diana, crossing her arms, clearly dubious.

Amma nodded as she felt a pricking at the back of her eyes. It would be too dangerous to allow them to aid her, but she also knew they would not accept that as an answer, and after a last, long look at the liathau statues and a deepening of her hatred of the crown, the lot of them were headed to the castle proper.

The entry was barred by more shadows, ones the imps could safely traverse, but when Amma broke through with her staff, the others could not seem to follow. She was privately relieved when Laurel and Perry were pushed backward by the hazy mist of noxscura, though troubled that Diana too could not break through.

The priestess went for her sword, but as soon as it was even partially unsheathed, the infernals all around turned on her, gnashing teeth and bearing claws. Amma threw herself over the woman to try and block the divine aura, and she just as quickly stuffed the sword back into its scabbard.

"I can cut through them," Diana insisted.

"Not all of them." Amma assessed the hazy wall only she could cross then the others. "I will do what I can from inside, but there is something to be done out here as well. Lady Winnifred Solonedy of Buckhead is somewhere in Eirengaard. She's been suspicious of the crown for a while and may have information, and, I hate to say this, but I think we're going to need someone with some noble standing to vouch for us after all of this is over." Amma was proud of how sure her voice sounded, managing not to mention the help would only be needed if they survived.

Diana's steely eyes roved up to the castle's spires, anger there, but defeat as well. "You need us to find this woman? I can conjure—" Her brow went narrow. "Well, perhaps I can *convince*." The priestess went to a small flock of pigeons that could only be infernal and knelt near them. Red eyes turned on her, watching, and the woman held out a hand. One with faded plumage relented to the priestess. "I can send messages with doves," she told them, sighing but resigned. "If one of you knows this Lady Solonedy, we can follow our winged friend here, if she cooperates."

Amma's heart tugged, thinking of Corben. Damien had called the magic to summon him divine—how had neither of them realized it was a gift from his mother? "Yes, do that, Laurel knows her," Amma said, voice cracking. "And one last thing. Vanders?" In her outstretched hands, the vaxin appeared in a poof of fur. His paws were curled beneath his chin, and he peered up at her, so tiny. "Take care of them for me," she said, giving him a kiss and handing him off to Laurel.

With only the imps gathered around her, Amma crossed through the barrier and into Eirengaard Keep. The silence in the castle's antechamber was even greater than in the city. Like in the catacombs, a sense of dread shrouded the room, shining eyes peeking out from the shadows. The silvery light inside her staff guided her, flickering flames in enchanted sconces dim and high on the castle walls.

Then there came a scuffing, a noise like claws on tile floors, and Amma's stomach twisted. Abject horror burst into her memory at the sound, fear flooding her veins, telling her to run, but her legs were leaden and held her to the spot.

From a connecting chamber, they came, an entire pack skidding around the corner, fangs bared, ears back, snouts wet. Long-bodied and low to the ground, the queen's band of miniature, herding hounds barreled toward Amma. She could feel their teeth in her all over again, biting and swarming. She had only been a child, just wanting to play, but the dogs were out for blood. They'd gotten a taste for her then, and they apparently hadn't forgotten.

Even the infernal creatures hid in the shadows from the snarling, snapping pack. Clutching her staff, Amma froze. But at her feet, the imps were prepared, and arcana sizzled around them.

Well, the imps had been half prepared. Only having been in existence for a night, they were not entirely ready to transform, bodies morphing strangely. Kaz took on his dog form from his head to his torso, big bulbous eyes and huge, pointy ears, but his bottom half remained firmly imp. Katz, who Amma had never seen transform, did so with a little more gusto, his canine appearance a bit more believable if his ears were so long that they trailed on the ground and he had so much extra skin that it fell into his eyes. Quaz, of course, became a ginger cat instead but retained his wings.

None of this, however, impeded them from defending Amma. The imps-turned-domesticated-creatures charged, and the entire pack swerved. The imps gave chase, and many taloned paws scurried away over the tile, the terrifying noise fading into the distance of the keep.

When her heartbeat finally slowed, Amma glanced about, truly alone then. She had felt small many times in her life, vulnerable, helpless, weak. The antechamber of Eirengaard Keep would have been dwarfing if even the others had been with her, but alone, she stared up at the doors to the throne room, hulking slabs of wood at least twenty feet high, wondering how she could even open them all by herself.

But a shut door had never stood in Ammalie Avington's way, and she simply placed her hand upon it and asked.

The throne room was laid out before her, cloaked in the ruddy light that the eclipse insisted upon casting through the massive windows at its back. It was an imposing, monumental place, meant to inspire awe, perhaps fear, but Amma was interested only in the figure atop the throne. Damien was seated there, alone, solemn, yet even surrounded by that which intended to dwarf, he was imposing.

The carpeting muffled Amma's steps as she drew nearer, staff swallowing itself up from her hand. The things in the shadows did not move to swarm her, only watch as she continued. Damien didn't move, but she could hear his voice, a quiet rumble, punctuated now and again with silence or a scoff. There was no one to be speaking to, it had to be himself, but then she wasn't terribly surprised. There had been so much talk of vessels and containment, it would have been a bigger shock for this to have not happened.

Amma reached the stairs to the dais but still hadn't drawn his eye. She stood for a moment on the platform below, gazing upward. If she were to turn back, now would be the moment, but really, that had never been an option, and she began up the second set of stairs.

A cat hopped down from Damien's lap, and she was hopeful for a moment that perhaps he was not possessed, that he had only been speaking to the creature, but then his eyes snapped to her, and they were dark.

"Damien?"

He was shaking his head, sitting up slowly from his slouched position, not happy to see her. "What are you doing here?" he asked, voice a whisper, desperate.

She said nothing because it was obvious; she was there for him. She reached the throne's level and went to stand just before it, a spot no one was ever meant to take up, never so close to a king.

"Amma, you can't be here." Damien's voice dropped with severity, fingers finding the armrests and curling into the wood.

"Yes, I can. They let me." She raised her chin to gesture to one of the infernal things skittering along the domed ceiling high above them.

Damien took a breath, head jerking, eye twitching. "E'nloc is inside me," he said, stalwart but tinged with shame. "It isn't safe here— I'm not safe. You have to go."

She only stood there shaking her head.

"Leave!" he shouted, voice echoing into the entirety of the throne room and cutting right through her, but she remained. Damien's strength, his act of being indestructible, had always been a shield. He had a softness that could be exploited, and someone had done just that. It was up to her to protect it, to protect him. "I promised I would stay with you no matter what," she said simply. "So I am."

"Amma, this is not—" He cut himself off as she took another step toward him. Pushing himself back into the throne, his eyes would not find hers, hazy smoke seeping out from under his palms. "It knows you're here, and It isn't...It isn't happy."

Black wisps of arcana floated out from around Damien, crawling across the ground and slithering up her legs, feeling every inch of her body. She stood under it, unmoving, taking steady breaths, watching him.

"It wants you dead," he said through grit teeth, and she felt the magic tighten around her limbs. "I can't...I won't let it, but I can't hold it back forever."

"You don't need to." Amma stepped forward, breaking from the arcana's haze. It couldn't hold her if she didn't want it to. She slipped her hand under his chin, tipping his head up to her. He looked awful, so sullen and drained and sad. Yet she still saw him, inside, trapped. "But you do need to force It out."

He shook his head, moving slightly in her grasp. "Impossible. And even if I could, I can't let It be free to destroy the realm. The luxerna in It is eating away at me, making me weak." His hand shot up, grabbing her so tightly about the wrist she thought he had to be lying. There was nothing weak about the hold he had on her as he tugged her forward. "Every second closer to death I am, the easier it is for me to succumb to It, and It won't. Fucking. Shut. Up."

Amma's wrist felt like the bones might snap, and she whimpered. His hold on her lessened, but just barely. It was dangerous, getting closer, but she had to. She lifted her knee, sliding it alongside his thigh onto the throne.

"Amma, please, you have to go," he begged even as he held her so tightly she could never escape. His breaths were shallow as she brought her other knee up, boxing him in with her body though she knew he could simply throw her to the ground or pitch her right off the top of the daises like he had said he'd wanted to do from the top of Anomalous's tower. Like he had said when he confessed that he loved her.

She touched his face, but he trapped that hand too, wrenching it away from the scar she meant to caress. Straddling him, she sunk closer still, and he fought whatever it was holding her, pulling her in one moment and holding her away the next. But he didn't pull away when she pressed her lips to his, gently, very gently. She would only give

Damien a soft kiss, a reminder of his own tenderness, of who he really was.

The magic encompassing him was even in his mouth, prodding at her lips as she pulled back. Some of it was his, that gentle but firm arcana she'd come to adore, and some of it was foreign, hateful, tasting of ash and death. She would drive it out, free him of it, return him to her, even if it was the last thing she did.

"I'm not leaving you, Damien," she said, pressing her body against his, arcana enveloping them both. "I love you."

"You love who I was, but I am no longer that person." He blew out a ragged breath, sunken eyes traveling down her, and then widening, grip going tight once again. "Amma, I am sorry, but you cannot be allowed to love this anymore."

CHAPTER 33
WHEN FUTILITY COMES FULL CIRCLE

*S*anguinisui," said Damien, the word hateful on his tongue, "forget you ever loved me."

Amma's eyes went glassy, her body hitching. "No, I—"

"*Sanguinisui*, remember, instead, the monster that abducted you, the blood mage who was cruel and vicious and deserving of your retribution for the Abyss you suffered at my hand."

She convulsed on his lap, arms trembling in the hold he had on both of her wrists. The magic of the talisman was stronger now with E'nloc behind it, though he knew it was only because he used it for further destruction.

"*Sanguinisui*, believe I enthralled you, coerced you, abused you, but you will regain solace once you finally kill me."

Amma exhaled sharply, gaze searching in bewilderment. She stiffened, and then the sparkling blue of her eyes fell on him. The adoration, the sympathy, the love, all drained away, replaced with fear, with anger, with hatred.

"No!" she screamed, thrashing. Stronger than she'd ever been, she tried to wrench away from his grasp, but he couldn't let her go, not yet.

"Get your hands *off* of me!" Her attempt to scramble backward was thwarted by his strength and the position she'd put herself in on his lap. Tears sprang to her eyes, from fear, from anger, it didn't matter, the rest of her was simply feral, but he kept her there, letting her fight, hating it but unable to release her. "I'll kill you," she screamed, voice echoing into the vast and empty throne room, and he realized that yes, that was the point, and finally let go of her arms.

Amma was quick—dark gods, she'd always been—and she grabbed the dagger holstered on her thigh in a flash. Her dagger, the one not meant for fighting but tending to the earth, the one Damien had blessed by the priestess with the spell he'd found in the Lux Codex what felt like ages ago. He'd sat beside Amma once, scribbling it down as she translated, and she hadn't even known what it could do.

As she raised it overhead, the dagger glinted with divine magic, a spell that would allow for a weapon to cast an unmendable wound, one even a blood mage could not heal from. Finally, her dagger would get its chance to plunge into him instead of save his life.

But as she sliced it down toward his chest, It took control. He'd been ignoring the voice, pushing E'nloc out, but there was only so much his weakening body could do. Damien caught her arm, holding her at bay. She sat straddling him, her face contorted with terror and rage, and she used all of her might to push through his hold and kill him. Both hands pressing down, just like when he'd enchanted her in The Wilds as a test. His arm shook beneath her attempt, noxscura wrapping around it as he fought his own body. He wanted to keep her just a moment longer—always one moment longer—and wrapped his other arm around her waist.

She growled at that, at the touch she would have nestled into only a moment earlier from the man she would have loved if destiny had deigned to be a little kinder to them both. He felt, a last time, the softness of her under his hands, even as every one of her muscles pulled taut, and he saw the sweetness in her heart even through his eyes, blurring with tears.

This was the only way. When she killed him, E'nloc's vessel would be no more, and she would be free of her villainous captor. Her heart would be unbroken, and she would be stronger without him. She would be the realm's hero, in fact, and no one deserved it more.

Perhaps it was a little cruel to take away the true things she felt—the things they both felt—but Damien was no stranger to cruelty, both given and received. And at least he would die knowing he had finally learned to love and given it to the woman who deserved so much more than what little he had to offer.

Blood poured out over Damien's chest as the pressure against his hold released. It was warm, just like when Amma embraced him, and at last a comfort to be drenched in his own gore. But his breath didn't slow, no pain came, and the dagger, her dagger, fell, clattering across the floor.

Amma's body slumped forward, and she collapsed against his chest, blood—her blood—pooling all over him.

"Oh, now that's it—that's the look." Xander's form, obscured by Damien's falling tears, stepped backward from where he stood at the throne's edge, a bloodied weapon in one hand, and a swath of fabric in the other. He lifted the material, but Damien didn't need to see Bloodthorne's Talisman of Enthrallment to know it was what he held protected inside, so much of Amma's blood dripping from it. "I do have to say,"—he swallowed, a hitch to his voice—"not as satisfying as I imagined." And then he took to the stairs and was gone.

"Amma?"

She is dead.

No. Damien gripped her under the chin to hold her head up, his arm still around her, but she was limp.

"Amma, please," he breathed, heart slamming into his chest, noxscura flooding out of him and surrounding her limbs. "*Sanguinisui,* wake up!"

She didn't move, not under his hands, his magic, his words.

Gone. As everything else should be.

No! Damien slid from the throne to the floor, laying her out and pressing hands to her chest. Her tunic was drenched in crimson, her skin slick as he floundered for the wound. Calling up the only healing spell he knew, Damien cast every ounce of magic he had into her body.

You will fail.

Frantic, he screamed for the priestess, still pulsing any bit of arcana he had into her chest, but she was leaden, her eyes not even finding his, not looking at all, hollow, empty. Blood pooled beneath her, thick, but he could no longer feel her inside it, could no longer touch that humanity they had shared, could no longer seek out the curiosity and the kindness that always flickered within. Why the fuck wasn't his magic working?

Destruction, It said. *It is all We are good for now.*

Damien gathered her up into his arms, and she slid into them easily so covered in her own blood. Blood that should have been his. "You can't," he pleaded as her head lolled away from him. "You've got to stay here. To stay with me." He took her by the jaw, turning her face to his, willing her eyes to find him. "You're *mine*, Ammalie! *Sanguinisui,* look at me! I didn't…I didn't mean to lose you like this. Please…please, come back."

"She's dead."

He lifted his eyes, the priestess standing over them, infernal creatures surrounding her, following Damien's will to be summoned. "Is Isldrah not your goddess?" he spat. "Does she not grant you the power to heal? Fix this. Now."

A terrible darkness surrounded the priestess, forcing her to her knees across from him. The shadows bit into her arms and thrust her hands onto Amma's chest.

"I cannot *fix* death." Pippa's fingers trembled as they were bathed in crimson. She sat there in her pointless robes, that useless symbol hanging from her neck, and she dared shed tears over the woman she refused to help.

Kill her.

Damien would. He would rip her to shreds, no point in her existence if she could not, *would* not, help. There was no point in *anything—*

"But Xander can."

The destruction pulsing under Damien's skin was quelled, and a voice inside him swore, but it was deadened by his own, much louder thoughts. How could Xander...

"By all that is grim and fucking unholy. That *bastard.*" Damien stood, Amma's body in his arms. She was so light, too light, and he pressed her to his chest as he raced down the steps to the platform beneath. Carefully, he laid her on the dais there. "You protect her," he snapped at Pippa who had hurried behind him, propelled by noxscura, then shouted at the hundreds of shadowy, infernal creatures who had flooded into the throne room under his sorrow and rage, waiting for his commands, "All of you, protect her."

He swept toward the vault and cast at the doors. They burst into splinters, the banner torn away, even the threshold ripped out of the wall leaving a massive hole to the disgusting room of trophies, and there was Xander Sephiran Shadowhart. Positively giddy, he sat in the chair that had once held Archibald, lounging in the mouth of a stuffed dragon's head, giggling.

The King of Eiren was across from him, doing his best to stand on his head, and immediately tumbling into a pile, groaning.

"Oh, Bloodthorne, this talisman of yours is delightful! *Sanguinisui,* sing me a song."

Archibald burst into an off-key baritone, words in Empyrean that likely praised some god or another. The gator-bears groaned in the corner, huge paws covering their ear flaps.

Damien's rage was muddied with confusion. "How the fuck are you—"

Xander held up the set of vials around his neck, and they clinked together. He always only wore one but had taken to a second since their stint in the Accursed Wastes. Damien thought nothing more of it than added precaution, but with a keener eye, he looked closer, and one was…well, it was different.

"You did wonder how I found you all those times, didn't you?" Xander tipped his head. "I feared you would feel it when I siphoned out your blood during our little sparring match, but I must have numbed you up just right by stabbing you in the spine. You didn't even notice the preservation spell I used, too distracted by your own, petty thoughts. I've wanted to use this so many times, but I needed to save it for when I finally had Archie and the talisman in the same place, but it is *so* worth it. *Sanguinisui*, shut up and go free Birzuma."

Archibald stiffened, and his body turned, marching toward the sapphire crystal.

"*Sanguinisui*, stop," Damien growled, and Archibald fell still. So, they could both command the king through the talisman, then.

Kill him.

His rage returned, and he strode across the room, glass cases and artifacts shattering as he went. Before Xander could react, Damien stood before him, a hand wrapped about his throat. "I should use arcana to avenge her, but I would rather choke the life out of you while your pathetic body attempts to heal itself. I wonder how many times you can survive."

Lifted from the chair, Xander kicked feebly in the air, but Damien's noxscura was all over him. Never had he been so powerful.

Destroy him.

Damien squeezed, and Xander's hands came up to his arm, holding on so weakly. "So…upset," he choked out. "Why?"

Vision tunneling, he felt Xander's life being crushed beneath his hand then relented just enough for the blood mage to begin healing.

Xander sucked in a breath, face reddened. "I've freed you," he coughed, "from your weakness."

Annihilate him.

"No." The priestess's words were louder in his mind than E'nloc's, and Damien released him in earnest. Xander crumpled into the chair, gasping and shaking. "Loving Amma never made me weak."

Xander's body heaved as he caught his breath, hands on his neck. His own arcana crawled over him, mending, and he turned his eyes up to Damien. "You can't," he said, but with none of the conviction his voice always held. "Neither of us can."

Damien simply shook his head, and for a brief and painful moment, he felt sorry for the other blood mage. His fingers clenched, wanting to take him by the throat again, to put him out of his misery.

"I can bring her back," Xander admitted, gaze held on Damien's threatening hand. "The resurrection spell, from the Lux Codex."

Of course he could. The bastard had kept the book once they abandoned him, and he would never waste something so powerful. But it still seemed impossible. "You need luxerna for that spell, and you can't even touch the stuff."

"But Pips can, and she's been carrying it around for me. Stole it off your kitten, in fact."

Where Amma had gotten luxerna in the first place was a mystery, but then he wasn't that surprised she came across some and pilfered it. "Then do it. Now."

Xander straightened, features shifting from nervous trepidation back to cunning. "Ah, but first, you have to free my dear, old mother."

"Fine. *Sanguinisui*, release Birzuma the Blasphemed from her occlusion crystal."

Archibald's body stiffened again and continued to the far side of the vault where the demoness's sapphire stood.

"Wait, what? Just like that?" Xander stared after the king. "You're going to give me exactly what I want?"

"Yes. Now, give Amma back to me."

"*Sanguinisui*, wait a moment, Archie." Xander leaned back into the chair. "You do realize that the moment that asshole finishes the ritual and Birzuma gets out of that crystal, she's going to *kill* him."

Damien nodded. "*Sanguinisui*, free Birzuma."

Xander scoffed. "*Sanguinisui*, hold on! I need to know that you grasp the gravity of this, Bloodthorne. I can only resurrect *one* person, and if it is your little baroness, Archibald will remain very much dead, leaving nobody to free Zagadoth."

"Yes, whatever. *Sanguinisui*, get on with letting Birzuma out."

"*Sanguinisui*, just one more moment!" Xander pushed himself from the chair, meeting Damien's gaze, standing but an inch away. He was getting just what he wanted, the asshole, but he was going to be a dick about it because he knew no other way to be. The man didn't look like he was enjoying it though, setting his jaw tight. "You know she is the reason, don't you? The reason for *all* of this."

Damien's chest prickled, eyes snapping to the sapphire crystal and the shadow inside.

"She tricked them. Both of them. Your mother and your father."

The vault's stagnant air felt especially heavy then, and Damien only glared back, allowing him to go on.

"You were probably too young to remember the taste, but I do. I can still taste it sometimes, especially when I look at you." Xander frowned, but Damien could feel it wasn't really for him. "The plan was to feed us the Elixir Eternea and convince your precious mother we were dead so she would take us out of Aszath Koth. There was no other way, she had to be the one to do it because of that stupid, fucking orb. Mother told me it was just a little prank we were playing. You didn't want to drink it—you were such a fucking baby." Xander snorted out a laugh. "But I told you it would be all right, and you did it."

"That's why Diana insisted we were dead." Damien's throat went dry, eyes shifting back to the crystal, noxscura climbing out of him to wrap around it.

"You remember being in Eirengaard after, don't you? You told me you did anyway. Birzuma only knew where to find us because she was the one who squirreled us away. Only after she convinced Zagadoth that your mother had actually stolen you, and he needed to march on the capital. But by then it was too late. That human loved you so much that when she thought you were dead, she let her weak, little mind be completely enthralled by that temple. Zagadoth didn't stand a chance against her once she was brainwashed into fighting for the crown against him. And then Aszath Koth was finally left to Birzuma. Sure, she lost it again, but she did have it, for a short while, and all it cost was your family."

Crush her.

Damien swallowed, feeling the tendrils of magic squeeze Birzuma's crystal. He could obliterate the demon into nothing, completely wipe her from existence. And knowing the truth now, he could free Zagadoth, he could free his mother, he could piece Aszath Koth back together, he could—

But Amma.

"*Sanguinisui*, free Birzuma."

Xander's mouth fell open, watching as Archibald took a final step toward the crystal and began to cast. There was magic in the vault then, but of a very different kind. Divine magic, but it was also slow and precise. It filtered through the chamber, and it crept over Damien with a slippery discomfort as it worked.

Xander felt it too, shuddering, but then he frowned at Damien again. He didn't lord his win over him, he didn't even grin, he just looked utterly broken. "You really *do* love her."

"Of course I do," said Damien.

Like he tasted the bitterness of the Elixir Eternea, Xander's tongue stuck out and he scoffed. "Well, I suppose it's time to explain this little misunderstanding to Kitten."

CHAPTER 34
THE USEFULNESS IN LEAVING EARLY TO AVOID THE RUSH

There wasn't darkness or cold or floating, but colors, a temperate feel to the air, and slightly springy ground underfoot—odd, considering Amma didn't really have feet anymore.

She gazed down at the thing that was herself. It looked like a body, but she knew that had been left behind. There should have been blood though, and a lot of it. She felt the knife go in, though she didn't know it at the time. It had pierced her heart from behind too quickly and completely for her to have known anything except what she felt seconds before: an unbridled fear and rage and desire to kill.

Amma gasped. "Oh, that jerk."

"Ammalie Avington, Baroness of Faebarrow, The Eclipse of Destruction and Heart of the Earth's Blood."

A woman stood before Amma. She hadn't been there a moment prior, or maybe she had, it was difficult to remember. She read from the book in her hands, so thick and old it seemed like it should have been difficult to hold, but she did it with ease, tips of long fingers curling around its edge. There was something familiar about her, the crimson to her hair stunningly deep as it floated about her shoulders and cascaded over the black cloak she wore. She was pretty—very pretty—too pretty to be human.

Beside her was a doorway. It grew up out of the ground but instead of wood or stone, a thin linen hung from the unanchored threshold, moving gently, shadows roving beyond it.

Amma blinked about at the place she'd appeared, something like a forest, but it couldn't exactly decide what time it wanted to exist in. Past the odd doorway, dying golden light streamed through thin branches, autumn on full display with leaves of maroon and auburn and saffron bending in a swift wind. That bled into a mound of snow just to the left. The trees there were pine, boughs covered in blankets of white that shimmered blue under the darkness of a night sky. Amma felt none of that cold, though, instead a gentle breeze at her back carrying the smell of roses. At her feet-that-weren't-feet, a sprawling of white and pink blossoms glowed with dawn's light, wet with morning dew. And to her right, the brilliance of a forest stood under full sun, intensely verdant and buzzing with unseen life.

A river ran through it all, encircling the place where Amma stood with the woman on an island of sorts. It was nearly frozen to her left, bubbling delicately behind her, raging on her right, and far off amongst the golden foliage it slowed.

"Why am I in the Everdarque?" The question came out before Amma's mind caught up, but she intrinsically knew where she was, having seen the woman who stood there before. She was one of the Autumn Court's fae, with her flaming hair and pallid skin, though they hadn't been introduced at the gathering.

"Well, you're dead," the fae said with a sort of sympathetic smile and an uncomfortable laugh. "Sorry, by the way, it's a pretty big bummer to most, which I really wasn't counting on when I came up with it."

Amma swallowed, eyes flicking to that odd doorway. She was afraid of that. "Oh, but still, why am I here?"

"This is where people go when they die, technically, this spot, where the courts come together." She pointed to the doorway. "But you'll end up in there. I made it. Isn't it pretty?"

The gossamer linen did have a beauty to it, shimmering with many colors, but it instilled a sort of dread in Amma too. "What's on the other side?"

"Oh, I don't know." The fae smiled, and it was too wide. "We don't die, so we've never gone through, and nobody ever comes back out."

"Ammalie? Is it really you?"

That voice. When last she had heard it, there was so much anger, so much pain and betrayal, but now it was as light as the morning of the party. The long and lithe form of King Wil of the Winter Court came sauntering out of the snow-covered pines. A shift of glittering frost blew around him though his silver gown and silver hair lay still, and his icy, blue eyes twinkled with delight.

"This one isn't yours, Tarwethen."

Amma's eyes felt like they might fall out of her head, though they weren't really eyes anymore, nor was it really a head her vision was located within. Unable to blink, she gazed from one fae form to the other. "What did you call him?"

"Tarwethen. But he's not meant to usher you off. It looks like you were one of..."—she checked her book—"Oh, Sestoth's? Interesting."

"Hi, hello, yes, I'm here, but I'm not sure why."

Amma jumped, the warm voice so close to her not-real-back. She turned, and there stood Rea, the soil-skinned, pink-haired fae who had been very friendly at Wil's gathering and given her a short-lived gift. Taller than Amma, her eyes, just as pink as her hair, fell on her, and she smiled. Warmth flooded Amma, quelling her fear, but only for a moment.

"This is...this is a trick," said Amma, though the words were strangled and the sentiment weak. She wanted it to be a trick, the kind of thing fae were known for, but in her heart, the truth began to burrow its way inside, like a slowly embedded thorn. But it *was* an absolutely mad truth, to be sure. "I've been here, I've seen your home, and...and I taught you how to have a snowball fight. You can't genuinely be telling me that you're *gods*?"

"I know, it can be very confusing when you meet us and you're still alive, but we can't let you in on it then," said Wil, or *Tarwethen* she guessed, though that felt ludicrous. "Have you formally introduced yourself, D?"

"Oh, no, I forgot that part!" The woman flipped her massive book closed, and it disappeared. She cleared her throat and threw back her shoulders, black cloak swept behind her to reveal a bone-white dress beneath. "I am Thea, goddess of death."

If Amma had had a stomach, it would have fallen right out of her. "Aren't you...aren't you a dark god? Supposedly locked away in the Abyss with the others?"

"Hmm? Oh, no, we just made that part up. You humans do *love* your lore."

There was a sparkling in the air then, and perhaps it had always been there, but Amma could see it very clearly, little specks of silver and gold. They fell like snowflakes in the wintery air about Tarwethen, they glided to the ground on the falling leaves in the autumn forest behind the door, they shimmered on every green leaf in the summery forest under full sun, and when she glanced at Rea again, who could really only be Sestoth, the goddess of trees and oaths, they glittered in her hair and eyelashes. Magic, pure and refined, dangerous, beautiful, and absolutely bullshit.

"I don't have time for this!" Amma threw what constituted her hands into the air. "Fine, you're gods, I accept how utterly weird and ridiculous that is. Now, send me back."

Sestoth's eyes went huge, but she grinned. Tarwethen, on the other hand, crossed over to the springy place they stood and grimaced. "Excuse me? What makes you think we can do that?"

"Because you're *gods*?" Amma screwed up her face. "And if you can't, get somegod who can, like Isldrah or Denonfy or Osurehm himself. I don't care, just make it happen."

A cacophony of voices burst into the island space as three beings appeared, two she recognized and a third whose name she didn't know but by the feathered wings on her back, she could only assume was Isldrah. Tertius, who had been behind giving the luxerna to Amma with Rae, who was actually Sestoth, was not looking at all surprised, but the Emperor of the Summer Court himself definitely was.

"Oh, this guy," Amma muttered, rolling her eyes at the bare-chested being she had known before as Norm, Wil's hated rival. Of course he was Osurehm, he could be no one else.

"We've been summoned?" Isldrah clasped her hands and her wings folded behind her.

"Yes, this one wants to *go back*," said Tarwethen, no attempt to hide his mocking tone.

"Oh, she can't do that," said Osurehm, and like that, he was gone.

Denonfy and Sestoth looked at one another sharply, and Amma grunted. "What a complete—"

"Here's the thing," Thea cut in, stepping away from her glittery threshold and coming nearer to Amma. "We aren't supposed to do anything on your plane. It was an agreement we came to ever since the *big* thing."

"You all call it *The Expulsion,* which is a very fancy name. We approve." Tarwethen and the others nodded.

"You guys interfere with the realm all the time." Amma slapped her not-hands onto her not-hips. "You grant magic to your followers and you answer prayers and…and you gave Fryn snake hair!"

"No, no, no," said Isldrah. "You all just pick up on the things we left behind the last time we were there."

"You let me summon imps in your temple!" Increasingly fearless, Amma pointed at the winged goddess and scowled.

"No, you just did that, and I *hated* it," she spat back.

"But your priestesses were being enthralled."

"Yeah, to *love* me." The goddess scoffed. "That little move of yours lost me seven thousand five hundred and twenty-nine points!"

Amma's next breath was excruciating as she wanted it to be a scream, but she knew she needed to negotiate. "Well, you're about to have a second expulsion because E'nloc is up on our plane, so maybe it's time to modify your agreement and do a little intervening."

Thea gasped. "Did you really let It out? Oh, is *that* what got those silly boys of Osurehm's? You weren't supposed to do that! We put it in the Abyss for a *reason*."

"Well, *I* didn't let it out."

"But that blood mage did, didn't he?" Thea glared at Tarwethen.

"No!" Amma was quick to retort, then grimaced. "Well, maybe a little, I wasn't there, but I'm sure Damien didn't mean to."

"It's going to destroy everything," moaned Thea.

"So?" Tarwethen flippantly gestured to the frozen forest. "We'll just make more of everything."

"Of course you'd say that since he's your fault." Her book appeared in her hands again, and she flipped through it as if it weighed nothing.

Amma blinked. "How is this your fault Wil?"

Tarwethen held his hands up, long fingers with too many knuckles spread wide. "Look, I didn't make him, okay, I just made Valgormoth, and all she did was turn everything to ice when she was on the plane. All of the rest of the demons in her lineage were her own doing."

"Oh, gods," Amma muttered, "I am not telling Damien that you're his however-many greats grandfather. He would hate that."

"You're not telling that blood mage anything because you're staying right here."

"Actually, she's going through the veil," said Thea.

"Actually," Sestoth interjected, "she's being resurrected."

Incensed, Tarwethen rounded on the goddess. "How?"

"Gave her essence to her when she was here last." Sestoth shrugged. "Denonfy had an inkling I should, so I did."

The other god nodded, lips drawn into a tight smile. It was strange he didn't speak, but she supposed he was saving up since he only retained two point three percent of his powers.

"But I wanted to keep her!" There was such a crankiness to Tarwethen's whine that Amma would have laughed if any of it were actually funny.

"Excuse me, can I go now? This doesn't have to do with me." Isldrah's wings flapped with impatience.

"No, we need one from each," Tarwethen snapped then he blew out a breath and seemed to compose himself. "Amma, I've a proposition for you. The gods will fulfill your request of once again removing E'nloc from your plane and trapping It in the Abyss."

"I didn't actually ask—"

"And in return, all you have to do is stay right here."

Amma's not-stomach sank to her not-toes. "I have to die?" she asked.

"No, here, in the Everdarque. You won't have your body, so you won't be able to get back to your plane, but you also won't technically die so long as you stay on this side of the veil. That all right with you, Thea?"

The goddess was still flipping through her book, harried. "Keep her here and get rid of E'nloc up there? If everything gets destroyed, I'm going to be *very* busy, so sure, that's fine with me."

"Wonderful, and the Autumn Court will surely follow your wishes. Isldrah, can you convince enough Summer gods to rid the realm of E'nloc one more time?"

"Sure, whatever." The goddess tapped a foot.

"And I'm sure you'll disagree," Tarwethen eyed Sestoth, "so I'll just summon another spring deity to—"

Sestoth raised a hand, and then gently placed it on Amma's shoulder. "If the decision she makes is to stay, I would not stand in the way of honoring that." Pink eyes found Amma's, flecks of gold swirling inside them. "She's mine, after all, and I would never dare not put what she wants first."

Amma's heartbeat, the one she was pretty sure she didn't have anymore, was in her ears, but Sestoth's voice echoed in her mind. What she wanted, put first. She had heard that once before.

"So," said Tarwethen, nudging Sestoth out of the way and replacing her before Amma, "it is your choice, and your choice alone to make, sweet, kind, altruistic Ammalie. Allow the apparent resurrection occurring over your body in your home plane, selfishly return to a world on the brink of destruction and watch it crumble around you, everyone you have ever known and loved as well as every other being and creature and even every, single tree succumb to a painful and agonizing death, *or* choose to save the whole of existence for the paltry price of immortality at the side of the gods."

"A real toughie," droned Isldrah, picking at her nails.

Amma's throat and lips couldn't go dry, but the panic was still there, coursing all around her and winking in and out like the sparkling silver and gold of arcana in the air. She looked from the god of winter and wealth urging her on the decision he knew she would make, to the goddess of death tapping fingers across her pages anxiously. Beside her, the goddess of birds and health also tapped, but there was no trepidation there, only impatience. The god of fortune and destiny who had given up nearly all of his powers to the oracle back in her plane only silently grinned at her as if he could wait forever and never tire of the present moment, glad to be in it always, and finally, there was the goddess of trees and oaths, the one by whom she had sworn.

"I'm going back."

Tarwethen smiled. "Of course, dear, now let's—" The god blinked. His fingers shifted to claws, teeth to fangs, limbs elongating, shadow growing. "How dare you, mor—"

"Stop that." Sestoth slapped his shoulder, and Tarwethen lost the terror that had been overcoming every inch of his being. "She made her choice."

"Yes, the disgustingly selfish one where she allows the entirety of existence to burn to ash just so she can, what, *live* a few seconds longer? Have you no, what is it called? *Humanity?*"

Amma swallowed, and this she really did as her throat was mending, and she shrugged shoulders that she would soon have again. "I don't care," she said, her own voice quieter in ears that were on another plane. "I would rather be with Damien for one moment longer than abandon him. I love him, and I made a promise that I would stay by his side. I can't break my oath, and even if I could: I don't want to."

Heart beating, Amma's vision clouded, and Sestoth's warm voice was in her ear. "That's my girl."

CHAPTER 35
HOW THE TURNTABLES

All of the good things on this and every other plane paled in comparison to life blossoming in Amma's eyes. The entirety of existence would be destroyed, but she had come back to him, and Damien would never allow her to be lost again for as long as he lived, which, admittedly, seemed to have a rather short forecast, but still.

There was a flash of fire, and the resurrection spell burnt itself out of the Lux Codex in Pippa's hands. She slammed the book shut and quickly shrouded it away, one less source of agony in the chamber, but barely an impression on the excruciating pain aching inside Damien. But there was Amma, alive, and nothing else mattered.

Gathered up in his arms, Amma's hand found its way to Damien's chest. Her lips parted, all of the love he'd rashly enchanted out of her returning to her face. She gripped his tunic, drawing her shoulders in, and then in a show of surprising strength, yanked him downward.

Amma's features shifted into malice, resentment, rage. The talisman was finally out of her, the enthrallment should have been broken, the last, horrible command he'd given her wiped clean, but she looked on him as if she would put an end to Damien's entire existence.

"Don't you *ever* try to make me stop loving you again," she hissed, and then she was kissing him.

Damien scooped her up against his body. Still covered in her blood, they slid against one another, but her arms were strong as they wrapped around his neck. He squeezed her back, hands roving over where the wound had been, now gone, and shifted away from where Xander sat, recovering on the dais from utilizing so much arcana. The other blood mage might have just broken everything either of them had ever understood about arcana and performed a divine spell of resurrection alongside a priestess, but he'd also been the one to make Amma dead in the first place.

Kill. Them. All.

"Shut up," Damien mumbled against her mouth.

Amma pulled back. "What?"

"Not you." He swallowed hard, throat still raw from screaming and crying.

She pouted. "That's still in there, huh?"

He went to nod, but there was a terrible crack that shook the entirety of the throne room. Pippa yelped, and even Xander started as Damien held Amma closer, pressing his back to the stairs. From the ruined opening into the vault, the bloody and terrified form of King Archibald Lumier came running. He fled past the others, a coarse scream echoing into the throne room as he stumbled down the stairs and fell to the carpeted floor below.

A dark and ominous cackle rose from the vault as a shadowy form stepped out of the swirling noxscura that flooded into the throne room. Birzuma the Blasphemed, Ninth Lord of the Accursed Wastes and Nefarious Harbinger of the Chthonic Tower, exhaled on the threshold of the vault of Eirengaard Keep, newly freed from her prison of over a decade, and obviously pissed. Skin blue like the depths of the night, her eyes shone with yellow light as they fell on the floundering form of the man who had just freed her. Horns curled back behind her ears, rigid and coming to points tipped with gold, growing out of a wild mane of black hair. She grinned, fangs glinting, and then struck out.

The demoness was standing beside them one moment and then hunching over Archibald in the next, faster than eyes could keep up with. A clawed hand came down on the back of his neck and lifted him from the ground, and the King of Eiren hung there in her grasp, sobbing in fear.

Birzuma inhaled deeply, and Damien knew that satisfaction, at least tangentially—there would be no stopping her. She growled and then took a long look out at the throne room filled with infernals that had crept out of the shadows to revel in her presence. A demon lord could not crawl out of a ripped veil between planes, she had to be summoned and with intensely powerful magic, yet she was there.

"Mother, dear!" Xander was back on his feet, gulping for air, a hand pressed to his chest, still drained from the resurrection yet beaming.

The demoness turned, features hard to read on skin dark as midnight, but her flickering, yellow eyes fell on the blood mage. "Xander." Her voice rippled through the throne room, thick and austere.

"Yes, it's me! I got you out," he panted, taking the steps two at a time and straightening when he reached her.

The blood mage wasn't short by any means, but Birzuma had at least a foot on him, her lithe form clad in layers of black clothing that moved ethereally around her like smoke. She held Archibald out of the way, his feet just scuffing the floor as he vainly attempted to flee. Birzuma brought a hand to her son's face to tip it up, black claws curling over the entirety of his jaw. "My son," she said, each word weighty and dreadful. "What took so long?"

Xander's eyes widened, for once at a loss as he stuttered. "I, uh, well?" He tried to look over at the others as if they could help, but she tightened her hold on him, leaning closer, waiting. "Zagadoth has been locked away for more than a decade longer than you, and—"

"What makes you think I would care about that?" Her jaws snapped, and Xander attempted to recoil but was trapped in her grip, a rivulet of blood seeping out from where one of her claws dug into his cheek. "Your incompetence left me to rot for far too long. Have you not grown to be more than worthless yet?"

"I-I still freed you," he said, voice wavering and small.

"Yes, wonderful, congratulations—you fulfilled your use, *barely*. I suppose this counts for one accomplishment in your miserable half life." When she released him, Xander brought his hands up, but whether it was in protection or desperation, it was hard to tell. He just as quickly balled fists and dropped them at his sides, face hardening as she turned away, a thin line of blood trickling down his face. "Now, for *you*."

Archibald was raised, and before he could scream, a claw tore through his chest. He let out a single, gurgling cry, blood raining across the burgundy carpet, the colors all melding into one under the reddened pall through the windows. A crystalline tinkling rang out in the room, and then Birzuma dropped the body of the slain king.

Damien was woken from his petrified stare by shifting in his pocket. Amma's hand had buried itself there, and he pressed lips to her ear to remain as quiet as possible. "Sweetness, is now really an appropriate time—"

Amma burst out of Damien's arms, too quick to be snatched back, and she was running. Damien shouted after her, and even Xander called out, telling her to stop as she flew toward the demoness, but she was faster than either could comprehend. A dose of luxerna will do that to a person who has just been dead, life renewed and fresh and requiring utilization, but none of them really knew that, they only knew that Amma was about to do something reckless and stupid.

She darted right for the demon, a flash of something white in her hand. Was she *mad*? She couldn't kill her, even if she could land a strike, and Xander's honor wasn't even worth it.

Birzuma turned, sensing the woman just as she was upon her. Claws were raised, and then noxscura blotted out the entire chamber. There was a scream in the darkness and the gnashing of jaws. Shimmering eyes flashed through the haze, pair after pair, the sounds of beating wings and scuffing talons as if a brawl had broken out in the shadows below. And then the chamber cleared.

Damien was on his feet, Pippa at his side, trembling but ready. Below, a horde of infernal beasts had descended upon Birzuma. A gator-bear had the demon's arm in its jaws, a serpent wrapped around her body, a flock of tiny wyverns covering a leg, the black cat flopping itself over her neck. She was completely restrained, and at her side, so was Xander.

Amma stood unscathed, breathing hard, eyes wide as if shocked at herself. The infernals had protected her, just as Damien had commanded them to do.

He scrambled down the stairs, practically falling on his face when his legs wanted to give up under intense pain and weakness. E'nloc's voice was loud, but he pushed it away, avoiding the mass of infernals restraining the demoness, and he took Amma by the arms gently, pulling her away. "Amma, what were you trying to do?"

She blinked away from the deadly place she had just been and up to him. "Do you trust me?"

"Yes, unequivocally, I just wish you'd tell me whatever the fuck it is you're doing," he said desperately.

"I can't, It'll probably try to stop me."

Kill her.

Damien nodded. "Fair."

Amma's nimble fingers took his hand, and her palm was pressed to his. There was something solid in his grasp, the handkerchief in her own as she pulled her hand away. Left in his palm was Bloodthorne's

Talisman of Enthrallment, recovered from Archibald's body, bloody, touching his skin.

"Amma," he breathed, staring at the stone. "This is my own creation. It isn't going to work on me, I'm—" The talisman glowed and began to burrow.

"No longer that person?"

His eyes shot up to hers, shocked, heart racing.

She grinned, absolutely wicked. "Are you ready to have some fun?"

Damien convulsed, the pain extraordinary. The talisman dug itself up his arm, across his chest, and slammed into his heart with such strength he fell to his knees, vision blacking out. Nope, that wasn't fun at all.

Amma's arms were around him as he fell, her yelp of surprise in his ear, and then many syrupy apologies followed as she tried to shake him back to consciousness.

"Damien?" she called, but it sounded far away, the twisting and gnawing at his guts intense, noxscura flooding behind but with much less fervor than it had before when it attempted to heal the luxerna's chewing.

This will kill Us, It said into his mind.

Good.

"*Sanguinisui*, wake up."

A warm flood of arcana raced around Damien's innards, and his vision sharpened, sitting up, totally alert.

Amma gasped, and then she looked on him with utter awe. "It worked."

"*Sanguinisui*, stab her!"

Damien snorted, glancing at Xander over his shoulder, still trapped beneath the pile of infernals.

"Worth a shot," the other blood mage groaned. "Oh, don't look at me like that, kitten, you could have stopped him, clearly."

Amma was sneering but only for a moment. She took Damien by the tunic once again and pulled him up to his feet. "Come on, we're fixing this. Pippa, you too!" She marched toward the doors, dragging him along behind her. She didn't have to do that, she could just order him to follow, or even just ask—he would do whatever she wanted.

No.

Damien's legs stiffened, and he lurched backward as noxscura held him to the spot. "Oh, fuck."

"Now," said Amma, brow sharp. "*Sanguinisui*, follow me."

A separate jolt of noxscura pushed at Damien's back, and his feet

327

thankfully decided to obey as well, but his guts were not happy about a damn thing, and he retched as he went.

"Oh, sorry, Damien," she said sweetly, rubbing his arm. Though his insides burned, at least half eaten away by now with the luxerna, there was that voice of hers, so warm and pleasant, saying his name and nestling into his chest, finding the place it belonged. *That*—that was worth suffering for. "But *sanguinisui*, hurry up."

More quickly, they passed through the throne room to the antechamber, the priestess following behind.

"Master?"

"Kaz?"

Kill it.

Damien growled at the voice and tried to grin at the imp, Quaz and Katz in various states of imp transformation alongside him, but he feared it came off as a grimace. "Where did you come from?"

"I summoned them in the temple," said Amma offhandedly. "They helped me free your mom."

"My *mother*?"

Amma pulled Damien out of Eirengaard Keep into the brighter redness of the outdoors, the eclipse still looming and the earth seemingly bathed in blood, silvery fissures drawn through the sky, a winged beast dropping out of one of them. "Yes, I brought her with me. She was enthralled, but I think she's better now. Did you know she has a sword? She's kind of a badass."

Damien wasn't sure what to say to that. "I've heard." He stumbled on the stairs, and she grabbed him, a shoulder under his arm for support, and Pippa was at his other side, helping him descend.

"Amma?" A horrified but familiar voice called out from the sprawling gardens before them. "Oh, you look awful!"

"Yeah, I died." Amma huffed, propping Damien up on a patch of soft grass. His vision was tunneling, but he could see Amma's friends, Laurel and Perry and another woman, a small contingency of horses behind, though he must have been losing consciousness again because none of them actually *were* horses, just creepy versions of the things. A few others came out from around the hedges, dressed in armor and wearing the crest of the Solonedys, and then there was his mother.

"Damien." He was drawn up into a tight embrace. Divine magic pricked at him, his stomach turned over, and everything hurt, but then none of that mattered because his mother was hugging him, and this time, he knew, she meant it.

Kill them all!

E'nloc hadn't stopped his crusade against Damien's will, but It

328

hadn't counted on how quickly It would destroy Its own vessel with so much urging. Damien had little left to give it, to give anything really, as the world around him went dark and blurry. Amma was saying something, the loveliness of her voice caressing what was left of him to caress, though it was firm. More voices prodded at the edges of his mind as he tried to blink back into the vigilance he'd had in the throne room. A discussion happened around him as he sat, no, fell back onto the grass.

"*Sanguinisui*, stay with me."

Damien's eyes shot open, noxscura swelling within him, and Amma pulled him back up to sit. Behind her stood a small crowd, Eirengaard Keep looming at their backs.

"Damien, I need you to open a portal to the Abyss."

He snorted. "I can't do that." It was a lie, of course, because if there was any power left in him at all, it was the power of destruction, and tearing a hole into the Abyss would surely swallow up all life. "The infernal plane, yes, lots of fissures to there,"—he pointed to a silver streak in the sky—"but the Abyss? Think of what will come out of it. Dark gods, literally, and then the end times."

"There's nothing there," she assured him, squeezing his arms, and even though it was obviously not true, he believed her. "Are you ready?"

Damien shook his head.

Amma's jaw went tight, glassiness to her eyes. "You want to stay with me, don't you?"

He did, more than anything else he'd ever desired despite the recent, stupid choices he'd made and how often he didn't allow himself the comfort of her presence. Existence would be destroyed if he remained alive, but…but he would have her for at least a few moments longer. "Yes."

"Good." She grinned though a tear rolled down her cheek. "*Sanguinisui*, open a portal to the Abyss."

Beneath Damien's hands, there was a rumbling in the earth, and then, all too easily, it split. Not a true split, not a crack into the soil and rock, but in all of existence. Amma pulled him to his feet, away from the fissure that spread through the garden, and they both could only stare into it. There was nothing inside but forever darkness, worse than even the pits they had encountered before.

Yes, It panted, practically giddy. *Destruction.*

Amma's fingers threaded into Damien's, a whipping wind hitting them both as they stood at its edge. She would be pushing him in, he knew it, the minor manipulation to make things easier something he instantly forgave her for. He wouldn't stop her, nor would he allow E'nloc to. It was at least less messy than being stabbed. He turned to her. "Thank you," he said, squeezing her hand.

She squeezed him back. "*Sanguinisui*, purge E'nloc into the Abyss."

Damien's chest tightened, and his breath stopped. If It got out, It would destroy everything, but he had no choice. Once again on his knees, the noxscura inside him pummeled and prodded, fighting luxerna. The voice of E'nloc laughed, it screamed, it cried, it shouted in triumph, and for a moment Damien was plunged into cold, lonely darkness once again.

The pendant hovered before him, and Damien was reaching out to it, taking it in his hand, and he crushed it into dust.

His vision returned, and two halves of an ugly gem on separate chains were in his feeble grip, and then they slipped, tumbling into the Abyss and swallowed up by the dark. His connection to E'nloc was severed, noxscura rushing to mend and heal his innards. It was freedom and light and goodness, but Damien's stomach still sank, because it wasn't only his freedom that had been given.

Inside the long fissure reaching away from them, blackness rose up, toppling the living things that teetered on the edge and reaching out with hundreds of tendrils. It had the voices of too many, and it spoke in Key and Chthonic and Empyrean all at once, and it said only *Destruction*.

Amma took Damien by the back of his tunic and drew him away from the fissure. "Stay here," she said, quickly pecking him on the lips. When she pulled back, there was her liathau staff in her hand, blossoming with tiny, pink buds on dark wood. She was covered in gore, hand prints of blood on her face, hair a mess, ragged circles under her eyes, and she was the most beautiful and powerful thing he'd ever seen. She turned from him and stepped up to the fissure, slamming the staff's end into the ground.

The garden burst into life under the red sky, grasses growing, limbs reaching, even the wooden statues bending. The flora creaked like trees in an oncoming storm, the wood twisting, limbs flourishing to reach out to one another and catch on. Together, the frenzy of plants joined in a spiral at the garden's edges and closed in on the tendrils of nothing that clawed at the edges of the Abyss, rooting for escape. More magic joined the fray, divine and irritating, but it was there at Damien's back, the earth rumbling with arcana.

Damien stood, and noxscura pooled in his hands. His body had been flooded with mending, urgency to fix what had been broken by

E'nloc's containment, and just as it had been begging him to do for moons, he released the noxscura fully.

Shadows wove themselves into the branches and blossoms, urging them on to close any gaps and fully come together. The vines and grasses and bits of statue coalesced, growing upward and over the fissure in a spiral. E'nloc's voice, that smattering of languages and terror, weakened to a din, muffled beneath the earth as the rift was encased.

And then, finally, silence.

The gardens were ruined, and yet better. In their place stood a single, massive tree. Its twisted trunk was nearly as wide across as the keep, branches bare, and it clawed upward, triumphant as the redness began to clear from the sky.

Amma fell to her knees, her staff disappearing. Damien went to her, falling at her side, and to his relief, she was smiling. "It's done," she breathed, taking his face in her hands. "And you're alive."

CHAPTER 36
HAPPY ENDINGS AND WHAT THEY ENTAIL

WE ARE HERE TO EXTEND AN OFFER.

Amma blinked, hearing the voice that was one and many at the same time. She looked out on the ruined gardens, now simply a tree, and standing at its base were five figures, swathed in heavy robes and looking terribly ominous with an even more ominous cloud hanging over their heads. Their faces were completely obscured, but that didn't make it feel any less like they were looking directly at her.

"That's the Grand Order of Dread." Damien swallowed, swinging an arm around her from their spot on the ground and drawing her close.

THERE IS NO NEED TO BE CONCERNED—THE TASK IS COMPLETE. HOWEVER, WE REQUEST AN AUDIENCE WITH THE FORCE THAT DESTROYED DESTRUCTION ITSELF.

Damien shook his head. "I didn't—"

NOT YOU.

"Me?" Amma asked in her meekest voice. She still had a hand on Damien's face, but her grip shifted down to his tunic, holding it tightly.

YES. THE SIXTH SEAT ON THE DREADCOUNCIL REQUIRES FULFILLMENT. WE WOULD LIKE TO OFFER IT TO YOU.

"Oh, uh, that's really sweet,"—Amma laughed nervously—"but no, thank you, I'm good."

I TOLD YOU SHE WOULD NOT BE INTERESTED. WELL, IT WAS WORTH ASKING. WAS IT, THOUGH? THIS IS VERY EMBARRASSING. YES, AND THIS CONVERSATION IS EVEN MORE EMBARRASSING.

"Um, actually, Dreadcouncil?" Amma sat a little straighter, Damien's grip on her tightening. "Since you're here, do you think you can break a demon out of prison for us?"

There was a short pause as the council members traded unseen glances. *NO. HOWEVER, WE CAN CLEAN UP THIS MESS. CONSIDER OUR DUTIES MET. YOU MAY WANT TO GO INSIDE.*

Lightning streaked across the sky, and thunder shook the city as the Grand Order of Dread all raised hands overhead.

Damien was on his feet, taking Amma with him and shouting at the others to head into the keep. Being bustled inside, Amma took a last look back at her giant liathau, the gnarled branches appearing dead though she could feel a strange and beautiful necrotic life thrumming through the tree, and above, the silver fissures to the infernal plane began to close as the creatures scattered about Eirengaard were drawn inside them.

The massive doors of Eirengaard Keep shut out the sounds as the planes were torn or mended or whatever in the Abyss it was GOoD was doing. Piled together in the antechamber, Amma's eyes took in those around her, those who had aided in closing the rift, and those who had stood by her side. Perry was recuperating as Laurel pat his back, Vanders on her shoulder and the knoggelvi and Stitches huddled behind. Winnifred and the mages she had brought from Buckhead were examining the imps who still looked at least a little like household pets as Pippa and Damien's mother took stock of one another's holy symbols. Amma squeezed Damien's hand, feeling the warmth that had almost been ripped away from her, breath finally catching, but then there was shouting from the throne room.

Carefully, Amma went to the entry, the door only cracked, and Damien stayed on her heels. Lifting herself from the ground was the form of Birzuma the Blasphemed, and she came to tower over Xander, screeching. The infernal creatures that had restrained them appeared to have been drawn away, a silver fissure still floating, open, in the hall's middle. Birzuma continued to berate her son about how long he'd taken to free her and what a disappointingly useless man he'd become.

Xander sputtered back, hands out, never able to completely form an excuse before she cut him off with another cutting remark.

"I feel like we should help him," Amma whispered.

"He *killed* you," Damien growled into her ear.

"Yeah, but he brought me back too, right?"

There was a hand on her shoulder, firm and strong, shifting her gently out of the way. Sword unsheathed, Diana marched past them and into the throne room, calling the demoness's name.

Vicious eyes snapped to the priestess, the spindly yet hulking form of Birzuma the Blasphemed turning, giving Xander a shove so he fell backward on the steps up to the throne. Exhausted, he remained there, face red and horrified.

"Oh, Diana Bloodthorne, it's been too long." She chuckled darkly, crossing arms and smirking. "Ventured out of your little cloister, I see. How's that goddess of yours? Still useless?"

"You," called Diana, her voice echoing into the room. "You took my family from me. You had me enthralled, you imprisoned my husband, and worst of all, you hurt my *son*."

Amma tapped Damien's chest from their spot at the edge of the door. "Aww, see, she was just enthralled, but she still loves you."

He was staring into the hall, wide-eyed and clearly worried, but he managed a nod.

Birzuma groaned. "Yeah, well, I'm a demon, Diana, what did you expect?"

"What you are has nothing to do with what I expect." The woman slashed her sword through the air, and the brilliance of it flared blindingly golden. "It's what you've chosen to be."

The demon began toward where Diana stood, and Amma's stomach clenched. Damien couldn't lose his mother, not so soon after getting her back.

"There's not much you can do about what I choose to be," said Birzuma, striding closer. "Not when I tricked your feeble mind into being heartbroken over your expendable spawn, and certainly not now either, *human*." The word fell from her tongue like ash, bitter and hateful.

Another slash, another flare of light, arcana hanging in the air in the wake of the sword. "I think you forget, Birzuma, because I was always so forgiving of your cruelty, that the reason I was originally sent to Aszath Koth was—"

"To destroy it, yes, yes, I know. And you failed at that too!" Birzuma stopped in the hall's middle to throw her head back and cackle.

"Not to destroy it," she called. "To banish its guardian. That is, after all, what I've been training for my entire life—to banish demons." With a final swing of her sword, the symbol she had been carving into the air out of arcana was complete. Diana slammed the tip of her blade into the floor, and a crack drew itself away from the weapon. Extending her palm, the priestess touched the symbol, and it flew through the air toward the demoness.

The fissure above and the new one below coalesced, catching Birzuma between them, and she sucked in a shocked breath, terrifying eyes now terrified. The arcane symbol slammed into her chest, light burst into the throne room of Eirengaard Keep, and when it cleared, the demon and the fissures were no more.

In the brimstoney air that was left, Diana huffed, and Xander lifted himself from the stairs where he'd been pushed.

The priestess pointed at him, making him fall still, her voice exacting. "Have you stopped being such a little shit?"

"Yes!" Xander was nodding, chest heaving with fear.

"No, mom, he killed Amma!" Damien pushed into the throne room, incensed, dragging Amma along with him.

"I resurrected her!" Xander snarled, shouting back. "It was all part of the plan. Pips, tell them!"

Creeping out of the antechamber, the priestess nodded. "I didn't condone any of it, but yes, he didn't want to kill her until he was pretty sure he could also bring her back. That's why he didn't do it in Buckhead when we were all in that estate."

"Pretty sure?" Damien growled, marching up to Diana's side. "You still stabbed her!"

"To get the talisman out." Xander was throwing around his hands. "To put a stop to that ridiculous order you gave to her. Why did you do that, Damien? You just look so...*sad.*"

The blood mages stared at one another, both utterly baffled, but the ire in the air fell away.

Diana blew out a sigh, shoulders relaxing. Sword left plunged into the ground, she wandered passed the burnt carpeting where the tear into the infernal plane had been, around Archibald's body and the pool of his blood, and didn't glimpse at Xander as she took to the stairs. The wall at the top of the platform had been torn away, and she entered the room beyond.

Amma was tugged along as Damien followed her, pointing to Xander as they went. "This isn't finished," he grumbled, but the blood mage only stuck out his tongue in response.

Inside the vault, Diana stood with her hand on what looked like a massive ruby, a human-shaped shadow inside. "I'm sorry," she said to it. "I wasn't strong enough."

Amma released Damien's hand, and he went to stand beside her. "Well, we can chip a piece of it off again, and The Brotherhood can enchant it so that we can at least talk to him in Aszath Koth."

"That would be nice," she said with a sigh, and the two stood before where Amma could only assume Zagadoth was trapped amongst broken glass and blood and dashed hope.

"Hey, uh, which one of you killed my father?"

In the wrecked entry to the vault, a very young, opulently-dressed woman with ginger hair and an awe-struck look stood. Amma swore under her breath and then scurried up to her, did half a curtsy, and then huffed, not bothering. "Princess Isabella," she said, clearing her throat. "We're truly sorry for your loss, but it was a demon who struck down King Archibald. And, uh, in vengeance, Priestess Diana has slain her." She held out an arm, gesturing vaguely to Damien's mother.

The princess didn't really seem to care though. "I've never been allowed in here before," she marveled, glass crunching below her feet as she wandered in. "He only ever let in Iggy, not me."

Amma stayed at her side. "Um, we *are* sorry about your father," she repeated carefully.

"Oh, yeah, well, he was a jerk." She lifted a broken crystal from a pedestal, looking it over. "This plan of his was *so* stupid, I'm not surprised it killed him."

Amma, Damien, and Diana traded awkward glances.

"Hey, you have your father's abilities, right?" Amma hopped in front of her and drew her attention away from the oddities and destruction in the room.

"Yes, not that he ever let me use them," she scoffed, tossing the broken crystal over her shoulder where it shattered in the rest of the mess.

"You wanna break something else of his?"

It took a few tries, but with a little coaxing and focus, the ruby in the vault cracked and arcana filled the air, dark and cloying and heavy, and then, there was a voice, deeper than the Abyss and rumbling up from the broken stone. "Kiddo?"

It went, of course, exactly as sweetly and strangely as one would imagine a reunion between a demon, a priestess, and their son could go after twenty-three years spent apart, imprisoned, enthralled, and toiling under half-truths. There were tears and embraces and frustrated sighs, and when the demon pulled the priestess into a deep and passionate kiss, Damien retched and covered his face.

Zagadoth was almost what Amma had imagined, about seven-and-a-half feet tall, with spiraling black horns, skin as red as liathau leaves in the heart of autumn, and, just as she predicted, a *tail.* But he was also a delightful surprise: warm, kind, and very good at giving hugs, picking up Amma the moment she was introduced and nearly squeezing the life out of her. Though, Amma supposed, she should have really expected all of those things since Damien was his son, after all.

But soon the sky through the windows in the throne room cleared and those who served in Eirengaard Keep began to venture out into the halls. Winnifred, Laurel, and Pippa had discussed next steps, intending to stay in the city to assist in cleaning things up and clearing names, but it wasn't exactly what any of them would consider safe for the others to stay.

Xander had not run off, watching the others with a keen eye. He composed himself and revealed a rolled parchment from his pocket. "To Aszath Koth?"

"Where did you get that?" Damien was peering at him dubiously.

"What do you think I was doing in the translocation closet at Yvlcon?" He waved the scroll in his face. "I knew we'd both need a way home after all of this. Don't worry, I won't stick around, I have other things to do."

"Well, I hope you at least stay for dinner," Diana cut in, and both Damien and Zagadoth grumbled at that, but it seemed there would be no arguing with her, especially once she'd retrieved her sword.

"All right, just a moment," Damien requested of the others, and he pulled Amma aside and into a shadowy corner of the throne room where it was quiet. He took a deep breath, clasping her hands in his, eyes turned down. "Amma, I am unsure what to say."

"Well, that's not like you."

He chuckled and looked up at her. "I promised to return you to Faebarrow, and I will, but first, would you please come with me to Aszath Koth? It is a dark and dreary place, especially in the winter, and it can be cold and brutal, but I want you to know the truth of it be—"

"Of course I'll go," she said, drawing him close, "and I'm going to love it because it's part of you."

He grinned that grin that brought such lightness to her heart, that one he never had when they'd first met but had become more frequent yet never common. "And then we'll go to Faebarrow, I swear it."

"As long as we're together," she said.

"Always," he promised.

Amma bit her lip, curious. "*Sanguinisui*, kiss me."

His lips were on hers, and they melted into one another.

"Oh, that's fun," she said as she pulled back.

"Amma, there are moral implications you should consider—"

"*Sanguinisui*, do not hurt yourself or anyone else and purge out Bloodthorne's Talisman of Enthrallment."

There was a thunk and the stone fell to the floor between them.

Damien stared at the talisman and screwed up his face. "Maybe I should have tried that back in the Sanctum."

Amma snorted. "Well, thank darkness you didn't." And she kissed him again.

INSERT CATCHY
ALTERNATIVE FOR
EPILOGUE HERE

Damien popped his head out from beneath the linens, rubbing the back of his hand over his mouth. He smirked down at the satisfied look on Amma's face, crawling up to meet her. "A great evil has come upon your land, Mistress Ammalie."

She blinked, dazed, senses slowly coming back. "It better not have yet," she said, taking him by the shoulders and rolling him to his back. "I intended to ride out and meet it." Amma climbed atop him, taking him by the wrists and pressing them back on either side of his head. She teased at him as she held him down, barely close enough to brush over the tip of his length.

"Surrender," he growled from beneath her. "You can't possibly resist the dark forces intending to penetrate—"

"Honey?" There was a sharp wrap at the bedchamber door. "Your father and I are headed to the Sanctum."

Damien squeezed his eyes shut, stomach twisting, ire rising. "Yes, mother, all right."

"We're taking the imps with us, just in case you're wondering where they are," she called.

"I'm sure we won't," he called back.

Amma snorted out a laugh, regrettably lifting her hips upward.

"And Gril just mopped the throne room, so do be careful if you go in there."

339

He grunted. "Fabulous. Thank you. Goodbye."

"Oh, and Ammalie, don't forget our training session tomorrow."

Amma grinned wide and called back, "I'm looking forward to it! Full armor or are we doing low contact?"

"Amma, please don't encourage this," Damien grumbled from beneath her, and she gave his wrists a squeeze.

"Well, that depends," his mother continued from the other side of the door, "do you want—"

"Basest beasts, the two of you can speak tomorrow!" he exploded, throwing his head back. "Just go already!"

"Goodness, you are so grumpy," Diana huffed, and he could practically hear the look she was giving the door. "All right, goodbye!"

Damien groaned, rolling his head forward to glower at Amma. "I know we have decided to split our time between Aszath Koth and Faebarrow, but we *must* acquire separate accommodations. Constant badgering about producing heirs from all four of our parents, yet never a damn moment of peace to make any."

Amma laughed, wiggling her hips as she dipped them back down. "Well, now that we're finally alone, do you want peace or do you want war?"

That woke up the blood that had gone dormant in his loins. "War, please."

Just as she pressed her lips to his, there was a flutter of black feathers that shot in through the window, crashing into the linens and rolling up in them. Amma squealed, sitting back and releasing him, and Damien buried his hand into the blankets to pull the bird out.

"Dark gods, Corben, have a little respect." He grabbed the bird about his middle and tried to cover his beady eyes with his other hand, but the raven bobbed his head around his palm.

Sitting back but sadly not on his length, naked breasts and belly exposed, Amma took the parchment from Corben's beak. "Oh, it's all right, Damien, you always say he's not even real."

"Real enough," he murmured and gave the arcane raven a toss back out the way he came.

Amma leaned against Damien's knees, his length nestled against her backside, and she unraveled the small scroll, blocking her breasts from him, but revealing a bit more of the slickness between her legs. He placed hands on her thighs and slid a thumb toward her center.

"She hatched!"

Damien's hand froze. "She did? When?"

"This morning!" Amma's eyes were wide and her grin wider as she scanned the note. "Three pounds, eleven inches, olive scales, eight

340

fangs, and they named her…oh." Her grin faltered, eyes pinging to Damien. "Her name's Murple. That's, um, pretty, I guess?"

"Translates to *hope* in draekin, so yes, it is. To other draekin."

Amma pressed the parchment to her chest, a glassy sheen to her eyes. "Oh, Damien, I was so worried because she was late, and they traveled so far."

"I know, but they're all accounted for now." He took the parchment from her and set it on the stand beside the bed. "Because of the food and gold you gave them." He slipped his hand between them, and she rocked backward as he curled his fingers inside her.

Amma's breath hitched, her ass rubbing against his length. "And the sanctuary you gave them," she gasped, hands bracing themselves on his chest. "Because you're so nice."

"Nice?" He worked her with a fervor and then pulled his hand away, dragging a gasp from her lips. Taking her by the wrists, he tugged her downward. "We'll see how nice you think I am after I'm through torturing you, my little prisoner of war."

"Oh, no," she said, all out of breath. "Please don't hurt me, Master Bloodthorne. I'll do *anything*."

"Anything?" His brow shifted up, and she nodded, lips parted eagerly and wet in anticipation.

There was very little Damien hadn't ordered her to do yet, all of which she obediently and ardently complied with, but there was one thing, one massive, hulking, looming thing, that he had yet to request.

Damien's grip on her went lax, and he reached up to place hands on either side of Amma's face. "You," he said, voice low, "you have changed me."

Her cheeks went red and warm under his fingers, and his heart squeezed, still able to pull a blush out of her after all this time. "I'm not the same as I was when we met either."

"Yes, you are," he said. "You are still thoughtful and kind and good. But I must request that you change me once more."

She tipped her head with that curiosity that pumped through her blood and back into him, making his pulse race.

"Will you marry me?"

Amma's eyes went wide, startled, and she sat up very quickly. Every bit of her stiffened in something like fear, even her nipples, but Damien only chuckled, the worry leeching away. As she worked through her sudden distress, he just folded his hands behind his head and waited.

Amma bit a nail, pressed a hand to her bare chest, and finally blew out a breath. "What am I thinking? Yes! Of course I will." She threw herself back down, wrapping arms around his neck and squeezing him. "Oh, I'm sorry," she said, apologizing for nothing like always. "I think I'm just so used to marriage being a bad thing that I panicked."

Damien chuckled in her ear, holding her against him. "It's fine, I already knew you would say yes."

"Ridiculously confident, as always," she mused, lifting her head to squint at him.

"No, I mean, I actually knew—the oracle told me."

"The Denonfy Oracle?"

Damien shrugged. "I think so anyway. I wasn't quite sure exactly what to ask them, so they told me the answer to my question without making me actually ask."

"How does that work?"

"I'm not sure, but at the time, I didn't want to know about any of the horrible things that I assumed would come to pass, I was only concerned about you and if you would be happy, in the end, and all I could think about was the very question you had said you would have asked once upon a time: *Who will Ammalie Avington marry*? And the oracle said, *You*."

"Me?"

"No, me." He grinned. "Now, do you consider our negotiations settled?"

She giggled and nestled into his chest. "Oh, I suppose we're getting peace after all then? That's fine, I'm a little sleepy anyway."

"Oh, no, my sweet, you must have forgotten." He rolled her over quickly and pinned her to the bed, purring up against her throat, "Evil will go so far as to convince you that you are safe, but it will always betray you, in the end."

And, because he was utterly abysmal at being as evil as he always said, Damien did the cruelest thing he could imagine and did not allow Amma one wink of sleep for the rest of the night.

Since Eiren had experienced the infernal plane being unleashed but also contained, the discourse surrounding the most superlatively evil being to have ever blighted the realm became slightly more complex and nuanced. New records were drawn up and beings were argued for and against, and the coveted spot of Supreme Evil was debated more fiercely than ever. Damien Maleficus Bloodthorne, demon spawn, blood mage, son of a priestess, and brand new fiance, however, never even made the list.

THANK YOU

I cannot express to you, Dear Reader, how grateful I am that you picked up this story, and you stayed with Damien and Amma until the very end.

You make the panic attacks and the sweating and the fact I have to live knowing my mother will read the steamy parts even though I'll ask her not to all worth it.

If you enjoyed this series, please consider leaving a review on your favorite site. If you didn't enjoy this series, I don't know why you tortured yourself to get to this point, but maybe you have more in common with the main characters than you think, and you actually do like a little pain, who knows?

From my heart to yours, thank you.

***

ALSO BY A. K. CAGGIANO

STANDALONE NOVELS:
The Korinniad - An ancient Greek romcom
She's All Thaumaturgy - A sword and sorcery romcom
The Association - A supernatural murder mystery

VACANCY
A CONTEMPORARY (SUB)URBAN FANTASY TRILOGY:
Book One: The Weary Traveler
Book Two: The Wayward Deed
Book Three: The Willful Inheritor

VILLAINS & VIRTUES
A FANTASY ROMCOM TRILOGY:
Book One: Throne in the Dark
Book Two: Summoned to the Wilds
Book Three: Eclipse of the Crown

FOR MORE, PLEASE VISIT:
WWW.AKCAGGIANO.COM

Made in the USA
Monee, IL
14 April 2024

56925178R00206